"YOU," FRANCE...
"ARE A ...

"What do you mean?"

"I mean I want to kiss you, but there's no reason I should. That's the mistake."

At her blunt statement, desire twisted in Charles's loins. By thunder, he'd just gotten himself under control and she set him off again. But the chance was too good to miss. "If you want to kiss me," he said carefully, "I won't stop you."

"Very well." She sat up quickly, and leaning over him, she pressed her lips to his. Her warmth penetrated to his soul as she explored his mouth with hers, softly searching. Her hands gripped his shoulders, and his strayed around her waist to draw her close.

"Very sweet," he whispered. "Frances, do you know what you're about?"

"Ummm. I'm kissing you. You're to lie still and do nothing." Her lips hovered over his, teasing and tantalizing.

He hardened between one breath and the next, feeling exactly as a hawk must when set to its prey. "You're driving me mad, you know."

⚡ TOPAZ

Journeys of Passion and Desire

☐ **TOMORROW'S DREAMS by Heather Cullman.** Beautiful singer Penelope Parrish—the darling of the New York stage—never forgot the night her golden life ended. The handsome businessman Seth Tyler, whom she loved beyond all reason, hurled wild accusations at her and walked out of her life. Years later, when Penelope and Seth meet again amid the boisterous uproar of a Denver dance hall, all their repressed passion struggles to break free once more. (406842—$5.50)

☐ **YESTERDAY'S ROSES by Heather Cullman.** Dr. Hallie Gardiner knows something is terribly wrong with the handsome, haunted-looking man in the great San Francisco mansion. The Civil War had wounded Jake "Young Midas" Parrish, just as it had left Serena, his once-beautiful bride, hopelessly lost in her private universe. But when Serena is found mysteriously dead, Hallie finds herself falling in love with Jake who is now a murder suspect. (405749—$4.99)

☐ **LOVE ME TONIGHT by Nan Ryan.** The war had robbed Helen Burke Courtney of her money and her husband. All she had left was her coastal Alabama farm. Captain Kurt Northway of the Union Army might be the answer to her prayers, or a way to get to hell a little faster. She needed a man's help to plant her crops; she didn't know if she could stand to have a damned handsome Yankee do it. (404831—$4.99)

☐ **FIRES OF HEAVEN by Chelley Kitzmiller.** Independence Taylor had not been raised to survive the rigors of the West, but she was determined to mend her relationship with her father—even if it meant journeying across dangerous frontier to the Arizona Territory. But nothing prepared her for the terrifying moment when her wagon train was attacked, and she was carried away from certain death by the mysterious Apache known only as Shatto. (404548—$4.99)

☐ **RAWHIDE AND LACE by Margaret Brownley.** Libby Summerhill couldn't wait to get out of Deadman's Gulch—a lawless mining town filled with gunfights, brawls, and uncivilized mountain men—men like Logan St. John. He knew his town was no place for a woman and the sooner Llbby and her precious baby left for Boston, the better. But how could he bare to lose this spirited woman who melted his heart of stone forever? (404610—$4.99)

*Prices slightly higher in Canada

Buy them at your local bookstore or use this convenient coupon for ordering.

PENGUIN USA
P.O. Box 999 — Dept. #17109
Bergenfield, New Jersey 07621

Please send me the books I have checked above.
I am enclosing $_____ (please add $2.00 to cover postage and handling). Send check or money order (no cash or C.O.D.'s) or charge by Mastercard or VISA (with a $15.00 minimum). Prices and numbers are subject to change without notice.

Card #_____ Exp. Date _____
Signature_____
Name_____
Address_____
City _____ State _____ Zip Code _____

For faster service when ordering by credit card call **1-800-253-6476**

Allow a minimum of 4-6 weeks for delivery. This offer is subject to change without notice.

Lady Shadowhawk

by

Janet Lynnford

A TOPAZ BOOK

TOPAZ
Published by the Penguin Group
Penguin Books USA Inc., 375 Hudson Street,
New York, New York 10014, U.S.A.
Penguin Books Ltd, 27 Wrights Lane,
London W8 5TZ, England
Penguin Books Australia Ltd, Ringwood,
Victoria, Australia
Penguin Books Canada Ltd, 10 Alcorn Avenue,
Toronto, Ontario, Canada M4V 3B2
Penguin Books (N.Z.) Ltd, 182–190 Wairau Road,
Auckland 10, New Zealand

Penguin Books Ltd, Registered Offices:
Harmondsworth, Middlesex, England

First published by Topaz, an imprint of Dutton Signet,
a division of Penguin Books USA Inc.

First Printing, June, 1997
10   9   8   7   6   5   4   3   2   1

Copyright © Janet Ciccone, 1997
All rights reserved

 REGISTERED TRADEMARK — MARCA REGISTRADA

Printed in the United States of America

Without limiting the rights under copyright reserved above, no part of this publication
may be reproduced, stored in or introduced into a retrieval system, or transmitted, in
any form, or by any means (electronic, mechanical, photocopying, recording, or otherwise), without the prior written permission of both the copyright owner and the above
publisher of this book.

BOOKS ARE AVAILABLE AT QUANTITY DISCOUNTS WHEN USED TO PROMOTE PRODUCTS
OR SERVICES. FOR INFORMATION PLEASE WRITE TO PREMIUM MARKETING DIVISION,
PENGUIN BOOKS USA INC., 375 HUDSON STREET, NEW YORK, NEW YORK 10014.

If you purchased this book without a cover you should be aware that this book is stolen
property. It was reported as "unsold and destroyed" to the publisher and neither the
author nor the publisher has received any payment for this "stripped book."

This book is dedicated to Connie Rinehold
(who also writes as Eve Byron),
a talented author,
a loving friend,
and a devoted mentor without peer.

And to Dana, David, and my mother,
with regrets for the many hours spent apart
while this work was written,
and appreciation for your loving support.

Women and falcons are easily tamed:
If you lure them the right way,
they come to meet their man.
Kürenberc, southern Germany, mid twelfth century
[from Peter Dronke, *The Medieval Lyric*
(New York: Harper & Row, 1968), p. 115]

Prologue

"Wait, George. Females are nervous, high-strung creatures. You have to make your move at just the right time." Charles Cavandish put a hand on his friend's arm to steady and reassure him. He was good at this. No, he was better than good. In this area, all the town lads agreed his skill exceeded theirs. "You want to be sure you're firm and in control when you begin."

"Yes, yes, I'm listening. Just tell me when." George almost stuttered in his excitement. "Lord, isn't she a beauty? Look at her," he breathed, his voice filled with awe. "What a catch she'll be."

"*If* you get her," Charles warned. "Overconfidence can be your downfall. You can't be sure of success in advance."

"That's half the fun of it, though, isn't it?" George countered. "It wouldn't be a challenge if you were sure of success. Every time is a new chance."

A new chance, Charles thought. Yes, each time was a new chance. Each time the familiar anticipation stoked the fire in his blood. Though this time he was teaching and George would reap the reward, Charles still savored every bit of the pleasure . . . well, almost every bit. Of course he preferred to be in control. But he felt a special vigor this morning, a vitality made even more pleasurable by the splendid day.

Late summer lay heavily on the rolling Dorset land with just a hint of the coming autumn. The freshening breeze rumpled his hair as he turned his head. It might have been chill, that breeze, except for the dazzle of sun that beat on the back of his neck, warming him through his light leather jerkin and shirt.

Suddenly, his two spaniels at the far end of the marsh

broke into a frenzy of barking. Flushed from its cover, a magnificent heron rose from a tall stand of marsh grass. "Now," Charles urged his friend. "Go!"

George lifted his heavily gloved arm and snatched the hood from the marsh hawk's head, giving the bird her sight. "Away," he cried as he tossed her into the air. "There's your prey!"

The fierce little hawk mounted the air in a flurry of wings and sped after the heron.

Charles spotted a strange black dog ahead of his two spaniels, but he paid it no heed. As always, he concentrated on the flight of his bird, feeling the powerful beat of wings, as if part of him rose with her, as if he were the one straining in flight. For a full year since he had received the young hawk for his thirteenth birthday, he had thrown his heart into working with her. Now, she would fell her prey without trouble, despite the heron's superior size. Charles tracked her with his gaze, imagining that night's feast of roast bird. The fragrant, moist meat melting on his tongue, dripping with . . .

A black blur shot out of nowhere and cut into his bird's flight path. Thrown off her mark, the marsh hawk wavered and fell back. Rude as a cutpurse, a female goshawk of enormous proportions cannoned toward the heron.

"What the—" Charles leaped forward.

"That's my heron," George cried.

The second hawk hit the heron like a load of brick, breaking the heron's neck. Locking her talons into its back and wings, she rode it to ground and disappeared into the reeds bordering the marsh.

"Damn!" Stagnant water flew from beneath his heavy boot soles as Charles ran through the marsh pools. "I'm going to kill whoever owns that bird."

"That makes two of us," George yelled, pelting after him, holding the heavy glove before him.

"Stay where you are and recover my bird," Charles ordered over his shoulder. "Swing the lure and she'll come to you."

George stopped dead and searched the sky for the hawk. Charles ran on, knowing he should recall the bird himself. But anger drove him. He would confront whoever dared steal his prey.

A dog broke from the reeds to his right, making a straight

track for the heron and the falcon. It was the same great black hound he'd seen earlier, Charles noted, as he thrashed through the reeds. He reached the birds mere seconds after the dog.

Perched on the heron's back, the goshawk cocked her head at him. Her sharp, haughty eyes and the arrogant tilt of her head seemed to say, "This one's mine. Too bad for you." The black dog assumed a protective stance beside the heron and stared at Charles, a fierce expression in its eyes.

"That's what you say now," Charles snarled, his gaze searching the woods. Since the dog had come from that direction, so would the owner. It was part of the old Morley property, but no one lived there these days. Not since Lady Morley had died some years ago.

The dense woods shivered as someone pushed through the overgrown bracken, coming down the hill. Charles clenched his fists and shifted on his feet, ready to fight. At fourteen, he was strong enough to beat any lad, though this wouldn't be any boy he knew. In fact, no one in this area possessed such a perfectly trained bird.

As the interloper drew nearer, Charles froze, puzzled by the high, pure notes of singing. Snatches of some wild song echoed eerily among the trees, wending their way to him on the wind. The branches parted, and a slim figure stepped forth.

Charles stared, dumbstruck. It wasn't a lad, but a girl.

Or was it a nymph?

She had hair the color of night wind, rich and smoky, the tendrils curling around her face like a dark nimbus and hanging to her waist. Absently, she reached up to pull a lock free from a branch and brush away leaves that clung to the strands. Snowy feathers tucked behind her left ear gleamed white against the dark wings of her hair. A rent in her plain, dark kirtle skirt revealed a slim ankle. And her smock hung nonchalantly off one shoulder, as if she didn't care in the least that it bared her white skin. Or that it drew his gaze to her small, firm breasts beneath the thin cloth.

Oddest of all, the nymph wore a thickly padded falconer's glove.

Charles swallowed hard, fighting the excitement that stabbed through his loins. He shouldn't feel this for a strange girl met in the wood. Especially one who had just snatched his prey. Yet he thought a good deal about females these days. So much so, he often couldn't sleep at night.

This female seemed aloof and calm. Her appearance was free and wild . . . and inviting.

Lifting her gloved hand, she sent him a ghost of a smile. Then she pursed her lips and let loose a sharp, shrill whistle.

The hawk left the heron without hesitation, flapping straight to her wrist. It settled contentedly on her arm, the tiny bells on its jesses tinkling. Drawing a chunk of raw meat from the pouch at her waist, she fed the bird. While it gulped the reward, she wiped her bloody fingers on a rag. Her gaze meandered back to rest on Charles again. As bold as you please, as if she had a right to snatch his prey from beneath his nose without so much as a *by your leave*.

"That was incredibly rude, you know," Charles called out, determined to overcome the ridiculous excitement he felt at her appearance. "I expect an apology."

Without answering, she strolled down the hill toward him, her step stately and confident. "Pharaoh's foot, but you're a cross one," she said as she drew up opposite him. With a low growl, the dog placed himself between them.

"I'm not cross," he snapped at her. "I'm furious. You stole my prey."

"I did not," she said calmly. "You sent up your bird too late." She smiled again, just the hint of a curve to her lips, challenging him.

Had he signaled George too late? Charles asked himself, enraged by the possibility. His family had always plagued him about being late—for church, for breaking his fast, for lessons with his tutor. But he was never, ever late for anything to do with his birds. In fact, his birds made him late for everything else.

"My hawk had been waiting on for a good long time before you launched yours." She rubbed the bird's snowy breast, and the creature returned the caress, bobbing against her hand, chittering softly in reply.

"I didn't see her," Charles stated sullenly.

"You would have if you'd looked. She was up quite high. Where's your bird now?"

He was supposed to care about his bird more than the kill, but he was too furious. He clenched and unclenched his fists as he lowered his gaze from the girl's serene, beautiful face to her neck. He could wrap his hands entirely around that slender stem without trouble. His fingers itched to do just that. Her lips looked smooth and ripe for kissing, and from the few such treasures he had stolen from the dairymaid, he knew he would like to sample this forest nymph's.

"How old are you," he demanded, still fighting his uncomfortable, dismaying interest, "that you think to know so much about birds?"

"Thirteen," she said, tilting up her chin regally. "And you?"

"We're not exchanging pleasantries." He put on his angriest countenance, locking his gaze with hers. Up close and lit by the sun, her eyes were a pure, ripe green. They made him think of cool, deep fields of clover on a hot summer's day, or of dew-brushed glades in early spring. He shook his head, all the more furious that she reduced him to foolish whimsy and lustful imaginings. Choler further inflamed his blood as he realized she didn't seem the least intimidated by his irate glare.

She bent over to scoop up the heron and draped it over her shoulder, careful not to disarray the pure white feathers. The dog moved protectively to her side as she headed back toward the hill.

"Stop! Where are you going with that?" Charles shouted as he ran after her. "You should at least offer to share the prize."

"I am quite certain I'm in greater need of the meat than you," she said, turning back to him. "I am alone at Morley Place for a few days. There is nothing there to eat except what we hunt." She indicated the hawk on her fist.

He stopped in his tracks at the sad, haunted quality of her expression, at the way her shoulders drooped as she walked away. "Why are you alone?" he called after her retreating back, his anger mixing strangely with pangs of doubt. "Where is your father? Why is there nothing to eat?"

"My father and uncle are at Poole, getting ready to leave for Paris. They've joined the train of the English ambassador," she answered without turning around. "I'll be going with them, but first I had to see Morley Place. They couldn't bear to come. My mother died here, you know."

"But what of money," Charles called. "Your father gave you money, didn't he? And why did you come alone?"

As she mounted the hill and entered the trees, a sunbeam slanted down through the branches, like an open door into the next world, illuminating the spot where she stood. She was so dazzling in that ray of light, the sight of her hurt his eyes.

"I gave the money to some starving children," she said. "And I lost my servant along the way on purpose. I *wanted* to come alone."

He blinked in surprise. When he looked again, she had stepped into shadow, along with her bird.

Charles's dogs had come up behind him and sat at his heels. He felt their snuffling on the backs of his calves, but he didn't look down. "Are you mad?" He muttered under his breath as he stared after her. "You gave away all your money? You *wanted* to come here with no company but a hawk?"

It struck him then—she wasn't mad. She was wild. Like an untamed hawk, she flew off on her own. She fended for herself and refused all aid.

She continued up the hill, moving from shadow to light to shadow again. Just before the undergrowth began, she stopped in another slash of sun. She turned and waved with her free hand while molten rays burnished her dark hair to a blue-black glow against her pale smock and skin. The bird balanced on her fist rose to stretch its wings to their full, magnificent length.

Odd feelings coiled through his middle, arousing and frustrating him. She was too beautiful and infuriating, too independent for his peace of mind.

He hauled himself around as she disappeared into the shadowy undergrowth, disgusted by his distraction. *Bested by a girl,* he thought angrily as he slogged through the water back to George and his own bird. Worse than that, she accused him of being late.

He would be any damn thing he wanted to be, late or otherwise, he growled to himself, unable to shake the conflicting emotions she aroused in him. But he wouldn't be late with his birds.

Silently, he made another vow as he glanced over his shoulder at the growth that barely rustled with her passing.

Never again will you best me, Lady Shadowhawk.

Chapter 1

"Mistress Morley, I regret that I can wait no longer. I am expected back at Sir Humphrey's by seven of the clock."

Frances netted her thoughts from where they soared in daydreams, bringing them back to the young man before her in the entry of her Paris lodgings. Her *former* Paris lodgings. "No, I suppose you can't. 'Tis growing late."

She stood, smoothed her serviceable, black mourning skirt, and picked up the wicker cage holding Oriana in her right hand, her equipment bag in her left. Casting the empty house a last look, she bid it farewell.

She had called this place home for the past nine years and loved every part of it—the open, airy entry with its curving staircase, the parlor to the left, enriched by its rose marble hearth. So many pleasant evenings she'd spent in that parlor, content with a game of cards or simple conversation with her uncle's friends and government associates, both English and French.

Now a sense of foreboding clung to the house, changing everything. Nerves roiled in her stomach at the thought of staying here alone for the night. With all the household staff gone, instinct told her she'd best leave. Fast.

Tears gathered in her eyes as her gaze swept the familiar rooms she had shared with her uncle after her father died three years ago. Now, fate had cruelly robbed her of the last person she loved.

If only she could turn back the clock, hear once more her uncle's cheerful whistle piping down the stair as he dressed for the day. How she longed for one of his loving pecks on her cheek, bestowed each morning before he strolled off to work for the English ambassador. Longing tightened inside her, wringing her heart. She could not turn back the clock, nor could she undo his death—a death by murder, or so she believed.

She couldn't prove her theory. "Set on by thieves," the Paris authorities had announced, after dragging his body out of the Seine by early morning's light. Only she knew they were wrong.

Never would she forget the night before—her uncle's wrenching cry that shocked her out of sleep. The scuffle in their entry had propelled her from bed at a run. Shivering in her night shift, feet bare, she had raced for the entry . . .

To find the front door standing wide and her uncle gone.

"We must learn who did it!" she had cried to the English ambassador. "No one should commit such a crime and escape."

"There, there, my dear," he had soothed her. "All steps will be taken to catch the guilty party."

At the time, Frances had believed him. But now, six days later, with nothing discovered, she had serious doubts.

"Hadn't I better take your trunk to Sir Humphrey's?" the man asked, reclaiming her attention as he indicated her modest pile of belongings. "He can send it on to London for you."

Frances agreed as he obligingly lifted the trunk. "Sir Humphrey is most generous to help me. I will keep only my bird and this bag."

Sighing, Frances followed the serving man down the steep steps into the street. While he loaded his barrow, tightening a strap around the trunk, she considered her dilemma.

When she lost her uncle, she had also lost her income. Given the choice, she would have stayed on and sought the murderers. But now her options narrowed. Pressed for a decision, she had spent the last of her precious, hoarded funds and booked passage back to England. Reasons to leave outweighed reasons to stay.

The state of the city added to her anxiety. The Duke of Guise threatened the king, his cousin, wanting the crown. The streets seethed with civil unrest. Something bad was about to happen; Frances felt it deep inside.

Sir Humphrey's man clearly shared her discomfort. With his barrow ready to travel, he stood at attention, casting nervous glances up and down the street. She dared not change her mind now.

But she was supposed to have an escort, and blast the man,

he hadn't shown up. Yesterday, she had kissed her friends farewell, assuring them she was in good hands. She had also promised the owner of this house to be out. He expected a new tenant on the morrow.

"Tell Sir Humphrey that if my escort does not arrive within the hour, I would be grateful to lodge with him tonight," she said. "If he does arrive, we will leave straight from here."

"He will always welcome you, mistress," the man murmured, checking the strap a last time.

That was only half true, Frances thought as she put down the bird cage and opened her purse. Sir Humphrey Perkins had worked for six years with her uncle. As a family friend, he would welcome her with delight, but not her hawk. She knew he preferred that birds remain in the mews. His did.

But Oriana was her special charge. They must not be parted. Which meant she, Frances, would want to sleep in Sir Humphrey's mews, and as a good host, he would be shamed.

"This is for you. My thanks for your help." She pressed a small coin into the serving man's hand.

The man bowed. "I'll tell Sir Humphrey you'll be along within the hour if your escort doesn't come. Otherwise, we'll expect you're on your way to the coast."

"Aye," she agreed, nodding. "If he comes, we'll be off at once."

She accepted his wishes for a safe journey, then watched him trundle off down the busy Paris street, the barrow rattling on the cobblestones. The tide of sabots and shoes that usually flowed along the Rue Saint Jacques had dwindled to a trickle as evening approached. The sky above the city looked as if a broad brush had washed it with clouds of dusky blue-gray and rose against a pale, silvery blue backdrop. The familiar view that once gave her pleasure now filled her with pain.

Retreating into the house, Frances set down the cage and ensconced herself on the stairs. Here she sat, all alone, squeezed between two unacceptable choices. She could wait for someone who probably wasn't coming. Or she could show up on Sir Humphrey's doorstep, begging his indulgence, which was highly embarrassing.

It was entirely the fault of this fellow, this . . . what was his name? She searched the pouch strapped to her belt for the queen's letter, just to assure herself for the hundredth time she hadn't read it wrong. No, the clerk's scrawl stated the name clearly: Baron Milborne, the royal Master Falconer, would arrive on the eighth of May to escort her to Dieppe. From there, they would take ship to England. Today was the eighth, it was late in the day, and he still wasn't here.

Mayhap he had had trouble crossing the Channel. Mayhap he couldn't find her lodging. Mayhap any one of a hundred things had happened that couldn't be helped. Whatever it was, it had best be a good excuse, Frances told herself. She couldn't sit here all night.

Pharaoh's foot, she had heard things about this Baron Milborne. Several women from Queen Elizabeth's court had spoken at length about him, carrying on about his vast physical attraction and the thrill of his kiss. He was unwed and a master of seduction. Those attributes alone would have bored Frances to tears.

But the post of royal falconer was highly revered. The man who held it must possess superior skill with birds of prey. The thought of meeting a man who had a way with both birds and women tied her stomach in knots.

She'd also heard the Master Falconer's name was Charles Cavandish. Could he be the same boy she'd met nine years ago, near where Cavandish and Morley lands met? Memory swept her back through time. A hop and a skip and she was thirteen again, full of mischief, her interest piqued by the boy who was slightly inept with birds. Inept enough to let himself be distracted from his own hawk to find out who had usurped his kill. And when he saw who it was, he seemed more distracted still. Almost fascinated.

Or had he been merely enraged?

Her thirteen-year-old instincts had told her it was something more.

Which made him fascinating to *her.* How many people in her life put her before their work or other interests? Just now, exactly none.

Besides, he had brought out something else in her—made her want to tease him and taunt him so he would spill the tightly checked emotion she saw seething in his eyes.

Those forest brown eyes had spoken legions to her that day. Not his looks—his face as beautiful as an angel's, his form perfectly proportioned, his leg well-turned. But his eyes . . . they said he wanted to possess her, to master her as he would a bird so she would fly to him willingly, offering her body and soul.

And heaven help her, at thirteen, having lost her mother at nine, she was starved to belong to someone as intimately as that.

No longer.

Now, she was two and twenty and finished with such nonsense. Offering yourself to a man meant ruin, tragedy, or both.

Shoving away the thoughts of the falconer, she tucked the letter in her purse and withdrew a gold button. Just after her uncle's abduction, she had found it, rolled into a corner of their entry hall.

Holding it close, she studied its unusual, embossed design. It was Spanish. She would stake her life on it. Which meant one thing to Frances: the Spanish had done this terrible deed.

No Englishman would listen to her convictions. The idea that officials might be abducted and murdered in the depth of night for conducting their work was entirely too frightening. She understood that.

A shiver rippled over her skin as the sun sank lower and the streets quieted into an ominous hush. The longer she sat here, alone in the echoing house, the more unsettled she felt.

It hadn't been bad so long as she'd had a maid, three house lads, the cook, and the steward for company. But she had had to let them go. Her uncle's last pay had scarcely covered a decent wage to keep them until they found new work. This morning, she had paid them a final time and sent them on their way.

Reaching for her equipment bag, she pulled it closer. The sheaf of papers concealed in the bag's secret compartment heightened her nervousness. She had to get them to England within the next few days. In fact, she couldn't wait to hand them over to Queen Elizabeth and be quit of them.

For the first time, she admitted the truth as she sat alone in the empty house. She was more than unsettled. She was genuinely afraid. Because if the men who had killed her uncle even suspected all she knew of his secrets, they would come back for her.

Chapter 2

Late again.

Furious at the events that delayed him, Charles Cavandish, Baron Milborne, wound his way through the crowded Paris streets, looking for the Rue Saint Jacques. By thunder, he couldn't believe it had taken so long to calm Arcturus and bind the hawk's broken leg. The bird had been caught in a trap set by Ralph Stokes, the new owner of the old Morley Place. What possessed the man to set traps and bait them with raw meat unless he'd known Charles was in residence with his hawks? Any bird would be tempted to pick up such a tidbit.

Sure enough, he had found Arcturus with the big steel jaws of the trap closed on its leg. It had taken all of his care to release the frantic bird and see it on the mend. By then he was several hours late for his ship to Dieppe. Lucky for him the ship belonged to his brother-in-law and had waited for him. Otherwise he wouldn't have gotten here at all.

Intent on his thoughts, Charles turned into the Rue Saint Jacques and collided with a giant going the opposite way.

"*Imbecile.*" The fellow's voice stung the air like a lash. "Do you think you own the street?"

"I'd ask the same of you." Charles jerked back, noted the swarthy complexion and foreign accent, and cursed under his breath. Another damned Spaniard. He'd had his fill of them in the Caribbean and sworn to avoid them to the end of his days. But they insinuated themselves everywhere, plotting to invade England, maneuvering for power in France. This one sized him up and down, as if primed for a clash. In response, hatred poured into Charles's veins, whipping up his sour mood. "Why don't you go back to Spain?" He assumed a fighting stance, feet braced, one hand wrapped around his rapier hilt, the other on the haft of his knife.

The man narrowed dark beady eyes that looked like a

beetle's, apparently debating the odds of winning a fight and what he would gain. Silently, Charles promised him a split head.

With a sneer of derision, the Spaniard bowed mockingly, as if to say he would gladly see him dead but couldn't be troubled right now, and detoured around Charles. With a flick of his black cloak, he vanished around the turn.

Pushing his hat forward to a more determined angle, Charles strode on. Gradually he tightened the control on his temper, bringing it to heel. With pleasure, Spanish soldiers would have torn him apart in the Caribbean. They'd done exactly that to his best friend, and he wouldn't forget it, though he often wished he could.

Bury the thoughts. He retreated from the raw pain that steamed just below the surface. If only he could weight the tormenting memories with stones and sink them in a dark lagoon. In his mind's eye he wrapped them in canvas and pushed them over the edge. They descended, falling deep and deeper until they settled into the black, all-encompassing mud of the bottom. They ought to stay there, leave him in peace.

But the next moment, they sprang to life again.

Small chance of ever escaping those memories, he snorted in self-depreciating mockery, moving on to consider his hawk and its broken leg.

As it often did, worry about his ailing bird temporarily edged out other thoughts. Birds died of such things, and he had raised Arcturus from an egg. He didn't feel the least charitable toward the man who had caused the trouble. In fact, he didn't feel charitable toward anyone, least of all the wench he'd been coerced into escorting back to England.

He was a master of hawks, not a nursemaid.

Full of his foul mood, he searched for the Sillington house and cursed to find he'd almost walked past it in his preoccupation. No light showed at any of the windows. He rang and knocked repeatedly, but received no reply. Thunderation, where was she? Hadn't she waited for him?

He heartily regretted giving in to his brother. He had no one else to spare, Jonathan had pleaded, so would Charles please escort the poor child home? Her uncle, aide to the English ambassador Sir Edward Stafford, had died; she was alone in the world. In his work for the queen, Jonathan must see her safely returned. Have pity on the girl.

He'd had pity, that was sure, Charles thought, gripping his rapier. He'd left his favorite hawk and come all the way to Paris. In return for his trouble, he found the wench missing. Stifling yet another string of curses, Charles knocked on the door of the neighboring house.

The servant who answered didn't know anything, but he sent Charles to the house on the left. Sure enough, the owner of the Sillington house lived there.

"Ah, Mademoiselle Frances. I spoke to her earlier." The gray-haired landlord introduced himself as Monsieur Jean La Blanche and settled his huge belly more comfortably over his belt as he stood in the entry. "She went to an inn for the night. I will write down the directions, yes? Pray come in and sit down. You've traveled far?"

"Across the Channel and down from Dieppe since this morning." Charles sank into a cushioned chair in the entry. Hang the wench. If she was settled somewhere, he could certainly sit for a minute. "Your direction to the inn would be appreciated. The girl's name is Frances, you say?"

"*Oui,* Frances. She will be glad you are here, I'm sure. I tried to convince her to stay one more night at the house, but she had no bedding nor anything else. I fed her supper and offered her the hospitality of my home, but she insisted on the inn for the night." He shrugged as he handed Charles the directions he'd prepared.

Charles scanned them briefly. By thunder, she'd gone halfway across the city. No wonder La Blanche insisted on writing them out. Reluctantly, he stood. With gracious courtesy, the landlord accompanied him to the door.

"My thanks for your trouble." Charles shook the gentleman's hand.

Monsieur nodded his gray head. "Have a care how you go, Baron Milborne. And take care of Mademoiselle Frances. An ugly thing, the way she was left in the world."

"I'm sure she's sad to lose her uncle," Charles agreed, wondering at the man's choice of words. He clapped on his hat and adjusted it as he regarded Monsieur La Blanche by the lantern light.

"Worse than sad, in this case. Very bad business. Have a care," monsieur advised again. "*Au revoir.*"

A nasty feeling ate at Charles as he descended the steps. Very bad business? He couldn't think what that meant.

As he set out for the inn, he glimpsed the Spaniard he'd

clashed with earlier. The man loitered with a woman across the street, stealing furtive glances at him.

Charles's hand itched to draw his rapier. In his bitter experience, Spaniards meant worse than trouble. He felt the dung beetle's gaze dig into his back all the way down the street. At the turn, Charles glanced behind him once more. Despite the increasing gloom, the Spaniard still watched him.

The man's interest in him struck Charles as distinctly odd—and sinister.

But he couldn't think about it right now. A young lady awaited him, desperate for his aid. She would undoubtedly be glad to see him. At least she'd better be. He was in no mood for nonsense from a maid.

Chapter 3

"Baron Milborne, you're late."

The young lady didn't sound glad to see him. Charles flipped a coin to the servant who had shown him to the chamber. The man withdrew, closing the door as he went.

"And *you're* not where you're supposed to be, Mistress Frances." Charles pulled off his cloak and tossed it over one arm. "I had a devil of a time finding this inn. Couldn't you have chosen something in a better part of the city?" He noted the lack of hangings at the window and the sparse furnishings.

"I have friends in this district. I chose it to be near them."

He grimaced. "You were told I would come for you. Better to have stayed at your home."

"And just why should I have done that? It had grown dark. I had no reason to believe you would come."

Her voice was belligerent—more than any woman's had a right to be. A warning flashed through his head—that he was in for a long, disagreeable journey back to England. But when she stepped forward into the light of the one candle and he saw her more clearly, he knew he was in for an arduous journey of another kind.

First of all, a large goshawk perched on her shoulder. A female, unhooded, with beautiful markings of deep brown. The bird was a rare beauty, but it couldn't compare to the woman.

She wore a nondescript kirtle skirt and bodice of black with a white smock beneath, the sort of thing suitable for a young woman of modest means in mourning. But her face . . . and hair . . . and body. The sight struck him dumb, held him rooted to the spot, his gaze drinking her in as if he could never get his fill.

Long, dark tresses flowed over her shoulder opposite the bird, reaching to her waist. They fanned across her arm as if she had been brushing them. Ah, she had been. He glimpsed the brush in her hand—a slender, tapering hand, white and fine. She gripped the brush in front of her, which led his eye back to her bodice. The plain fabric with its snug fit accentuated rather than hid her lushly curved bosom that flowed down to a tiny waist.

Now that he looked closer, he noticed a pad laced to her shoulder that kept her bird's talons from needling her flesh. A wise measure, but it partially blocked his view of her assets. So did her full skirt, which undoubtedly hid slender hips and thighs.

Charles gave himself a swift mental shake, wondering at the direction of his thoughts. Something was wrong here, that Mistress Sillington should have him conjuring up visions of her unclothed the moment he laid eyes on her. Already he imagined uncovering the parts of her that were covered, piece by piece. The idea sent spikes of interest shooting through his loins. He forced his gaze back to her face—a face that held unusual beauty, as if she were a wild thing spawned in the forests and marshes like her hawk.

Or a nymph. Yes, that was it. As if she dwelled in wild places, untouched by human hand. She was enough to drive a man to ruin, luring him to think he might tame the untamable.

Surrounded by her dark cloud of hair, her face was small boned and delicate, with a slightly tipped-up nose and arched brows. Her flesh was pale, accented dramatically by her stark black-and-white garments, colors that turned many women's skin sallow and sick. Not Mistress Sillington. They fit her to perfection, repeating her raven and alabaster coloring, making her a vivid vision of shadow and snow.

And her eyes . . . those wide, clear eyes of deep, earthy green. They reminded him of rolling pastures of new clover in spring, or of emerald forests where no man had ever trod, or even of . . .

He scowled as a memory emerged from the recesses of his mind.

"You don't go by Sillington," he began, unwilling to believe what he suspected. "I asked for that name below stairs, to no avail. Yet when I asked for an English woman who had just arrived alone, I was directed to you."

"I am Master Sillington's niece, but my name is Morley," she stated. "Frances Morley. You were late nine years ago in

Dorset, Charles Cavandish, and you're late still. I should have known 'twas you had become the queen's Master Falconer and a baron as well. I had hoped it was not."

Realization stung him. This was the wench who had bested him all those years ago. Or rather her bird had bested his.

It was a good thing he recognized her before giving in to the interest affecting his nether parts. She was the last person he wanted anything to do with. But he'd promised to see her safely back to England. *Blast.*

"I am late," he snapped. "For good reason, too. You should be glad I came at all."

"Should I? You haven't yet given me a reason to be."

Her flippant tone pushed his patience. "I came because I was told you needed help, Mistress Morley," he said curtly. "But if you don't want it, good night." He whirled and headed for the chamber door. No wonder Jonathan couldn't get anyone else to come for the wench. First she reproached him, then she entranced him, then she irritated him worse than a cockleburr under the saddle.

"Where are you going?"

The fear in her voice stopped him. Charles turned back in time to glimpse it in her eyes before she hooded them as she would her hawk, masking all trace of what she felt. So she was vulnerable, he thought, faintly surprised. Then understanding took over. She wasn't as bold as she liked to pretend.

But she was a shrew, he reminded himself harshly. And she was also seductive. She might not intend to be, but for some reason, one look at her scattered his thoughts like grain blown to the four winds. He couldn't think rationally in her presence; he could only stare . . . and feel.

Her torrent of luxurious hair drew his gaze again. He moved from there to the white embroidered neckline of her smock. It was threaded with a lace that was undone, exposing her slender, creamy throat. How well he remembered the feeling as a lad, the white-hot desire to put his hands on that lovely neck. The wish burned him still. But now his adult imagination leaped beyond the tame touch he'd craved as a youth.

A sudden vision assaulted him—of this beautiful nymph, beckoning to him in the wild Dorset woods where they first had met, suggesting many things. Smoldering kisses beneath a canopy of forest leaves. The touch of her flesh setting his on fire . . .

Charles brought himself up short. "I'll take another chamber and see you on the morrow," he snapped, leashing the outrageous image. The look of relief that flashed across her face surprised him yet again. Had she thought he would leave her for good? He didn't desert his duty because of a shrew. "We'll depart for the return trip early," he said to set her mind at ease. "I'll expect you dressed, your fast broken, and your things ready precisely at the stroke of seven of the clock."

"Despot." She turned her back on him with an injured sniff. All traces of her relief had vanished. Using graceful, deliberate motions that would not upset her hawk, she put down the brush. Again working on the side opposite her bird, she began to plait her hair.

Charles shook his head at the irony of it. No use offering kindness. She resented him—her proud, straight back told him that as clearly as her face. She scorned his aid, though she was forced to accept it. For that, she would cut him and bring their interview to an end.

Well and good. The sooner they parted, the better for them both. But as he moved toward the door, realization halted him once more. He'd almost forgotten her bird, an unforgivable lapse. "How will your goshawk travel?" he asked, kicking himself mentally, cursing her influence. He returned to inspect the bird.

Though Mistress Morley refused to turn around, the bird's head swiveled, its sharp, yellow eyes missing nothing. Again he noted the pad on her shoulder, and wondered why this added sign of her vulnerability reassured him. Even she couldn't perch a hawk on her shoulder without protection. A bird's talons were dangerous enough to rip out a person's eyes in a single swipe. "She needs to be safe and dry, preferably at your side, in something large enough that her feathers won't break," he said, more softly than he'd intended.

She turned around to regard him. "Do you really care?"

"It's my duty as a Master Falconer," he said shortly. "A valuable bird requires transport. I intend to see it done right."

Her lips curved into the faintest ghost of a smile at his statement.

He wasn't sure if he'd pleased her or amused her, but a perverse pleasure filled him. He liked making her smile. Why, he couldn't fathom. The women he knew used such things as bait to set a snare and lure men into reach.

"There is the cage I intend to use." She nodded toward the bed, indicating a wicker affair on the floor. "Do you approve, Baron Milborne, sir?" The double pair of eyes— hers and her hawk's—studied him intently.

He ignored the sarcasm she applied to his title and went to examine the cage. It looked clean and well ventilated. He tested the door, noting it opened and closed smoothly on leather hinges. "What happened to the hawk you had nine years ago?" he asked, putting down the cage and returning to the table. He pulled out a chair and sat, confident that he now controlled himself and the situation. Birds were his livelihood.

Frances struggled to subdue the emotions thrashing inside her. The instant he had entered her room, she'd recognized Baron Milborne as the boy from Dorset, known him by the arrogant stance of his well-made body and the splendor of his piercing brown eyes.

That very beauty made him dangerous to her—as dangerous as a baited net to a wild hawk. *Beware*, the caution sounded inside her. *Beware. Guard your heart.*

Unfortunately, her heart ignored her. It quickened in response to him, almost the way it did when she flew Oriana. It surged with excitement, ever willful, breaking free of her restraints. Fascinated, she continued to study him by the candlelight's golden glow.

His features had softened as they talked about her hawk, suggesting a kindness that had to be false. And he was marvelously tall and beautifully proportioned, with broad, strong shoulders that dwarfed the chair where he sat. How she longed for a man whose outer strength and beauty delighted the eye the way his did.

But inward strength and integrity must match the outer, and such qualities didn't exist in so striking a man. From her past experience, she ought to know. "Barley water?" she offered, delaying her response to his question.

He nodded his assent.

She poured from an earthen jug, then took a chair opposite, sitting straight and alert, as if she were meeting an opponent at the negotiating table. He watched her as he drank, his gaze probing over the flagon's rim. Finished, he set it down, leaned across the small table, and put out one hand.

She angled back, away from him.

"I'm not going to bite you." He chuckled at her involuntary reaction and shifted his hand to rest on Oriana's head.

Pharaoh's foot, but he had audacity to touch her bird. "I know that," she snapped, bracing herself for Oriana's displeasure. "But she might bite you." His fingers were within inches of her nose. "She doesn't like strangers. She especially doesn't like being touched on the back."

Flaunting her counsel, he slid his fingers down Oriana's feathered back in a slow, sensual movement.

Horrors, her hawk tolerated him, making a liar of her. Worse yet, prickles of fear and fascination raced up Frances's spine, as if he caressed her rather than the bird. Even as an inept boy, he had possessed some magic that had lingered in her memory for nine long years. Now, as a woman, she found him far more unsettling. His wizardry had grown strong.

She closed her eyes to shield herself from his presence. To her surprise, Oriana's weight lifted; the bird fluttered from her shoulder. Frances snapped her eyes open again to see her goshawk settle on the devil's arm and begin to preen.

She barely choked back her outrage at the defection. "She's never done that with anyone else before."

Charles grinned as he admired the goshawk's feathers, the pattern of the primary and secondary wing feathers perfect in their rows. Though he admired the woman sitting across from him more, so proud and stiff. "Had her since she was young, I see. Take her from the nest?"

"Yes," she said shortly. "I raised her from an eyas. She loves me."

"Hmm. Don't worry, she won't go to anyone else, just you and me."

"Why has she gone to *you* at all?"

Charles wanted to laugh outright. Fury and chagrin showed openly on her pretty face. He couldn't help it if her bird liked him. They all took to him, some faster than others. But he wouldn't tell her that. It was small enough revenge for the humiliation he'd suffered at her hands nine years ago. He noted that the hawk was barely needling his arm with her talons, something most goshawks did if alarmed. His quilted sleeve protected him adequately. It pleased him well.

"You didn't answer my question," he said, looking from the bird back to her, his hand lingering on the hawk's breast. Her eyes watched him, wide and stricken. "What happened to your other hawk?" he asked, unaccountably moved by her mute admission of distress.

"She strangled on a piece of meat three years later," she said starkly.

Charles heard the agony of loss in her voice. One's first bird, trained and responsive to you alone, was a treasure and a triumph never to be found again.

"The goshawk I had left me one day," he confided, taking himself by surprise. "I set her at some grouse, and off she flew, never to return." He braced himself for more of her mockery.

Instead, her deep green gaze filled with pain. "That hurt," she whispered.

"Did you lose a bird that way?"

"No. But I know how it feels . . . being left."

He stared at her, at the midnight ripple of her hair and the sorrow marring her face. She had lost something . . . or someone. Suddenly, he was sorry for coaxing Oriana away from her. A sharp urge tugged at him, unusual in its intensity—the wish to hold her in his arms and woo away her pain.

The uncharacteristic, charitable feeling surprised him. He was the least likely candidate to comfort a grieving woman. Furthermore, he refused to try.

Because if he did, she would fight him. She was mourning her uncle. She was thoroughly wild. And like all wild things, instinct drove her to suffer alone. He moved his arm, sending the bird back to her shoulder. "Master Sillington was your mother's brother?" he asked, changing the subject, giving her what refuge he could from her grief.

At his question, her face shuttered again. The moment of confidence fell away as a shadow dropped between them. "My mother was a Sillington." She stood up. "You had best get some rest now, hadn't you?"

"Aren't you afraid to be alone?"

Her gaze dropped as she shrugged, indifferent.

It rankled, how easily she rejected him. Like a wild bird

that was only half trained, only half trusting—or not trusting at all.

Annoyed by the shadow between them, frustrated with how much it bothered him, he leaped up and strode to the door. He opened it, then paused, for some reason reluctant to leave on this note. Turning back, he formed words on his tongue, but none seemed right. What could he say to banish that shadow? Why did he even want to try?

He never had a chance to decide, because suddenly, pain exploded in the back of his head.

Chapter 4

Charles reeled as something hard connected with his skull. "By thunder, what the—" He staggered and fell into a crouch, instinctively groping for his rapier hilt.

Dimly, he saw four men leap into the chamber and pull the door shut behind them. He landed a solid blow to the chin of the first fellow who came at him, noting with surprise that his attacker wore a mask.

With no room or time to draw his rapier, Charles found the haft of his knife and whipped it out. Lunging, he laid an ugly gash down one man's arm and nicked the second. "What do you want?" he demanded of the man who circled him warily, just out of reach of his blade. "Money? I'll give you mine. She has none."

Frances shrieked in pain. Jerking around, Charles saw the third man yank her arms behind her back while the fourth grabbed for her bird.

The goshawk launched itself from her shoulder and fought back, aiming its razor-sharp talons for the man's eyes. He screamed and beat at the bird with both hands.

"No, no! Don't hurt my hawk," Frances cried, struggling against the cloaked monster who held her arms. "You'll break her wings."

"Then hood her," he snarled, gesturing for the others to draw back.

Charles took advantage of their momentary distraction to catch up a small table. Using it like a shield, he braced himself against a wall.

Frances called her hawk to a perch and hooded her, then submitted to being tied. For the sake of her bird, she'd given in to these rogues.

As soon as she was secured to a chair, all four shifted their evil gazes to him.

The table legs kept them at arm's length, but it also made

his knife less effective. His mind raced as the four sidled around him, looking for a weak point. All were masked. All were of considerable height and breadth.

Hired thieves.

They rushed him en masse. Charles thrust to meet them. The table legs gouged the face of one, the chest of another. The remaining two angled in from the sides, clutching for him.

Swinging the table high, Charles crashed it over one's head. The man slumped to the floor.

"Good table," Charles muttered, casting a glance at Frances as he retrieved it. Her green eyes were full of fear in the gloom.

The remaining three men returned to the attack. One of them now wielded a poker.

The first blow of the metal cudgel landed on the table, cutting a deep scar. Charles twisted away, then lunged forward again, catching the men off guard. Once more the table legs stabbed, landing its blows. But his head throbbed from the earlier attack, and he couldn't best four men, not in these close quarters and without more resources. He would have to summon help. "Thieves," he bellowed at the top of his lungs.

Frances joined in with shrill screams. "Cheats! Scoundrels! Call the night watch."

The attack ceased. "Silence!" One of the men addressed them with a thick Spanish accent. He stood with his poker poised over Frances's head. "Be silent or she receives the blow."

Charles recognized the Spaniard from the Rue Saint Jacques and bristled. "What do you want?" he growled.

"We want this woman . . . and you. Depart with us quietly, and you will both remain unscathed."

Spaniards wanting Frances? Why Frances? "You can't have her." Charles inched toward the door. "You can find comelier and more accommodating wenches below stairs. Take one of them."

The speaker growled a warning and motioned to one of his fellows to block Charles's escape. Before the man could advance, Charles dived for the door handle, twisted it, and flung the door wide. Stumbling into the passage, he shouted, hoping someone—anyone—was nearby. No good. No reply.

He sensed more than saw the poker descend toward his head and dodged out of its path. Legs tangled with his, tripping him. The table flew from his grasp as he crashed to the floor, his breath whooshing out of him. The poker made another assault.

His head exploded in fireworks. With a grunt of pain, he fought a wave of dizziness and sudden nausea. With a last effort, he wrapped his hands tightly around his hunting knife and swung at anything within reach. He must have hit someone, because he heard a yelp, but he didn't know who . . .

Darkness blotted his vision. Like grains of black sand, it sifted in thick layers before his eyes, robbing him of consciousness. The last thing he remembered was the jolt of the wooden floor as it flew up to meet him. And then he knew no more.

Even in repose, his face reminds me of a hawk's, with thick brows slanted over his eyes, fierce and proud. Frances studied Baron Milborne where he lay in the jolting wagon, trying desperately to think of anything but the fate awaiting them at the hands of these men. Trying, too, not to give in to her fear that Baron Milborne might die.

She was angry with him for being late, but she never wished him dead.

He'd been so full of aggression toward her when they first met at the inn—as she'd been toward him. Angry pride had lit his eyes and stiffened his back when he realized who she was. Yet his expression had softened when he handled Oriana, just as the goshawk had softened toward him, responding to his magical touch so quickly, it put her in awe of his skill.

Still, fierceness seemed to dominate his nature. It had returned, redoubled in strength when the Spanish attacked. Never had she seen anyone fight with such fury. If she were romantic, she would imagine him her champion, fighting on her behalf.

A pleasant fantasy for those who could afford it, but all her life, death had stolen away the people who cared for her. She had been forced to champion her own causes, so she imagined no such nonsense. The baron had fought because he had to, not as a special favor to her—a woman who was no relation, a mere responsibility to be escorted back to England. Worse yet, she had once bested him, costing him his pride in front of his friend.

At the time, she'd enjoyed her triumph and his palpable rage. After all, he *had* been late. But once grown, she understood the folly of her youthful rashness. A man bested by a woman could never be a friend.

She cradled his head in her lap as the wagon lurched, doing all she could to protect him from the jolts of the road. He had opened his eyes briefly when the Spanish heaved him into the wagon, but had succumbed to unconsciousness again.

She leaned over to examine the ugly gash to his head, but saw little in the dark. His failure to revive frightened her. What would happen if he did not survive?

She would be alone in the world once more.

Nonsense, she told herself. She was already alone in the world. Dragging the baron into danger with her didn't change that.

And *she* had put him in danger. It was thus her responsibility to ensure he escaped, when the time was right. She was quite sure she could arrange to slip away. Her friends Pierre and Louis would have seen them abducted by the Spanish. Yes, all would be well . . . *if* she had the time to manage things . . . and *if* Baron Milborne didn't die first.

Quickly, she checked his breathing. His pulse thudded, reassuring and steady, in his wrist. His chest rose and fell in shallow but rhythmic cadence. He might well revive and be fine.

But what if his mind were addled? What if he didn't remember who he was?

Rejecting the possibility, desperate to think of something else, she recaptured a memory instead—of how he'd looked on that day in Dorset so long ago. It was hard to believe, but age had further perfected him, turning the angel-faced boy into a handsome man with a wealth of thick brown hair and the muscular form of a god. How would he look with the barrier of his garments peeled away?

A dangerous thought, that one. She forced herself away from it and plunged back into the more innocent past. That day on the marsh when she'd met him, he had captured her interest. Just looking at him had made plumes of pleasure unfurl deep inside her. She couldn't have stopped those feelings then. She couldn't stop them earlier at the inn, when she realized who he was. Now, in spite of their danger, in spite of the danger to her from him, she felt that same weak-kneed pleasure. With his head nestled so intimately in her lap, she willed the rest of the world far away.

She touched his nose lightly, sliding the tip of her first finger along its smooth plane, perfect except for the odd bump in the middle. How had he broken his nose? she wondered. Defending whom or what?

Which brought her back to fear and their danger. They were in dire circumstances. Yet she didn't want to think about it, couldn't even plan an escape until Charles returned to awareness. He would need care.

He would need her, as the only ally available.

That complicated everything. He would resent being dependent on her, and she had never wanted such a responsibility. Still, it couldn't be helped.

She sighed as she gazed at his handsome face and swore not to repeat the mistake she had made at the inn. He *had* been late, but she should have done something when the Spaniards first attacked him. Instead, she'd frozen with fear, just as she had the night her uncle died. Sorrow and guilt at that insistent memory clenched at her stomach, almost too much to bear.

Charles shifted in her lap and ran his tongue over his lips, a sensual motion that sent pleasure tingling through her middle again, as subtle as the tinkling of bells on her hawk's legs. Oddly enough, he distracted her from her pain. His long, dark lashes etched their feathery pattern on his cheeks, so entrancing she couldn't help but wish he would raise his lids and gaze on her with caring warmth.

He wouldn't, though. When next he opened his eyes—assuming he did open them—she would see pain. She would see his displeasure at being involved with her, mixed with that barely veiled awareness of her she had noted at thirteen. On some obscure level, she had understood his awareness. She'd felt the same thing for him, though she hadn't recognized it as desire until now.

She licked her lips nervously, her own feelings for him as mixed as his responses to her—angry and impatient one moment, solicitous the next.

How she would welcome any of those reactions right now, even his anger. Anything to assure herself that he would recover and go his own way without her.

His wound worried her. So did their captors, who were taking them south. Whatever they intended, they were deadly serious about it, moving out of Paris with efficient stealth.

Please, Charles, wake up, she prayed silently, as she again leaned close to his face, trying for the dozenth time to determine the severity of his wound. But it was too dim in the wagon with its canvas cover that hid them. She could barely make out the blood-matted hair plastered around the gash. Since she was as helpless as he was, she could do nothing for him except try to reason with their captors. They had ignored her earlier pleas, but she would try again. Eventually, they had to stop to rest.

"Good sir, I pray you," she called to the man trudging behind the wagon as they rattled over the rutted road away from Paris. "Might we stop for some water to revive monsieur?"

The guard looked up briefly, then shook his head to show he didn't understand.

Frances tried again in Spanish. This time he grunted in the negative and cast his gaze down.

No, Frances sighed, they wouldn't do anything for the man who had caused them injury. But she wouldn't desert Charles. Not when his ankles were shackled, leaving him like a duck bound for the spit.

As she scooted around on the hard wagon bed, wincing at the discomfort from the long sit, she chided herself for thinking of him by his first name. She ought to call him Baron Milborne, even in her thoughts, but somehow it didn't fit. Her head bumped against the canvas stretched overhead between the two tall wagon sides, and she sighed again, wishing for the hundredth time that he hadn't been late.

She should have known the Spanish would find her if she lingered in Paris. If only she had gone to Sir Humphrey's to wait, this might not have happened.

But she'd chosen the inn so she could see Pierre and Louis again. The two waifs she'd adopted off the streets were her most loyal friends, even above her uncle's colleagues. Which landed her here, captured, with the duty to help this man.

"You must listen." Using her Spanish, she renewed her assault on the sensibilities of the guard. "I am of no use to you without this gentleman's assistance. He has vital information, and the blow to his head might have destroyed what he knew. We must be sure he is well."

The guard, called Diego by the others, frowned and seemed to come to a decision. He disappeared from her view. The wagon pulled off the rutted track and drew to a halt.

She heard a rapid exchange in Spanish, then knew a burst of hope as water gurgled into a container.

The fellow who had clouted Charles with the poker lumbered around to the back of the wagon, climbed in under the canvas cover, and thrust a wooden mug in her face.

She took it from him without thanks and dipped her handkerchief in the water. Charles moaned as she dabbed it against his brow and trickled a few drops in his mouth, leaving the wound for later. First he must regain consciousness and full use of his wits.

Frances started to lower his head to the wagon bed, then thought better of it as the wagon jerked into motion again. He was going to feel bad enough when he came around. At least she could continue to cushion him from the rough ride. She resettled his head on her lap.

They would both need the full use of their wits when the time came to escape.

Chapter 5

Black ink of tropical midnight. Heat . . . always the incessant heat . . . bore down with the strength of an enslaving fist. So many nights Charles skulked through this nightmare. Tonight it pursued him, and he fled before it, drowning in horror, begging to cast off his guilt.

Once again the dank walls of the Spanish garrison reared before him, thick and impenetrable. He pressed both hands against the chill stone and prayed. Blood from his broken nose trickled down his lip and into his mouth, the acrid taste a bitter reminder—even his captain said he couldn't help his friend.

Richard's scream split the air. Tormented, Charles clenched both hands to his head and squeezed. The hot odor of Caribbean soil pierced his brain, along with his shipmate's pain. Visions of white hot pincers writhed through his mind until he, too, cried for mercy. Anguish rendered him impotent, robbed him of power. He had failed to help when it mattered most.

The nightmare changed its countenance. God, how he fought it, wanting to escape. It pinned him down with relentless brutality, drowning him in the sultry tropical nights of his past.

Lush growth thick with flowers swayed around him, deceptively fair. Ocean breeze caressed his face, just the way Inez had. How she burned in his memory, her beauty rich and exotic. Suddenly he saw her stroll in a clearing, a scarlet blossom tucked in her dark hair. She hung on her father's arm while Charles watched in secret, peering through dense banks of leaves. He could tell she pleaded for something, her cajoling like a pretty toy. Her father nodded in answer, and her laughter bubbled forth, a vibrant reward to the man granting her wish.

Child of a rich, Spanish planter, she was pampered by

slaves and intent on her own indulgence. She had demanded his blind devotion, and heaven help him, he had shut his eyes to all else.

Richard . . . forgive me . . . what have I done?

He fled through the jungle to escape his own stupidity. Vines snaked around his legs, a constant reminder. A man who would do anything under the sun for a woman became a vulnerable fool. Guilt wrapped him in thick clouds of vapor, as dense as the jungle foliage, as cloying as fog.

Charles fought his way deeper into the rain forest. The vapor resisted him, something it shouldn't do if it were normal and brought by weather. He wanted to shout Richard's name, to tell him he would wrest his friend from Spanish hands.

But the vapor obscured his vision and weighed down his limbs.

Then he realized the dense, foggy feeling was inside his head. It created a pounding pressure that threatened to split his brain like an overripe peascod.

In contrast, someone had taken the trouble to cushion him on something warm and soft . . . and alive.

Inez?

No, not Inez. She had refused to share his life.

He opened his eyes and confronted more darkness. A jolting, rattling motion shook his body and resounded in his ears. Blinking, he tried to focus on the odd, swaying roof above him. The dim light must mean night was coming. Or was it morning?

A shadow floated above him. Slowly, it took on form and texture until it become a face . . . Frances . . . it was her bewitching face seeming to drift above him, her eyes wide and searching and eloquent with concern.

Memory of another past haunted him, of the thirteen-year-old nymph, passing from sun to shadow in the autumn Dorset woods. Sun to shadow . . . always moving from light to dark . . .

Lady Shadowhawk.

Awareness of the present crept into his mind, burning off visions from the past as well as the confusing fog.

His head must be resting in her lap. They were moving in some kind of vehicle. Memory banished the rest of his confusion—memory of being attacked, of his unsuccessful clash with four brutes. Spaniards . . .

Bracing himself for the effort, Charles tried to sit up. Hot knives of agony cut through his head. "Where the devil are we?" he gasped.

"Don't try to move," Frances whispered. "I'm not sure where we are, but we'll know soon. Please lie still."

Something about her answer didn't bode well, but he sagged back, unable to do more until the pain subsided.

In the meantime, her fingers stroked his brow with a soothing pressure, soft and cool and welcome. If only this were heaven, for she was surely an angel, in looks if not in speech . . .

"They didn't hurt you, did they?" he mumbled, catching her hand and holding it against his temple so she couldn't withdraw.

"Not at all," she reassured him. "I'm quite well. Try to rest."

Willingly, he followed her orders, wanting to lie here forever in the illusion of tranquility she created. But then something occurred to him. She said she was well, but things must still be dire indeed for her to hold his head in her lap and caress his face so sweetly. Nothing else would induce her to be that kind.

"Where are we?" he gritted out, determined to hear the worst. His head ached so much, even moving his mouth hurt.

"We're in a wain, escorted by the four Spaniards," she said in an apologetic tone. "We're their prisoners, I regret to say."

"The devil we are!" He tried to move his legs and found he couldn't. "Thunderation! What's this on my ankles? What in the—"

"You're leg shackled," she answered, smoothing his hair back from his eyes. "I tried to convince them you were no threat, but—"

"No threat!" he snarled. "I'll kill them." Clenching his jaw against the pain, he levered into a half-sitting position with one heave.

Damn. They were being smuggled out of Paris like sacks of beans.

"Why do the Spanish want you?" he demanded. "You haven't enough money to be worth their while."

"They killed my uncle before they realized he was worth

more to them alive. Now they want me alive . . . At least
that's my guess."

"I repeat, *why* do they want you?" Charles gingerly probed
his pounding head and found a wet spot. It hurt when he
dabbed at it. He squinted at his fingers, trying to see if it was
blood.

"I . . . suppose they think I know as much as my uncle
did."

Her slight hesitation raised his suspicions. "And what do
you know, if anything?" He couldn't imagine it was of any
importance. Young ladies weren't privy to state affairs.

"I know everything my uncle knew."

Charles groaned. By heaven, he resented being dragged
into this business. All he'd wanted was to be left alone.

"You're bleeding again. You really must lie still," she
said. Her milk-pale forehead creased with concern as
she blotted the wound with a soft cloth—a handkerchief, he
guessed—moistened in cool water.

He closed his eyes and gave in to her touch. It felt good to
have her hands on him, even though her dabbing made the
wound throb anew.

Wings rustled. Dissonant bells tinkled, and as Frances
turned away from him, he realized Oriana had not been left
behind. He stifled the urge to laugh at the absurdity of it. Not
only were he and Frances prisoners of the Spanish, but the
goshawk was, too.

"Does your head hurt much?" she asked, bending back
over him.

"It will probably hurt more after you answer my next
question. Not meaning to be callous, but why did they take
me if you were the one wanted?"

"I . . . I told the innkeeper a man would be meeting me,"
she said, her expression solemn. "He looked at me so oddly,
I was afraid he thought I was . . . you know, not the sort of
customer he wanted. So I said I expected my husband."

"Your hus—"

She placed one finger to his lips, shushing him. "Don't let
them hear you. I think—"

"Hist, Frank," a voice hissed from outside the wagon.

"Who's Frank?" Charles breathed with as little sound as
possible.

"I am." She leaned over and rapped several times on the

side of the wagon, then sat back. "Thank heaven they know where we are."

"Who are *they*?"

"Pierre and Louis."

"Stout Englishmen with weapons?" he asked, hope rising.

"No."

"Stout Frenchmen with weapons?"

"They're French and they're stout, but they're not men. And they don't need weapons. They'll help us escape."

A foreboding jolted through Charles. "How old are these two?"

"I'm not sure. Mayhap . . ."—she tilted her head to one side, considering—"eleven or twelve. But don't trouble yourself," she said brightly, sending him an encouraging grin in the dimness. "All will be well."

Chapter 6

"All will be well!" Charles cried, heedless of who overheard them. "The Spanish have got us. I'm leg shackled. There's no one to help us who's worth anything, and you say all will be well? Are you mad?"

"Softly. Hush please!" Her long fingers fluttered like the wings of a distraught bird. "You really must—"

"I won't be ordered about, mistress, and I won't hush," Charles hissed, lowering his voice anyway. "You're going to tell me why you're taking this so lightly. Then you're going to tell me what you have planned, every detail, starting now."

"I'm sorry. I can't tell you anything. But I swear that all will be well."

"Oh, magnificent. She won't tell me." Charles squeezed his eyes shut and concentrated on banishing the raging crescendo of pain in his head. "How did I get mixed up in this," he muttered to himself. "More to the point"—he opened one eye and accused Frances—"how did you?"

"I didn't mean it to happen. I didn't mean to get either of us involved, but you were . . . oh, never mind that now." She sighed and bundled up the loose hair that tumbled over one shoulder. "In a few hours they'll have to stop and rest the horses. And they won't travel with us by day. Not much, anyway, since we might be seen and questions asked."

She had been about to say "late," Charles realized, thoroughly vexed. She blamed their situation on his being late. "Just what am I to do when they try to make me tell the things your husband is supposed to know?"

"They won't get the chance," Frances whispered back with an assurance he couldn't share. "We'll be away before that. And if they do get a chance, they'll start with me, not you."

His first peevish thought was that that seemed fair enough,

though hardly desirable. No, it wasn't desirable at all. Being taken by the Spanish was no jest. With his legs shackled together, he could defend neither himself nor her. "What's their excuse for this wagon?" he demanded, trying to find a comfortable position in the leg shackles. His boots saved him from the metal cuffs' chafing, but the iron bar between them held his legs at a set width, rigid and utterly maddening. His head throbbed like a drum to the movement of the wagon. "These men are soldiers, aren't they? How is it they're allowed in France?"

"They're probably posing as servants to the Spanish ambassador to France. They've been assigned to take a load of special provisions to meet the Archbishop of Toledo, who is arriving from the south. His Eminence doesn't travel by sea if he can help it." She prodded one of the bags surrounding them. "This is fine quality, unground wheat for manchet bread. His Eminence prefers the best."

She seemed remarkably well informed about the details, Charles thought. Too well informed. He didn't like what that implied. Trying not to think about it, he began turning over escape plans in his mind.

"Rest, now," she urged. "We'll have no other chance to sleep. Later, we'll need to be alert in order to escape."

He loathed the idea of giving in to sleep, leaving himself vulnerable.

But her lap was deliciously warm, cradling his head in a manner he could never hope for under better circumstances. Besides, he did have to clear his brain of this confounded dizziness if he hoped to get them to safety. As a last precaution, he roused himself to grope at his belt to check his knife. At least they'd left his hands unbound. Then he realized why.

"Thunderation! They've taken my knife. My rapier as well."

"I fear so." She bent her face closer to muffle her words. As she did so, her thick braid came untucked again. It tumbled over her shoulder and knocked him in the nose. He winced.

"Oh, your pardon. My foolish hair. It's so unruly." Her nimble hands nipped away the braid and caressed his face again, soft and soothing. "I don't hold much hope for recovering your weapons, but I believe I can manage to unlock your leg shackles."

It made no sense that he should enjoy having her face so near his, not when she made him ragingly angry with her insane confidence and her evasive answers. But the faintest breath of honeysuckle wafted from her, mingling with the nutty smell from the sacks of wheat. Warmth and intimacy. A cradling nest. Along with the splendid heat of her thighs.

The thought of what the Spanish would do to them later interrupted his lapse into pleasure. This was no jaunt for the joy of it. Damn his brother, tricking him into coming to escort her. Given Jonathan's penchant for intrigue, especially as one of the queen's spy masters, he must have known about the danger all along.

Which left Charles with no help but a couple of urchins and a woman nicknamed Frank. "You'll have to pardon my lack of optimism, mistress, but I would rather think the English ambassador will send a search party for us. I have faith in his men."

"He won't do that," she said with unfailing logic, stroking his hair with that damned soothing motion. "They will think that you arrived, as planned, and that we caught our ship to England."

"You have the most irritating manner of contradicting me."

"And you"—she made a moue at him with her full lips—"have the most arrogant way of discounting everything I say."

Charles closed his eyes, more to escape her lovely face than to rest. Her beauty lulled him into a false sense of security, and he couldn't afford to be off guard.

He breathed deeply to steady himself as her fingertips and palms glided along his temple and cheek, as tender as eyas down. Her hands descended, brushing against his neck as she straightened his collar. She moved them away too soon, instead turning her attention to ordering his hair. Vainly, she attempted to restore the part and direct it away from his wound.

His head did throb so . . . and he could use the sleep. With a last luxurious glimpse of her nymph's face, he drifted off, reaching for a splendid dream. If only he had never gone to the Caribbean, if only he had never been devoured by such passion for a woman that nothing else mattered. He yearned for the days before he'd known that destructive hunger, when he'd been at peace with himself.

But such days were long gone. As the fog of his injury

closed around him, the image of Inez's beauty haunted him. If that voyage to the Spanish West Indies had made a man of him, it had also corrupted him beyond hope. Inez couldn't be blamed. He had failed his best friend when he was most needed, and his poor judgment would torment him for the rest of his days.

Something had changed. Awareness leaped into Charles's mind, chasing away sleep. He snapped his eyes open, then winced at the light flooding the canvas overhead. They were still in the moving wagon, prisoners of the Spanish. He'd hoped it was only a bad dream.

Wiggling his legs, he felt the ankle cuffs and the rigid bar. *Damn. No dream, for sure.* His legs were still shackled. His mouth had grown as dry as the sands of the Turkish desert, and he had to relieve himself something fierce.

But he still had the soft warmth of a female lap cradling his head—Frances's lap. He shifted his gaze and found her sleeping, her head pillowed against the sacks of wheat. The fingers of her one hand curled in a death grip around a handful of his doublet. Her other hand rested on her hawk's cage.

Such a sweet face, so innocent in slumber, belying the haughty arrogance she displayed when awake. The lids of her eyes, closed now, were like shorn cream velvet with a dark border of lacy lashes for fringe. Her opulent lips, so tempting last night at the inn, were pinched into a tight bud. He pondered those lips, then decided no one would ever believe the things that issued from them when she was awake—neither the insults nor her insane optimism. Every time she opened her mouth, his head ached.

That reminded him, his throbbing pain had left. Charles carefully moved his head from side to side, experimenting. His vision had cleared, too. The roaring in his ears was gone. Tightening his neck muscles, he raised his head and scanned the interior of the wagon. He felt alert, sharp—ready to plan their escape.

The creaking rhythm of the wagon slowed. He'd suspected they were about to stop. Focusing his attention on the voices outside, he heard clipped orders from the captain directing them off the road. As the wagon wheels bounced out of the road ruts and lurched across rough meadow, Frances jerked awake.

"What's happening?" Her death grip on his doublet half strangled him as she looked frantically around.

"Nothing, yet. We're stopping, but there's no danger. Not now, anyway." Charles motioned for her to let go of his doublet. "You're choking me. Would you be so kind . . ." The canvas roof darkened as they passed into something—a deserted barn, Charles supposed.

Looking sheepish, Frances released his doublet. "Do you feel any better?"

"Well enough to arrange our escape."

"I'll handle that with Pierre and Louis," she informed him. "You're wounded. We'll have it planned by tonight."

He started to upbraid her for her idiotic notions, but fell silent as Spanish voices closed in on them. They remained still as their captors unhitched the horses. But one look at her and Charles could almost hear her thoughts racing. No doubt she was thinking how she and her fierce eleven-year-olds would effect a miraculous flight.

The goshawk fluttered in its cage. Instantly, she turned to it, all tender murmurings, even as she placed a hand on Charles's temple, soothing both her charges.

Damn, but her touch felt good. Too good. Charles wished she would leave him alone so he could think straight. The horses were being led away, probably for water, then to graze. When would it be their turn?

A hand yanked up the canvas covering of the wagon. A coarse, unshaven fellow addressed them in Spanish, ordering them out. Charles came alert instantly, knowing this was one of last night's attackers, now minus his mask.

"He needs the shackles off before he can get up, Diego," Frances said sweetly to the man in Spanish. Apparently, he knew no English. But he understood a woman's charm, especially with Frances turning a considerable amount in his direction. The buffoon all but drooled over her dazzling smile and soft voice, not even aware that she issued him a command.

Inez had been like that, Charles remembered sourly. She'd used her appeal as ammunition to get her way, withholding it to punish him when he refused to cave in.

He banished thoughts of Inez as Frances removed her hand from his brow and continued to bewitch the Spaniard. "Come now," she coaxed in Spanish, "give me the key."

Charles almost had to stifle a grin as the man shook his

head and backed away. He must have learned already that Frances would badger him until she had her way. He disappeared. The captain came to bicker in his stead.

"*Que?*" The leader planted his burly frame at the end of the wagon and grunted at Frances. His long leather jerkin and bulky galligaskins didn't conceal his bullish proportions, formidable in his solid height and imposing breadth.

A bonfire of anger ignited inside Charles as he remembered the dung beetle from the Rue Saint Jacques. He'd been there hunting Frances. This same devil and his men had then ambushed her at the inn.

Narrowing his eyes to slits, Charles assessed his opponent. For a halfpenny, he would strangle the captain with his bare hands and relish doing it. And he wouldn't have to wait long. Without question, they would come to blows.

"Good captain," wheedled Frances. "Won't you unlock these shackles? How is a man to take care of his needs?"

The captain spat on the ground and turned away, unimpressed by her wiles.

"Captain Landa, you would be wise to humor me," she called after him in that beguiling voice of hers—though now the guile turned to a taunt. "I know everything about your recent error regarding my uncle. When I see the archbishop, you wouldn't want me to tell him about it, would you?"

The man halted abruptly and swung around.

Charles muttered a curse. The wench gave as good as she got, that was sure. The Bull thought so, too, because he glowered and leaned over the wagon. He closed one of his huge hands around her arm and jerked her toward him.

Charles's head slid from her lap and banged on the hard boards. Groaning, he sat up and clutched his wound at the wave of pain.

"Gently, Captain Landa," Frances admonished as he jerked her again toward the end of the wagon. Gripping her arms, the Bull wrenched her to her knees, bringing them face-to-face.

"You know nothing," he snarled.

Charles could barely contain himself. He wanted to fling himself on the man and tear him apart—how dare he maul the woman assigned to his protection. But he forced himself to stay still, watching for signs of the man's weakness. Strategy could save them; he'd learned that truth the hard way.

JANET LYNNFORD

"But I do," Frances said calmly as she faced her enemy. "I know your king wants me whole and able to talk, just as he wanted my uncle. You don't dare fail him twice."

Her sheer gall fascinated Charles as she balled her fists against her thighs, showing no reaction to the captain's deepening scowl and threatening stance. Crouched at the end of the wagon, she looked fierce enough to spring on him and wrestle him to the ground. "Give me the key to the leg irons," she demanded in a flat voice.

With a growl, the Bull pushed her away. She fell back against the wheat sacks, but scrambled up again until she saw he summoned Diego. A glimmer of a triumphant smile hovered at her lips as the captain thrust a ring of keys into his underling's hands.

"Remove the bar between his feet," he barked in Spanish. "Replace it with the chain so he can walk." He cast Frances an ugly look, then spun around and left Diego to execute the command.

She scowled at the captain's retreating back as she dusted wheat chaff from her hands.

Charles clenched his teeth. He understood the promise of retaliation in the Bull's look. During his duty in the Spanish West Indies, he'd learned more than he wanted about Spanish tempers.

They must be away from these men within the hour, or Frances, too, would know the full measure of a Spaniard's wrath.

Chapter 7

By the bright heavens, he's changed more than I thought.

Frances knelt on the ground several feet from the heavy wain and tried not to stare. But she couldn't help it. The entire time she opened Oriana's cage and urged the bird onto her gloved fist, pretending to be absorbed in her work, she watched Charles from the corner of her eye. Diego knelt at his feet, exchanging the rigid bar of his shackles for a chain so he could walk.

Before, with him lying hurt and vulnerable in the dim wagon, she had forgotten he wasn't fourteen anymore, not as easily put in his place as he was nine years ago.

Now, as he uncoiled from his seat on the wagon tail and stretched to his full height, she realized her error. The full light of day revealed what she had only guessed at in the dim candlelight of the inn last night; he was more than just handsome. Although he wasn't unusually tall, the thick contours of his thigh muscles, along with the width of his chest and shoulders, suggested a dangerous strength. He radiated an assured power despite his head wound and fatigue.

Clearly, from the stance he took, poised for action, and from the way he sized up their opponents, he was a menace to anyone he decided had crossed him . . . including her, though in an entirely different way.

Dangerous pleasure from watching him swept a path through her middle like the mating flight of a hawk. The warning sounded again in her mind. *Beware. This man seduces women as easily and naturally as most people eat and drink.*

She swallowed thickly and shifted her gaze, concentrating instead on Diego as he joined his fellows. Studying each man in turn, she noted the third Spaniard now wore his arm in a sling. Charles had done that damage during last night's fight.

Apparently, the captain recognized his prisoner's potential threat. Loaded gun in hand, he personally hustled Charles out of the barn to take care of necessary business. She understood the precaution, but it left her alone with the other three men.

Like a rough gang of scoundrels, they huddled together, jabbering in Spanish punctuated by slang she didn't understand. Their pointed leers thrown her way made her stomach tighten with fear. She mustn't show it, though. She must put them in their place.

She marched over and regally demanded they build a fire for boiling water. They met her command with mute, astonished stares. But after several uneasy seconds, they obeyed. Two dispersed to gather wood. Another collected stones for a fire ring just beyond the barn door. The one with the sling searched the wagon, hauled a black kettle from a sack, and filled it with water from a nearby pond.

Trembling inside, relieved that her bid for authority had worked, Frances sat on the wagon tail with Oriana, gripped her equipment bag, and awaited Charles's return.

"Sit," she ordered the minute he appeared. "I want to bathe your wound."

He complained fiercely throughout her ministrations. His irritated snarls made giggles tickle her throat. How could she laugh at a time like this?

Baron Milborne's dangerous charm made her giddy, she decided while bandaging his head. Couple that with their danger, and something close to hysteria built inside her.

They needed food, she told herself firmly. Something hot and bracing to keep up their strength. Determined to procure some, she finished with Charles and sought the captain. "We must hunt, sir. My hawk requires raw meat with a bit of fur and bone to keep her fit. Otherwise her weight falls. This is an expensive bird."

The captain's eyes flickered with interest. Frances recognized his look. He dreamed of claiming her valuable hawk once she was in prison. Or once she was dead.

Ignoring the cold waves of fear that flowed through her, she rallied her strength, smiled prettily, and tempted him further with a description of steaming hot rabbit stew. If she had to kill fresh meat, she might as well fill their pot. She craved something hot and bracing herself.

The captain was a man; his stomach ruled, though even

that with caution. He ordered his men to pick up their guns—one of them a heavy arquebus that could blow a man to pieces, the others, smaller hand calivers—and ordered them to follow her. Even Charles had to come, so he couldn't escape while they were gone.

Frances slowed her pace to accommodate his leg shackles. Yet despite them, he walked proud and angry at her side, seeming freer and fiercer than the men who guarded him with loaded guns.

As she trudged through the meadow east of the road, Oriana on her fist, her equipment bag with the precious papers slung over the other shoulder, Frances bid farewell to the interlude of closeness she had shared with Charles in the wagon. While dawn crept over the horizon, she considered her reaction to him and decided it was best banished from her mind.

Yet she had taken comfort from their brief intimacy, when his head had lain snuggled in her lap. Robbed of her uncle's presence in her life, she had shed tears of self-pity and wanted to cling to Charles. Especially when, in his sleep, he had shifted to his side, pillowed his cheek on her lap, and linked one arm around her waist.

After that, she couldn't rest again. His touch had sent her heart racing and great wings of longing fluttering in her belly. He completely destroyed her inner calm.

Unfortunately, his movement had told her something else as well. He was used to closeness with women, probably used to bedding with them. Whereas she had never had such closeness with a man, except once with Antoine, and not through the night. Later, she had regretted it—it was a harsh way to learn a lesson, but she *had* learned it. If she wanted loyalty, she should rely on her hawk, not on a man.

Yet Charles was honest with her, though sometimes brusque as well. In fact, he often bordered on rudeness. But she would far rather another man's rudeness than Antoine's honeyed company. Her former betrothed had oiled his every word with lies.

Suddenly, she chafed with impatience, needing the work with her bird to clear her confused thoughts.

Oriana craned her neck, alert and eager. The air smelled of sedge crushed beneath her feet as they swished through the vegetation bordering the shimmering pond. The fierce joy of the chase coursed through her, setting her alight like the sun's rays burnishing the land. Despite their watchful captors, despite the fear of them icing the pit of her stomach, she was still alive, she was going to hunt, and for her, while there was the hunt, there was hope.

Her anxiety lessened further when the captain wandered off to relieve himself in some bushes and didn't rejoin them. He was obviously confident that she and Charles couldn't escape. The two other Spaniards dropped back, seeming to enjoy the sunshine and the chance to talk. That left only the arquebus bearer one pace behind her.

Relieved that things were going so well, she scanned the meadow intently, pretending to look for game. In reality, she searched for the telltale rustle of tall grass. Pierre and Louis should be nearby.

"Now's our moment to plan our escape," Charles hissed at her side. "Here's what you're to do."

She started to find him so close beside her, his jaw clenched, his eyes burning like a wild animal's when caged. No wonder. He had a hundred reasons to be furious with both her and the Spanish. One of those reasons was around his ankles, shortening his steps.

"*I* have it all planned," she informed him as they walked, pretending more assurance than she felt. "But we can't talk just now." She indicated their guard with a tilt of her head. "Blessedly, he doesn't know English. I tested him every chance I got. But 'tis best not to speak too freely." She sent him a smile of confidence. "You'll be happier once you have a full stomach. Men always are."

"I'll be happier once I've made blood pudding of these whoresons," Charles snapped. "Which I intend to do first chance *I* get. But we have to understand our parts for this escape to work. We'll talk about it now."

For no good reason, his anger turned her thirteen again and full of mischief. "No, we're going to hunt, and I'm to serve as the dog." She grinned cheekily at him. "I'll see what we can flush from these grasses. I hope some rabbit, because I'm starved. There's wild onion everywhere, so we'll put that in the stew as well." She almost laughed at the frown lines cut by irritation in his handsome brow.

"Are you refusing to cooperate with me?" he growled.

"Yes," she said brightly. "I am."

"Tell me about your plan."

"I can't," she said primly.

"If you're trying to make me angry, you're succeeding marvelously. Exactly why can't you tell me?"

"The more you know, the more like you are to ruin it." Unfortunately, he had an unsettling way of bringing out the worst in her. Why, she didn't know. Mayhap because it took little to make him like the arquebus, primed and ready to explode.

The frown lines deepened, adding a hard crease between his eyes. "Mistress Morley"—sarcasm boiled behind the formality of his tone—"I do not intend to wait meekly until our hosts decide to question us. If you don't tell me what you plan, I'll take charge and do it my way."

Pharaoh's foot, but he was determined to master her. She was equally determined he would not. "And do you expect to escape right now with our friend Arquebus following?" She made a moue at him and was rewarded by his snarl. "I, for one, am going nowhere until Oriana is fed."

She turned to her bird, finished with Charles and his choler. If he refused to trust her, it wasn't her affair. She would lose herself in the passion of flying her bird. The hunt's age-old ritual would bring her release.

Adjusting the heavy glove on which Oriana perched, she whispered sweet syllables to her bird and began to walk.

"Why don't you hood your hawk?" he asked, still close at her side.

"No need for one, Master Falconer, sir," she murmured, getting his point only too well. "Since Oriana trusts me, I don't keep her blind."

"Yet you do me." His sharp expulsion of breath told her she had pressed him too far. His next words proved it. "I'll agree to your scheme only on one condition."

"What?" she asked warily.

"I fly Oriana from now on."

He might as well have asked to bed her on the spot. She stared at him in shock. "She won't let you."

"You know better than that." He chuckled wickedly and swept her with an assessing gaze. "She *will* let me. She'll want me to."

He loomed over her, exuding a pungent, masculine magic that made birds and women submit to him. Foolish desire winged through her blood at the thought of his subduing her in like manner. Frances stared at him, unable to tear her gaze from his, wanting him in a mindless, primitive way that thoroughly frightened her. Without question, after he mastered Oriana, he would come after her.

Turning away in panic, she fiddled with Oriana's jesses and bells to be sure they weren't tangled.

"I'm also warning you," he continued, "I'll not wait any longer to be quit of these shackles. Your scheme to get me out of them didn't work. Now I intend to take the key by force."

"I said I'd get it for you."

"How, damn it? If you have a plan, out with it straight."

"Y-You're impossible." Her stutter ruined the drama of her accusation. She rushed to cover it up. "Is this how you behave with all the women you take hunting, as cross as an old bear?"

"Women prefer to be the quarry when I hunt."

She whirled to face him, a biting retort ready on her lips. The desire smoldering in his eyes brought her up short, increasing the heat of her own arousal, doubling her fear of his power over her. "I suppose you think women are only good for bedding," she flung at him, relieved that her voice remained steady.

"They *are* good for bedding. I can think of one in particular who would be superb."

She wanted to shout with indignation, but refused to succumb to the humiliation. To be insulted so, in front of their enemies, no less! Arquebus stood just behind Charles, vainly trying to follow their exchange. The two other men had caught up and watched them, smirks on their faces. The sizzle of excitement between her and Charles leaped like a live flame, obvious to any within range. "You're preposterous," she hissed.

"You raised the subject."

She *had* raised the subject. But it was his fault. If she held anything back from him—even something she needed to keep private—he blackmailed her with his magical voice. Terrified of yielding to him in greater matters, she relented on this smaller one. "Once we start off again tonight, one of the boys will slip you the key," she whispered. "There. I've told you the plan. Now please, I beg you, leave me alone!"

Holding Oriana closer for protection, she communed with her creature, urgently trying to shut Charles out. Oriana shook her feathers, swelling to twice her normal size.

Charles chuckled to himself. He'd found a second of Mistress Morley's vulnerable spots. Before long, he would know every weak point and unprotected chink in her formidable armor. Then this bold wench might learn she couldn't toss him tiny details of her plan like crumbs to a rat.

While she cooed and talked to her hawk, he drank in her beauty. Despite the dark smudges under her eyes from lack of sleep, despite their long night on the road, she looked fresh and appetizing in the late morning sun. The wrinkles in her black kirtle skirt and dirt-smudged smock added to the wild air about her. Her thick braid wound into a rough coil exposed the white nape of her neck. How he burned to place his hand there, just at the top of her smock where the rays of light shone on her porcelain flesh.

Slowly, his hand would descend, his fingers pushing away the fabric, exploring her bare skin. In fact, he would like to remove her torn bodice and smock entirely to see her full breasts and tapering waist. Lust shot through him, fueled by his earlier experience in the wagon: he'd awoken to find his cheek cushioned so close to the apex of her pliant, desirable thighs that he'd caught the scent of her woman's warmth. It was enough to drive any man over the edge.

But then, she'd been crying. Quietly, so as not to disturb him, but he'd felt the shake of her sobs. Probably mourning her uncle, which stopped him in his tracks. Any liberties he might have taken dried up inside him in the face of her grief.

The remnants of tears on her cheeks moved him unaccountably, more than he cared to admit. And although he wasn't accustomed to comforting grieving women, a strong desire to drive away her pain had seized him, taking him by surprise.

The contrast of that noble feeling against the lust she fueled in him now pitched him on the horns of a dilemma—to console or seduce? She changed so rapidly from one demeanor to the other, he wasn't sure. But right now, without question, lust prevailed . . .

He wondered if she understood her effect on him as she crooned to her bird while they walked. The creature puffed out her feathers and ruffled her crest, chuckling to her mistress in reply.

Half closing his lids against the late morning sun, he studied the goshawk. When she flew, he would know for certain, but he judged her to be tough, hardy, and perfectly trained. Amazing that a woman had prepared her so well.

But of course that was what had outraged him most when he'd first met Frances. She insisted on excelling at something he felt belonged to the domain of men.

Now she heightened his dilemma by first arousing him, then infuriating him, even as she forced him to admire her skill with her bird.

With an impatient thrust, he pushed the entire issue from his mind, concentrating instead on his chain so it didn't snag. He wanted nothing to do with women other than an occasional bedding. He wanted to be left alone. And he wanted to hunt.

They walked until Oriana had cast up the pellet of fur and feathers from her last feeding. She was ready to fly.

"What are you waiting for?" he urged. "Give her her wings."

Frances sent him a mulish glance, as if she understood exactly what he wanted and delighted in withholding it. "Most men are in no hurry to give females their wings."

"I am *not* like most men."

"I hadn't noticed." With that taunt, she turned her haughty back on him and launched the gos.

The bird left her fist with a powerful thrust and the beat of great wings. Her rise into the dazzling sky launched something within Charles as well—a lonely hunger seeking release in the relentless drive for the prey.

For three years that same hunger had kept him awake nights, its pain driving him to fill an elusive need. It was like this every time he joined the chase—for woman or for game. Each time his blood heated. Excitement flared.

The presence of the Spaniards heightened the feeling in him. Primitive emotions merged with anticipation of the hunt and threatened to consume him—fury at the shackles, the driving urge to attack the Spaniards and tear them apart with his bare hands, the insane desire to beguile Frances until she begged for his touch.

He hesitated on the next step and frowned at her back. What was it about her that turned him into a foolhardy youth, one with more daring than sense?

She was driving him mad.

Moving as fast as he could in his hobbled state, he caught up with her, determined to take charge again. He clapped a hand on her shoulder, and she nearly vaulted out of her smock.

Suppressing a grin, he searched her face as she turned. She

slapped on a glare as fast as a speeding bird. Too late. He'd already glimpsed her desire for him—with the urgent leap of fire, it flared in her emerald eyes.

Who was driving whom mad?

Amused by her efforts to hide her interest, he gestured toward the hawk's flight path. "You're supposed to be the dog in this hunt," he chided her. "Go flush the game."

From his vantage point, Charles watched Frances catch up a stick and move forward, stirring grass and bracken in a vigorous rush. Rabbits should be plentiful here. Oriana hovered directly above as if she were connected to her mistress by an invisible thread. In the brief minutes at the inn last night, he had bonded with the hawk in the strange, magical way that his old teacher, Master Dickon, had taught him was his gift. Now, thanks to that bonding, he felt the exhilaration of the bird as she pumped her wings to reach her pitch. As if suspended in the heavens, she hung on high, waiting for her mistress to flush the quarry so she might attack and kill.

His blood heated. He moved after Frances, conscious only of the hunt and the change that swept over Frances's face as swiftly as the flicker of a wing. Suddenly, she was no longer an earth-bound woman, prisoner of the Spanish. She was a wild creature belonging to field and sky. Her feet flashed beneath her skirts as she ran, beating the tall grass with a long branch.

He grinned and lengthened his stride until he hit the limit of the chain. Despite the impediment, energy charged his limbs. Flying birds of prey meant fever-pitched races through the wilds in pursuit of blood. It was about hunger, keen and urgent. It was about passion—for the chase . . . for a woman who fired his lust . . . for the freedom to break loose from the bondage of daily cares and soar at her side. With the pain in his head receded, he threw his heart, if not his leg-shackled body, into the infinite promise of the hunt.

A rabbit erupted from its cover. Frances loosed a special whistle. As the coney's brown fur flashed like a skein of yarn, unraveling at dizzying speed through the grass, Oriana dived and homed in on her target.

Charles changed course, ready for the zigzag dodges of the rabbit. He knew that when it veered away from Frances and the hawk, it would come straight for him.

In a flash, the coney whipped by him, followed by the hawk. He gave chase, instinctively finding a loping stride in

spite of the shackles. Frances panted at his heels, breathing
hot and quick. Obviously, she could pass him if she wished,
but she held back so he could go first. He imagined the pair
of them side by side, doing something other than hunting,
their blood speeding, their lungs laboring for air, their need
for each other rising. The lust of the moment seized him in a
grasp so intense, it was almost unbearable.

Suddenly, the hawk fell on her target like a stone.

Fur flew in all directions as he reached them. Sensing
Frances right behind him, Charles watched Oriana fight the
wounded rabbit for all she was worth while it kicked and
bucked, trying to throw her off. Quickly, he moved in with a
stick and angled for a blow that would miss the hawk. Recognizing his move to help her, the hawk let go. He struck once,
then twice, rendering the rabbit senseless. He pulled back.

Oriana dropped on the head, tore past fur in one swift rip
of her razor-sharp beak, and began to feed.

"Good girl." Panting, Frances sank into a crouch before
the kill.

"Well trained," he said briefly, though he wasn't watching
the bird. He eyed Frances, the way the bared flesh of her
throat and bosom heaved as she drew in and expelled air, the
brilliant flush of her face. His loins flamed at the sight of her
rapt attention to her bird's feeding. The meat was their survival—their food and sustenance. Yet his physical desire for
this woman surmounted all else. He wanted to grasp her the
way the hawk had grasped its prey, pull her into his arms,
and make her his own.

"Clean kill," he forced himself to say instead. "How much
do you want her to have?"

" 'Tis best she stop now," Frances said after a minute.
"We could use another rabbit or two, so she'll have more."

Without another word, he stretched out his arm to the
hawk. Taking a last tidbit, Oriana docilely mounted his arm.
Just as at the inn, she didn't needle him with her talons, but
settled her feathers as he rose to his feet. Satisfied by the
welcome weight on his arm, he murmured to the bird, then
glanced at Frances.

She smoldered, fury rippling from her in almost tangible
waves.

She was jealous again.

Stepping forward, she thrust out her fist to Oriana in an
imperious gesture.

Grinning wider, he held the hawk away. "I'm to fly her, remember? You wouldn't deny me this. I'm only half a man without a bird."

Her eyes widened, and she stumbled back a pace, her haughty expression chased by one of sympathetic confusion. It proved she wasn't as immune to him as she liked to pretend. New surges of appetite fueled his lust as he held her gaze, awareness firing between them like gunpowder flashing in the pan.

Yet nothing could come of it—not with Arquebus behind them and peril dogging their heels. He tamped down his frustration as he took the glove from Frances and resettled Oriana. "Get along," he ordered the bird, barely concealing the catch in his voice as he launched her again. Relieved that she obeyed him implicitly, he held out his stick to Frances. "One rabbit won't feed six people and a hungry hawk. We need several more."

Frances glanced around her, as if coming out of a trance, and nodded mutely. She turned at his order, focused on her bird, and moved off.

Charles clamped his mouth shut and shook his head in self-mockery. Hunting game—hunting women—he'd always thought them fine sport. But they'd never affected him this intensely before.

Thankfully, the hunt, plans for escape, and the vile Spaniards kept his mind too occupied to dwell overly long on Frances, on the way she had run her moist, pink flower of a tongue over her lips as she'd stared at him. He stored the thought away for later consideration when he had time.

Two rabbits later, they approached the far side of the pond. Arquebus caught up, as did the other Spaniards, all three with their weapons primed. The captain rounded the pond from the other direction, cutting them off. As if they could escape in this open, flat country with his legs shackled, Charles thought in disgust.

A large stone caught his eye. It begged him to throw it and smash the Spaniard's head. With extreme difficulty, he restrained himself. And only because Frances had promised him the key. How she would manage it, he had no idea, but he was forced to try her plan since she refused to cooperate with his.

"*Frank, ici,*" came a sharp hiss. "*Maintenant?*"

Charles knew better than to turn his head as he traced the voice to the reeds ringing the pond.

"Non!" Frances kept her answer to a loud whisper. She stepped closer to Charles and stroked the bird perched on his fist. "Not now," she murmured, pretending she spoke to Oriana. "Tonight, when we travel again."

From the corner of his eye, Charles spied two ferretlike faces peering out from among the cattails. Scruffy hair and smudged faces—little more showed. He set his teeth as hope plummeted. Just as he'd suspected; Frances's saviors were nothing more than street vermin. No chance these two could help.

He must take charge of their escape.

Except that Frances refused to cooperate, wouldn't even hear what he had planned. Her resistance made his blood boil. As the queen's Master Falconer, he was accustomed to obedience, not to his orders being shrugged aside.

"Tonight, then," the one whispered to Frances, "when you are under way, we will . . ."

The boy reverted to French, and Charles couldn't translate his slang, except to know he intended to create a stir of some sort.

"Go ahead, launch her a last time," Frances ordered Charles, as calmly as if they strolled by the Dorset shore, as if no men stood over them, armed and eager to shoot if they made a wrong move.

Charles launched Oriana, but this time he took no pleasure from the bird's flight.

While the gos rose in the air, Frances held her hand-kerchief to her nose to conceal the movement of her lips. "My companion is leg shackled," she told the boys. "We require the key carried by the biggest man, the captain. It's the tiniest one on the ring at his waist. Get it for us first. The rest of your plan pleases me well."

The cattails rustled in seeming agreement, and they heard no more from the lads.

Damn the pair of pestilence. And blast Frances for thinking them capable of organizing an escape, much less besting four Spaniards. It was all up to him.

He bit back a groan as he eyed their captors and wondered how in thunder he would manage it without getting himself maimed or killed.

Chapter 8

A magical air of unreality hung about Charles as he reluctantly led the way back to camp, carrying Oriana and two of the rabbits. How could they be in mortal danger in this quiet countryside full of early spring greening? How could he be lifted out of himself by the hunt one moment, then plummeted into frustration and despair the next?

Back at the barn, he dressed the rabbits while Frances watched. The pounding in his head had started afresh from his running after the bird.

Fool, he chided himself. He should have rested while Frances worked Oriana, but he never could resist the hunt. Now he needed more rest before they escaped. And he needed food.

What they got was some hard bread and a few bites of cheese while the water for cooking heated. Hardly enough for an injured man. Soon after, though, the perfume of simmering meat and wild onion washed the air.

Arquebus chose that moment to come at him with the bar shackle.

"Don't come near me," he snarled, leaping from his seat and sinking into a crouch.

"Diego," the squat man flung over his shoulder. "Come here."

The Bull came, too, summoning the fourth man and closing in on Charles. *Curse it,* he couldn't fight them all, no matter how much anger fueled his strength. Yet he couldn't sit meekly, either. With that damned bar, he could take only mincing steps. Hate for the Spaniards roared through him. Hate, too, for his helplessness and dependence on a woman.

"Do something, damn it," he snarled at Frances. She dropped the stick she was using to stir the stew, her face turning ashen as her eyes widened with alarm.

"Captain, I beg you to leave the chain for now." She

mastered her fear as she approached them, but he heard the frantic edge to her voice.

The Bull ignored her pleas and thrust her aside. She landed in a heap on the barn floor.

Charles roared his outrage and lunged toward the closest man. All four rushed him at once. He landed a punch to Arquebus's jaw, then kicked out and hit the other one squarely on the knee. As the man doubled over, Charles dived under Diego's arm and broke into a stumbling run.

He burst out of the barn into the welcome sun. Where he was going or what he thought to achieve by fleeing, he had no idea. He only knew they would not kill Frances, and he had to be free. Once at liberty, he would find a way to liberate her, and then he would grind those scurvy devils into dust.

"Stop or she dies!" the captain called.

Charles knew better and charged on.

Frances cried out, a frightened, pleading sound without words.

He whirled back. The Bull stood in the barn entry, one arm gripping Frances around the collarbone. Charles's own hunting knife nicked her throat, releasing a trickle of blood.

"You can't kill her," Charles challenged. "She is required by your king."

"I could mark her with a few cuts," the Bull sneered. With lazy insolence, he shifted the knife and began to cut away the fabric over Frances's heaving breast. In another minute she would be bared for all the men to see . . . and to use.

Defeated by the threat and the panic in her eyes, he held out his upturned palms and returned to the barn. Step by step agonizing step, he endured his fury, forcing himself to remain outwardly calm. Because of his duty to the woman he'd been sent to protect, he had to do it. They would not kill her, but they might do far worse.

Two of the three lackeys surged into the open to surround him. The third must still be incapacitated from his blow. At least he had done some harm.

"Let her go." He halted directly in front of the Bull and Frances.

The Bull grunted, gesturing for the Spaniard with the bar.

"Release her first," Charles insisted.

The captain shoved Frances. He grinned as she stumbled to his left.

Though he burned with inner fury, Charles stood firm, never taking his gaze from his opponent.

Diego bent over and reached for Charles's left ankle. Reason told him not to resist, but reason be damned.

He dived for the Bull, his fist connecting with the captain's nose. Blood spurted everywhere. The man reeled backward and crashed to the ground. Charles leaped on him, groping for his hunting knife as two others jumped him from behind. Pulling the knife free, he drove straight for the Bull's chest.

His opponent rolled away, the knife grazing a shoulder instead. Thrown off balance, Charles recovered and hurtled himself for a strike at the throat. The captain caught his wrist, stopping the knife just short of piercing his flesh. Muscle pitted against muscle, they wrestled. His arm shook with exertion as Charles forced the knife up . . . up . . .

Diego raced in with a log and raised it for a blow. Charles plunged to one side. The log struck his arm a glancing blow, knocking the knife from his grasp. It skittered away into a pile of loose straw.

Charles lost sight of it as he collapsed beneath the assault of the three Spaniards. He fought them with feral madness. The bone in one man's arm cracked. More blood flowed. Arquebus howled with pain.

Charles's advantage didn't last long. His strength waned as his head pulsed, ready to explode. His blows weakened and missed more often than not.

The Spaniards overpowered him at last. Curling himself into a ball, he steeled himself to endure their kicks and blows. Every bruise and cut tormented him—his right rib throbbed, his left eye burned. They replaced the bar while he lay spent, then dragged him back to the wain.

Hauling himself in under the canvas covering, he collapsed and closed his eyes, willing consciousness to leave him. Blessed forgetfulness, take him away from this torment. He was too hot-headed, letting emotion overcome sense.

Wet, warm drops fell on his face, accompanied by muffled sobs. To his astonishment, Frances bent over him, weeping. When he tried to open his eyes, only the right one responded. He touched the other gingerly, feeling the tortured flesh.

"Why did you do that? Why did you resist?" Frances's tears on his face were somehow infinitely more disturbing than her teasing taunts.

"Did you expect me to sit by while they batted you around? Should I smile pleasantly and let them put on this damned bar?" He gnashed his teeth, enraged by the blood smeared on her white neck, infuriated by the rigid metal holding his legs apart.

"They put the bar on you, nonetheless. And you got beaten in the bargain."

"So did they." With grim satisfaction he remembered the ugly crack of the one man's arm.

She knuckled away her tears with the back of one hand. "Why couldn't you wait for the boys to get the key?"

He closed his good eye. "I'm not in the habit of waiting for women and children to do my work."

"It's our work, too. Why do you have to be so bull-headed about it? You charge in and strike with no thought as to what might happen to you."

" 'Tis a habit I picked up."

"Where did you learn to be so foolhardy?" Her voice was hesitant, as if she were afraid to know.

She ought to be, he thought grimly. The memories plagued him without ceasing. "The Spanish West Indies," he said, refusing to elaborate or to move his mouth any more than necessary. One of his teeth might be loose. Or was he just too numb to feel it properly? He raised one hand to investigate. *Praise heaven,* he'd been mistaken. The tooth was still solidly in place.

"What were you doing there? You must have been very young."

"I was all of seventeen and thought to win fame and glory," he growled, hating the star-struck boy he'd been, longing for fortune and a chance to become great. "My older brother, Matthew, and I signed on with the great Sir Francis Drake. We sailed on his famous raid of the Spanish isles."

"I'm amazed your father let you go."

"Unfortunately, my father had nothing to say about it. He died of apoplexy when I was thirteen."

"Oh. I'm terribly sorry. I suppose that's why you went." When he refused to elaborate, she continued. "Can you tell me about the West Indies? What was it like? I don't know much."

"You don't want to know more. The West Indian islands are beautiful to look upon but deceptively harsh."

"I have heard a few ugly things about them. I heard the Spaniards are worse than the ones here."

"Double what you know of their brutality. They fight to win and damn the rules of fairness."

"You were a prisoner?"

"My best friend was until he died. I tried to rescue him, but I was too stupid to manage it. All I could do was smuggle in a knife to him." The familiar, gut-wrenching anguish claimed him as he spoke. "The Spanish invent highly imaginative tortures."

"Oh, God." Frances bent over, laid her cheek against his brow, and embraced him with both arms. "How terrible. I didn't know."

A tremor shook him at her touch. He didn't deserve anyone's sympathy—he should have saved his friend. Yet she poured blessed balm on his raw wound of self-hate, and he'd spilled his story, something he rarely did.

He was sorry in the next moment as he realized she shouldn't have to know about Richard since they, too, were prisoners of the Spanish. His experience left him little hope that the similarities would end there. Yet the pleasure of her cheek against his forehead drove him to prolong the embrace. With a shaky hand, he stroked her hair. She felt good against him, cool and smooth against the heat of his pain.

"I see it hurts you to talk about it," she whispered. "I won't ask any more, but I'm sorry you lost your friend. He must have been dear to your heart."

Her gentle acceptance was wholly unmerited. He changed the subject with a grunt. "We should have escaped earlier instead of hunting."

"One of us would have been shot. We couldn't take the risk."

"Sometimes the hope of dodging gunshot is the better choice," he said gruffly, torn between surprise and irritation that she concerned herself so over him, a stranger who had not been particularly kind. A warm, salty drop plunked down on the corner of his mouth, and he touched it, marveling. Why was she weeping so for him?

"Why did you cut the captain?" she asked, raising her head at last and wiping her eyes. "He'll repay you in like coin."

"I meant to kill him. Failing that, there was another reason. Did you get the knife?"

She grimaced at him, shook her head, and held one finger to her lips. "The knife? I didn't think about it," she said in a helpless tone he'd never before heard from her.

He stared, baffled by her answer. Had she gotten the weapon or hadn't she? *Blast!* Their captors would miss that knife and search until they found it.

She reached down and worked up the hem of her gown. What was the mad wench doing, showing her leg at a time like this?

It was an exceedingly pretty leg, muscled at the calf. His gaze lingered on her flesh, moving higher until he was arrested by something more important. Stuck in her garter was his knife. He lifted his gaze to the mischievous grin on her face.

He grinned back, both relieved and amazed. Not only had she gotten the knife, she'd had the sense to say aloud that she hadn't. "Never mind, foolish woman," he growled for the benefit of any Spaniard listening. "I see you're far too addle-witted to understand such important affairs. Leave me alone. I want to sleep."

Her answering smile met his, and she pulled down her skirt again to conceal the knife. "Eat first," she said quietly, pulling a bowl from among the grain bags.

Glories, she'd saved him some stew!

He devoured it in minutes, then closed his eyes, exhausted. He must rest and regain some strength, or he would never manage to free them, much less carry out his plan for escape.

As weariness claimed his body, he felt Frances stretch out beside him to sleep. Visions turned in his mind, of how she had looked during the hunt earlier, at the moment when her hawk left her fist. Molten light had bathed her as she tilted her face to the rising sun. She was like that sun, so pure and faithful and courageous, she burned as if lit from within.

The image memorized, he treasured it for a moment. Then he released it and slid into sleep.

Chapter 9

Why had she wept over him? Frances wondered as she sat in the wagon next to Charles and watched him sleep.

Because it was my fault he was beaten, she admitted miserably. Every time they met, something went wrong for him.

She shook her head to dislodge her guilt. No, it wasn't guilt. It was really self-pity. She wanted to keep him at her side. But the fact was, everyone she'd ever cared about died sooner than they ought to. Charles needed to be as far away as possible from her before she ruined his life . . . or worse.

A maudlin half laugh rose to her lips. How absurd, the way fate had brought them together again. Absurd to be thrown with him into prolonged intimacy when they disliked each other on sight. She abhorred his arrogant assumption that he, as a man, made all the decisions. And she quite as clearly enraged him when she took command.

Despite these things, she had a compelling desire to tear off both their clothes and lie naked in his arms. Which made not one whit of sense.

One hand to her mouth, she swallowed back her hysteria. She must quell thoughts of this nonsense, stay calm, and manage things properly as her uncle had taught her. And with Pierre and Louis to help, they should be able to escape. A pity her uncle had never approved of the boys enough to bring them into his household. She considered her lads more valuable than gold.

She slipped out and sat on the wagon tail. Captain Landa had stationed two guards at the barn door to watch over the wagon and their prisoners. But as soon as their superior had climbed to the loft above to sleep, they plunked down to devour the last of their meal.

The stew had been delicious. Frances would have liked more, and the portion for Charles had been too small, but she didn't dare ask. The men had fussed at her about the cut of raw meat and fur she had insisted on giving Oriana. *Fools.* The bird had filled their pot, yet they didn't want to share with her.

Satisfied that the men were too occupied with their gluttony to object, she slipped from the wagon and sat in the shadows behind the ladder to the loft. Pierre or Louis would be along soon and might need her help.

Diego heaved to his feet, his face grim, a caliver ready in his hand. "Here, what are you doing?"

"Just sitting," she said blandly. As long as she didn't try to escape, surely he wouldn't object.

"Back in the wagon," he ordered, pointing with the gun muzzle.

The Bull's face appeared over the edge of the loft, his hair littered with straw. He had been sleeping, or trying, it seemed. "If she wants to sit there, I give her leave. Guard the door."

"Thank you, Captain Landa. 'Tis most kind of you." She couldn't think why he would be kind, but she accepted without hesitation. "I'll stay right here."

"See that you do," he warned. "Try anything and I'll tie you up." The Bull's head disappeared back into the loft. Diego returned to his place by the door.

Leaning her head against the ladder, Frances shut her eyes and listened to the voices drifting down from the loft. If only she might overhear something of use.

"How many days till we're back in Paris?" Arquebus said, not bothering to lower his voice. She knew his medium-toned voice with its peasant accents by now.

"Nights, you mean. A good many. We have four to Nantes. From there we go straight down the coast to meet the archbishop at the border of France and Spain," the captain replied. "His Eminence will want to question the woman before we take her on to His Majesty."

Frances swallowed hard. His Eminence, the Archbishop of Toledo, intended to question her? Her blood ran cold at the thought. From the condition of her uncle's body, she knew firsthand how the Spanish acquired information. The terror of the nightmare returned to her. She hadn't even looked carefully at his corpse, but turned away, weeping uncontrollably. The sight had been too atrocious for words.

"A pity we couldn't beat more out of the fellow before we

sent him on," the captain continued. "We should have tried more extreme measures. His Eminence will."

Him? Frances froze. *Who did they mean?*

"He'll tell more when his niece shows up."

"*Sí.* He'll talk when she screams loud enough. They always do," the captain grunted. Their talk subsided. Hay rustled as the men settled themselves.

Frances sat in shock, hand to her mouth, staring at the barn's rough board wall. By the bright heavens, had she heard right—that her uncle wasn't dead? That meant some other man must have been buried in his place.

She lurched to her feet, suddenly exhilarated. Her beloved uncle lived! She had to get to him at once. And what better way than to go with the Spaniards. They would take her straight to him. She would go willingly, and then, she and her uncle would escape!

One difficulty remained. She would have to force Charles to escape without her. He wouldn't like it, but her uncle was her problem, not his.

"Messieurs," a young French voice whined, interrupting her urgent thoughts. "Share your food with a poor lad? I have had naught to eat for the past two days."

Frances stilled by the ladder, stifling the urge to call out. Louis had come for the key at last. She tensed, ready to help if required. For all her bravado in front of Charles, she couldn't swear their scheme would work.

"Get away, scum." One man kicked out at Louis, but he danced beyond reach. "We've nothing for the likes of you."

"But monsieur, I beg you"—Louis pulled at his rags and sagged pathetically—"I'm near starved."

"You heard the man." Diego stood up and swiped at him. Louis jumped out of reach faster than his groveling, undernourished appearance suggested was possible. "The food's all gone. Take yourself off."

"A coin, then," Louis wheedled, louder and even more irritating. "Alms?"

Frances shifted her gaze upward, toward the loft where the captain rested. She bit her lip hard and waited, her heart in her throat.

"I'll show you to trouble your betters!" Diego leaped for Louis, caught him by one arm, and boxed his ear.

Louis released a bloodcurdling howl that hurt Frances's ears almost as much as the blow. "Why don't you give the boy some bread," she called loudly, stepping forward, pretending a boldness she didn't feel. "You have some to spare."

"Stay out of this," the other guard growled as he caught her by the arm.

Louis shrieked as if Diego were killing him.

"What the devil is going on?" Charles emerged from the wagon and tottered toward her like a wooden soldier, his steps regulated by the bar between his feet.

Frances groaned inwardly and wrenched away from the guard. She didn't need Charles involved in this. She hurried to him, twisted both hands in his doublet, and buried her face in his sleeve, feigning distress.

"Quiet down there," another voice roared. "A man can't sleep with fools on duty. *Madre de Diós,* I have to settle everything myself."

Frances sighed with relief. Here was Captain Landa at last. The giant eased his bulk onto the ladder and descended, one rung at a time. Louis still wailed, though Diego had stopped cuffing him.

"Shut your damned noise," Diego yelled in Spanish.

Louis pretended not to understand him. Blubbering at the top of his lungs, he rushed forward and threw himself at the captain's feet, locking his arms around one of the man's legs. "*Mon seigneur,* save me from this horrible beast. I only begged a scrap of food and he tries to kill me, *vraiment.* And to kill is a sin against God, *n'est-ce pas*? I beg you to help me, *mon seigneur.*"

"Get me my whip," ordered the captain.

"*Sí, mi capitán.*" Diego slapped it into his superior's hand.

"Throw the beggar out and we'll give him a taste." The captain rolled his mouth into an ugly smile.

Louis blanched, but didn't let go of the captain's leg. "*Mon seigneur,* you would not beat a poor lad, would you?" His hands grasped and scrambled all over the captain, picking and plucking at his clothing, everywhere at once.

"Get him off me," the captain shouted, tugging at Louis with one hand while flourishing the whip with the other.

Louis obviously knew the captain couldn't strike at such close range. He hung on like a river leech. Diego and Arquebus each gripped an arm, but Louis bit one and kicked the other in the gut.

Charles scowled at the scene before him, heartily

disgusted by the men's callous attitude toward the boy. "Let me go to his aid," he chastened Frances, trying to pry her hands from his doublet. "No one should treat a child so, especially a hungry child."

"Pray do not interfere," she begged in his ear. "The lad can take care of himself." She hauled back on him with all her strength.

He stopped straining against her hands and stared at her. The oddest, guilty look adorned her face. Whipping his gaze back to the fight, he studied the boy more closely. It must be one of Frances's street urchins. And by thunder, though he hated to admit it, the scrawny lad looked likely to accomplish what Charles, for all his military training, could not. The seasoned cutpurse was about to snatch the unsuspecting captain's keys.

The lad wiggled and fought, using his feet as adroitly as he would his hands. He kicked one man in the throat, barrelled into Diego, knocking him over, then grasped the third one's jerkin, tearing it open and spilling buttons all over the floor. The lad turned to run, but the captain tripped him. Curling into a ball, the boy rolled, bounded up again, twisted around, and sank his teeth into the captain's hand. The whip flew from the captain's grasp. As it skidded away, the youngster let out a horrifying shriek as if he had been bitten and not the other way around.

"Let me help him," Charles whispered to Frances. "Here," he called loudly. "I'll handle the little pest." He started forward, intending to do just the opposite. Hindered by the bar, he collided with Arquebus and crashed to the floor.

As Charles struggled to gain his feet, he saw the captain cradle his hand against his middle while the other two fought for a hold on their slippery fish. The captain's ring of keys clanked to the floor. The boy swept them up and ran.

Diego caught up and tackled him. The keys flew through the air, a shining rush of metal, and disappeared into the grass. Louis howled and fought and kicked. Then, as if the fish grew too strong for the line, he broke free and sprinted away across the rippling sea of green field.

Diego lumbered to his feet, cursing and groping in the grass. With a shout of triumph, he straightened, holding up the ring of keys for the captain to see.

"Scurvy beggar." The captain refastened the ring to his belt. He held out his hand, examining the bite. "*Madre de*

Diós. First I'm bloodied and knifed by a scurvy whoreson, then bitten by a rabid dog. Someone will pay for this." He glared at Charles.

Charles ignored him, too full of mixed emotions—grudging admiration for the lad's nimble fingers, frustration with the hated leg shackles, fury with Frances for refusing to use his plan, then excluding him from hers.

As the men scrambled about their duties, Charles turned away from the captain and let Frances hustle him back to the wagon. It chafed to let her guide and coddle him, but the shackles offered him no other choice.

"Please lie down and keep out of the captain's way," Frances ordered. "You really must conserve your strength."

His blood boiled at her order and he sat down on the wagon tail, refusing to obey. "I have to step out for a minute," he grumbled. "You lie down."

"They won't allow you to go anywhere. You would be mad to try." Her beautiful, wide eyes narrowed at him.

"Must I be blunt about it. I have to relieve myself."

"Oh." Color crept into her face.

He stared at her, intrigued. So she could falter and blush, too. He'd not thought her too toughened to be capable of either reaction.

He grinned and winked at her with his good eye.

Amazingly, her blush deepened. Her gaze skittered and fluttered like a hooded bird trying to fly, totally out of control.

He added this new, small show of her vulnerability to his horde. He could still count on one hand the few she'd shown to date. Even so, they offered comfort—and eased his self-disgust.

Chapter 10

Pissing at gunpoint took a devilish amount of nerve and concentration. Charles muttered to himself while he managed the feat. The gun-mad lackey they'd nicknamed Arquebus poked him in the small of the back with the weapon's cold muzzle the entire time. The others sat around the remains of the fire outside the barn. Charles's stomach growled as he craned his neck to see if any stew was left. He'd had only that small serving from Frances, and his insides were still as empty as a deserted guard post.

To his disappointment, all he saw was the kettle full of boiling water that Diego was using to bathe the captain's bitten hand.

"*Madre de Diós,* I look forward to Spain," Captain Landa said. "Wait until I tell His Eminence the trouble these English monsters make. Not to mention miserable French beggars. Scurvy little whoreson even drew blood. He jerked his hand away as Diego applied a steaming cloth. "*Imbecile!* That's too hot!"

Diego waved the cloth to cool it, then again applied it to the wound.

"What I did should ease things, though. Did she hear me earlier?" the captain demanded.

Diego finished the cleansing, put away the cloth, and picked up a roll of clean bandage. "She was sitting beneath the ladder," he grunted, frowning at the linen that bunched and twisted as he struggled to make a neat wrap. "Couldn't help but hear."

"*Bueno.*" The captain nodded his approval. "She'll be led astray by what I said. She should be docile as a lamb from here on, but don't relax your guard around her."

Charles prolonged buttoning his trunk hose, his mind urgently piecing together these words. The captain had fed Frances wrong information earlier? About what?

Arquebus poked him with the gun. "You're done. Get along."

"Look," Charles said to Arquebus, wanting to delay. "There are some early berries on those bushes. They would make a welcome sweet after the stew."

As the man stepped into the bushes to check, Charles strained to hear more.

Unfortunately, Diego finished wrapping the bandage, tucked the end in place, then straightened and sent Charles a pointed stare.

The captain glanced over his shoulder, following the direction of his underling's gaze. "Then there's the husband," he said loudly as he twisted his mouth into a sneer. "He's more and more trouble as we go along, Diego. I never did find the knife. If it doesn't turn up soon, we'll strip them both and do a thorough search."

The vivid image that sprang into his mind—of Frances, bleeding and weeping after the monsters were done with her—horrified Charles. With a jolt of helpless anger, he realized he had to drop the knife somewhere so their captors could recover it. Though he desperately wanted a weapon, keeping it exposed Frances to a danger he couldn't permit.

"Don't know what these are." Arquebus thrust a branch of red berries at him. "Not sure I want to eat 'em, either. Might be poison."

Charles took the branch and examined it. "I agree it wouldn't be wise to eat something that could make us ill." He gave the berries a cursory glance, then tossed the branch away. He'd known from the start they weren't edible. They were just an excuse to linger. "I'm going back to the wagon," he growled, heading for the barn. "I want to lie down."

Hunger gnawed at Charles's stomach, a vivid reminder of his prisoner status. To forget it, to pass the time before they moved on at dark, he tunneled in beneath the canvas roof and stretched at full length beside Frances. Curled on her right side against the grain bags, she slept, hugging her equipment bag tightly to her chest.

Such heaven to lie at her side. It filled him with hunger of a different kind.

His gaze devoured her as she slumbered in the dim light, all sleek, haunting curves. She had removed the hawk's protective pad and her bodice while he was out. He spotted them draped across a grain sack. The embroidered neckline of her smock drooped gracefully to reveal one tantalizing shoulder. Her flesh seemed to shimmer white, just as on that day in Dorset nine years ago.

Fighting the urge to touch her more than was necessary, he eased onto his right side, seeking a better position, and found . . . *blast it,* her body would fit his to perfection—like the tender-sweet core of an orange nestled against its outer flesh. It would fit . . . if he let it.

But he couldn't. The lads had secured the key. The guards would be lax once they resumed their journey at nightfall. They would think him shackled and helpless. He must concentrate, be ready for the lads' signal when it came.

Yet the old hunger threatened reason—the hunger to caress her beautiful shoulder, to push away that blasted bag and cup her swelling breast with his hand as he removed her clothes and bared her tantalizing . . .

Charles cut off the thoughts before they could build. How he could think such things while shackled and imprisoned was beyond him. He had to resist, for she presented a far more lasting threat to him than the Spaniards.

Since returning from the West Indies, he hadn't courted any woman with an eye toward permanence. Instead, if he wanted a female, he sought some married court lady known to favor multiple bed partners and gave her a straightforward proposal—a favor of her choosing, within reason, in exchange for a few nights of shared lust.

He supposed his reputation as a considerate, creative lover ensured that he'd never been turned down.

As he resettled on his back, Frances's sweet thigh pressed against his.

Charles stifled a groan. He twisted and willed himself not to think about her, but the nether part of his body refused to cooperate. His gaze wandered back to her lush body again and again and . . . *thunderation,* he'd forgotten the knife. 'Twould be best to take it from her while she slept. He would drop it in the straw so the Spaniards could find it. Though he hated to give up the weapon, duty required he put Frances's safety above the edge it would give him in escape.

With cautious fingers, he inched up her kirtle skirt. Slowly . . . silently . . . like a thief.

The blade tucked in her garter glinted dully. He reached for it over a ripple in her linen skirt and couldn't help but notice the rise and fall of her fetching breasts straining beneath the thin veil of her smock.

Excitement shot through him, heating his blood and hardening the flesh between his thighs. His fingers itched to stroke the peaks of her breasts, to feel her desire mount in response to him. Like the falconer working in tandem with a fierce, wild hawk, he craved the ecstasy of the moment when their wills would blend, when they would unite in the hunt for passion's release.

The knife, he reminded himself grimly. This was no time to lose control. His pulse pounded in his ears as he slowly reached for the leather haft.

"Just what do you think you're about?" she hissed. She reared up and twisted to confront him.

He started and yanked back his hand. Had she been awake the entire time? The tremor of her breath wavered against his face, quick and shallow. Her parted lips, the smoldering desire leaping in her eyes, told him she was as aroused as he! *Perdition,* he had to calm them both down. "Nothing that need concern you." He groped for the right words. Should he tell her the truth? Or let her think he lusted for her flesh?

"Nothing?" she repeated with a sniff. "It felt like something." She cast a glance at his hand—a glance brimming with distrust.

It hit him like a blow, that distrust. He wasn't perfect, but he wouldn't ravish her in a situation like this. The idea that she thought otherwise diminished him, left him not quite whole. He had to have her trust, if nothing else. "The truth is, I was after the knife."

"The knife?" She frowned, tightening her mouth into a skeptical line. "You weren't interested in anything else?"

"No," he forced out, feeling quite the liar. Of course he was interested in that "something else" she referred to. "What I meant to do was take it without troubling you. But since you're awake, pray be so good as to hand it to me."

To his astonishment, her distrust vanished. With all the faith of a child, she plucked the knife from her garter, placed it in his hands, and closed his fingers around it. "I took it for you in the first place. Here. It's yours." A fleeting smile brightened her face. "I could tell it was your favorite from the way you wore it at your belt and the way you handled it. I wanted you to have it back."

The caring in her voice amazed him. *Ye gods,* she'd

regained his knife because she knew it was his favorite? Not because he needed a weapon to defend them, but because she yearned to give him a treasure he'd lost? He was so stymied by her generosity, he could hardly move. He had to force himself to accept the knife from her hand and inch his way toward the wagon end.

"Where are you going?" she whispered after him.

He felt like a knave as he answered, "I'm going to put it out where 'twill be found."

"But why?" She grabbed his doublet to stay him. "I got it back for you. I want you to keep it. You'll need it once you escape."

Relief went through him. At least she still had a scrap of practicality. "I must do it," he said, knowing the whole truth was essential. "Because they think one of us has it. They'll strip us to check."

"Whist." She waved away the threat of the Spaniards with that cocky nonchalance of hers. "I'll pass it off to Louis and Pierre. They'll keep it for you."

Once again, she touched him—with her courage, with her sudden valor and show of strength. "I can't let you take that risk," he said firmly, guarding his reaction. "They won't stop with a search. Not with you."

She sank back, seeming shocked at his blunt words. He took advantage of her momentary silence to slide out of the wagon. A quick study of the now-snoring guards, a few awkward steps from the wagon, and he'd done the deed. The knife blade protruded slightly from a heap of straw.

Satisfied that the Spaniards would find it and leave them alone, he wriggled back into the wagon, feeling as foul as a worm. But why should he? He hadn't violated her. He'd given up the knife to keep her safe.

Back among the warmth of the grain sacks, she curled on her right side once more, as if sleeping. But he knew she wasn't. She was every bit as aware of his presence as he was of hers.

With a sigh, he settled beside her, found her hand, and laced his fingers with hers. "I thank you for the knife," he whispered, squeezing gently. "I've never had such a generous gift. I'm sorry I had to give it back to them."

"You're welcome." She returned the pressure of his hand. "I thank you for sacrificing it for my sake."

He closed his eyes, but it was no use. He was more aware

of her than ever. Releasing her hand, he placed it at her side and turned away. If they ever escaped alive, he hoped he would have the time to learn why this woman sent him flying from irritation, to sympathy, to lust, and back again so quickly. And the wisdom to understand what the intense, disturbing effect she had on him meant.

Chapter 11

Just before dusk, Frances crossed the line between sleep and waking, nudged by the minute rustle of a grain bag. Along with the feeling that someone friendly hovered nearby.

Crawling cautiously to the end of the wagon, she glimpsed Pierre's shadowy form as he slipped through the barn door. Then he was gone. Nothing else stirred.

With a smile of victory, she searched beneath the grain bags and found the key. Both her lads, with their stealthy feet and light fingers, had been stealing things for years. Since she firmly believed every God-given talent had a purpose, she but redirected their efforts, ensuring noble use of their skills.

The hard part was, she thought, clutching the precious key as she checked the barn, to teach them the difference between base and noble use. Some days she despaired. Yet they were her lads. She would not give up.

Indeed, Pierre had chosen the wisest moment to deliver the key—he understood that well. By the barn door, Diego and the sling-armed guard snored, heads pillowed on their packs, never suspecting a thing. The captain and Arquebus must still be in the loft.

Praise heaven they were her lads and not minions of the Spanish. She nodded with satisfaction as she envisioned the mortified guards when they discovered their prisoner's escape. How she would hate to be in their boots then.

She inched back into the wagon and bent over Charles, her hand poised to shake him awake and tell him the news. But he looked so angelic in sleep, her hand stilled. Tousled hair fell across his forehead; his mouth had relaxed. With one cheek cushioned on his arm, he seemed young and innocent again, no older than her boys. Except for the two-day growth of whiskers that marred the clean line of his chin and jaw. It reminded her of where he'd been and what he'd seen.

He wasn't a boy anymore. He was a man—a man she'd touched with her gift of the knife. Yet minutes later, he'd put her hand away and turned his back to her. After confiding in her, after spilling a tiny drop of his pain, he'd rejected her.

Inside, her yearning for companionship, honed by years of loneliness, expanded into a deep-seated ache.

But Charles hadn't the sensitivity to help her. She must bear that ache alone. Steeling herself against it, she shook him gently by the arm.

"Wh-wh- . . . Oh, coz, it's you." He stared at her through bleary, sleep-heavy eyes. "What is it? Is the house afire?"

"You're not at home, Charles. And I'm not your cousin."

"Damn." He looked around as if reluctant to remember where he was and why. When he did, the peace she'd seen in his features melted away, replaced by a grim frown.

"I know. I feel the same as you on the matter. But this will help your mood." She held up the little key.

His eyes lit from within. He snatched it from her and struggled to reach the shackles.

"Not yet," she cautioned, catching his hand. "Later."

"Now," he growled, hot with impatience. "I'll have them off now."

"We've no chance of getting away now. After we're on the road and they think we're sleeping, they'll suspect nothing. The boys will create a distraction and we can slip away." She felt supremely guilty saying "we." As if she would go, too. But he had no reason to doubt her. Not yet.

He searched his clothes for a good hiding place and concealed the key. "Let's pray they don't miss it."

"They won't." She grimaced. "They'll be too excited over finding the knife."

Just as she predicted, Arquebus stumbled on the knife while the Spaniards broke camp and prepared to travel.

"*Mi capitán,* I found it!" He presented the missing blade to his superior with a flourish and salute.

Charles breathed easier after that. With the key pressed against his flesh inside his netherstock, he felt almost cheerful. He swallowed the light meal of stale bread, more rock hard cheese, and water from a nearby spring, making sure Frances ate her share. Then they again took to the road.

As night deepened over the vast French countryside, they passed few people. A group of field workers traveling home cheered themselves with bawdy songs. But after they passed, the rattle of the wagon drowned them out. No one else seemed to be abroad on the lonely road, from what Charles could see out the back. No one they could appeal to for help. At this time of day, people sought their homes or a local ale-house, craving ease after a hard day's work.

Charles no longer minded. Their escape was set. Now he wanted to focus on this forced intimacy with Frances—he wished it could go on and on, even as he anticipated breaking free. As they lay in the jolting, moving wagon, he stared at the canvas overhead and decided he must be mad. This couldn't continue. It wouldn't once they escaped.

But he liked her closeness.

And for an unexplained reason, a burning need to have her consumed him. Why, he didn't know, except he hadn't had a woman for some time. Thrown into close confines with her, his lust was a natural response. And she did need someone to look after her. Those reasons must suffice.

With a tentative movement, he eased one arm around Frances's shoulders. She didn't reject him, so he tried his other arm. Without a word, she nestled against him, and he pressed her close, rubbing his face against her tickly hair. Spikes of excitement awakened in his groin.

He tamped down his lust, determined to contain himself. Anything more at a time like this would be mad.

Yet she felt like more to him.

Tightening his arms around her in a fierce embrace, he steeled himself to await the signal to escape.

A horse shrilled in pain. Charles bolted upright and knocked into Frances as the wagon lurched forward. Spooked, the team charged into a gallop amid Spanish curses and angry commands to bring them under control.

"Now!" Charles shouted at Frances over the deafening clatter as the wagon increased its speed. "Take your bird and jump."

"The key first," she cried, gripping him with frantic fingers.

Charles fumbled at the lock and cursed the careening wagon. It bounced him so that the key refused to fit in the hole. "Go ahead of me," he bellowed over the surrounding din. "I'll be free in a minute." The first cuff snapped open. As he tussled with the second, he noticed Frances digging frantically among the grain sacks. "What's wrong?"

"My equipment bag. I can't find it. It has to be here."

"The devil with the bag." The second lock sprang open, and he tore off the cuff. With the hated bar in hand, he crawled toward the wagon's end to check on their captors. The vehicle jerked wildly, almost knocking him flat.

Outside, a Spaniard shrieked, his words unintelligible.

Charles stuck out his head from under the canvas. Ahead of the team galloped a flaming, shrieking rider. Thunderation, the boys had torched a Spaniard. How ever they'd managed it, he admitted he couldn't have created a better diversion. Two men tailed the torch, flailing him with their doublets to stifle the flames. Their mounts fought for their heads, terrified of the fire.

Amid the chaos, Charles felt Frances bump against his shoulder. She put her lips near his ear. "Go now. Slip into the ditch and lie low until the wagon is out of sight. They won't see you."

"We'll go together!" Urgency made him rough. Despite the bone-jarring shake of the wagon, he felt it begin to slow. He grasped Frances around the waist and hauled her to him. To his astonishment, she pulled back.

"I'm staying. You go."

"Staying?" he echoed. "The devil you are."

"I have to." She yanked away from him and huddled against the wheat sacks. "My uncle is still alive."

"Alive?" She must have taken leave of her senses. "You told me he was dead."

"I overheard them talking. They said he's still alive," she cried, trembling as if on the verge of tears.

He clamped down his jaw as he remembered what he'd heard by the campfire. The captain had wanted her to believe something false. "He's not alive." He grasped her arm, but the wagon wheel hit a rock and knocked her from his grip. "Your uncle is well and truly dead."

"No, he isn't. I'm going to him. Take this for me." She thrust her equipment bag in his hands, flung herself on a grain bag, and wrapped both arms around it in a stranglehold.

Alarm filled him. Their moment was slipping away, but he'd be damned if he'd leave her behind. Ahead he saw the burning Spaniard had been doused by his fellows, and they had stopped by the road. Only another hundred yards or so and the wagon would reach them.

"Go while you can," she insisted, half raving. "He's not your uncle. He's not your affair. He's mine."

The wagon slowed further as the horses lost the edge of their panic. Charles dared not waste more time arguing. In another second their chance would be gone. Yet she had a death grip on the grain bag, as if he would drag her away against her will. He would, too, except a scuffle would alert the Spaniards. He could either escape without her or stay. He had to choose.

Desperate for a way around the dilemma, he balanced at the edge of the bucking wagon, holding her equipment bag, his gaze jumping from her to the Spaniards and back again. All he wanted was to carry her to freedom, yet she thwarted him. If only he could . . .

Her foot lashed out so fast, he felt rather than saw it. The smashing blow to his hip knocked him off balance. Bar shackle still gripped in one hand, he plummeted into the road and landed with a painful jolt.

Spurred by instinct, he rolled into the ditch and lay flat on his belly in the dark, praying no one had seen him fall.

He cursed in silent outrage. The madness of the wench! All day long he'd been looking forward to *their* escape, *their* freedom. And then to *their* safe arrival back in England. Now he wasn't going anywhere. He would find another way to free her, and next time he would carry her bodily. He refused to leave her to the Spanish. Her uncle was dead. He knew that for sure.

Chapter 12

If someone had told Charles six months ago that he would lie facedown in a ditch full of mud for a woman, he would have called them crazed. But here he was, mud and all. Thunderation, his bruised face was begrimed, his clothing fouled, and the ditch smelled like a pig trough . . . or something worse.

Scarcely allowing himself to breathe, he listened as the wagon raced away, putting more distance between them every minute. Blast it all, but she'd pushed him, forcing him to leave her. And the devils had tricked her. Loyal to the end, she'd fallen right into her trap.

"Bloody hell, where is Frank?" whispered a voice in strangled English. "What have you done with her?"

It was one of the French urchins. He butchered the language so, Charles could scarcely make him out. He sat up and examined the beggar, feeling rather friendly. "*Bonsoir,* Louis"—he picked one of their names at random—"I applaud your escape plan, setting the man on fire. How did you manage it?"

"Louis did it. *I* am Pierre." The child squatted on his haunches and reached out to finger Charles's white shirt in the dark. "Nice cloth, Monsieur Millstone. Now where's Frank?"

"The name is Milborne. And Frank, as you call her, refused to come."

Pierre's eyes sprang wide with horror. "*Diable!* You lie!"

"I wish I did, but they suggested to her that her uncle is still alive," Charles said grimly. "She thinks they're taking her to him."

"*Merde!*" The cocky self-assurance vanished. The thin face crumpled as the boy surged from the ditch.

Charles was ready for him. He snagged Pierre by the ankle and dragged him back, kicking and fighting. "Quiet," he hissed, holding the boy tightly. "You can't save her by running after them, shouting for the Spaniards to let her go. You need a strategy as you had before."

"But they'll destroy her. How could she think to stay?" The lad collapsed in the mud and loosed another string of curses both colorful and inventive.

Charles knew they were inventive because he couldn't translate half of them. "I never knew such a wrongheaded woman," he agreed, his own frustration and concern for Frances hitting him with unexpected force. "Gets something in her mind and there's no stopping her. But I'm sure her uncle's dead."

The boy's thin ribs heaved in a spasm. *God's blood,* but he was crying for Frances. "Don't worry. We'll go after her," Charles soothed, feeling as awkward as an untried nursemaid with a sobbing infant. "I'll be sure she's set free."

"*You* don't have to go," another voice said.

Charles spun around. It was the other urchin, Louis. This lad stood half a foot taller than Pierre and looked older by a year or two, which made him about twelve. Other than that, they seemed almost identical in the dark, with their dirty spikes of hair and ragged clothes. "Of course I do," he contradicted. "I'm hardly going to leave her to those barbarians. They smashed my head and eye. Heaven knows what they'll do to her."

Louis squinted at him in the dark. "Better you than her," he observed without a trace of sympathy. "But you still don't have to go after her."

"I do. We're both English." Charles winced at his feeble excuse. It seemed Louis doubted him, too, for he responded with only one word.

"*Vraiment?*"

Uncomfortable with the lad's disbelieving stare, Charles turned his back on him, found a stick, and started to dig.

"Be still, Pierre," Louis ordered his compatriot whose stifled crying punctuated the night. "We must plan a new attempt. But first we will see if *monsieur le baron* is fit to assist us or no."

Fit to assist them? Charles gripped the stick in fury and dug harder. He'd be damned if he'd turn his task over to two children, no matter what they thought.

"What *are* you doing, *monsieur le baron*?" Louis asked sharply.

"I'm burying this blasted Spanish shackle so it'll never

touch human flesh again." Without ceremony, he dumped the iron bar and cuffs into the long, shallow hole he'd carved out. He covered them with mud and packed it down.

"*Très bien,*" Louis congratulated him. "You can go home to England now."

"You listen to me." Charles whirled on the boy. "Mademoiselle Frances arranged for me to go free. I expect to do the same for her. Understand? I'm not going home. I'm going to free her if it's the last thing I do."

A sudden grin split the urchin's thin face. He nodded wisely to Pierre as if some deep-seated belief were confirmed. "He passes muster, agreed?" Pierre assented, and Louis turned back to Charles. He assumed a stern expression by wrinkling his forehead and tightening his childish mouth. "*Écoutez, Baron Millstone.* We agree to let you help us, but I warn you, if you think to tangle in Frank's jesses, you'd best have a care. We only approve, how do you say, honorable intentions. Yours are honorable, *oui?*"

Charles resisted the urge to grab Louis by the collar, or what passed for a collar on his ragged shirt, and shake him. "The name is Milborne, and don't you dare to speak of such things about the mademoiselle," he said stiffly instead. "She is responsible for her own choices, and they're no business of yours."

Louis winked at him knowingly, not the least intimidated. "Just what I would expect from the likes of you. Frank said you were a . . . what was the word she used . . . ah, a hot head." He pronounced it without any h's, in the French manner. "No patience at all."

With a curse, Charles slung Frances's equipment bag over his shoulder, pulled himself out of the ditch, and started walking. No patience? He'd show them patience when it came to rescuing Frances. He'd worked with too many birds and had too much military training to lack that trait. But how patient would anyone be when forced to accept help from a motley gang of rude-mouthed street infants?

As he strode along the dark, uneven track, he muttered to himself. Just what he needed—an advocate for Frances, trying to insinuate the woman into his good graces.

Unfortunately, Louis's tactic was working. It had been bad enough, wanting Frances in bed, but now his rage threatened to lash out—rage at her captors fueled by fear for her well-being. He knew quite well what the Spaniards did to their captives. That fear drove him forward through the chill night, lending him strength. Even when his head throbbed anew, he pushed one foot ahead of the other, never pausing. His mind churned as he assembled his plans. Unfortunately, he needed to quiz Louis, but one worked with the raw material at hand.

"How did you spook the horses?" he began.

"Stones," Pierre spoke up proudly. "Does nasty things to horses. Makes 'em run."

"I noticed." Charles frowned at the lad's poor English grammar and pronunciation. Yet it was a miracle he spoke English at all. "How did you set the man on fire?" he again addressed Louis.

"With burning straw bound to stones," answered the lad. "I have more here." He patted a ragged purse tied around his waist with a length of rope.

Charles noted the resource and continued. "The one man will be burned. They'll have to seek a physician for him. Do you know the name of the next town?"

"Aix-des-Choix. We have friends there. They'll help us save Frank."

"Then we'd best hurry. We should come to that town by morning, if my memory of geography serves me. Do you think your friends can get me some gunpowder?"

"Depends on how much you want," Louis said.

"Just enough to rescue Frances."

"Frank," the lads reminded him in unison. "She prefers to be called Frank."

They walked for two hours. At this rate, Charles knew they would be exhausted by the time Aix-des-Choix appeared. But the resourceful Louis knew someone he claimed owed him a favor. He found the farmer's lad sleeping in a barn loft. A short time later, they trotted down the road in a borrowed, two-wheeled cart, the lad driving. Pierre immediately curled into a ball on a canvas sack and fell asleep. But Louis remained alert and seemingly intent on driving Charles mad.

"How did you meet Frank, Baron Millstone?" the boy wheedled.

"I was sent to fetch her back to England," Charles

answered shortly. Intent on conserving his strength, he dangled his feet over the back of the cart and tried to relax.

"Sure you never met her before?" Louis probed, sitting beside him and dangling his legs, too, aping Charles's every move.

"Once."

"When? Where?"

"It's not important that you know," Charles growled in his sternest manner. He would end this interrogation posthaste.

"It's important to you, Baron Millstone," Louis crowed in triumph. "I can tell. Frank says I'm good at noticing such things."

"Go to sleep. You need the rest. And the name is Milborne." He focused on ignoring the boy.

Louis grinned at him and charged into his next observation. "So your brother is *El Mágico Demoníaco,* the queen's spymaster. You don't look like him."

"How would you know?" Charles snapped to attention, despite his resolve not to. "Who told you about him?"

"He did himself. I met him twice. He came to see the English ambassador. Then he came to see Frank."

Charles suppressed a silent groan. Blast Jonathan, he'd throttle him when he got back to England. *If* he ever got back to England. "How do you come to be so well informed?" he demanded. "And what the devil were you doing at the English ambassador's?"

"Très simple," Louis swung his legs and laced his hands in his lap, playing innocent. "Frank gives me errands for him. She promises to make a gentleman of me some day."

She hasn't progressed much, Charles thought, appraising Louis's torn, soiled trunk hose and stocks. "How does she expect to do that?"

"I learn English. I work hard and use my money for a clean room and food. Pierre, he goes to the church school, then cooks and markets for us each day."

Charles shook his head in wonder. If Frances wanted to adopt children, why had she chosen these two? "What about your family? Don't they object?"

"Got no family. What're you doing with Frank's bag?"

Charles's gaze slipped to the equipment bag lying beside him in the cart. "She asked me to take it. Blast if I know why, when she still has the hawk."

Louis put a protective hand on the leather bag. "Best have a care for it. She's attached to this bag."

Charles frowned. "She takes that attachment too far, if you ask me. Wears the damned thing as if it's part of her clothing. Even sleeps with it in her arms."

Louis grinned at him, as if he knew exactly what Charles preferred Frances to sleep with in her arms. *"Naturallement,"* he offered in explanation, "she keeps it close. It has all her bird's equipment in it—jesses, leash, hood."

"I know that." Charles let loose his sarcasm in response to the lad's sly grin. "But she doesn't have to act as if she's wed to the blasted thing."

"No? Who should she act wed to?"

Charles scowled at the lad and refused to be trapped into a faux pas.

Louis wouldn't give up. "You kissed Frank yet?"

Charles grimaced at the bald question. "I warned you, Louis. You're not to—"

"I meant nothing," Louis protested, clearly delighted by Charles's disgust with the topic. "But all the men want to kiss Frank. I think so do you."

"Which men?" Charles demanded, unable to suppress a surge of jealousy. The sudden image of some lout with no feelings for her kissing Frances . . . it drove him insane.

Louis took his time in answering. "The ones at the ambassador's. The ones in the market. Most men who see her want to kiss her. Why do you wish to know?"

"Did she let them?"

Louis peered at him shrewdly. "Only Monsieur Antoine, the one she was to wed."

Charles's mind whirled. "She was supposed to wed? Then why didn't she?"

"Je ne sais pas." Pierre tilted his head and scowled, as if he, too, wondered. "He never came to the church at the time set. He left Paris instead."

Left at the altar? Frances had been abandoned on her wedding day? Charles gripped the side of the cart and rubbed his aching head, hating what he'd just heard. "Damn it, why are you telling me this?"

"Because you asked me." Louis continued to watch him closely. "And because she'll never tell you herself."

* * *

The sun had risen and shone with irritating brilliance by the time they reached the outskirts of Aix-des-Choix. Charles was muddy and disheveled, his hair awry, his doublet torn, with no money at all. Their captors had thoughtfully removed his gold earlier. As for food ... he was starved. If he expected to rescue Frances, he had to eat. But he intended to move quickly. Eat, gather weapons and resources, and get to the rescue. During their journey, he had solidified his plan.

"Samuel and Gaby'll see we eat," Pierre responded to his queries. "They owe us a favor or two, so they'll help us. You'll like them, too, I'll vow."

With reluctance, Charles again schooled himself to accept the boys' favors. And the favors of unknown people who might think him a beggar, just like these lads. "Lead on," he growled. He would eat what was offered, whatever it was. After all, he had done worse on his voyages. He'd been known to dine on cooked rat, when pressed. But it *did* have to be cooked. Once his belly was satisfied, he would see if Samuel and Gaby would agree to his scheme.

"I truly know nothing, Captain!" Frances cringed in her chair, trying to appease her tormentor. "I know nothing about any papers in Spanish. Nor did my uncle, to my knowledge. I swear."

"Bitch." He slapped her again, so hard that her head whipped back. "If His Eminence, the archbishop, were here, he would make you talk."

With that, the captain slammed out of the inn room and locked the door from without. With a moan, Frances bent double in her chair and cradled her aching face in both hands. With her mind still numb from the blows, her flesh already swelling, she tried to think what to do. How could she avoid being beaten and battered to a mass of blood and bruises before they got to Nantes?

If she had gone with Charles, she could never have convinced him to let her follow the Spaniards alone. And he would never have consented to go with her. It wasn't *his* uncle. Why should he risk his neck?

She didn't want him to risk anything. He'd had trouble enough from her as it was.

For the first time, fear coursed through her, freezing her

insides. She hadn't realized how she depended on Charles until he was gone. Just knowing he was near had given her a sense of security and false courage.

How she longed for his arms right now, his touch that sent fire storming through her blood and created a moment to cherish in the midst of fear. Though that was a ridiculous thought. First of all, he'd been as much a prisoner as she was—more so with his shackles. Second, she doubted he considered their encounter cherished. Now she would never know, because Pierre and Louis had managed his release.

Triumph replaced fear for a moment. She had shown Charles her lads' skill, she thought proudly. If only he would appreciate them the way she did. He might, since they had set him free.

Cautiously exploring the bruises on her face, she decided the skin was swollen but not broken. Why had the Spaniards dared stop here? Probably because they desperately needed a physician for the burned man. He might even die.

She looked around her room and studied the single tiny window. Could she get someone's attention? If she could escape, she might follow the Spaniards to Nantes and on to Spain. There she would find her uncle, and . . . no, that wouldn't work either. If she appealed to someone for help, they would report her to the authorities of the town. They, in turn, would insist on notifying the English in Paris, who would come for her and end her attempts to free her uncle. Like Charles, they wouldn't listen to her, convinced as they were that the body they had buried was her uncle's.

She wasn't convinced. She loved her uncle with a devotion that defied their logic and arguments. Even now she could imagine him lying in a dank cell, alone, deserted, believing he would never see his niece again. The pain of the thought sent agonies through her. She opened Oriana's cage door and caressed her friend as she made a vow. She must not, under any circumstances, give up her quest to set her uncle free.

Nothing could have astonished Charles more than the handsome stone dwelling that Louis and Pierre led him to in the best part of town. How did the lads have friends among the gentry? A fine lady greeted them in the parlor with grace and civility. She wore a well-cut gown with fashionable farthingale and a pretty lace ruff, though she wore excessive paint on her cheeks. He bent over her hand in his best manner, then shook the hand of her equally resplendent husband. They were introduced as Monsieur Samuel and Madam Gaby. No other names were said.

Pierre and Louis introduced Charles as Master John, an English gentleman on a jaunt to see rural France. The couple treated them with great courtesy, though to his way of thinking, they ought to get down to business. He couldn't chase the image of Frances from his mind—of her bound and helpless at the hands of the captain.

Charles ate quickly whatever passed his way at table— capon with onion, spinach pie. "Stop that," he cuffed Louis, who was fiddling with the table candles. Madam had excused herself from the dining chamber, and the master had followed. "Don't play with fire. 'Tis dangerous." He caught a hand that snaked back toward the candle. Louis turned up a guileless face, and their eyes met. "Exactly how do you come to have such fine friends?" Charles demanded. "Or are they Frances's friends?"

"They're our friends, from Paris," Louis said. "Lemme go."

"I will if you'll leave the candles be. You'll set their house afire." Charles released him and took a bite of bread, wondering if he should press for more information or just talk to the couple himself. They seemed to know some English, and he knew enough French.

"They're experts at Crossbiting Law," Louis informed him. "That's what you call it in England. Frank said so."

Charles choked on his bread, and bent double, coughing. His host and hostess weren't gentry, they swindled people for a living?

"Don't go playing hoity-toity on us." Louis pounded Charles on the back. "How else do you expect us to get at Frank? Gaby's got skill in the black art, besides."

Charles rubbed his aching head and groaned. The woman picked locks as well. Splendid. "Then have them get me the gunpowder." He might as well take care of all his problems at once.

"How much did you say you wanted?" Louis asked, as calmly as if he'd been asked for ale or wine.

"Enough to fire a dozen muskets," Charles told him. It wouldn't take much to do what he had in mind. He would control that part of the rescue, at least, but the rest ... He rubbed his head again, which was aching. He didn't like entrusting the rest of the scheme to Samuel and Gaby. But it seemed he had to. Desperate measures were required.

Chapter 13

"They'd better know what they're doing," Charles muttered under his breath several hours later. It was past noon as he and Louis approached the inn where the Spaniards had lodged. Samuel and Gaby had sent their servants about town to gather news of the travelers. Then they added some thoroughly creative pieces to his plan. Everyone was briefed in his or her part, but nerves plagued Charles. The thing could go wrong in dozens of ways; however, he still had his original scheme. A packet of gunpowder nestled in the leather purse strapped at his waist.

He and Louis entered the tavern by the kitchens, pretending they were too poor to enter the common room. Heaven knew they looked it. But in reality, they would watch events in the common room until their turn in the scheme came.

For a small coin, Charles bought a pint of ale and the right to sit by the kitchen fire. Louis pulled out a pair of dice and shook them temptingly in his hand. Would he play to pass the time? Charles took the ivory cubes, shook them, and breathed on them for luck. As they spun from his hand, he heard the Spanish captain in the nearby common room call for more beer.

Twin beady eyes of the snake stared up at him as he realized his foe was within his grasp. His heart raced in his chest like runaway horses, pounding with urgency as he thought of Frances, so close and locked away above stairs.

At that moment Gaby arrived. Charles heard her greet the host and imagined how she looked in her fashionable blue and green gown, as pretty and proper as one could wish. He stole a look into the common room and saw her sit at a table, sulking prettily. The captain would be sitting by the fire, beyond his sight, but within clear view of the attractive Gaby.

"What, all alone, *madam?*" the host asked as he requested her order.

"Bien sûr," she sighed, looking all the prettier in her distress. She reached up to rearrange her pert little hat with a rakish feather. It tipped at a saucy angle on her honey-colored hair. "All alone. With no one to care for me. No one at all."

"Surely someone as lovely as yourself will not remain alone for long," said the host, as if well versed in the ritual.

Loyalty must run deep among thieves, Charles thought. Samuel and Gaby had agreed to help free Frances, even though there would be no profit for them in the scheme. At least not just yet, though of course he had promised them funds aplenty when he returned to England.

"I fear I lead a lonely life." Gaby's glossy lips trembled. "But I value my solitude. Only the most splendid of men could tempt me to change my forlorn state. Pray bring me some ale."

The host had his lad bring the ale as he went about his business. The lad happened to be Pierre, cleaned up and with a linen cloth over his arm. The other men in the room eyed Gaby covertly, but left her alone, as if used to her presence. She proceeded to drink in a series of dainty, breathless gulps, pausing between each to draw her bowed lips into a pout and dab them with her handkerchief, alternately letting out soft sobs and wiping her eyes. She seemed the perfect solitary lady, distressed and awaiting rescue by a shining knight.

Though Charles couldn't see the Spaniard, he felt sure the man had noticed Gaby's arrival. What male would not?

Gaby ignored the others in the room and concentrated on emptying her tankard. Done, she rose to her feet and stood for several minutes, wobbling dizzily, a vague expression on her pretty face. Then she staggered across the common room, her step woefully unsteady as she threaded her way through the crowd of occupied tables, benches, and stools.

She disappeared from Charles's view. Quickly he slung Frances's equipment bag over his shoulder and tiptoed to the door, holding his breath. Just as Gaby passed before the captain, she tripped on a stool leg and sprawled. Her skirts flew up, showing an ample swath of plump calf.

The captain leaped up, put his meaty hands on her waist and arm, and helped her to her feet.

"Oh, my ankle." She wobbled and clung to him, her face distorted with pain. "I cannot stand."

Without hesitation, he swung her into his arms. "You must see a physician, my lady. You have had a grave fall."

"I can provide a chamber," the host suggested helpfully.

"I already have one," the captain said. "If the charming lady will permit. I even have the village physician attending one of my men. He can serve you as well."

"Alas, my ankle does hurt so," Gaby sighed. She locked her gaze with that of the Spaniard. The attraction between them leaped in the room, a palpable thing. Gaby let herself be borne away upstairs.

Charles ducked back into the kitchen and sat down before the hearth again.

They were gone a good long time. So long, Charles began to sweat. He cast a glance at Louis, but he seemed unconcerned, continuing to play at dice as if absorbed by the game. Charles had been losing for some time now, but he didn't care.

"Two francs."

Louis's voice snapped Charles back to doings in the kitchen.

"You've lost two francs. Pay me." Louis offered a grimy palm.

"I thought this was a gentleman's game," Charles protested.

"It is." Louis grinned. "Gentlemen pay their debts. Two francs."

"I'll pay you later." Charles batted away the hand. Samuel ought to arrive soon. On stealthy feet, he slunk back to the door. The cook and kitchen maid eyed him curiously, but he ignored them. Beyond, Pierre sat on a stool, ready to fill orders.

A prosperously dressed gentleman in a scarlet doublet pushed open the inn door, bringing a ray of sun and a breath of air that cut through the tobacco smoke from several pipes. *Samuel, at last.*

"Have you seen my wife?" he demanded of one of the tapsters as the man ran by with his tray.

"Good sir," Pierre hopped up, as if eager to be of service, "is she the fair-skinned lady with pale hair and a blue and green gown?"

"*Oui, certainment.* And a hat with a feather in it."

"She was here earlier, but she . . ." He smirked at Samuel. ". . . went upstairs with a gentleman."

Samuel's face darkened. Without another word, he put his hand on his sword and stalked toward the host. "Which room?" he demanded.

As Samuel ascended the stairs, Charles motioned to Louis. They approached the host and begged to earn some money by cleaning rooms.

"If you'll empty the slop jars in the chambers," the man agreed readily, "I'll give you a sou."

They trailed up the stairs behind Samuel, pretending they didn't know him. At the upper landing, Charles and Louis went one way, Samuel, the other. Charles sauntered down the passage, pretending to be about his work, bracing himself for what would happen next.

A shriek broke out loud enough to wake the dead. "*Eeeeeouuu,* I didn't do it. I'm innocent, I say." A door flew open and banged against the wall. Samuel dragged Gaby into the passage by her hair.

"Lying jade," Samuel cried. "You were with a man. Everyone below stairs knows it. Where is he? I'll kill him! Damn your eyes. Every time I turn my back, you're at it again. I ought to kill you as well."

"There's no one here, as you can see," Gaby shrieked as she bucked and fought her husband's hold. "I sprained my ankle and a kind gentleman loaned me his chamber until the physician could see to it. I swear 'tis the truth."

"No one here? Then whose clothes are these?" Samuel shook the captain's doublet and trunk hose in her face, cast them aside, and backhanded her with a blow that sent her flying back into the room.

She wailed in a series of loud, broken sobs.

"Where is the captain?" Charles asked Louis uneasily as they ducked into a dark corner of the passage.

"In the closet. Naked, too." Louis pinched his arm. "Get ready. Here they come."

"I'm taking you home and locking you in your chamber, bitch. Send for the priest, man," Samuel shouted at the host, who had ventured to the top stair as if concerned by the stir.

"You wish the priest?" the host asked. He pointed urgently to the door next to the captain's chamber.

"Yes. He can shrive the scoundrel who dared dishonor my

wife," Samuel continued loudly. "Because when I get back, I'm going to kill him."

They clattered down the passage, Gaby wailing as Samuel pommeled her, ensuring that anyone within hearing recognized the sound of two people leaving. Then, Samuel stomped down the stairs alone with the host while Gaby moved backward toward Charles and Louis. Kneeling before the door the host had indicated, she pulled out a metal tool and fit it into the lock.

"I'll check the captain's room for the key," Charles whispered to her. Sure enough, the captain's clothing yielded the key. He gave the door to the chamber's sole closet a glare as he left. The captain cowered in there, waiting for the outraged husband to be gone.

There was no time to lose. Charles ducked out of the bedchamber and relieved Gaby of her task. The door swung open to reveal Frances, lying on the bed, her eyes closed.

Charles crossed the room swiftly, gathered her in his arms, and strode toward the stairs.

"Damn it, I left my sword." Samuel met them as they were ready to head down.

"Ow, you beast," Gaby wept, continuing the charade loudly enough for the captain to hear from his closet. If he'd even considered coming out of his hiding place, he wouldn't dare now.

"Get the hawk," Charles commanded Louis in a loud whisper as he tossed the packet of gunpowder to the boy. "Then put this in Gaby's chamber, light the fuse, and run."

Louis caught the packet with a pleased grin and wheeled around to obey.

Charles charged down the stairs, bearing the half-unconscious Frances. "Fire!" he shouted to everyone in the common room. "Everyone out, straight!" He hurried through the tavern kitchen and into the stable yard.

Pierre was already atop a fine coach loaned for the occasion by Samuel and Gaby. Louis streaked past and clambered up with Pierre and the coachman. Charles laid Frances inside on the seat, tossed the equipment bag in a corner, and climbed in after her.

The coach lurched into motion and rumbled down the road. Through the cloud of dust it raised, Charles glimpsed people pouring from the inn. In their midst, the feather on Gaby's pert hat bobbed.

With a sigh of relief, he turned to Frances. She moaned. Looking down, he saw the entire left side of her face was swollen in an ugly, purple-black bruise. "By thunder, what have they done to you?" Full of fury, he caressed her face with a trembling hand. "Frances, can you hear me? Have they hurt you anywhere else."

She opened her green eyes and met his gaze. "Oh, God. Charles."

He enfolded her in his arms and cradled her against him, feeling a fierce relief so vast, it shocked him. "Never mind. You're safe now. We'll get back to Paris and from there, back to England."

"No, she said weakly. "You must take me back."

"I will, sweet. But not just now. You must rest first."

"You don't understand." She struggled to sit up. "I mean back to the inn."

"No," he growled, irritated that even now she would believe the Spaniard's lies and brave their cruelty. "Frances, your uncle is dead. Trust me."

She shook her head vehemently. "I told you before, I have to go with them. I want to go back. I must!"

Chapter 14

"You're *not* going back to those monsters and that's final," Charles ground out as Frances dived for the coach door. Barely able to contain his fury, he launched himself after her and clamped a hand around one of her wrists.

"Let me go! I have to find my uncle," she cried. Her voice brimmed with hysteria as her head whipped down. She bit him squarely on the hand.

Charles shouted in pain. Pushed to the breaking point, he clenched her around the waist and hauled her back to the middle of the seat. "Have they beaten all the wit out of you? You can't go back to them."

She blindly swung her fists at him. One of them connected with his injured eye.

Pain overtook what was left of his reason.

Half standing, he wrestled her squirming body down on the seat, planted a knee on either side of her thighs, and pinned her with his weight. "By thunder, I've just risked my life getting you away from them." His chest heaving with the exertion, he clamped her arms to her sides. "I've been starved for you, shackled and beaten for you. I've even been kicked out of a speeding wagon *by* you, and all you can do is bite the hand that rescued you." He cast a furious glance at the marks on his wrist. "I'll not have it. If I have to truss you up, you're coming with me to Paris, and—"

An explosion shattered the late afternoon peace.

Frances shrieked and jerked free. She rolled into a ball, arms crossed over her head, as if expecting the coach to fly to pieces.

As the echoes of the blast reverberated through the sundrenched countryside, then died away, Frances cautiously opened her eyes. "We're still alive."

"Aye," Charles answered with a wry grimace. "But our Spanish friends are not."

She stared at him in horror. "You didn't—"

"I blew up the inn," he explained with satisfaction, hoping the other inhabitants had heeded his warning and vacated the doomed building. "Of course I'll pay the host for his loss as soon as I can."

To his surprise, the fight went out of her. She slouched against the seat and began to weep, tears rolling down the puffed skin of her damaged cheek. "Now I'll never find my uncle."

Her misery sliced through him, becoming part of him as she babbled between sobs.

"He's the only person who loves me. If they were going to kill someone, it should have been me rather than him. I wish I were dead."

Charles eased his weight off her. Unsure what to do, he lifted her onto his lap and cradled her in his arms, his heart wracked by the urgent wish to stop her crying. Despair welled inside him, wrenching like her sobs, as he remembered how it had been at thirteen to lose his father, the strength in his life. Despite the presence of his mother and many siblings, he had felt orphaned and alone.

"I've opened your wound again," Frances said in a small voice, her fingers brushing his scalp. " 'Twas unforgivable of me when you were trying to help. I lost my head."

Charles held her against him so tightly, he felt her racing heart against his chest. God, another of her sweet vulnerabilities. He hadn't imagined she ever let her passion rule her. Not as he had in the past. "I am sorry, Frances, but your uncle is dead. I overheard the captain say he hoped to trick you into thinking otherwise. It was a deliberate ruse on their part."

"Why do you say this!" she cried fiercely, rearing up her head.

Such a creature of extremes, he marveled. Soft and vulnerable one moment, defiant the next. He tensed, prepared to hold her fast if she lunged for the door again.

She pushed him away, but didn't try to escape. Instead, she glared at him with such anger, he saw the tendons tighten in her neck. "He's alive, and you won't stop me from going to him. I'll go to the border alone and find a way to free him. I vow I will."

"No," he said firmly. "If he were alive, I would help you find him. But the man you buried was your uncle."

"How can you be sure?" A twinge of doubt weakened her voice and flickered in her eyes.

Her pain wrenched at him with unexpected strength. He'd thought life in the West Indies had hardened him to all emotion, yet he felt it now. It couldn't have come at a worse time in his life. "You're the one who should be sure," he said, fighting the feelings stirred by this woman. "Didn't you see him laid out?"

"No." She swallowed hard and clenched her jaw in a visible effort not to cry again. "His body was terribly mutilated. It was so horrible, I looked for only a second." A shudder racked her and her expression twisted with grief. "He was always so full of life, always urging me to see the bright side of things. I couldn't bear to see a desecrated hull with his spirit gone." Her next words were choked. "Sir Humphrey, his friend, looked more closely and t-t-told me it was my uncle. I never asked him how he could be certain. I let him see to the coffin and other details. I went to the funeral and the grave site . . . b-but I didn't look again." She hid her face in her hands.

Charles blinked and swallowed. He stroked her hair, fighting the hurt he felt for her, wishing to escape the emotions he'd buried long ago. He would get past them, he swore inwardly. He wanted to help her, but while doing it, he would feel nothing at all.

"Now do you understand?" she continued brokenly. "If I have any reason at all to think he lives, I have to take the risk and search for him. Otherwise, I abandon him to a certain, horrible death."

He understood only too well the overwhelming need to help someone dear. God knew he'd tried to help Richard. And right now he burned with the wish to heal Frances's battered face and her tortured spirit. Sweet heaven, even with the damage done to her, she was still beautiful enough to have men flocking to her side.

"Be assured I will help you," he said hoarsely. "I will prove to you that your uncle is dead."

"H-how?" she sobbed.

"We'll have the authorities exhume his body."

Her head jerked up. Her green eyes, always startling, pierced him like sharp emeralds, demanding the truth. "We'll what?" she asked, her voice high with disbelief.

"I said, we'll have him dug up."

"Pharaoh's foot."

He couldn't tell whether she didn't want to do it or didn't believe he wanted to. He took both her hands in his. "I think it's the only way for you to find peace. You can't move forward with your life until you're sure about the past. None of us can." Lord help him, he knew he hadn't. He hadn't been able to consider loving another woman since he'd lost Inez. "I'm not certain they'll agree readily, but we'll see it done. Now will you agree to come quietly to Paris? Without a fuss?"

She studied his expression, seeming to search for something. Sincerity, he guessed. Earnestly, he met her gaze and held it with his own. Fear and uncertainty still shone in her eyes, and he wanted to banish them both. Finally, she looked away and, with a shudder, admitted defeat.

"I agree." Her voice sank to a low rasp. "But Charles, what if it's not my uncle buried in the churchyard? What then?"

Charles released her hands and sank back in the seat, staring at her. A small rise of impatience ran through him at her stubbornness, her refusal to accept the truth. A fresh recognition chased away the first emotion: she refused out of devotion. He admired that. "Try to rest and recoup your strength," he said to circumvent further argument. "When we know more, we'll decide the next best course."

"But what of the Spaniards?" she asked, veering in a new direction. "The death of the captain and his men will be reported to the Spanish delegation in Paris. They'll have a new dispatch of men after us soon."

"Not that soon." Suddenly, a weariness overcame him, weighing more heavily with every breath he took. At the moment, he didn't care a fig what happened on the morrow. Their immediate pursuers were dead, and he intended to enjoy the respite. "Word won't arrive in Paris for some days." Her doubting expression exhausted him. "I assure you," he insisted, "we are safe for now. Including the brats."

"You mean *Pierre* and *Louis*?"

"I call them the brats," he said, amused at how protective she was of the boys, especially since they seemed to need far less care than she did. "They behave like brats, so don't scold. Now what was I going to say? Oh, their two friends, Gaby and Samuel, are safe as well. I saw them as we left, standing in the inn yard. I wish you could have seen them

work." He considered telling her the entire tale, of coaxing
her to laugh at the idea of the Bull, stark naked in Gaby's
closet and shivering with fear, but she interrupted before he
could begin.

"I know well enough how they do things. I *have* met
Samuel and Gaby," she said with a flicker of a smile.

"You have?"

"I've known Louis and Pierre for five years. They taught
me whom I can trust and whom I cannot."

For some unknown reason, her words reminded him of
Louis's irritating question last night. *You kissed Frank yet?*
The urge to do just that surged through him. Her soft lips,
unmarred by the beating, hovered tantalizingly near.

"Why don't you lie down? I'm going to," he said instead.
He set her firmly on the cushioned seat and swung over to
the opposite side. With his back wedged into the corner, he
propped up his feet. "When 'tis safe to stop, I'll get some
cool compresses for your cheek. 'Twill bring down the
swelling. You look a fright."

"My thanks. So do you."

It took him a moment to realize she wasn't really insulted,
merely teasing him. He fell silent, feeling out of his depth
with her, never knowing what to expect.

Tilting his hat over his good eye, he pretended to sleep. In
truth, he watched her covertly as she slid her slender hips
along the green velvet seat and brought up her legs. Then she
rearranged her torn, rumpled plumage, as if she weren't covered discreetly enough in his presence, curled into a sleeping
position, and closed her eyes.

She looked so innocent, lying there exposed to his stare.
The tear tracks on her cheeks and the bruises marring her
flesh signaled him like a beacon fire, stimulating his instinct
to respond with help.

He grimaced and snapped his gaze away from her soft,
tempting mouth and slender form. How much longer, he
wondered stoically as he closed his eyes, could he keep from
doing what that meddler Louis had had the audacity to say
aloud? And would Frances let him? Or was she just as likely
to slap his face?

The coach bounced and lurched over the road like some
great lumbering monster groaning over every rock in its
path. Unable to relax, Frances snatched glances at Charles,

who had tipped his hat over his eyes to block the light. Even in repose, he looked tired. Lines of tension bracketed his mouth, as if he worried and plotted even in his sleep. In spite of his reassurance, she couldn't imagine he wasn't alert to the dangers that lay ahead.

How could this be happening? she wondered. Why would a stranger fight for her so valiantly, suffer such physical abuse, then rescue her at risk to his own life?

And how could she have imagined him nothing but a thoughtless, inconsiderate bore who wanted to rule a woman? He wasn't that at all.

But he wasn't entirely thoughtful either, because he'd left her bird behind. A new sob tightened in her throat as she finally acknowledged what was too terrible to accept, even now. Oriana was gone. Sweet Oriana, who had bonded with her mere days after she hatched. The fluffy, endearing eyas had spent the following months trailing Frances about the house, begging for tidbits, as devoted as a puppy. She had grown into a beautiful, strong creature, full of fierce love for her mistress, as if Frances were both mother and mate.

Now she would never again see her beloved friend, nor hold her on her fist. Nor would they ever again experience the glory of the hunt.

It hurt her face and nose abominably to weep, but her tears demanded release. Frances tried to suppress the whimpers, hoping the rattle of the coach masked what sounds escaped. She had lost her uncle *and* Oriana. It was too much pain to bear.

"Does your face hurt?" Charles asked, his voice stark.

"No," she whispered, afraid to say more for fear the flood would break loose again. Apparently, he hadn't been sleeping at all. So of course he'd heard her crying.

"I am sorry that whoreson struck you."

She couldn't answer. Swallowing a sob, she struggled onto her other side to hide her face. She wanted to hate him for sacrificing her bird, yet she couldn't. He was a falconer, and she knew very well what it had cost him, forced to choose between saving her or the hawk. Instinct and training would have urged him to choose the bird. Yet he had rescued her.

He sighed heavily. "Obviously something is bothering you. Tell me what it is and I'll see what I can do."

"O-Oriana's gone," she choked out. "But please don't think I blame you. It's not your fault."

Silence followed, except for the squeak and bang of the vehicle. And the guilt that whispered inside her head, calling her a churl for adding another care to his heavy load.

"Your hawk is up top with Pierre and Louis," he growled at last.

She jerked around, her gaze leaping to his face, only to encounter the intense irritation radiating from him.

"I don't know why they took her up there," he said. "The wind is bad for her, but we haven't stopped once since we started so I let it go. It was more important to put distance between us and any possible surviving Spaniards. When we do stop, I'll bring her inside."

"Oh!" She levered into a sitting position. "She really is with us?"

"I *am* a master of hawks," he said haughtily. "It's my habit to think of their welfare first."

Of course it was. Hadn't she thought nearly the same thing only a moment ago? She flew at him and flung her arms around him, anointing his face with kisses. "Thank you, thank you! You *are* wonderful! How can I ever repay you for saving her? And I thought you a rude-mouthed bully. I'm sorry. I was wrong."

Thunderation, Charles thought as he awkwardly patted her hair. She was the most baffling, irritating wench he had ever met, thanking him and even kissing him for saving her hawk, though not once had she thanked him for saving her own skin.

Chapter 15

She was also outrageously outspoken, Charles thought gloomily as they rode on. So Frances had thought him a rude-mouthed bully. He'd known that, but he'd flinched anyway when she confirmed it aloud.

Still, her kisses were adequate compensation for the affront—kisses that had ended too soon as far as he was concerned. He would have liked to change them into caresses of a more intimate nature. Her very touch set him on fire.

But she'd retreated to her former place and resettled on the seat, this time with smiles wreathing her face. Would she have smiled like that if he'd kissed her back? he wondered. Probably not.

The coach swayed and bounced over the road toward Paris. Beyond the leather blinds covering the windows, the countryside hummed with activity, men and women working the fields, travelers on the road. No doubt they eyed the passing coach with suspicion. Only the wealthy traveled in such luxury. Their passage would be noted and reported. . . .

Thankfully, he had a plan.

Dust permeated the air, and Charles closed his eyes, needing to conserve his strength. But the sweetness of Frances's kisses, added to the memory of their intimacy in the wagon, fired his lust. This engaging, enraging wench stirred up a tempest inside him, conjuring multiple images in his head. In his mind's eye, he saw her lying on white linen, her sleek hair as dark as his desire, her porcelain flesh gleaming, awaiting his touch as he knelt on the bed. But no prospect of bed awaited them in Paris. Their midnight would be spent in a graveyard with a pair of spades.

"How will we do what you propose?" she asked, echoing his very thoughts.

"I was just considering." He mulled over the latest worry.

"Our chief trouble will be the authorities. They won't approve of digging up consecrated ground. They'll want consultations with dozens of officials, both English and French." He paused, searching for the right words to explain what they might have to do. But devil take it, there were no right words. "We'll probably have to dig him up ourselves," he stated baldly.

"You're jesting," she said, stunned. "You couldn't . . . we couldn't . . . could we?"

He squinted at her through his good eye, noting that though she remained prone, her eyes were wide, staring at the coach roof. "I know it sounds macabre." He wondered if he'd outraged her. "But it's the quickest way to know the truth. If you think about it, the digging isn't the hard part. The hard part is opening the coffin and looking inside." He stopped after that, reluctant to voice more persistent concerns. What if the man they exhumed was completely unrecognizable? Or what if Frances could tell with surety that the body *wasn't* her uncle's, as she'd mentioned before? By the gods, he prayed neither of these things would happen. He had assured her this would solve her problem, but he hadn't convinced himself. Things could go wrong.

"Does your uncle have any distinguishing features?" he asked. "Something that would help you recognize him if . . ." He didn't want to say if the man's face was destroyed.

"Yes, I know what you mean," she answered bravely. "He did have a strangely shaped scar on his right ring finger."

"We'll check for that. Anything more?"

"No, except that I'm sure I'll recognize him if I truly look this time."

Should he tell her what an eight-day-old body could look like, especially after being in water overnight? No, there was no reason to disgust her. Time enough for that when she had to look for herself. "We'll manage," he promised. "Now try to sleep. Neither of us has had more than restless snatches in the last thirty-two hours."

It was good advice, but try as he would, he couldn't follow it himself. His gaze kept wandering back to her graceful form as she slept, flat on her back so her face wouldn't be touched. Her long eyelashes rested like feathery wings on the ruined flesh of her cheek. Damn the captain for handling her so. Charles was glad he'd destroyed the brute. He'd done it for himself, but also for her, which was madness, because he'd promised to protect Inez the same way three years ago, to be her gallant knight in all things, to the death if required. No such sacrifice had been asked of him. Instead, he'd destroyed his own chances to perform brave deeds, and despite her faults, he didn't blame Inez. She had simply put her faith in the wrong man.

And now here he was, asking another woman to trust him. *Pure madness!* As the razor talons of his old wounds tore at him, he advised himself to stay away from her. Trust came easily only the first time. Once betrayed, as Frances had been, it came hard or not at all. He would not ask her to take a chance on him.

Still, he couldn't keep his gaze from devouring the sight of her. Again he wondered why his proposal to help had stunned her. Because in offering, he would have to go out of his way?

The last thought amazed him. Had she received so little support during her life? She certainly exhibited a fierce loyalty to her uncle that suggested she had been well taught. It ran strong and deep in her, like a wild river that had dug its bed well. And she didn't give that loyalty lightly. He imagined what a person must mean to her to deserve that gift. God, he would give his right hand for such a thing.

He had given it once; he had wagered all and lost. He had wagered that Inez would be loyal to him over Richard. Though she'd chosen him, their idea of loyalty hadn't matched. In the end, he hadn't won a thing.

His friend had taken his loss of the wager well. As shipmates, they had shared much, almost starving to death together on the voyage over, then basking in the splendor of Hispaniola once they arrived to plunder Spanish ships and towns under his commander, Drake. It had been a rare time until they met Inez. Curse the day they'd gone swimming at that isolated, inland lake and discovered her. Unaware that they watched, she'd frolicked in the shining water, her sleek, nude curves firing their lust. Later, they'd made asses of themselves, competing for her favor, when they both should have realized she was forbidden fruit. They were English, and because she was Spanish, any future between them was doomed.

His bad judgment, along with its damning consequences, festered within, augmented by the annoying road dust, making it impossible to sleep.

Charles flicked open the leather window cover and studied the countryside as they passed. He hadn't told Frances, but they weren't going to Paris—at least not yet. First they must rest, so he'd directed the coachman to St. Augustine's monastery, which his sister visited regularly to sell their family's cloth. There they could bathe, have their wounds dressed, sleep, and eat their fill. They required strength for digging, and unless he missed his guess, Frances had no inkling how taxing their midnight foray in the graveyard would be.

Frances awoke to Oriana's deafening squawks. High-pitched screams of indignation rose from above on the driver's seat, deafening the hearer. Not that Frances wasn't used to it. It meant her hawk wanted her mistress, food, and attention, in that order. Now.

"Are we almost there?" She sat up and tidied her disheveled dress and hair. A day and a half of traveling had done nothing to improve her appearance—and her face. She groaned as she touched her injuries. Her cheek had swollen as big as a hawk's croup stuffed with fresh meat. It felt like fresh meat too, radiating raw pain.

"Almost." Charles had been gazing out the window, his face hidden by the window flap. He closed the flap and turned to face her. "We're stopping for a minute to rest the horses."

He opened the door and leaped out as soon as the coach ground to a halt. "I'll get you some water," he said over his shoulder. "Stay here and don't move."

"Get Oriana, too," she called after him, wetting her dry lips. She was thirsty, but she wanted her bird.

He brought the drink first, imposing his own priorities. She took the dipper and, trying to be grateful, drank down the contents in several gulps. Charles wrung out his wet handkerchief and handed it to her.

"Lie down," he advised, "and lay this across your cheek."

"I would rather a piece of raw beef." She grinned at him ruefully.

With a chuckle, he backed away from the coach door. "So would Oriana, but we dare not tarry here. We need to arrive at our destination before dark."

"You're not going to Sir Humphrey, are you?" Louis put in, weaseling his way past Charles and into the coach. He plunked down across from Frances. *"Quel salaud,"* he swore as he looked closer at her face. "I'd kill the rotter for doing that to you, if he weren't already dead."

"I'd kill him myself if necessary," she answered, then noted Charles's expression at their exchange. She'd shocked him again.

"Voici Oriana," Pierre put in, poking Charles in the back with the cage.

Oriana screamed her impatience, and Frances laughed, reaching for her friend. "Come here, love," she crooned, settling the cage on her lap and opening the little door. Oriana fluttered straight to her shoulder and began to preen. Frances felt Charles's gaze on her from outside the coach, but he didn't interrupt as Louis leaned over and whispered in her ear.

"Oh!" Frances blanched as Louis finished speaking. Word had come just as she'd been abducted by the Spaniards—her uncle's special messenger from Spain was due in Paris soon. She must convey the expected message on to the queen. Should she tell Charles?

Silently, she debated. Just now she must convince him not to go to Sir Humphrey or the English ambassador when they arrived in Paris. Since she sensed a battle coming, the messenger news must wait. Besides, she would far rather not involve him at all. She'd endangered him too much as it was. "Why didn't you tell me sooner?" she whispered to Louis. "That's only two days away."

"When did I have a chance?" he demanded, slightly indignant and much too loud.

"A chance to do what?" Charles asked. "What's only two days away?"

Frances glanced up to find his narrowed, suspicious gaze locked on her face. "Thursday is two days away," she said brightly, recovering quickly.

"So what if it is. What are you up to now?"

"Aren't you thirsty, Louis?" She ignored Charles's question and turned to the lad. "Shall we walk to the well?"

"After he tells us where we're going." Louis glared at Charles belligerently. "This isn't the road to Paris. Where's he taking us, I'd like to know?"

Frances turned to Charles, baffled by this new development. "But you said we were going to Paris? Why would you—"

"Get to the well, you ruffians, and have some water." Charles prodded the boys from the coach, as if eager to be quit of them. They moved reluctantly, but didn't fight him. After a minute's hesitation, they crossed the field to the nearby barnyard and its well. Charles blocked Frances's attempt to follow. "Now," he demanded, "what's in two days?"

"Charles"—she wet her lips nervously—"where are we going if not to Paris? We *are* going there, are we not?"

"Of course," he agreed. "But first I've something else in mind."

I see," she said, tilting her chin haughtily. "And am I to know about this something or do you insist on yet another surprise?"

"I'll tell you about it when you tell me about Thursday," he gritted out.

Frances tossed her head and turned away. She could be every bit as stubborn as he was. "Charles, I believe the boys are right. I don't think we ought to go to Sir Humphrey's or the ambassador's. The Spaniards will hear of us immediately if we do. We'd best hide in the boys' lodgings instead, and we'd best go there now."

"*I* decide where we're going and when. I've given the coachman instructions. Be quiet and wait."

"You just don't like them," she accused. "They're too base born for you."

"Why is it you don't object to the things they do?" he countered. "Or to what their friends do for their livelihood?"

"I do. Often." She looked at him in surprise. "But they're not prepared to live any other life yet. I'm working to change them, little by little."

"How?"

"I'm teaching them to read. And to speak English."

"Oh, no." He put up both hands. "You're not taking them back to England with us. I won't have them. Paris is their home."

"Their home is where I am," she declared with indignation. "As if I would leave them alone to fend for themselves. I was going to ask permission to bring them when you first arrived, but I didn't have a chance."

To her dismay, he crossed his arms, a surly expression on his face. "I won't have them. They're dirty and lousy, and their manners are terrible. They'll filch things everywhere we go. Not to mention wanting to work this Crossbiting Law thing."

"I notice you didn't object when Samuel and Gaby served you well."

"Desperate measures were required."

"That's my point. Their entire lives call for desperate measures, or they would have died long ago. You have no idea what it's like being born to a life like theirs."

"And you do?" He sounded cross.

"I don't either," she hastened to add, "not firsthand. But I've seen enough to understand. And I can imagine what it's like."

"So can I when I want to."

"We'll stay at their lodging when we get to Paris," she insisted. "They'll also find us men to help with the grave. We can't dig it up alone in one night, you know."

He looked angry, but said nothing more. Obviously he didn't like her taking charge, but they desperately needed help with their plans.

And she wouldn't tell him about the messenger. He was so stubborn, so domineering, he would undoubtedly try to usurp her responsibility, saying it was men's work. Yet the messenger would communicate with her alone.

She had taken her uncle's place before; she would do so again. The information from this messenger could make all the difference to England's future. She would not fail her queen or her uncle now.

Chapter 16

Paris must wait. Frances resigned herself to Charles's change of plans and tried to appreciate the benefits brought by delay. He insisted that a hearty dinner and a good night's sleep would not be amiss.

She did admit to a certain hunger as their coach rolled through a broad valley bisected by a silver, chattering stream. Truth be told, her stomach churned as if an entire troupe of tumblers performed inside. And though she refused to admit it to Charles, she welcomed the sight of St. Augustine's monastery when its ancient, solid walls loomed ahead. A brief solitude in this spirit-touched haven appealed to her. She needed time to heal, if only for a night.

The abbot recognized the name Cavandish immediately, Frances noted. As Charles explained, his sister and her factors visited the place regularly on their trade journeys to supply the abbey with cloth.

Based on that firm friendship, sweetened with Charles's promise of gold pieces to come, the kindly old ecclesiastic expressed a gracious willingness to host them in his private dining parlor. He saw them seated around the heavy oak table and their trenchers heaped with food.

Louis and Pierre fell to and stuffed away more edibles in shorter order than Frances had ever seen, which was saying a good deal. Charles engaged the abbot in discourse about trade and politics while the meal progressed. Oriana perched on the wood block provided and happily ripped at a hunk of raw pigeon complete with feathers. Frances was left blissfully to herself.

Safe for the time being, she gave over her attention to bodily needs. *Pharaoh's foot,* but her stomach felt as empty as a deep game bag. Trying her best to remain ladylike, she attacked a huge slab of smoking hot mutton, a wedge of pigeon pie dripping gravy, crisp-crusted bread, and new-picked peascod from the monastery gardens. The sharp edge of her appetite dulled, but her stomach clamored for more as she plied her spoon to a bowl of thick, steaming soup floating with parsnips, barley, and she knew not what else. She only knew her stomach grew heavy with ecstasy. Her spoon slowed.

She lingered over a slice of dried apple tart laced with nutmeg and sugar syrup, letting each bite melt on her tongue. A sense of temporary security permeated her being, gratefully greeted by her weary body and aching soul. No Spaniards dared attack them here.

She washed down the food with frequent quaffs of a hot, cinnamon-scented brew the abbot referred to as his "very special mulled spice." The drink slid down her throat in the most delightful manner, warming her insides. Without hesitation, she downed a full wooden tankard of the beverage and the good half of a second, forgetting all about where she was going on the morrow.

She put down her spoon, leaned back in her chair, and let her eyelids drift closed, her mouth stretched in a contented grin. Why she smiled, she couldn't imagine. Being a refugee from the Spaniards was no jest.

Oh dear, she thought sleepily, the abbot's "mulled spice" must have been wine, sweetened and spiced till she failed to recognize its potent tang. With shameless abandon, she had swilled those tankards. It had gone straight to her head, making her feel magnanimously, expansively appreciative of everything and afraid of nothing.

Poof! A fig for trouble. Folding her hands over her full belly, Frances envisioned the bliss of a clean, quiet room with a roost for her hawk, a bed heaped with blankets, and a roaring fire.

She got the last three, but the room wasn't quiet. It had Charles in it. Botheration on the man for telling the abbot they were wed. Still, what did it matter? They had already traveled unchaperoned and shared the bed of a wagon for several days now. And the wagon was far smaller than this room. Dismissing the need for concern, she tottered into the chamber and surveyed it unsteadily while a brother built up the fire and conversed with Charles about their needs.

"Oriana," she whispered to the bird perched on her shoulder. "Are you making this room spin? Pray tell it to stop."

But it wasn't Oriana. The room itself insisted on making lazy revolutions like a cartwheel, refusing to be still.

It wasn't so unpleasant, Frances decided, as she managed to bring the furnishings of the chamber into focus. She moaned softly at the welcome sight of a wide bed of sturdy oak with an inviting eiderdown.

Deciding that Oriana could perch on a chair, she reached for the one nearest her. But blast the thing, it wavered and bobbed in the most irritating manner. When she finally cornered it, she groped for its back to hold it still. The gos eyed the oak rail with first one eye, then the other. *Praise heaven it passed muster,* Frances thought, as Oriana settled on the topmost rung and began to preen. With a look around, Frances realized the brother had left them. She was alone with Charles.

"You shouldn't have told the abbot we are wed," she said. Her words, as she pushed them out, felt as slow and ponderous as sticky sweets still gummed to her tongue.

Charles sank down on the bed and tugged at his right boot. The room spun pleasantly with him at the center, which tickled her insides, prompting her to laugh. "We ought," she said, "to sleep in separate rooms."

"I refuse to repent." Charles grunted as his boot came off. He appeared unaware of her struggle with the unruly chair or the sticky words. "Besides, you did it first, telling the innkeeper you expected your husband. Why shouldn't I fuel your myth? You are to be known for the remainder of our journey"—he made an expansive gesture—"as Baroness Milborne, my wife."

"But you lied to the good brothers," she said as piously as possible, fighting a grin. "And they believed you. You've committed a terrible sin."

"What would you prefer I say, Mistress Scold? 'She's not my wife and I don't give a damn that we're traveling without adequate escort. Oh, and the two lads are ruffians and thieves. I hope you don't mind.' "

He seemed serious, which meant she should be, too. But Frances fought a losing battle with the building giggles. One of them erupted through her nose in a thoroughly unrefined snort. She clapped a hand to her face.

He looked up sharply from his left boot. "My dear Frances, are you well?"

The room spun crazily. She liked the way he looked at the

center of that spin. "I wish you'd call me Frank as the boys do," she said solemnly.

He frowned for a minute, as if sensing something amiss, but let it pass. "Blasted boot," he grunted, returning to his task. "Sticks like glue. Ouch!" He clutched his side. "This isn't helping my sore ribs. Suppose you lend a hand."

Sighing deeply, Frances traversed the gulf between them on unsteady legs. He seemed a long space away, and her path wandered, as crooked as a dog's hind leg. Stopping before him, she bent her knees, braced herself, and held out both hands. "Give me your foot."

He obliged.

Frances staggered as she grasped his heavy heel with both hands. "Do you keep bricks in your boot?" She wrestled it back and forth. Why did the room insist on twirling when she needed her balance? As she scowled at the recalcitrant boot, she was seized by a sudden attack of titters. "Did you really say that Pierre and Louis were thieves?"

"No, I asked if you wanted me to say they were."

"Yes, please." Bubbles of laughter tickled her nose. She shook all over from them. "And I want to watch the abbot's face when you do."

"You're not taking this at all seriously," he said, apparently quite annoyed with her. "Now listen carefully and remember. I said they were your uncle's children on your father's side. Both parents died of the fever, so we're fetching them back to England to live with us. Shocking, the way they were cared for. But since they were orphaned, 'twas no surprise." He waved one hand to get her attention. "Frances? Would you get back to my boot? It won't come off unless you pull."

"Oh." She glanced down, surprised to find the boot hadn't budged. Bracing herself and setting her jaw, she pulled. Suddenly, the boot popped free. She staggered backward and sat down hard on the stone floor with the boot in her lap.

Charles's guffaw filled the room as his stern expression melted, replaced by a devilish grin. "By thunder, look at you."

"I got your damn boot off," she said with all the injured dignity she could muster.

He laughed harder, clutched his bruised side, and fell over backward on the bed.

"Swine," she muttered. "I might have injured my backside."

"You didn't, did you?" He raised his neck and peered at her from the bed.

"I don't know. I can't feel anything down there."

He brayed with laughter and pounded the bed.

"It's not my fault," she declared, looking hard at her legs, hoping they would get her up of their own accord.

"It most assuredly is," he chortled, propping himself up on one elbow. "You drank too much mulled wine at supper. When I saw you downing it, I assumed you were accustomed to it. It didn't come to me what was wrong with you until . . ." He paused, gave his boot a significant look, then broke into another guffaw while she glared.

A tap sounded at the door.

"Enter," he called through his merriment. Sitting up, he wiped his eyes and smoothed out his face. Then he rose and offered her his hand.

He deserved a thorough tongue lashing, she thought, struggling to her feet and dropping the boot in the process. But she couldn't give it now, because a stout brother draped in the brown robes of the order waddled in bearing a steaming pot.

"I have brought your poultice, Baron Milborne. It is my own special mix."

"Many thanks, Brother Denis," Charles greeted the newcomer. "How good of you to oblige us with your special concoction. Nothing like a fresh herb poultice to draw out the pain of a bruise and reduce swelling."

"Nothing like it," the brother agreed. He chattered happily as he placed the pot on the table and demonstrated to Charles how to spread the poultice on fresh linen.

Frances heard few of their words. Gripped by a sudden fatigue, she realized she'd better lie down before she fell down. The idea seemed an exceptionally sound one. Concentrating hard on the bed so it couldn't evade her, she staggered across the chamber and fell, full length and fully clothed, on the soft eiderdown.

The brother glanced at her in surprise. "Baroness Milborne, shall I withdraw so you might first disrobe? Once you are comfortably abed, I can assist you in applying the poultice."

"Many thanks, but I'll assist my wife," Charles cut in smoothly. He escorted the brother to the door, tendering

many words of gratitude that neatly covered Frances's need
to explain why she slept in her clothes.

Frances heard the bump of the door as it closed behind the
brother. Though she kept her eyes closed, she could feel
Charles's gaze bore into her on the bed.

"I'm not taking my clothes off." She squeezed her eyes
tighter, wishing she could hide.

"Nor should you," he said in that calm, calculating tone of
his. "Lie still whilst I minister to you."

She knit her brow in worry as she wondered what minis-
tering he intended. Suddenly, something wet and damp
plopped on the bruised side of her face. "That's hot!" she
yelped, smelling herbs and knowing it was the poultice. She
tried to push it away.

"It won't burn you." Charles's strong hands pressed her
back against the bed. "I tested it on my own face first. Lie
still, Madam Hawk, and let the herbs do their work."

"What's *in* this blasted thing?" Frances muttered, sub-
siding with a show of reluctance. The warm linen settled to
the contours of her face, surprisingly soothing.

"Comfrey, pennyroyal, onion, and Solomon's seal root,"
Charles repeated the brother's recipe, "stamped fine and,
since he had not the time to steep it in vinegar overnight,
boiled lightly in wine."

More wine, France thought as her eyes watered. Exactly
what she needed. She inhaled deeply and felt the pungent
vapors renew her giddiness. The room revolved with
delightful grace. "What of you?" she asked as a contented
grin, so wide it probably looked idiotic, threatened to split
her face in two.

Charles chuckled again and stroked the undamaged side of
her face. "I'm not done with you yet. I intend to remove your
shoes and nether stocks next. At least you'll not sleep in
those."

She held her breath as he slipped off her shoes and rolled
down her stockings. Praise heaven he tried nothing untoward
. . . until both shoes and stockings were gone. Suddenly, his
hands closed around both her calves. "Such beauty," he murmured. "Would that it were mine." He drew both palms in a
languid, tingling caress down the full length of her bare legs.

His touch lit up her core like a magic torch.

"Charles, stop," she cried, terrified of her response to
him. Clutching the poultice to her face, she half sat. As she

struggled to find him in the spinning room, to pin him with an accusing stare, something dripped on her chest. Distracted, her mind muddled, she plucked at the brown stain spreading on her white smock. "Where did this come from?"

He leaned over and blotted her chest with a clean piece of cloth. " 'Tis nothing. Your poultice is leaking. A rather unromantic thing for it to do just now."

Another bout of drunken giggles convulsed her as she imagined how she looked, the poultice dripping down her face, her hair askew. She flopped back on the bed, tittering uncontrollably. "Oh, Charles, I'm of no use to anyone tonight. I'm certainly not romantic. Why don't you just cover me up and forget I'm here?"

Obediently, he spread a gray blanket over her, but she thought he looked annoyed as he tucked it around her feet. Could he be disappointed she failed to succumb to his wiles?

She snuggled beneath the blanket in safety, blessing her escape. He probably had no inkling what he did to her—how when he touched her, he kindled flames that urged her to touch him in return. Like the instinct that drove the hungry hawk to hunt, she'd felt that powerful drive just now . . . the wild, mindless urge to guide his hands up her bare legs until he discovered her woman's core. Praise the dripping poultice for saving them both.

She tried to watch him with one eye while he went to the table and prepared his own poultice, but the chamber rotated, so she gave up and let herself drift. "By heaven," she sighed, thinking of the Spaniards, "I feel safer than I have in days."

"I'm glad to hear that, but I should remind you this is your first night as my wife," he said, bringing them back to the dangerous subject. The bed creaked, and she felt the mattress sag as he lay down and rolled to her side. "You seem entirely too unaffected for a new bride. Aren't you afraid I'll take advantage of you in your sleep?"

"I did wonder before," she murmured, not the least alarmed by his banter. It was nice lying there, talking to him, but not having to look at him, well fed and warm at last. Sleep hovered near, taming the tingles caused by his closeness. "But now I know you'll not. You're much too kind."

"I'm not kind." The light teasing vanished from his voice as swiftly as it had come. "I have the most overpowering desire to seduce you, Frances Morley." He leaned over her and she felt the warmth of his breath on her cheek. "When are you going to admit that you want me, too?"

"Poultice pate," she giggled, keeping her eyes tightly closed. "If you're serious about seducing me, you'd best leave off your onion hat." She delivered the insult nearly to perfection, but another snort slipped out at the end, ruining it.

He sighed, as if deeply mortified.

She suppressed a laugh. "You smell like a wine head."

"That's what you'll have on the morrow," he warned as he rolled back on his side of the bed. "You have the most effective manner of squashing a man's ardor, you know."

"Good."

"Are you sure it's good?"

"Umm," she expanded, feeling positively eloquent in her response. She breathed deeply and the giddiness increased.

"At any rate, I'm glad to know you feel safe now." His voice drifted from a long way off.

"Forbidden subject. Talk about something else," she ordered. "What did you tell the abbot about our wounds?"

"Accident at a strange inn. We clashed quite hard in the dark."

"You knocked me out cold with your hard head." Frances giggled. "It is hard, too. As hard and stubborn as . . . as . . ." She groped for the right words, but like the scaly, awkward fish she had caught at six, they bucked and slid away before she could grasp them.

A sudden notion that she yearned to kiss him came out of nowhere. It warmed her insides like an inspiration. She imagined tasting his lips—they would be like the mulled wine from supper, their exotic spice urging her to indulge again and again.

Charles opened his good eye, observed Frances's relaxed state, and chuckled to himself. Frank was tipsy. She laughed so hard, he couldn't seduce her properly. Most puzzling of all, he didn't care. He liked being with her when she was this way—relaxed and too fuzzy-headed to order everyone about.

"Anyway," she murmured, in a tone implying a confidence, "the comfrey is doing its task."

"Is it?" he prompted.

"Umm," she said dreamily. "My face feels better already. And don't they say comfrey makes you wiser? Well, it's doing it. I see everything as clearly as can be."

"It's not the comfrey. The wine has made you daft."

"You're just jealous." She slurred the words together. "You want to be as wise as I."

"Are you wise about anything in particular?"

"All things!" She gestured widely with one arm and clouted him in the face. "Oh dear, did I hurt your bad eye?"

"Not at all," he assured her. "You merely put out my remaining good one. What specifically are you feeling wise about? Anything to do with me?"

A long pause ensued, and he thought she'd gone to sleep.

"You," she said succinctly of a sudden, "are a mistake."

"What do you mean?"

"I mean I want to kiss you, but there's no reason I should. That's the mistake."

At her blunt statement, desire twisted in Charles's loins. By thunder, he'd just gotten himself under control and she set him off again. But the chance was too good to miss. "If you want to kiss me," he said carefully, "I won't stop you."

"Very well." She sat up so quickly, he had no chance to remove his poultice. Leaning over him, she pressed her lips to his. Her warmth penetrated to his soul as she explored his mouth with hers, softly searching. Her hands gripped his shoulders, and his strayed around her waist to draw her close.

"Very sweet," he whispered. He wanted more as she ended the kiss and nuzzled his cheek with her nose.

"If I'm the sweet, then you're the savory," she chuckled in his ear, catching his lobe in her teeth and worrying it.

Excitement spiked in his groin. Some primitive emotion bottled up inside him for three years cried for release. "Frank, do you know what you're about?"

"Umm. I'm kissing you. You're to lie still and do nothing." Her lips hovered over his, teasing and tantalizing. "You taste splendid, just as I thought you would." The coil of her dark hair spilled from its knot and tickled his face.

He hardened between one breath and the next, feeling exactly as a hawk must when set to its prey. "You're driving me mad, you know."

She answered not a word, but stripped off her torn kirtle bodice as she mumbled something about being hot. Her thin linen smock drooped, and her bare, white shoulder tantalized him once more. He groaned.

"Are you unwell?" she asked, all solicitous care.

"I'm worse than unwell." He reached out to caress her

beautiful shoulder with one hand while the other enjoyed the feminine swell of her hip. The temperature increased in the chamber.

Charles began to sweat.

She laughed with a tinkling sound like hawk bells and bent over to rub her cheek against his. Her eyes had glazed over, and her lids fluttered.

She was so tipsy, Charles realized, she didn't know what she was doing. And in another minute she would be asleep. She seemed tragically vulnerable just then, with her hair bristling on one side, the poultice she'd replaced slipping and her other cheek too red in her pale, weary face. Her innocent trust reminded him she'd been betrayed by Antoine, that perfidious Frenchman.

His urge to seduce her disappeared, replaced by a far stronger desire to hold her in his arms and make love to her . . . sweetly, tenderly. But he couldn't do that, either, not given her past, or his. Realizing it, he cursed his luck. For a second he wished he'd been assigned a loose woman so he might have her without any qualms. Instead, a dull ache throbbed in his chest where he'd once had a heart. He would be a regular ale-sop by the time he reached England at this rate.

Gently, he pressed her back onto the bed. With a soft release of breath, she relaxed and lay still while he rearranged the poultice on her face.

"Aren't you going to ask me what my uncle knew?" she asked suddenly. She clutched his arm and squeezed, as if full of urgency, taking him by surprise.

"What your uncle—"

"Yes. You never asked me, though you've been panting to know."

He was panting to have his way with her, that's what. Though he supposed he must settle for this instead. "What did your uncle know?"

"Too much." Her volatile mood shifted again, and she giggled. "He has a friend who goes to Spain for him, a whore. She seduced a man and read his dispatches while he snored, dead drunk." She giggled again. "Whoever said whores were worthless?"

"What did the dispatches say?"

"Invasion of England," she pronounced solemnly. "Imminent."

"When."

"Soon enough."

"But when?"

"You're repeating yourself, you know."

"But I want to know."

"You know too much already." It seemed she would grow quarrelsome if he keep on. Mayhap he should let her sleep. But she had started this confession, and he had to know something else. "Why aren't you wed, Frances. You're so beautiful, it makes no sense."

Sure enough, her mood shifted to anger. "Don't you talk sweet to me, you scheming dog." Her words slurred. "Men are full of lies, promising marriage when they have no intention of wedding. I'll kill the man who tries that with me again."

Charles winced at the caged fury behind her words. Mayhap he'd opened a foul pot of worms, but if he proceeded carefully, he might pry from her what he wanted to know. "Tries what?" he asked with care.

"He was a whoreson. A lying, despicable, fatherless son of a female dung hill."

By heaven, such language, Charles thought. No doubt she had learned it from Pierre, whose mouth ran as foul as a gutter at times. "Who are you talking about?" he probed cautiously. "What did he do?"

"Do? Ha! He promised to wed me and told me he loved me. And I, like a fool, couldn't wait for him to prove it in bed. He had a honeyed tongue in the head of a lying wolf."

Charles winced as he digested her tirade. By thunder, his suspicions were confirmed. He struggled with renewed waves of rage while a long moment passed. By then he wasn't sure what she was thinking, or if she was even still awake, but he had to let her know he wasn't like Antoine. It was suddenly of vital importance that she not paint him with the same brush as the man who had destroyed her virginity as well as her trust. "Frances," he ventured, " 'tis your friend Charles."

She smiled. "Call me Frank, would you? Antoine never called me Frank. Mademoiselle Frances, he called me. His *belle trésor.* You wouldn't call me that, would you?"

"Well, not just now. Before you were bruised, I might have said it. And after you heal, I will, for certes. But not just now."

"Antoine called me that no matter what I looked like. I hate him. I hate the name Frances because he called me that. Call me Frank," she repeated. "What shall I call you?"

"You can call me anything you like. Cavandish would do. Or even Charles if you're inclined. But Frank"—he brushed back a lock of her hair—"I promise I'll keep you safe."

"No one can do that," she announced prophetically. "Not with those swine on our tails."

"They're not on our tails just now, nor will those particular individuals ever trouble us again. So put them out of your head and sleep."

She obeyed, and her lips parted slightly as her breathing evened out and her chest rose and fell in regular rhythm.

Satisfied that she rested, he rose, built up the fire again, then stood by the bed watching her. It wasn't fair, the way life had treated her. She had been left alone in the world over and over, first by her mother's death, then by her father's. As a young woman, her lover had betrayed her, then she had lost her protector uncle.

At the barrage of thoughts, a wave of pain hit him hard. Moisture started in his eyes, and he groped to find the bed.

It wasn't fair, he thought as he lay down beside her once more, wanting to hold her, knowing he dared not.

Dashing away his sentimental thoughts, he tucked the blanket more securely around her and turned away. The wool cover must separate them, despite his wish to feel her flesh against his in comfort and in need.

It was better this way, really. She deserved someone with a depth of spirit that matched hers, someone with an equally loyal heart. Look at what she'd done for her uncle, and at her decision to help Louis and Pierre. Over and over she gambled all to help them, despite the pain or disaster it might bring. She'd suffered for her uncle's sake. As for the boys, Charles predicted their background would lead them to hurt her bitterly in the end. Yet she reached out anyway to offer her gifts, her courage shining like a star in the dark sorrow of the world.

He, personally, wouldn't dream of taking such risks on purpose. Not at this point of his life.

Yes, better he stay aloof from her, he thought stoically as he stifled his own hungry need. No use arguing that his past wasn't his fault, that he'd been faced with impossible

choices. The fact was, he lacked the courage to put it behind
him and try again.

Ironic that he, who possessed bold physical courage, was a
coward when it came to emotion. Nothing in life, it seemed,
was fair.

Chapter 17

Silence stole through the monastery after the bells of matins. Huddled beneath her blanket, Frances moaned, fighting a dream. She was racing across bare fields, pursued by terror. Not a scrap of cover. Deserted and abandoned. With the Spanish murderers breathing hot on her heels.

As she fled before them, an immense pack of secrets, heavy and chafing, rubbed sores on her back. Was there no refuge? No place to hide?

Oriana! her heart called, yearning for her sole remaining friend. Searching blank skies the color of midnight, she stretched both hands to the stars and cried for her love.

The swift beat of wings startled her ears as a bird swooped low, streaking for her so fast, she could scarce make it out. Yet she knew it was Oriana. Her hawk brushed her head in a whirring blur, then remounted the wind.

Mistress of the skies. Pride of the air. Her hawk was her crowning glory, while she, the servant, waited below, living a vicarious pleasure in her bird's soaring flight.

Hawk of heaven, let me fly free like you.

The piercing blast of her own whistle broke from her lips. She sent the familiar signal over and over, keen and urgent, full of her need. *Come to me, beloved friend! Come to me!*

The frenzied sound of speeding wings preluded her answer. Frances searched the night skies, all her hopes pinned on one thing: her bird's trust and loyalty would bring her home to Frances's fist once more.

With a scream, a different bird answered her call—a huge tercel plunged out of nowhere. Swift and fierce, he attacked. And she . . . she was the prey. His shrill cry pierced her mind, paralyzing her like a foolish dove, ready to fall to his will. Eyes closed, heart pounding in terror, she braced herself for his strike.

The dream changed. A shrill whistle shredded the air—her

own keen cry. Suddenly, she flew at his side, her arms transformed to massive wings that pumped the air. Night fell away, replaced by dazzling light. How she reveled in the freedom of flight! She soared and dipped at his side, cutting circles in the sky. She was the mistress. She, the queen of heaven, taming the wind and owning the air.

The sun's bonfire kindled her heart, fueling her wings. Her mate flew beside her, prince among hawks. But the female always dominated a pair—in size and strength. She procreated. She accepted his homage—his strength mixed with loving care. This was her moment. This, her desire—the chance to claim the throne and rule her own life.

The dream shifted again. Just as she took up the reins of her destiny, her mate left her. The winds transformed him, granting him human form and the needs of a man.

She was the hawk, and he, the master, bidding her fly to his fist. Searching the wind, she found and rode the current. But his whistle cleaved the air, firm and commanding. He wanted to man her, to make his own.

A dark cloak flew from his shoulders, snapping in the wind, speaking his mastery. He lifted his fist and signaled her submission. No false lures. No lying promises. Blunt and honest, he stated his desire.

Submit to my will! His whistle summoned her across the distance. With his legs planted firmly on the earth, he stood solid and dependable, something she wanted. But no! No force under the sun could make her surrender. Her entire being yearned to fly.

Small chance of that when he brimmed with cunning. He possessed something surer than brute force. He wielded a magic that claimed her heart. The lure he swung was her own desire to belong to someone who offered her care.

With a sob, she spread her wings and plummeted for him, the man who was her fate. He had the power to catch and cage her, to force her to submit to the blinding hood. Yet even as her heart submitted, she longed to rise into the dazzling sky.

"No!" she cried, fighting his power. "I won't do it. I won't."

She screamed and thrashed, suddenly terrified, just as when the Spanish captain beat her, demanding she tell where Charles had gone. "I don't know where he is!" she cried. "He got away and I'm glad."

Strong arms grasped her, pinning her so she couldn't move. But the accompanying voice sounded unexpectedly gentle in her ear.

"Frank, can you hear me? 'Tis all right. You're having a bad dream. Wake up."

At the command, the fight left her. She blinked her eyes open to sunlight and Charles, holding her close, his voice soothing.

"There, now, you see," he gentled. " 'Twas a nightmare, no more."

"Hold me." She clung to him hard, needing his strength. But when he bent to kiss her, she pushed him away. "No! I can't! I-I'm sorry," she faltered, wanting him desperately yet burning with fear. The meaning of the dream was all too clear to her—she couldn't bear to be ruled.

"It's all right," he said calmly. "You don't have to kiss me this morning, though you did last night."

Had she done that? Sure enough, a foggy memory of her behavior lingered in her mind. She had kissed and teased him. How unnervingly forward, when nothing existed between them. Would he think her a jade?

But when she dared to meet his eyes, his forest brown gaze enfolded her—along with a forgiving smile. She let out a long breath of relief as he turned and extended his warmth to include Oriana, sitting on her nearby perch.

Oriana watched them with sharp, golden eyes. Frances smiled weakly and stretched out a hand to caress her bird. "I guess I did kiss you. 'Twas wanton of me, but I was grateful to you and wanted to show it." Though she knew that wasn't all she'd felt.

"How is your face?" Charles asked.

"Better," she admitted. "How does it look?"

"It's turning blue-green," he pronounced after a scrutiny, "but the swelling's down. A great improvement." He patted her on the arm.

"Thank you, Charles." She let the air out of her lungs with relief. Praise heaven he wasn't like Antoine, full of pretty compliments that were false. When she looked terrible, Charles didn't lie.

And his protection was real. He had snatched her from the Spaniards and destroyed them. Her expression must have tensed in anger at the thought of their abductors, because Charles's arms tightened around her.

"You're safe, sweetling." His hands soothed. His kind hands, gentling, taming. "Those devils won't trouble you again."

She closed her eyes, savoring the security of his touch for a moment. Then she pushed back the blankets and tried to sit up. "Oh, my head." Groaning, she cupped her head in her palms. "That mulled spice is wicked. I'll never touch another drop."

He chuckled softly. "You have a wine head, right and proper. But the bad dream is over. All gone."

"Everything is a bad dream these days. Even waking. And not just because of the wine."

"I know, but better times lie ahead if we can master our problems. Let us break our fast, then make our plans."

"Yes," she agreed, not wanting to face the day, knowing she must. "We should plan, but we'll likely disagree."

"Not if you're reasonable."

"Do you suggest I'm unreasonable?"

"Oh, no. Never that. A bit hardheaded at times, mayhap."

"Me!" She ruffled, indignant, not caring that she had puffed up exactly like a rattled bird. "You're the one who's hardheaded. I distinctly recall establishing that fact last night."

"I never agreed."

"That's the point. You never agree with me."

It was a bad start, Charles realized. They talked for some time after that, but settled nothing. She wanted to ride straight for Paris and search out friends to help. He wanted to wait until the morrow, after another good night's sleep. She insisted they required assistant grave diggers. He agreed. But they disagreed on who they should be.

"You can't hire an honest workman and ask him to dig up a grave," she ranted at him as they walked in the monastery gardens later that morning. "He'll take your money and do the job. But he'll also report you to the authorities. We'd be caught and have no end of explaining to do. And while we were explaining, the Spaniards would strike. I assure you, the captain's death will be known in Paris by the morrow. This time they'll just kill me and have done. Remember what they did to my uncle."

Charles regarded her evenly while he took all this in. "That's quite a chain of events," he said at last. "We start by hiring an honest workman to dig a hole and end with you dead. Are you sure it would happen that way?"

"I am."

He noted her jaw that jutted defiantly. Definitely a bad sign. The hawk balanced on her shoulder doubled the stare, adding her unblinking, yellow glare to Frank's.

"Whom do you think to hire instead?" he asked, holding hard to his temper.

"Friends of Pierre and Louis."

"And friends of yours, I assume," he said with disgust. "Are these the people you spent your time with for the last nine years? Murderers and counterfeiters? Cheaters of the hangman's noose?"

"You just cheated the noose yourself."

"Would you rather I hadn't?" Her implication infuriated him.

"No. But it proves my point." She threw him a smug glance. "We do what we must to survive. Don't sit in judgment on someone else."

They called a temporary truce when the dinner hour arrived. But by the time they had joined Pierre and Louis in the abbot's private dining chamber and eaten, Charles knew she was up to something. The winks and nods exchanged by the boys, not to mention the small objects passed back and forth under the table, put him on guard.

" 'Tis nothing," Frances assured him. No more than two boys quibbling over some sous. But once the meal was over, Frances bustled off with the excuse that the abbot had arranged a private space for her to bathe.

Surely, Charles assured himself, she told him the truth. She wouldn't get into trouble over something as simple as bathing. But he didn't trust her, no matter what she was doing.

He forced himself to leave her be, to return to their chamber and call for his own bath. With the dirt scrubbed away, he donned a new shirt provided by the brothers. Wishing he could have bathed *with* Frances instead of alone, he strolled in the garden and struggled with his choices. Should he wrest control from Frances and demand she obey him?

Ha! he scoffed in derision. He'd have to tie her up and haul her to Paris in a sack before that happened. She would never agree to do things his way.

At last she reemerged from the abbot's chambers with the boys, her dark hair, wet and plaited, hanging in a long tail down her back. Her mourning clothes had been cleaned and pressed, the slash in her bodice mended. Oriana sat on her shoulder pad, eying him sharply, as if daring him to cause Frances distress. No one seemed to care if it were the other way around.

The trio was plotting something. It was as plain to him as a hawk in the hand. Everything she did was secretive and suspicious. When Louis disappeared an hour later, Charles smelled trouble.

"Where is he?" he demanded, cornering her in the garden at the edge of the hyssop bed.

"He went to visit relations."

"He doesn't have relations. You're up to something. I want to know what it is."

She shrugged one shoulder—that beautiful, tantalizing shoulder he so loved to see bare. The gesture filled him with madness. He swelled with the desire to pull down her clothing, to possess her and lay bare her secrets as she answered his need with her own. But he dared not . . . would not risk such a thing.

He grasped her waist, nearly spanning it with his hands. "Tell me what you're doing," he demanded as he shook her—not hard. But her hair rippled loose and fell free to her waist.

Her glare brimmed with defiance. "Why are you so sure there's anything to tell?"

"Everything makes me think it. You sent Louis on an errand and don't deny it. If I'm to get us safely back to England and take care of this other business first, I believe I'm entitled to know."

"He's gone to Paris to arrange for the grave diggers," she relented.

"It's a long way to Paris."

"He'll find a ride. We must meet him tonight."

"Tonight? *Damn.* He realized then how much he'd wanted another night with her in the big bed, undisturbed and apart from the cares of their lives. Out the window went his opportunity, like an unleashed hawk. "Why tonight?" he demanded. "Tell me the rest."

"Would you tell *me* if you were in my place?"

"So you *are* keeping secrets from me," he snapped, his patience worn down to a raw, painful nub.

"If you say so."

"Damn it, you're the one who just said so. How am I to protect you if you keep secrets. It's the man's task to protect."

"And what is the woman's task?" Her green eyes shone like emeralds, hard and precise, demanding an answer.

He closed one hand around her wrist, but the shadow of her hair fell between them as she turned her head away. The shadow always fell between them. Lady Shadowhawk held herself aloof.

"Very well," he admitted defeat with a silent curse. "We'll ride for Paris tonight."

What was the woman's task? Charles wondered later as he sat in the monastery orchard and stolidly examined the cherry blossoms wreathing the trees. Until several years ago, he'd thought it the woman's task to adore the man, to agree with everything he wanted and be at his beck and call.

Inez had taught him otherwise, in a lesson he would never forget. But Frances was different . . . wasn't she?

Sinking onto a bench, he remembered Inez. The memory of her lush beauty smote him. All his hopes and dreams had resided in her, yet no measure of loyalty had hidden in either of their wretched hearts when the test came. Their differences had torn them apart.

But he knew once Frances's loyalty was won, she remained staunch unto death. Just consider her devotion to Pierre and Louis, two miserable thieves.

For the first time, he admitted he was jealous of the boys. Of the easy way her hand rested on their shoulders. Of the casual way they jested and bantered with her, of the enthusiasm with which they embraced her at will. He recalled the devoted way they had followed Frances after her capture, determined to free her, along with Pierre's childish sobs when he learned their rescue attempt had failed. Despite the strange code of honor they lived by, Charles couldn't deny the honesty of their love. And strangest of all, he, too, had ached to burst into tears like that small lad.

"My lord baron?"

The musical voice of the old abbot interrupted him. Charles pushed back his hat and rose.

"Don't let me disturb you, my lord. Sit," the robed religious urged him.

Charles sank back on the bench and the abbot took a place at his side. "That's quite a marvelous bird *madam la baroness* has. Did you train it for her, Baron Milborne?"

"Indeed, no. She trained the creature herself."

"Then she is possessed of marvelous skill, as you are yourself. Tell me, would you do me the honor of examining my falcon? She has not been eating well these days."

For the first time, Charles examined the old man with an eye to his personal life. Despite the abbot's advanced age and the austerity of his vocation, lust for life still burned in the man's gray eyes. And apparently he still enjoyed the hunt. "I am honored you ask my opinion. I will look at her with pleasure, if you wish."

The abbot led the way to a well-tended outbuilding. Outside, leashed to a bow perch, sat a gray peregrine falcon. A young brother sat beside the perch, anxiously attending her. He jumped up the instant his superior approached. Charles saw at once that the bird's head listed, her eyes dull. He called for a glove.

Then he deftly unleashed the bird and nudged her onto his fist. He carried her to the shade of a garden trellis and sat down. Around them twined rose vines, reminding him of Frances, fresh and vigorous and alive.

Charles studied the bird, advised a change of diet and a different perch by day, but something more than boredom ailed the bird. "How long have you had her?" he asked as the bird chittered to him softly.

"Nigh on six years."

"Who else handles her besides you?"

"Brother Sebastian used to tend her," the abbot answered slowly. "We netted her together when she was a young eyas. He was devoted to her as keeper of the mews, but he died last winter. He was nine and sixty."

The abbot moved his thin, refined hands as he spoke, and Charles sensed the patience of Job in him, to have seen and lost so much. "Your bird is in mourning," he said, gently stroking the bird's speckled breast.

The abbot sighed. "I was afraid of that. And I have made it worse for her, neglecting her of late since my own duties have increased with France's unrest."

Charles turned to the young brother. "Would you be so

good as to fetch another glove?" The fellow obligingly scuttled back to the mews, returning a second later with the required glove.

Charles handed it to the abbot, who slipped it on. The falcon went eagerly to the older man's fist.

"I prescribe feeding on the fist, by you only, daily. And you must carry her with you throughout your day. She should sleep on a perch in your chamber at night."

The abbot stroked the bird with his free hand. "And I had thought it a luxury I had to forgo."

"Once you are bonded to a bird, you must honor that bond. Without Brother Sebastian and without you, she is bereft. A bird doesn't give her trust lightly."

He thought of Arcturus as he spoke, languishing in England, but at least the bird had Master Dickon. Then he thought of Frances, and his gut contracted. Glancing away, his gaze settled on a wood carving in the center of the rose trellis, a beautiful rendering of two intertwined birds, wings outflung. "That carving on the trellis, what does it mean?" He nodded toward it.

"Ah, the hawk and the dove. They stand for the active life and the contemplative life, age-old symbols. You, my friend, have chosen the life of the hawk, the life of action. Like the hawk, you will have to fight and kill to survive in life."

"And the dove?"

"The contemplative life is one of thought or prayer. Religious life and the lives of women are usually represented by the dove."

Another question leaped from Charles as he again thought of Frances. "What must a dove do to survive?"

"Obey with meekness," answered the abbot readily. "The dove lives in the cote and becomes the sustenance to feed others. Or breeds more of its kind. It never fights. It accepts its fate."

Charles sank into thought, intent on his inner turmoil. "Then Frances . . . is no dove," he mused, unaware he'd actually spoken until the abbot chuckled in response.

"Nay, the baroness is not," he agreed. "She demands to fly free, the same as you."

Charles sucked in his breath as he remembered the way Frances had looked earlier in the garden, with Pierre on her one side, Louis on the other, one of her hands resting on each of their shoulders. Bonded with them, but never possessing.

Damn, but he hungered for such a bond with a woman.

But love was something Frances gave seldom or not at all. And never, since Antoine, would she give it to a man unless she knew it was returned.

Which made him unfit as her companion. *He* was the master of hawks and falcons; he demanded mastery of everything around him in order to survive. He could never trust himself enough to place his heart—his miserable, shriveled heart—in someone else's hands.

Far easier to claim women using primitive urges that leashed them to his side. Far easier compared to what Frances required. Even to be her friend, he had to desire her freedom as much as she did before she would fly back to him of her own accord.

Even as he recognized his obligation, he hated it. Tonight, sorrow lurked in a midnight graveyard, waiting for her. He wouldn't let her go alone, at least not physically. He would guard her person. Yet at the same time, he was supposed to let her walk her own path.

He wasn't sure he could do it the way she required. He was used to stepping in and taking control, as a man should.

With a grimace, he realized it would be one of the hardest nights of his life.

Chapter 18

The ride from the monastery to Paris took three full hours. Charles repeatedly coaxed Frances to tell him more of Spain's imminent invasion, but she refused to answer. "We'll both know more soon," was all she would say.

Twelve bells tolled midnight by the time Charles and Frances crept through the thick, muffling fog on the north side of the Seine. Charles jerked at the sound, then realized they approached yet another church.

"This is the one," he stated for what seemed the hundredth time. If she said no again, he might go mad. Impatience to be done with tonight's work gnawed at his nerves.

Without answering, she moved forward, looking like a wraith in the dark, barely illuminated by the lantern swinging from her hand.

That must mean yes, he decided. She'd only spoken briefly since they'd entered the city—"It's too quiet," she'd said. "The streets are deserted. Something is wrong."

Despite her concern, they had left their horses, Pierre, and the hawk with Louis at the boys' lodgings. The dark, ramshackle building where they claimed a single chamber had stared vacantly at Charles with broken windowpane eyes. It had turned his blood cold in his veins. Or was it their mission? The night's hush hugged them, as heavy as a shroud.

Catching up with her, he clasped Frances's hand in his and plowed across the road to the churchyard entry, pulling her behind him. They would settle all doubts about Edward Sillington here and now. No turning back.

Heavy iron gates leaped at them out of the fog, barring their way. A great chain with a lock bound the gates shut. *Give up,* it seemed to urge. *The dead welcome no one here.*

"We're up and over," he ordered her in a loud whisper, indicating the stone wall rimming the churchyard. "You first. I'll give you a boost."

"Shouldn't we wait for the diggers?" Her usually white skin seemed paler still in the dark. Wisps of fog turned her ghostly, half haunted, which she probably was. The morbid reality of tonight's mission had set in.

"They'll see us at the grave site. The yard isn't that large." He longed to reassure her, but he couldn't, in honesty. Either her uncle lived on in a Spanish prison or he had died at Spanish hands. Either answer would be grim news. He urged her to place one foot in his cupped hand. Amid flapping skirts and chemise, he tossed her up.

She struggled onto the broad wall. Once in a sitting position, she pushed off and disappeared from his sight.

With a surge, he jumped after her, caught the ledge, and levered himself up. He vaulted over the top with speed and little grace, wanting to keep Frances in his sight. Menacing shadows ornamented the churchyard, conjuring up visions of warlocks and witches snatching Frances from his grasp. Even he grew fanciful in this dismal place.

Frances waited for him beside a huge marble monument to some long-dead city father. Charles gazed at the ornament chosen to grace the tomb: heaven's gates standing wide. On the heaven side, Gabriel beckoned with outstretched hand. Let it be a sign, Charles hoped in silence—a good sign.

Feeling for his new hunting knife, a gift from the abbot, he moved toward Frances. If returning her safely to England required digging up graves at midnight, he would do it. No one accused him of shirking. Though he could use some of Gabriel's redemption to get him through tonight.

"Which way?" he asked.

She shook her head, as if uncertain, and pointed into the yard's depth.

"Was there a stone?"

Her single nod jerked like a stutter. Taking her free hand, he found it as cold as death.

He steeled himself to keep from pressing her fingers to his cheek. But the expression on her face wrenched words straight from his gut. "Whatever you find, I'll help you, Frank. Either way."

She remained silent, staring like a demented soul into the swirling fog, terrified of what she would find in the grave.

Wondering what had driven him to make that offer, he took the lantern from her and held it high. "I'll look for fresh-turned plots and when I find one . . ." He left the sentence unfinished. Like a gaping grave, the mystery of her uncle lay before them, beckoning with bony fingers. Tucking her hand beneath his arm, he forged ahead.

Frances drifted after him, as if she walked in her sleep.

The grass beneath their feet offered no impediment, being clipped short. The graves in this part of the churchyard were well tended. Not many had such elaborate ornaments as Gabriel's gate, but all had upright, substantial markers, many with limp clutches of flowers offered to angels carved in the flat stone.

As they ventured deeper, he quickened their pace. They passed clumps of scarcely budded trees and bushes standing like skeletons, their naked bones trembling in the breeze.

"Here's a fresh spot." He halted before a plot of raw earth. With the lantern, he found the stone and inspected the name. "This isn't it." Again, he sought her cold, unresponsive hand and led on.

Four wrong sites later, they stumbled on the right one. No mistaking the name—Edward Thomas Sillington—nor the dates engraved on the flat granite stone.

Putting down the lantern, he checked Frances and found torment flickering in her wide eyes. With a quick motion, he unstrapped the spade from his back and began to dig as Frances stood frozen like a pillar of solid ice.

Old leaves skittered around them in the wind, scraping and rattling against stones and the ground. Dank fingers of cold crept from the river to paralyze them deep into their bones. Charles threw his back into the work and dug with a vengeance.

Some minutes later, they were joined by five ragged men. Louis had done well, Charles admitted grudgingly, noting their size and strength. He shook hands and slipped the men coppers to start the work. As the breeze nipped their ears and fingers, he wished he'd also brought strong spirits. They could all use a stiff drink, including Frances. She would need it even more by the time they were done.

With six, the work went quickly. Soil flew, and they descended into the earth. Within the hour, they stood calf deep, then knee deep. Six men to dig six feet down.

Sweat streamed down Charles's face and glued his shirt to his back and chest. Now immune to the midnight chill, he flung off his doublet and worked in shirtsleeves. Three solid infernal hours passed before someone's tool finally clanged against lead.

"That'll be it." Charles uttered the first words since they'd begun. "Did someone bring rope?"

"Aye." One of the men nodded and climbed from the hole to fetch it.

With considerable struggle, they wormed the ropes under the coffin. Then the six of them lined up on both sides of the grave and hoisted until their joints screamed with the strain.

The ropes stretched taut, and Charles feared they would break, but fortune was with them. The hemp held as they landed the coffin on solid ground.

The men retreated to a respectful distance. The grisly ritual of opening the coffin belonged solely to Frances. Superstitious, they crossed themselves and huddled in a clump, wanting no part of what would come next.

Realizing he alone stood ready to help Frances, Charles swung his spade and broke the bar that held the lid shut. Then he stood and stared at the coffin, reluctant to go on. Yet it seemed he had no choice but to show her the body. She would hurt worse if she didn't look.

His hands fumbled at the lid, prying ineffectively. All the stories he had ever heard about hauntings and specters and the hands of the dead reaching out to claim the living raced through his mind, unsettling him for a moment. They were nothing but the products of too lively an imagination, but the reaction he expected from Frances would be intense and all too genuine. If only he might look in her stead to spare her. If only he'd known her uncle and could take the burden on himself. If only . . .

He'd spent too many days wishing his tomorrows different. He cast away the futile hopes, set his shoulder under the handle, and shoved up. The lid yielded with a groan, and he forced it open a crack.

The ghosts he might have imagined, but the odor that accosted him was utterly, disgustingly real. His head swam with the stench.

"Stand back," he warned Frances, lowering the lid hastily as he sensed her presence behind him. "I'll look first, then let you check the scar."

She obeyed without question, handed him the lantern, and retreated several steps, averting her face.

His first good look at the corpse—more grisly and

decayed than even he had expected—smote him almost as hard as his recurring nightmare. At least the maggots hadn't gotten to it yet, thanks to the coffin's lead.

"Which hand did you say the scar was on?" he asked as he raised the lantern high.

"Right," she answered on a sharp, inhaled breath. "Ring finger."

Charles cursed under his breath. It did have to be the hand away from him and thus the hardest to reach. Propping open the lid, he groped for the hand muffled in the thick burgundy doublet and searched for the scar. "Here it is. Come closer, but don't look yet. I'll ready the hand so you can see."

Her fingertips connected with his arm from behind. Their frigid cold penetrated.

"Is it bad?" Her voice quavered like the flame in the lantern.

"No, it's . . ." The lie died on his lips. "Yes," he said quietly. "It is."

"What of the smell?" she asked.

Her bravery tore at his resistance. "Perfectly normal," he assured her. "Come around on my left side." He shifted the lantern so it lit the hand and cast the body in shadow. "There's the scar. Is it the way you remember?"

"Yes." She turned away swiftly. "That's it."

"Did he have any other distinguishing features?"

"Not really. Just . . . let me look at his face. Does he have whiskers?"

"A small beard and mustache. I must tell you, his nose is almost gone. You might not recognize him."

"I will. Just let me . . . see."

He looped one arm around her waist and braced himself to catch her in case she fainted. She straightened, faced the coffin, and looked full on the dead man's face.

A horrified gasp escaped her. Her muscles stiffened, and he felt her limbs shake. Vainly, he held her close, offering his support and protection. But with a pang of despair, he knew nothing could shield her. "Is it your uncle?" he asked as gently as he could.

"It is." A strangled moan leaked from her lips. "He had a mole on his cheek. Is that it?" She pointed. "Or is it blood?"

He would have to release her to touch the spot, but he feared she might collapse if he did. "Hold the lantern for me," he directed instead, so he could keep his one arm braced around her waist. The light wavered in her hand as he quickly rubbed the spot. "It doesn't seem to be blood," he observed. " 'Tis slightly raised." He rubbed it the other way. "It must be a mole. Anything else?"

A violent tremor rippled through her, yet she lifted her chin valiantly. " 'Tis my uncle without question. I'd know him even without his nose. See the distinctive bow of his upper lip? And his hairline, the way it peaks." She traced the outline without quite touching the putrid flesh, as matter-of-fact as a physician studying a cadaver. But her composure lasted only a minute longer before she buried her face in one hand. "Oh, Uncle Edward."

Charles steeled himself against any reaction and reached for the coffin lid. As he lowered it into place, she wrenched away and dropped the lantern. The light sizzled out as she stumbled to his left.

A second later he heard her retch in the nearby bushes. Concerned for her, he turned toward the waiting men. "We're finished. Pray be so good as to lower the coffin." He pressed silver coins into their damp, dirty palms. "Then start filling the grave. I'll help you in a minute, but first I must attend the lady."

He found her leaning against a low gravestone. Though her frail body was racked by uncontrollable weeping, she made scarcely a sound.

He slid an arm around her waist, feeling useless in the face of her pain, exactly as he'd felt when his father died. He'd sat with his mother while the priest performed the last rites and tried in vain to help her. His mother had squeezed his hand hard and wept, twisted sounds of her anguish signaling the end of hope. A gaping hole had opened inside him, threatening to suck him into its black depths. Now it hovered near . . . so very near. "Do you wish to talk about it?" he asked Frances, very low, steeling himself against his emotions.

"No, thank you." She gulped and groped for a handkerchief. "I know for certain now that he's dead. At least he isn't somewhere being tortured by those stinking . . ."

"Don't." He half strangled the single word as he pressed her head against his shoulder and stroked her hair, now damp from the mist. "Take comfort that no one can hurt his empty shell."

"S-sometimes I wish I had died when he did. Is that evil?"

"No. You loved him, that's all."

She cried harder, and he ached worse than the time he'd had the ague as a child. Nothing he said could help.

"Who is Inez?" she gasped between sobs.

Charles stiffened in shock.

"You cursed her in your sleep last night."

He shouldn't have been surprised, by either Frances's abrupt change of subject or that he'd dreamed of Inez and said her name aloud. Her name was often on his lips, chased by an oath of despair. "I prefer not to talk about her."

"I have to talk about her," she said, sounding as desperate as if she dangled on the edge of a precipice. "What did she do to you?" She turned up her face, and by the faint moonlight, he saw her need to drown her pain in his. She did need to talk of Inez; she groped at anything that would overshadow the final, devastating grief from admitting her uncle's death.

"It wasn't her fault, what happened. It was mine." He shook his head at the confession, stunned that he was willing to feel pain in her stead.

"But what did she do?" She tightened her hold on his hand until her nails bit into his palm.

"She didn't do anything," he insisted, ignoring the sharp pain.

"And she should have?"

"Yes," he groaned, his torment shifting suddenly to rage. "No, she did what she had to. But we both loved her, Richard and I. We acted like raving lunatics, attempting to woo her—when there was no chance on earth she could ever wed with either of us."

"Why was she in the Caribbean?"

"Her father owned a huge plantation. We discovered her swimming at a secluded cove. God!" He clenched his teeth to keep from shouting his fury. "I don't want to talk about her."

"Please, Charles, I *need* to know." Her eyes were a fiery green like the spring's new growth, demanding the right to live.

"No!" The depth of his own self-hatred frightened him. "No more. Let the past be the past. Like you, at times I wish I were dead."

"Have a care what you wish for, friend. Such desires can be unexpectedly fulfilled," came a low voice.

Charles straightened, at once alert and ready to act.

A brace of men from the Paris citizen night watch confronted them. Light blinded him as several lanterns were brought to the fore. In their midst stood a tall man in a plumed hat.

"Sir Humphrey!" Frances struggled to her feet, her queasy stomach still churning. "Are you here to . . . help me?" Her question trailed off into doubt as she realized that could hardly be possible. Not accompanied as he was by men who trained calivers at her head.

"Mistress Frances, I am heartily sorry to inform you that you are wanted by the Paris magistrates." His voice was fatherly and troubled, his face sad.

"What is this about?" Charles demanded, his tone suspicious as he stepped forward to shield her.

"Yes, why do they want me?" Frances asked. Sir Humphrey had always been her friend. Bluff Sir Humphrey with his big, homely face like a mutton slab, his hearty manner, and his booming laugh. What could he possibly mean?

"The overwhelming evidence points to your having murdered your uncle," Sir Humphrey said simply.

Frances felt her jaw go slack. "W-what?"

"It broke my heart to hear it, but the night watch has proof." Sir Humphrey sighed heavily. "Now you must face the consequences of your actions. It grieves me so to—"

"But I loved my uncle," Frances cried. "I would never do such a thing."

"In truth? Yet your fond feelings haven't prevented you from trying to rob his grave."

"I'm not robbing his grave. I merely . . ." She stopped in confusion. How could she possibly convince them she hadn't thought her uncle dead and required proof.

"I always thought of you as affectionately as a daughter." Sir Humphrey shook his head ponderously. "I am deeply disappointed to think you did this deed, Frances. All to lay claim to your uncle's English estate."

Frances recoiled. "He didn't have an estate."

"He certainly did. Your mother's property in Dorset went to him upon your father's death."

"That property was mine," she insisted, thoroughly baffled and dismayed. "It has been for years."

"You see," Sir Humphrey spoke to the watchmen accompanying him. "She insists the property is hers, a blatant falsehood. The property only passed to her at her uncle's death. Which clearly she had to arrange."

"Just one moment," Charles interrupted, stepping forward with one hand on his knife hilt. "What proof do you have that Mistress Morley is guilty of this crime?"

"More misfortune," Sir Humphrey intoned. "The watch was called to the house in the Rue Saint Jacques by the new family. It seems a bloody knife, the death weapon, was found on the property. As Mistress Morley was the last known inhabitant of the house . . ." He let the significance of his statement sink in.

" 'Tis all a mistake," Frances assured him. "Truly." She turned to Charles. "I shall go with them and explain everything and all will be put to rights."

"You show an honest desire to atone for your sins." Sir Humphrey nodded in approval. "In which case, I myself will do whatever I can for you, since I always favored you as a child. If you come along quietly, mayhap the magistrates will go easy on you. You might merely be deported rather than hanged."

Deported? Hanged? Frances shook her head in a daze as her hope of setting things right dissolved. How could this be? Her father's property had come to her at his death, though she had stayed in France instead of returning to it in England. She'd wanted to be with her uncle; she'd stayed out of love. Her mind spun in confusion. "Sir Humphrey, you don't believe this of me, do you?" She stepped toward him. "You have known me for nine years now. Surely, you don't think I have done such a foul thing." She clasped his cloak with both hands, pleading. "I beg you, do not—"

"Unhand me, wench," he ordered as he raised both hands to push her away. His cloak flipped back over one shoulder as he moved. "I refuse to acknowledge any claim to friendship as long as you persist in this evil. If you would confess your sins, I will do all I can to defend you. But if not, I must leave you to your fate."

Frances no longer listened to his words. Instead, she stared hard at him, her stomach churning with dismay. For she saw his doublet lacked one gold button right in the middle. The remaining buttons shone, their gold embossing plain in the lantern light. She recognized the pattern instantly. It matched the one she had found in the entry after her uncle disappeared that night. "Your doublet has Spanish buttons!" she cried in disbelief.

Sir Humphrey glanced down at his doublet, then back at her. "Of course it does. 'Tis a gift from His Eminence, the Archbishop of Toledo. He sent it to me weeks ago. Pray don't change the subject, my dear."

"No!" she shrieked, grasping the doublet and shaking him. "You've arranged all this to discredit me. Why?" Her voice rose to a shrill scream.

A flit of movement caught her eye, but anger riveted her attention on her former benefactor. "Why, Sir Humphrey?" she cried again, tugging at him while he tried to fight her off. "Why, oh why," she sobbed, misery filling her as one of the last bastions of affection in her life fell to enemy Spain. "What have you to gain?"

Suddenly, one of the civil patrol yelped. Men erupted into action around her.

Frances wheeled, but Sir Humphrey twisted her arm in an iron grip and hauled her away from the melee.

Terrified, she searched for Charles and saw him fly at one of the patrol with his knife. A blurred, rag-clad figure attacked another as the grave diggers were discovered by the patrol and attacked in self-defense.

Suddenly, her captor lurched heavily to his knees, jerking Frances with him. One of Louis's friends had clouted him on the back of the head.

She struggled to rise, but Sir Humphrey held fast. Another clout from her savior broke his grip. She wrenched free and ran for the churchyard gate.

Tears stung her eyes, clouding her sight. She swiped at them with her sleeve as her heart bled at the new betrayal. One of the few friends she possessed, someone she had always counted on, failed her now. Was there no one left in the world whom she could trust?

Sobs shuddered from her lips as she lunged at the wall surrounding the graveyard, but she lacked the height to reach the top. Frantic, she searched for the gates. They were locked, as before, no doubt by Sir Humphrey and his escort to keep their victims in. She tried for the wall again, leaping as high as she could.

It was no use.

Suddenly, she was clasped from behind and lifted. Her breath whooshed out of her in surprise.

"Grab the top," Charles panted.

She wanted to scream with relief. Instead, she obeyed and scrambled to the top of the wall. Landing on her stomach, she twisted until her feet hung down, then toppled from the wall onto the free side, falling to her knees. Charles landed beside her, caught her around the waist, and lifted her to her feet.

"Run," he ordered, clasping her shaking hand in his strong one. "Make for the Seine."

Frances ran, knowing she must trust Charles to lead her to safety. And though she hated entrusting her life to anyone else, just now she had no choice.

Chapter 19

Frances clutched her equipment bag under her arm and pelted down the fog-filled Paris street with Sir Humphrey and his henchmen mere yards behind. Their pursuers' threatening shouts and the clatter of their racing feet bounced around the eerie, oddly empty streets, amplified by the tall stone buildings on either side. Terrified, numb with shock, Frances ran blindly, trusting Charles to guide her.

The man she had thought was her friend had accused her of murder. He wished her beneath a gibbet, her hands bound, a coarse rope tightening around her neck as crowds of people leered.

"In here," Charles hissed at her. They swerved and dodged down a narrow street. Her heart crashed against her ribs in a wild rhythm of panic. *Dieu,* let them not be caught.

At the end of the street, the River Seine loomed. Charles secured her hand in his own and lunged onto the bridge. Thick vapors from the river swallowed them whole. Despite the welcome cover, fear propelled Frances to match Charles's huge strides. On the other side of the bridge, they pelted across the Place Maubert and headed west, entering the student quarter where streets narrowed and houses huddled like rats. The chase became a dizzying flight through the confusing warren of dank alleys and rough byways bordering the riverbank.

Frances's throat stung, raw and dry from her frantic gasps for air. Broken cobblestones cut through her thin shoes and into her tender soles. They charged past a butcher's yard and into another alley. The noisome odor of rotted animal entrails slapped her in the face as she tripped over dark mounds of refuse. Steeling herself against rising nausea, she took strength from Charles's grasp and raced on.

Please let us lose them. Make Sir Humphrey give up and go home.

Her ardent prayer rose as she zigzagged at Charles's side. As if in a crazed game of fox and geese, he led her up one street, then doubled back into the next. They crossed and recrossed the Seine once more. To her joy, the sounds of pursuit faded behind them.

Still, Charles refused to rest. Not until the city bells tolled half past three did he slow their pace. He descended stone steps to water level and drew her under a bridge. Frances collapsed against the stone arch, the air she inhaled searing her lungs. Her heart slammed against her chest like a smith's hammer at the forge. Around them, derelict warehouses on the quays loomed, the water-rotted structures like slimy, sleeping dragons that could wake at any time.

"I still say there's something odd about the city," she said between teeth that chattered from nerves and chill. "No one about, as if people were hiding in their houses. Deathly silence everywhere." She glanced around her, shuddered, and hugged her old leather bag to her chest with both arms.

"We'd best find shelter. Where can we go to sleep for a few hours?" Charles wrapped his arm around her shoulders, offering unexpected support.

"I know the owner of a barge," Frances rasped. She burrowed against him, disliking her need for him, but desperately glad he was there. "For a coin or two, he'll hide us until noon."

Charles snorted. "I intend to be quit of this city long before noon. We'll fetch Oriana and make for a port city that no one expects. If there is something about to happen here, we'd best leave. Besides, we need to tell the queen about the imminent invasion of the Spanish. She must call the country to arms."

"Uh . . . Charles . . . I can't leave Paris yet." Frances blundered over the confession. She dared not tell him about the messenger. Yesterday, she'd withheld the information out of irritation, but today she felt obliged to protect him. If he knew of her errand, he wouldn't hesitate to leap into danger's path.

With ease she imagined Sir Humphrey naming Charles an accessory to her crime, forcing him to the gibbet at her side. "You must head for the port after you've rested," she urged. "I'll follow later tonight." The words out, she bit her tongue and hoped for divine intervention. Nothing else would make him agree.

As expected, he waxed choleric. Displeasure radiated from him, emphasized by his silence and the grim set of his mouth. "So are you finally going to tell me what's to happen on Thursday?" he asked at last, removing his arm.

How she ached for the sheltering warmth of his arm around her shoulders, yet she must not yield and tell. "I dare not," she whispered in a tiny voice.

"That's some improvement. Before you refused to tell me. Out of stubborn spite, I thought at the time." His stare was speculative and all too discerning. "No matter. I'll guess. You've taken your uncle's place since he died. What task have you inherited now? Something at noon, you said. Where?"

His rapid fire of questions and accurate deductions robbed Frances of a reply. She swayed, dizzied by exhaustion, the chill wind blowing off the stagnant Seine, and the finality of her uncle's death. Too tired to argue further, she leaned against the cold stone, hoping he would leave the city as she asked. Because despite his strength, even he wasn't invincible to harm, even he couldn't control the men who pursued them, even he . . .

"I was sent to deliver you back to England, and I plan to fulfill my duty," he announced, breaking into her agonies with that calm confidence of his. "I'll go with you at noon to whatever appointment requires your presence. We'll leave the city together when you're done." He offered his embrace once more.

Frances moved into his arms wearily, unable to refuse. To what lengths would she go, she wondered, to remain in his embrace? Such a simple need, yet so complex. By giving in to her own need for comfort, she again compromised his safety. She also compromised her freedom. "What now?" she asked, settling her cheek against his chest.

"Sleep," Charles advised without pause. "That's the best thing when you're exhausted. Where do we find this bargeman of yours?"

"This way." She rose to her feet and tottered downstream, unsure how she would survive the meeting with the messenger. Sir Humphrey had known far too much about her uncle's secrets. It seemed she was doomed to be taken by either the Spaniards or the Paris magistrates. Which meant she faced diabolical torture for information or hanging for imaginary crimes.

But for the first time she didn't feel completely abandoned, though she had lost her uncle once and for all. Charles was at her side. He had proved he intended to stick there, too, whether she willed it or no. Though most of the time he irritated and dominated her, and though she dared not stay with him permanently, for now, his presence comforted her.

Deep in her heart, a tiny beak like a hatching hawk's pecked at its encasing shell, full of the desire to someday see the sun.

For the next half hour, Charles drowsed beside Frances on a pile of straw in the low-roofed stern of a dingy boat. Bad smells abounded at the anchorage—decaying cabbage, polluted water, rotten fish.

Charles pinched his nostrils shut with thumb and first finger and sucked in the next breath of air. It cut off some of the smell. But bad odors were the least of his worries just now.

Blast it all, he was involved with a woman—after he'd sworn never to do such a foolish thing again. But his painful response to her grief at the graveyard told him all too clearly that he had taken the fatal step across the forbidden boundary—he had let himself feel something for a female, and not just in bed.

Though he resented it fiercely, one saving grace remained; he wasn't in love. How well he recalled his ache of adoration for Inez. It drove him to idiotic lengths to satisfy her smallest wish. Never again, he had vowed.

Further, he had this encounter with the messenger to manage. With a massive effort, he refocused his mind and his energy on that task. Anything so he would forget to be aroused by Frances.

His body, however, remembered all too well.

As she rolled to face him, her eyes closed, her coil of dark hair spilled from its knot, tumbled over her shoulder, and tickled his face. A pang of desire twisted in his groin. His attention to the problems at hand dispersed like a covey of flushed quail.

"Your hair is attacking me again," he breathed so as not to be heard above deck.

"It's not," she contradicted sleepily, burrowing against

him, both arms drawn in to her chest. "Um, keep me warm. I'm chilled through. You smell like rotten fish."

"The boat and water smell of rotten fish," he muttered, relishing the sensations that streaked through him, despite his oath not to. "Don't pin the blame on me, Lady Hawk."

"Is that my new name?"

"Hmm," Charles murmured, wanting to ignore the shadow that still wavered between them. For now, he would pretend it didn't exist.

Soft as feathers, her body molded to his. Soft breasts begged his hands to fondle, slender hips pressed against his desire. Allure in the depths of her limpid green eyes dared him to taste her wild warmth. Something keenly elemental about her spoke to him—she was pure like earth, water, fire, and air. Yes, she was definitely the air, the teasing, taunting wind, bidding him seek release with her in flight.

Pushed by instinct, he bent over and covered her lips with his own.

She moaned softly and responded, opening to his demand. Her mouth tasted savory and sweet, and he imagined her lips, rosy and plump, teased by his onslaught. He nipped and feasted and delighted in her, then slid down to sample her cheek and ear. All notice of foul odors flew from his mind.

"Such sweet favors you offer, Frances," he spoke against the petal-soft flesh of her neck, which gleamed like pearl luster by the light of their flickering lantern. "You have no idea how much I want them from you."

"No?" She rolled her hips against his hardness in a motion that inflamed him. Groping for her skirt, he pulled it up and sought her thighs with his hand.

Immediately, her body stiffened, though she had provoked him. She quivered in terror, like a bird trembling on his fist.

Blast. He moved too fast.

A full day of reasoning wouldn't have stopped him, but her fear slammed him to a halt. Her distrust smote him like the hawk's clean kill. He must mend the damage with all speed.

Focusing on Frances, he exerted his power. "There now," he soothed, pulling down her skirt and patting it into place. "I told you before I'm not like Antoine." He lulled and reassured her the way he would Arcturus. To his relief, she relaxed. "I have a better way of doing these things," he teased, feeling the tight muscles in her back ease in response to his gentle spell. How he loved to inspire trust—in the past, any bird or woman would do. But now, thoughts of other women paled beside Frances. He ought to stay away from her. It was folly to do otherwise. Yet he burned to have her trust.

"Of doing what things?" She sucked in a breath, as if hesitating, then teased him back. "If you think to seduce me, you likely could, you're such a sorcerer. You do things by fell arts."

"You're brave to offer, but I don't intend to seduce you," he said chuckling, pleased to tell her outright. "I intend to provoke you. You'll decide how to respond."

Her fingers uncurled from around his arms as she stared at him, surprised. "Provoke me? Why?" she demanded. She propped up her head with one arm and studied him in bemusement.

"You'll see soon enough." He caught her free hand and rubbed her fingers against his cheek. She giggled and pretended to wince at the rasp of his sprouting whiskers. But Charles could tell she liked the gesture. It was intimate, but not too much so.

"You're as hairy as an old ox," she jested.

"So are you." He brushed one of her bristling locks out of his face. "Your hair tickles me every time I come near."

"It does not. You tickle it by coming close." She pursed her lips in a mock pout.

He chuckled. "As if your hair had a mind of its own?"

"My mother said it did, always pleasing itself. It refused to stay where she put it, tucked up with pins."

"I can imagine your mother telling you that, my mad wench with your wild, willful hair."

She sighed deeply as a wistful look crept into her eyes. "My father called my mother that—his willful wench. She was the one with the mind of her own, yet my father always took her counsel. I have tried to be like her, so patient and calm. I don't know whether I've succeeded or not."

He heard the longing in her voice, the pain of loss, and tightened his arms around her. The poignancy of her mood spoke to him, though at the same time her hair tickled him something fierce. *Blast it.* He fussed and fussed with it and had just managed to tuck the bushy end back into its knot when she reached to help him.

The bush sprang loose and poked him in the nose. She grinned.

"You little mischief maker," he scolded. "Your hair is unmannerly. 'Tis time you taught it to behave." He pushed the bush away, but it refused to cooperate. "I'll whack it off with my knife."

"Beast. I'll not have you speaking rudely of my hair." She donned an injured look, then shifted to an impish smile. "Whack it off, indeed. I'd see you paid a price if you did."

"Hmm, what would be my punishment, sweetling?" He enjoyed her delight in their banter, but he wanted more than that from her. His gaze fastened on her lips and refused to leave. "Now *you're* being provoking. Though I've had more practice, your skill is not bad," he challenged, wondering how she would respond.

To his amazement, she giggled behind one hand and stole a sidelong glance at his groin. His arousal undoubtedly showed through his trunk hose, but as long as he didn't behave like Antoine, it didn't matter.

"Such a braggart, Master Falconer," she said with a sniff and a wink, "always wanting to best others. I say you aren't the most skilled. Let me show you what *I* mean." In a bold motion, she placed one hand on his chest, and he tensed. With what he swore was eagerness, she traced the muscled contours beneath his shirt.

As her hand moved, he winced on purpose, then sent her an apologetic look. "That's a tender spot where the bastard . . . pardon me, the captain . . . kicked me."

"Oh, no!" Forgetting their contest, she gazed into his eyes. "May I see?"

"No need," he protested. " 'Twill be better soon, I'm certain."

"Let me see," she insisted. "You're wounded and you didn't even tell me." She grasped the lower part of his shirt and pulled as he attempted to hold it down. "You should have let me tend you at the abbey. I would have . . . oh my!" She jerked the shirt from his hands and gasped at the bruise that marred his ribs.

"Your hands are cool. Here." He caught one and placed her soft palm over the bruise. "Ah." He closed his eyes and swam in the delicious sensations she aroused. "That feels wondrous fine."

"I am sorry they hurt you. 'Twas all my fault."

He sneaked a peek at her through half-closed lids. His arousal throbbed more insistently as he noted the regret for his bruise shimmering in her eyes. The strain of her breasts against confining cloth kindled more fire in his loins. The lovely secret locked between her thighs beckoned, her woman's fragrance singing a siren's song until his blood hummed in his ears.

Just then, she bent over and put her warm lips to his bruise. *Thunderation,* what had he started? His heartbeat increased to a raging tempo as her mouth and fingers stroked his sore side. More sensation jolted through him, primitive and compelling. He groaned aloud.

"Did I hurt you?" She jerked up to meet his gaze.

He staved off the impulse to crush her full length against him as her concern filled him with an illicit sense of joy. "You didn't hurt me," he hastened to assure her through clenched teeth. "Pray continue. You can't imagine how much it helps. One of them also kicked me here." Pulling off his shirt was a struggle in their close quarters. He managed it quickly, for all that. He flipped onto his stomach to display his back. Tugging down the waistband of his trunk hose, he showed her the bruise just below.

"Oh!" Her cry mixed both regret and pain. She wrapped her wonderful hands around his waist and scattered kisses across his aching flesh.

Charles panted, wanting to feel her mouth and hands on every part of his body, touching, caressing, pleasuring. "Here, too." He adjusted his trunk hose to expose the small of his back.

She dipped her fingers into the twin dimples at the base of his spine, just above his buttocks. But then nothing further happened. Charles twisted to look over his shoulder and found she stared at his naked torso, a fascinated, bewitched expression on her face. Then she bent to kiss the bruise.

Lord, am I the provocative one, or is she?

He no longer cared which. "Ah, yes." His body jerked involuntarily with pleasure as her fingers brushed his lower thighs. How he wanted to rip up her flimsy skirts and bury himself in her sweet, hot depths. "Don't stop now," he beseeched her.

As she again put her lips to the other bruise, he tried to gauge her enthusiasm. Her sweet mouth danced over his flesh with the whisper of eyas down. Then, to his further amazement, she laved his bruise with her tongue. He imagined that pink flower of flesh, darting from her mouth, warm and wet as she stroked him. Her assault on his senses, combined with the images in his mind, made him so hard he clenched his fists to keep from culminating then and there.

By thunder, he ought to stop her. If he didn't, he would ravish her on the spot, which would involve them to a degree he'd promised to avoid. "I believe you'll agree I've won our wager," he ground out. He'd never dreamed, when he challenged her, that she would show such zeal. Quickly, before he could change his mind or regret it, he rolled over and sat up . . . and stilled at the expression on her face.

A fierce, wild yearning filled her gaze, illuminated by the dim lantern light.

"Charles, in a few hours, I may be dead or a prisoner," she whispered urgently. "Do me one favor before then."

"You won't be taken prisoner. I won't allow it."

"Sir Humphrey knows exactly where my uncle always met his messenger. He'll be waiting for me, and so will his Spanish friends. Before I die, let me make love to you. Please?"

He ought to deny her, but his body refused to reject the latest of her impetuous notions. His arousal stiffened further with jubilation. "You'll regret it after," he forced out, reaching for her even as he mouthed the words.

"This is my choice. Think of it as a thank-you, or an apology for what you've been through on my behalf."

He didn't care what she called it. Any justification would do right now. He wanted her with a single-minded ferocity that defied all else.

Apparently the belief that she would die soon drove her to want him, too. He recognized the fear of death mixed with lust for life as it quivered through her slender frame and flashed in her eyes. She stripped off her bodice, placed one hand, palm flat against his chest, and as she pushed him down . . . down . . . until he lay prone on his back, he decided he, too, would die content if he could have her just this once.

Need shuddered through him as she drew one bare leg across his pelvis and straddled him. The warmth between her thighs as she settled against his arousal charged his blood. It shot to his brain, so potent and dizzying that his mind whirled with unfulfilled lust. Gripping her pliant waist with both hands, his gaze feasted on the beauty of her smock-covered breasts.

"Charles, Charles, you're so impatient," she murmured, clearly noticing his rapid breathing and the massive bulge in his trunk hose. She couldn't well miss it, sitting on it the way she was. To heat him further, she caressed his bare arms and chest with her hands, then slid down to uncover his nether parts. "It's mad for me to want you; you have such domineering ways." She lifted her kirtle skirt and offered him the sweetness lodged between her creamy, smooth thighs.

He groaned aloud as she found him with one hand and guided him inside. He squeezed her waist spasmodically as she sank down on him, as her slick, hot flesh closed around his.

The long hours of lying with her and not having her overcame him. He thrust once, twice, half a dozen times until the spasms of culmination rushed over him. He groaned and shuddered as he soared over the top. By heaven, she dazzled him with her incredible gift. The ecstasy went on and on.

Unfortunately, the pleasure ebbed at last; it always did. He breathed deeply and opened his eyes, only to find her staring at him, disappointment written clearly across her lovely face. He'd gone much too fast for her. She hadn't had a chance to feel a thing.

Frances gazed down at Charles and wondered why she had done it, now that it was over. But the thought of Sir Humphrey arresting her, then turning her over to the Spaniards, reminded her all too poignantly. Desperation gripped her again—she wanted Charles's arms around her, holding her tightly, to blot that fear from her body and her mind. But it wasn't supposed to be over so soon, was it? It hadn't been with Antoine.

"It's your turn, Frances. Now you must let me pleasure you," he said.

She gaped at his words, not knowing what he meant. Yet the sight of his beautiful, bare torso still inspired unusual, exciting sensations within her. Between her legs, she tingled and burned.

"For all your bold talk about lovemaking, you have little knowledge of it, have you." He chuckled as he sat up and refastened his trunk hose. Then his welcome embrace closed around her, and he drew her against his chest. "A few kisses for starters. That's the way the real pleasure is supposed to begin."

"But I thought we were finished."

"My dear, we've hardly started." He cut off any further protest by covering her mouth with his own.

Whatever she'd expected, within minutes, she realized that Antoine hadn't initiated her to the finer points of intimacy. He'd kissed and groped for his own satisfaction, not hers.

Charles shocked her with his difference. Now that his own bodily wants were met, he trained his complete attention on hers. While his lips busily teased her mouth, his fingers lowered her smock to discover her breasts, stroking them until she shivered with delight. Those same clever, teasing fingers then dipped between her thighs. There, they caressed the core of her womanhood until she wilted across his lap, weak and breathless, her heart racing like the throb of a hawk's wings. Antoine had never pleasured her like this.

"Now sweet, you shall soar." The husky warmth of Charles's voice tickled her cheek. His teeth tugged at the soft part of her ear as he pressed her down on the pallet and parted her legs. The entire time, his fingers teased her. Their languid strokes drew heat and pressure to her center until she writhed and wiggled, filled with the impulse to cry out her delight.

"Oh, Charles, you make me feel so . . . so . . ." Her exclamation faded into astonishment as he traded his fingers for his tongue. Frances sank back, closed her eyes, and gave in to the storm of sensations he aroused in her. Lights pulsed like stars exploding behind her closed lids as he flicked his wet, pliant tongue against her female center. She felt as if she walked on a dizzyingly high cliff, looking down on the vast tapestry of the world. The pressure of her pleasure built within her, filling her with the urge to leap from the height. Charles drew her on toward the edge. His hands pressed her damp thighs apart, insisting she feel. His tongue laved the core of her being.

"Pharaoh's foot," she cried as she suddenly launched from the cliff's edge. She rose in exaltation, as if lifted by strong wings. Currents of sensation swept her to the heights. She never wanted to see earth again, but lusted to dance on the wind, to dwell in the heavens as queen of the sky and air.

She cried aloud and clasped his head with both hands, holding him tightly to her. He continued to stroke her for a long time, until the last delicious shudder shook her . . . until the final remnant of completion slid away.

Charles moved to lie at her side, full of intense wonder at what had just transpired. He had found her ultimate vulnerability—she wanted him. The enormity of her body's silent admission swept over him, filling him with an insane but equally intense pride. For she would want no other man the way she wanted him. "What is it I made you feel?" he whispered against her hair, unable to resist stoking his pleasure some more.

"Pure magic." Like a graceful, exultant bird, she sighed and stretched her arms, as if spreading her wings in flight. "I never imagined anything could be so wonderful," she murmured almost shyly, eyes cast down, "but it was just as when I fly Oriana. I was lifted above common things of the world, as if I could fly, too. I felt a power so great, so wondrous . . ." She lifted her face and met his gaze. Her emerald eyes glittered with passionate intensity. "But why am I trying to explain to you how it felt? You know what it is to soar with your bird."

Incredulous, Charles let Frances's praise rush through him. Women had called him skilled in bed, unusually stimulating, even wonderfully satisfying. Of course they'd sworn they loved him as well. Frances said nothing of love, which was for the best. But she did something even more amazing instead. She described her experience with words so extraordinary, he couldn't quite believe they applied to him.

"Did I please you?" she asked, her eyes anxious. "Did you feel the magic, too?"

He bent to kiss her brow and velvety cheek, at a loss for adequate words.

"Oh, well, I suppose it was rather routine for you," she said, reading his lack of reply as a negative response, "but for me, it was the most incredible experience of my life. I'll die happy now."

"You're not going to die," he said more sharply than he'd intended. He was gratified to know he pleased her better than Antoine. He was astonished she considered what he'd just done the high point of her life. But he didn't like her fatalistic belief that this was their last time in bed. In fact, he intended to have her again.

"You're correct, of course," she said plaintively. "I won't be dead. I'll be in a French prison, I suppose."

"You won't." He swore vehemently. "I won't permit such a thing."

"I don't see how you'll stop them. I wish I did."

"Frances, enough of this talk. You belong to me now, and I guard what's mine." The statement leaped from his mouth without his permission. But *damn it,* she was his. With only a small pang, he resigned himself to the inevitable. He had to claim her. Because not only did his body still want her, but she'd declared he gave her pure magic. He wasn't going to give that up.

But Frances seemed stunned by his words. She stared at him. Her mouth worked as if to challenge him, but no sound came out. "Exactly what do you mean," she said when she found her voice at last, "that I belong to you?"

She looked delectable in the dim light of the barge. Charles enjoyed the view of her porcelain skin and black hair. They reminded him of sweet whipped cream and hot coals brought together in a sizzle of sensuality. The more he thought about keeping her permanently, the more he liked the idea. He wanted to have her again. Now . . . before they had to leave the temporary sanctuary of the barge and get on with their dangerous lives. He wanted to evoke that pure magic in her again. And this time, he wanted to bring her to completion at the same moment he found his. This time, he wanted some of that magic for himself. "What I mean"—he tinkered with the idea, firming it in his mind—"is that since we've been so intimate, you must now be my wife."

Color flooded her face, the same hue as one of those exotic pink flowers from the Netherlands. A tulip, he thought, staring with fascination at her flushed skin. She was just like a tulip, delicately tinted, tenderly fleshed, and alive. More to the point, her high color proved he'd shocked her again, something he enjoyed no end.

"I . . . but . . . You expect me to be your wife?" she blurted. She sat up and adjusted her smock to cover her breasts. "Because of what I just did, you expect us to wed?"

"Because of what *we* just did. I told you I'm not like Antoine. I meant it, Frances." He threw caution to the winds. He'd made her feel magic. He wanted to do it again and again.

"I can't be your wife while the Spaniards and Sir Humphrey are after me." She crossed her arms and gazed at him, as defiantly as if he were the one she had to stop, not the Spaniards. "You'd be wiser to save yourself and let the matter rest."

Chapter 20

"Let the matter rest? What kind of mad advice is that?" Charles glared at Frances, thoroughly displeased that she intended to prove difficult. "It's my duty to protect you, and I intend to fulfill it. Especially since we're to wed. You'll tell me every detail you know about meeting this messenger, and I'll handle it from here."

"You'll not handle it. You don't know a thing about it."

"I don't know because you refuse to tell me," he snapped, recognizing the pokerlike stiffening of her back that signaled resistance. "But a wife's place is to obey." Even as he spoke, he remembered his talk with the abbot and knew he faced another hawk, not a dove. But blast it, he would squeeze the information from her any way he could.

"Charles Cavandish, do you mean to say you let me *have* you just so you could force me to tell you about the messenger?" cried Frances, the warrior in her leaping to the fore just as he'd expected. "I never dreamed you would be so coldhearted."

Charles studied her tempting breasts as they rose and fell in agitation beneath her light smock and knew he hadn't done any such thing. He'd let her "have" him, as she put it, because of his raging desire for her, but he wouldn't tell her that. "The details if you please," he ordered tersely. "Now."

"No!" She plunked down with her back to him and refused to say another word.

Blast the wench, he wanted to shake her. "This could be a matter of life or death, Frances," he warned. "I insist you tell me. I'll dog you until you do."

"Threaten all you like. I won't say a word." She lay down on her pallet, her stubborn back to him.

Clearly, he would get nothing further from her. He lay down on his own lumpy pallet and frowned at the wall. This woman aroused his lust and his ire so quickly, he lost control of what he was doing. Look at what had happened—she'd driven him to propose marriage after knowing her only four short days.

The magnitude of his action struck him suddenly with the force of a bludgeon, and he was appalled. He'd vowed never to succumb to a woman after Inez. He'd sworn to stay unwed forever. His gut clenched with disapproval at the thought of Frances's impulsive decisions and insane logic. He would have to endure them for the rest of his life. . . .

Even as his mind opposed the marriage, his body argued vigorously in its favor. His loins heated as visions flashed through his brain—visions of her on their wedding night. He would strip away her marriage finery and explore every inch of her tender flesh—the graceful column of her neck, the glory of her firm, full breasts, the welcoming entrance to heaven between her legs. The knowledge that he could then couple with her over and over in his infinite hunt for the intangible, in his attempt to satisfy his insatiable hunger for something—perhaps it was for that pure magic she described—firmed his decision.

He would wed with her.

He would be impaled for life on the horns of his dilemma.

Blast it, she was enough to run a man to ruin.

Frances drowsed alone on her pallet, prickled by the straw and lulled by the lap of water against the boat until the city bells tolled half past four. She roused then, driven by hunger and thirst to be up and about.

Stretching, she turned to find Charles lounging on his own pallet, wide awake and watching her. She shrank into herself as his thick eyebrows tightened into their hawklike ridges and his gaze brimmed with the poignant hunger for her she'd seen ever since they met. Apparently their earlier coupling hadn't lessened his interest in her. In fact, it seemed to have intensified.

As for her own interest . . . the image of his sculpted back and shoulders rippled through her mind again. Heaven forbid, but she wanted to tear off both their clothes and worship every muscle and sinew of his naked body with her lips. Urgently, she groped to stanch the flow of such mad ideas.

"I just thought of something," she murmured, pinched by the imp of mischief to tease him before he tried to beguile her again. "You haven't been late once since your first night in France."

He scowled. "I'm only late for things when I'm with my birds." He left the obvious unsaid—that his birds had stayed behind when he came to France.

"Why didn't you bring one along?" she asked, irritated with herself for failing to note this oddity sooner—a master of hawks was never without a hawk in hand.

"I would have, but Arcturus broke his leg."

She flinched at his revelation. "You left a bird with a broken leg because of me?" His cold expression, coupled with the steely note in his voice, told her it was his favorite bird, too. She wanted to weep for the forlorn bird left behind, as well as for the master who hid his pain so well, probably even denied he felt anything at all.

"Don't let it trouble you," he said, evidently marking her concern. "My hawk is in good hands. He's almost as attached to Master Dickon as he is to me. Though not quite."

His "not quite" spoke volumes of the pair's devotion. "I'll make it up to you," she promised earnestly. "I'll . . . I'll mate Oriana with your tercel. After he's better, of course, and when the season is right. You would like that, wouldn't you? Having a new eyas to raise?"

"I might like it. The question is, will they? You can't just mate them at your whim."

"It's no whim," she assured him, shivering as she imagined the pair of hawks, acting out their owners' desires.

She sought a safer subject. "What was it like, growing up with so many brothers and sisters?" She'd wanted to ask for some time. "I saw your house in West Lulworth the few times I went to market with my mother. It's huge, isn't it? But then you had, what, six brothers and sisters? It must have been a luxury—having someone to play with every time you turned around."

Charles heard longing lace her voice as she hurried into the new topic. The vast difference between the warmth of his childhood and the loneliness of hers needled him with regret. "My childhood was bedlam most of the time," he agreed, seeking something amusing to share. "Once Matthew and I dressed a pig in Lucina's coif and smock and set it in her chair with a bowl of porridge and a spoon propped in its hoof. Frightened the cook half to death. She vowed for weeks after that Lucina had been stolen by fairies and a changling left in her place, even after she saw Lucina was quite well."

He smoothed Frances's unruly hair and decided that she, too, was a fairy, delightfully disheveled, as she'd been at thirteen. She'd stolen something from him, too—his ability to remain aloof and masterful in her presence. And when the fairy smiled and her soft lips curved like a half moon that gleamed through the mist, the urge to have her besieged him, as if he'd been struck by moon madness. He wanted to pluck the pins from her hair until it floated around her shoulders, then lower her bodice and smock and bury his face between her soft, bare breasts. With a massive effort, he forced himself to attend her words.

"I never got into mischief," she said wistfully. "The maids or Mama were with me all the time—though I did like being with Mama. She worked the most exquisite embroidery in silks of all colors—blue, scarlet, green—and told stories while I watched her needle move like magic, painting a picture in thread. I do wish I'd had a brother or sister, though. Even an older one."

He grimaced. "You wouldn't have liked an older brother or sister, I promise. Mine ordered us younger ones about until I thought I had an extra father and mother. I was fast friends with Matthew and Lucina though, who were closer to my age." He remembered playing bowls and cards with them, then pictured Frances all alone at Morley Place, and wished she'd had a friend. "You never came to West Lulworth. Why?"

"We had everything at Morley. If not, it was brought to us. And we did have many enjoyable pastimes. My father helped me net my own hawk when I was seven and taught me to handle her. We hunted often together, and I explored every inch of Morley land. One day I found a hawk's nest in the woods near the marsh."

He noticed she didn't mention which marsh, though it was probably the one where they'd first met. "How high was the nest?"

"Quite high. I climbed the tree."

She leaned against the boat as they talked, close enough that her hair tickled his cheek. He could just imagine her, back skirts pulled forward between her legs and tucked in her waistband, her feet bare as she climbed from limb to limb. "And that's how you found Oriana?"

"No, that bird died young. I found Oriana in a woodland outside Paris and climbed to that nest as well. I was sixteen."

Charles calculated rapidly. "That makes Oriana six years old." No wonder her bond with the bird was so fierce, so loving. "And you were nine when your mother died?" She winced, and he regretted his careless wording. "I mean when you left Morley Place to live in London," he amended, trying to cushion the words.

She nodded, her eyes clouded with grief. "You probably heard when my mother died of smallpox. They wouldn't let me see her while the physician, my father, and the maids ran in and out of her chamber in a frenzy. I knew she was dying, though, when they all left her except my father. I slipped in that night after he'd fallen asleep, exhausted, at her side. She was just barely conscious, so I lay beside her on the bed. I kissed her and wept, and though she could barely talk, she comforted me and said good-bye. I can't quite explain how she did it, but she did. Ironic, isn't it, the dying comforting the living. But she had such a loving heart." Her voice lowered at the end, her sorrow like the willows trailing their weeping limbs in the waters of Morley marsh.

" 'Tis a wonder you didn't get the pox yourself."

"I did," she said fiercely, "and I wanted it, because my mother had had it. I thought it just that I should share everything with her."

Charles flinched as he imagined Frances as a child, believing she ought to suffer a fever so she might share with someone she adored. It was another sign of her fierce loyalty, even in her youth. He tilted up her chin with his forefinger and studied her face, with her high, noble forehead and intelligent eyes. "I wish I had known you then."

"We would have hated each other on sight. We did when we met on the marsh."

That wasn't entirely true, but Charles had no desire to correct her or talk about that first meeting. He would rather she never knew the intense, sexual excitement she had roused in him that day, despite her tender age. "You have a scar." He touched her cheek. "From the pox?"

"Yes. And here." She pointed to another shallow mark at the base of her brow.

He leaned forward and kissed the scar. "Have you more? Mayhap down here?" He lifted the neck of her smock and peered down, catching a glimpse of her lovely breasts.

"Stop that." She slapped his hand away. "Men want only one thing." She closed her eyes and shook her head, as if to will away her error. "I'm sorry, that popped out by mistake."

He understood exactly why it had popped out—old beliefs often refused to die. In that moment, he hated Antoine more than ever. "Frances," he whispered, "I told you I would take you as my wife. I meant it. I won't let anyone do to you what Antoine did."

"Rest assured, *I* won't let anyone do what he did, including you." Bitterness swelled in her voice. "Curse my loose tongue for ever telling you about him."

"I'm glad you did. I needed to know."

"I didn't want you to know. Everyone around me knew at the time it happened, and it was horrible." She shuddered, and from the ripple he felt run through her body, he realized she was close to tears. He drew her closer, wishing he could exorcise the past from her soul.

"But your father and uncle stood by you, didn't they?" he placated. "And surely people in France are less strict about when a woman . . . does such things. And he promised marriage, so it wasn't your fault."

"You don't understand at all, do you?" She pulled away, took up her leather bag, and smoothed it across her knees. "Losing my virginity was nothing . . . nothing!" Her anger built until she nearly shouted the last word. "I loved him, and when he said he loved me in return, I believed him." Her face twisted at the ugly memory. With a supreme effort, she calmed herself and faced him. "I never doubted him for a second. Even when he failed to arrive at the church, I was so blinded by my own emotions, I thought something urgent had kept him away. I refused to believe ill of him and defended him to everyone. I couldn't imagine he'd lied to us all, including the priest, until my uncle had him followed and learned all. He'd left Paris for his estates in the south— estates I'd never known he had. Nor did I know about his wife."

Charles bit back an exclamation of rage. He burned to hunt down the swine and run him through with his blade. But revenge and murder couldn't help Frances now, while comforting would. "Put him out of your mind, sweetling, and start anew." Good advice; would that he could follow it himself.

She seemed to think so, too, for she studied him intently,

as if uncertain whether to go on. He lifted his eyebrows and nodded encouragingly. He liked her to confide in him.

"There's no more to say. I just wanted you to know why I refuse your offer to wed."

He narrowed his eyes in annoyance. "Frances, if this is another of your foolish notions, I don't like it. You haven't refused me, nor shall you. We'll be married as soon as we reach England." *Damn it,* she wouldn't shake off his offer as if he'd meant it lightly. He had his pride.

"But why would you want to marry me?" she demanded, apparently determined to argue. "Dozens of beauties back in England are probably sighing for you this instant. And me . . . I'm a bitter old woman who's been destroyed by life."

"You, old and bitter?" He couldn't contain a shout of laughter, her words contrasted so poignantly with her beauty. "That's nonsense, Frank. You're not bitter. Think of the way you are with Louis and Pierre."

Affection softened her face like a ray of sun after heavy rain. "They're mere babes. I can feel for them. But—"

"Babes?" He snorted derogatorily. "That pair were conniving old men the moment they entered the world. That you believe otherwise proves my point."

"I'm sorry to differ with you." She drew herself up in that haughty manner he hated when they disagreed. "But what I'm trying to tell you is, most men want to be adored by their wives, even if they don't return the feeling. I can never adore any man."

Charles's jovial good humor shriveled. Why shouldn't she adore him when she had no trouble worshipping those two unwashed brats? Choler twined with jealousy reared its ugly head. "Now see here," he began. "You're going to wed with me."

Her eyebrows rose, slightly condescending. "You forget that the French magistrates or the Spaniards will be waiting for me this afternoon. I see no way I'll be anyone's wife after today, so this discussion is pure rhetoric. I thank you for your kindness in offering for me. In truth, I've never imagined you could be so kind, but I—"

"Stop! That's the second time you've said that. I'm not kind." He stared at her, confounded by yet another of her crazy notions. He wasn't known for his kindness. It wasn't a characteristic he'd cultivated over the years. Prowess in bed with women, masterful feats in the chase—those he had fostered. But kindness . . . hardly.

"But you are kind." She drew closer and took both his hands in hers. "At least you've been kind to me. So let me savor it in my last hours."

Charles felt the pressure of her hands and looked deeply into her eyes. Her haunted gaze captured his and drew him in. Suddenly, the vivid sensation of stepping across a barrier assailed him. The outer world went dark. Down he fell, sucked out of himself and out of control into a black vortex where flashes of light like stars rained around him until . . . his mind cleared and an image formed.

He was a wild bird, caught in a net . . . or was Frances the bird? The myriad emotions seething through him so overwhelmed, he couldn't tell himself from her. All he could do was fight the net. He ripped at it with talons and beak, desperate to break away to freedom, but succeeded only in tangling painfully in its grasp. Fear, anger, and hopelessness attacked him, wearing down his resistance, yet he struggled on, fighting to be free, until . . .

. . . Suddenly, the net lifted. He spread his wings and launched himself with a powerful thrust. Muscles pumping, he mounted the air to seek the freedom of flight. Earth sank away beneath him, its petty cares disappeared. He ruled the skies, he triumphed. Ecstasy pulsed in his veins, until he could bear no more . . .

With a supreme effort, Charles broke the mental bond with Frances and returned to himself with a jolt. In the dim light of the barge, he sat, shaken and blinking, unable to accept what had just transpired. During the years since Inez, he'd stayed solitary in his thoughts and feelings. And although he craved the release Frances offered when they coupled, the mere idea of merging emotionally with her brought a cold sweat to his flesh.

"I'd best ask the boatman if he can offer us some food." He clambered to his feet, needing to escape, to put distance between him and the woman who aroused a tumult of feelings he would rather forget. "You should rest."

"Go on, be stubborn. Don't admit to emotions if you don't want to. But you have them, just the same." Her voice devoid of feeling, she trained her gaze on the floor.

But he saw the shadow cross her face. He knew she was hurt and angry, and his gut clenched. He hated himself for paining her, the very thing he'd sworn to avoid. "I told you I wouldn't do what Antoine did. That's as far as I go," he grated out. "I have my limits. Rest now while I fetch some food."

"You're always telling me to rest."

The more she resented him, the more he wanted to escape. "That's because you need it," he said, far too patronizinly. "You'll be glad you had it come noon when we meet this messenger. Where do we find him, by the by? I need to lay some plans."

"My uncle usually met *her* near the Carmelite nunnery just off the Place Maubert."

"Her?" Charles halted in surprise. "The messenger is female?"

Frances didn't even favor him by meeting his gaze with her own. "I did tell you my uncle received information from a whore."

Charles swallowed this disquieting news. Though any distraction from his earlier emotions was welcome, what he heard didn't go down well. A woman conveying secret information to another woman in an open square? Now that Humphrey knew they were in Paris, he would be watching for Frances, might even know about her uncle's expected messenger. They would be easily spotted. That thought led him directly to another troubling fact. "The city is still too quiet. Folks would normally be up and about by now, but not a soul is stirring. I'm going to have to look into this and find out why."

Frances sat erect. "I think there's going to be a battle."

"Between the Duke of Guise and the king?"

"Yes, and the Spaniards have backed Guise. They intend to put him on the throne of France, then control him." Her voice rose as her previous anger transferred to the new subject. "They're everywhere in Paris and throughout the country. That's why word traveled back here the minute you blew up that inn. It's not enough for them to invade England. They're scheming to rule the Continent as well."

As he digested this new information, he sensed her agony. The pain of her uncle's death was etched permanently in her posture. The secret information she carried, whatever it was, weighed on her soul; within hours she must gather more secrets. A minute ago she had opened to him and shared her emotions. Now she returned to her former behavior, showing no more than glimpses of what she felt, and those by accident. She was like a miser, refusing to share a scrap of her cache.

Irrationally, he wanted more.

"I hadn't realized the extent to which the invasion of England and this trouble were connected," he said at last, determined to tamp down his useless feelings.

"They must be," she said harshly. "Now that I know Sir Humphrey was working with Spain, it seems clear. How much more Uncle Ned told him, I hate to think."

A warning went off in Charles's mind. "How much more was there to tell?"

Frances pulled her knees up to her chest, wrapped both arms around them, and didn't reply.

His gaze fell on her leather bag, clasped between her knees and her chest, and a new suspicion filled him. "Frances," he demanded, wondering why he had been so blind, "what have you in that bag?"

She lifted her head and blinked at him. "Nothing much. Oriana's leash and hood, some spare jesses, and a jar of healing ointment. My handkerchief and a comb."

"Then why do you hold on to it so tightly? Oriana isn't even with us just now."

She shrugged her slim, tantalizing shoulder. "The bag was my father's, and I'm fond of it. Are you going to fetch us something to eat or no?"

Belligerent, infuriating female, he cursed inwardly. As usual she evaded the question. "What else is in that bag?"

"What makes you think there's anything else?"

"Because you always keep secrets from me."

"And you try to pry them out of me with all the tact of a thief beating a locked chest to splinters with an ax," she said with rancor to the barge wall.

He jerked around and left her at that. If she thought he had no tact, he didn't care. She knew his foibles by now, and he didn't intend to change.

He went to the hatch and stuck out his head to look for the bargeman. A few stars still twinkled in the predawn sky, and he gazed at them as frustration, desire, and misgivings churned his insides to a pulp. For a hairsbreadth moment in time, he'd thought to improve his life by claiming a woman for his own. Simpleton! he wanted to shout. He was an addlepated fool to imagine he was in control.

How he wished to be back in England, none of this having happened, sleeping peacefully in his featherbed in Dorset with Arcturus perched at his side. But the thought of being in bed—any bed, anywhere—conjured visions of bedding Frances and inflamed his desire once more.

Tact be damned. If he were really as tactless as she claimed, he would have told her what he knew about Morley Place—that it had been sold and was no longer hers, despite what she thought. But to spare her feelings, he hadn't said a word. He'd kept his mouth shut, unwilling to hurt her if she didn't need to know.

He muttered to himself, cursing the injustice. If he were really so tactless, he would also have been the first to demand she lie with him instead of the other way around. He would have demanded she lie with him a second time just now to relieve his ungodly lust for her. After she bared her vulnerabilities by sharing her emotions with him, she would have yielded. He could have had her again. The urge to do that very thing ate at him all the time, especially then. Especially now.

Charles procured from the bargeman a less than tempting meal of bread and milk, but all the while he cursed the fates that kept putting him in prone positions next to Frances—first in the wagon, then in the monastery, then in a damned barge with rotten fish. That irresistible temptation had pushed him to claim her, yet mating with her once hadn't lessened his desire one whit. If anything, it made him want her even more.

Then there was this matter of emotions that she brought up. He winced, hating the topic. He didn't like to think about emotions, especially not the kind most women prized. He'd indulged in his share with Inez and look where they had led. That wonderful thing called love had destroyed his reason and his best friend.

It was wiser to keep an emotional distance. Frances should understand that after her experience with Antoine. He would explain it to her, rationally and intelligently, and she would agree to his terms. He would provide her with security; she would satisfy his physical needs. Most of all, she must never again expose him to an excess of emotion the way she'd done earlier, forcing him to lose his identity in hers. With that understood, they could live comfortably, side by side. It seemed the perfect match . . .

Except for Frances's impossible, impulsive nature and her infuriatingly contrary ideas, prompted a voice within. Except for the pure magic she claimed he evoked in her. Where did those things fit?

Blast it all! Charles ousted the thoughts from his mind with an angry shake of his head. He had more pressing matters to attend. In a scant few hours, the Spaniards and Sir Humphrey would be after Frances, and he would have to defend her.

For the first time, Charles acknowledged his brother's wisdom in sending him on this errand. Given the chance that trouble might develop, Jonathan had chosen someone strong who could step in.

But Jonathan hadn't known a civil battle between rival factions was about to erupt on the streets of Paris, catching them in the middle. If they didn't get killed, they must convey the messenger's news—along with whatever was in Frances's blasted bag—in all haste back to England and Queen Elizabeth. Spain's invasion of England was imminent—he could smell it in the air.

It was as rank and as unwelcome to him as the putrid breeze blowing off this part of the Seine.

Chapter 21

Frances's prediction of a confrontation was confirmed. By five of the clock, hundreds of feet tramped through the streets of the city, accompanied by the thunder of tabours and the squealing of fifes. They signaled the entry into the city of King Henri's Swiss and French Guard. The king intended to meet the threat of a coup d'etat with his own coup. He might hold his capital against the Duke of Guise and his Spanish supporters. Then again, he might not.

At half past six, Charles informed Frances that they must leave the barge.

She held herself aloof, still wary from their earlier disagreements. If he had felt the things between them as she had, why wouldn't he admit it? Or had he refused to acknowledge their intimacy and changed the subject because he didn't feel anything? Had she misjudged the degree of warmth hiding beneath his cold exterior and hoped for too much?

Such questions brought discomfort and no answers. As Frances followed Charles on deck, she wiped them from her mind, like poorly formed letters from a slate. Accepting the mantle he'd purchased for her from the bargeman's wife, she huddled in its black depths. She had told him about the magic and revealed her own emotions because she couldn't help it. She'd been too thrilled by his touch to hold back.

But it hadn't been wise. Like most males, he had turned possessive afterward. Worse still, he had blocked her out. She could never wed a man like that.

"Where are we going?" she asked as he handed her across the gap between barge and land.

"The Place Maubert." He linked his arm firmly with hers and led the way, as if expecting her to protest.

Frances pondered as they walked. The Place Maubert was exactly where many of the soldiers would be stationed, but it was also where she must meet the messenger. She supposed it was logical, yet should they go so soon?

She dared not disagree, given their tenuous rapport. Instead, as the sun rose over the city, she studied the houses and shops lining the silent, narrow streets. Shutters that would ordinarily be removed as dawn crept into the sky still blinded the windows. No tempting aroma of baking bread filled the air the way it usually did. Doors to houses she had visited in better days stood barred. The once familiar neighborhood waited, as if holding its breath, though Frances could have sworn she glimpsed faces peering from upper windows. With the arrival of the soldiers, all of Paris feared that violence would erupt in the streets.

As they turned into the Rue Saint Jacques, the site of her former home, Frances's wave of nostalgia disappeared. She stopped suddenly at what she saw, jerking Charles to an abrupt halt as well.

At the far end of the street, a group of men silently erected a barricade. Topsy-turvy piles of furniture, barrows, and carts cluttered the passage into the Place Maubert. But the primary building blocks were huge hogsheads, rolled into place and standing tall on their ends. Frances knew dirt or cobbles loaded inside transformed them into barriers for use in battle. If every street leading into the place were so barricaded, the French soldiers were penned in the square, unable to escape let alone attack.

The French king was about to be outmaneuvered.

It meant one thing to Frances—the Spanish-backed party would have the upper hand in Paris by the time she must meet the messenger. Her chances of safely receiving the message dwindled.

The realization filled her with grave misgivings. But with the misgivings came an idea—one she must act on quickly. Ripping her arm from Charles's hold, Frances whirled around and ran. She must move before she missed her chance.

At Frances's abrupt defection, Charles twisted around and followed. What had gotten into the wench, that she would take to her heels so suddenly? The erection of the barricade might be ominous, but hardly unexpected. For the last two hundred years, the citizens of Paris had used chains twined from building to building, piles of rubble, and anything else at hand to cut off the retreat or advance of threatening forces.

He supposed another of Frances's crazy notions had hold of her again.

She bolted down the street ahead of him, but aggravation lent speed to his feet and he gained on her. Just as he thought he would catch her, she veered and dodged down an alley. As he rounded the corner, she stopped at a door and shouted, "Open, Jean-Claude. 'Tis Mademoiselle Frank."

The door sprang open, and Frances whisked inside. Charles caught up just in time to wedge his shoulders in the opening before the door could slam in his face.

"Were you going to leave me out in the street?" he demanded, thoroughly incensed with her capricious behavior. He leaned against a huge cupboard to catch his breath, assailed by the odor of fresh bread in a dim, warm kitchen.

Frances sent him a saucy glance as she embraced a young lad. "I knew you would follow. You always do."

"Who is this man, Jean-Claude?" An elderly lady in black robes stared at him, her eyes wide with fright. Her gaze locked on the haft of the huge hunting knife in his belt.

It took him several minutes to realize, from her white headdress, that she was a nun, and they had entered the pristine clean kitchens of the Carmelite nunnery. The lad seemed overjoyed to see Frances, as if he knew her well. The nun showed a similar familiarity, for she patted Frances on the shoulder and asked how she fared. *He* was the one the woman objected to.

It could have been worse, he told himself, as he reassured the good woman he meant no harm and was the protector of Mademoiselle Frances. But his temper rebelled. Frances had lived in this part of Paris for years and knew these people. She should have introduced him, instead of pretending he didn't exist—though she might have every good reason to wish he did not.

Assured that he would not hurt them, the nun invited him to sit by the fire and offered him fresh bread, ripe berries with churned cream, and hard-cooked eggs. But instead of feeling appeased as he bit through the crisp bread crust to the fragrant sponge inside, Charles fumed. Frances might have told him where she was going. He'd left the barge in the hope of finding just such a place as this to watch from and wait for the messenger.

But no, she bowed to her impulsive nature. She flew off

for the nunnery without a word, all but forgetting him and shutting him out in the street.

An hour later, though he still blamed her, he finally acknowledged his own fault in the affair. Not being familiar with this part of Paris, he should have asked Frances for advice to begin with. But pride prevented him. It prevented him from doing a great many things. Pride, temper, and intolerance, Master Dickon often told him, made him a fit companion only for hawks.

He had to bite his tongue at the sight of Frances sitting with the kitchen lad on a bench. Another of her adopted waifs, no doubt. She had wheedled the boy until he let her wash his hair, clearly not the first time she had done so for him. Now she straddled the bench with him before her, humming to herself as if she hadn't a care in the world while she trimmed his scraggly locks. Where had her anxiety gone?

He supposed he had enough for them both since she refused to share more about the messenger with him. The many questions requiring answers for a successful campaign churned through his head. What did the messenger look like? How would Frances know her? If the square was completely cut off from the outside, how would a woman dare enter without making herself fair game for the bored soldiers stationed there? How might he distract Sir Humphrey or any other waiting men so that Frances might meet the messenger safely and escape? "What time are you to meet her?" The last of his questions fell from his lips by accident. He hadn't meant to speak aloud.

"Three of the clock," she answered, looking up from the lad's hair.

"I thought you said 'twas noon."

"I did. That was to be sure I arrived in time."

Charles suppressed a scowl, again irritated that she hid the full truth. More than that, she wore a contented expression as she fussed over the lad. At a time like this, it bothered him no end. But then she probably felt safe here, with friends who knew her well.

The kitchens grew chaotic as the dinner hour approached and more nuns poured in to prepare the midday meal. With them came word from outside that the French king had ordered his soldiers to protect Paris, not attack it. No bloodshed of innocent citizens would be allowed.

The nuns applied themselves to their work. Sharp knives

lew as they prepared fresh fruit, herbs, and vegetables, and delectable scents of roasting meat rose in the air. Women rushed to and fro across the flagstone floor. Charles felt at ea in this feminine domain, so he asked for a room overlooking the square where he and Frances might retire. His request was granted, most likely to get them out of the way. Since her lad now had work to perform, Frances left without protest.

From the upper story, Charles studied the men in the Place Maubert. Soldiers packed the square, some lounging at their ease, others swaggering about in pairs and trios, shouting insults at the citizens beyond the barricades. Hemmed in, they could do little more. The barriers blocked the mouth of every street leaving the square.

"That's Louis de Crillon, head of the French Guards." Frances leaned against the window ledge and pointed out the commander. "They say he's as stupid as he is brave. I see he's fuming because the Duke of Guise sent the Comte de Brissac to reinforce the Sorbonne, but he can't tear out of the square and confront him in battle."

"In his place, I would fume, too." Charles noted that her previous tension had returned. He saw it in the rigid set of her neck and shoulders. Her respite in the kitchens was over; her calm, a ruse. He understood that now as she shifted from one foot to the other, her concern apparent. She knew as well as he what must be done.

But how, in this chaos, would they manage it? Which of the numerous plans that churned through his head would work?

He examined them thoroughly, one by one, analyzing their strengths and weaknesses. Despite the importance of his task, time hung heavily on his hands. Seated at the table, Frances drummed her fingers while she examined a book of prayers. Her nails clicked in an annoying rhythm until he wanted to shout at her to stop.

He propped one foot on a stool and leaned against the window ledge. Below him in the square, men stripped off doublets and jerkins as the sun beat down on them and they began to sweat. Hunger and thirst no doubt plagued them, Charles speculated, as he and Frances ate the repast provided them by the abbess.

As the dinner hour came and went, no provision wagons arrived for the soldiers. No drink, not even water, was

available to them. The barricades played their part, as they
were meant to do. Nothing came into the square; nothing
went out.

By then, the men in the square were bored and wanting
action. They paced or fidgeted, restless and without purpose.
Their voices rose as they complained, fought among them
selves, or sat in silent anger. Charles noticed a handful had
gathered at one of the barricades to shout at a motley crowd
of the duke's supporters on the other side. Monks, students,
watermen, and porters returned the soldier's insults with
taunts of their own. Tension mounted on both sides of the
barricade until the air fairly crackled with it; a similar ten
sion mounted inside Charles. The duke's supporters knew
full well the king's men had orders not to fight. If threatened,
what would the soldiers do?

By two of the clock, Charles had failed to devise a flaw
less plan for meeting the messenger, and he raged with impa
tience at his inadequacy. His best idea was to go in Frances'
place, but he knew she wouldn't permit it. Besides, the mes
senger wouldn't acknowledge him, or so she said.

From his place by the window, he frowned at her, wishing
she would ask his advice or guidance. But she sat at the table
and refused to speak to him, fiddling with a rosary and the
prayer book instead. She looked immeasurably tired after
their near-sleepless night. He longed to talk over the plan
with her, if only she would bring up the subject first. Curse
her uncommunicative, stubborn ways.

As if she heard his silent dissatisfaction, Frances lifted her
head and gazed at him. Despite fatigue, her movements were
graceful as she rose and joined him at the window. "The time
grows short. 'Tis almost three of the clock." She leaned
against the embrasure and studied the men milling below.

"It does indeed," he said tersely. "I have some thoughts on
how we should proceed."

"In truth?" She regarded him with raised brows, as if ques
tioning his right to have any thoughts at all, let alone on how
they should proceed.

He decided to pretend she had expressed interest. "Here's
what we'll do. I'll go into the square and wait for the mes
senger while you stay here. I'll be in no danger among all
those men, whereas you would be."

Frances didn't seem to be paying him much attention

"Look." She pointed toward one of the barricades. "There's a monk bringing the soldiers water."

Charles glanced at the brown-robed, hooded friar as he mounted a barricade, a wooden yoke balanced on his shoulders with a bucket on either side. The religious descended carefully into the square and offered water to the eager soldiers. The men crowded around the buckets to drink from the dippers or fill their own cups, paying the monk himself little heed.

"Exercising his Christian charity, no doubt," Charles said before rushing on with his plan. "Now here's your part in the plan. Once I'm in the square and I spot the messenger, I'll point you out at the window. She'll recognize you, as she ought, and you will—"

"I don't see how *you* will recognize the messenger," Frances interrupted. She left the window and returned to the table. "You might diagram this plan of yours for me." She riffled in a drawer, found a quill and paper, then uncorked the ink pot in its stand.

"She'll be the only female in the square. I would have to be blind not to notice her," he snapped, taking the quill and dipping it in the ink while Frances stepped back. "You'll be here." He sketched in the Place Maubert, then labeled the Carmelite nunnery along one side. "I'll be here. You'll nod to her, and she'll tell me the message. I'll leave the square and meet you at a rendezvous point. I think we should return to the barge, since we both know its location. From there, we'll collect Oriana and leave Paris. Thus far we've seen nothing of Humphrey, so we have nothing to fear from that quarter. He's undoubtedly busy elsewhere in Paris, working with the Spanish. As for your messenger, I know you're worried about her safety"—he broke off with a gesture to suggest she need have no fear—"but you said she's a prostitute. The men will be so delighted to see her, they'll never suspect why she's there. After we leave, she can peddle her wares and make a few coins." Charles chuckled at his own cleverness as he turned for Frances's approval.

The chuckle died in his throat as he discovered he'd been talking to no one.

The door to the chamber stood open a crack, and Frances was gone.

Chapter 22

Frances rushed down the back stairs of the nunnery toward the kitchens. Nervous energy coiled in her stomach as she planned her next moves. She felt quite sure the monk dispensing water to the troops was no man.

"Jean-Claude, I need a monk's robe. Can you help?"

The kitchens were empty save for the little lad, bent over a trough of soapy water. He looked up from the pot he scrubbed, agog at the urgency in her voice.

"What about one of the nuns' robes?" Frances urged. "An old one, mayhap, that's no longer wanted. You must stop what you're doing and help me. I need a dark hood as well."

"We can look in the laundry." Jean-Claude seemed pleased at the excuse to put down his pot. "Are they fighting in the square yet?" He led the way to the nearby washroom.

"They're not and you should pray they don't," Frances admonished as she sorted through a heap of old clothing designated as rags. "There's no glory in being shot with an arquebus at close range, you know. Ah, here's what I need."

Minutes later, Frances stood at the kitchen door, garbed in an old black robe with a tattered hem. Jean-Claude tore a wide sleeve from another frayed habit and pushed the narrow end down over Frances's head. The wide end fell open around her face like a hood.

"Do I look enough like a monk?" she asked the lad anxiously.

"I suppose, if no one looks hard." Jean-Claude yanked at the improvised hood so it fell over her forehead, half hiding her face. "Where are you going, dressed like this?"

Frances briefly explained her plan. Jean-Claude's face lit up with glee. "I'll help. I'll wait at the little door on the square and refill your buckets when they're empty. You can count on me." His face glowed with pleasure at finding an important part to play.

"I'll knock when I need you, then." Frances ruffled his clean hair and donned her most confident manner, but she couldn't hide a shiver as Jean-Claude lifted the nun's heavy wooden yoke to her shoulders. He attached the empty buckets to their hooks and pointed out the well to her. Frances kissed him, then slipped out the kitchen door.

If ever man wished to strangle woman, Charles thought in desperation, he did now. Whatever reason Frances had for sneaking out on him, he knew he wouldn't like it.

He failed to find her in the empty, clean-scrubbed kitchens, deserted now that the meal was done. He failed to find her in the empty, echoing great hall where the nuns dined three times a day. His boot heels clicked on the stone floor as he crossed from one end to the other, increasing his pace to match his frantic nerves until he ran. He flashed by the chapel entrance, where the nuns were praying. Frances wouldn't be there.

An ominous feeling harassed him as he found the front entry and peered out one of the windows flanking the barred door. With close attention he scanned the crowd of men. He spotted Crillon, looking hot and distracted as he moved among his men on horseback, soothing tempers and reinforcing orders to maintain the peace. The commander shouted at the citizens beyond the barricades every time he came near enough, warning them to leave his men alone. The monk was still there, doling out water. He'd been joined by another, and together the two made their way through the crowd.

But of Frances, Charles saw not a trace.

Common sense told him a woman would have to be mad to go out there.

She's mad, sure enough, he thought grimly, wishing he were wrong. Three of the clock had passed mere minutes ago. Without question she was somewhere in the square. He must find her and get her out.

An uproar at one of the barricades caught his attention. A group of men approached the citizens guarding that entrance to the square. After a time, the citizens parted to let one man pass. As he climbed over a brace of barrels, Charles recognized Sir Humphrey Perkins.

Hatred leaped in Charles; it seethed from his every pore. The man didn't deserve to be thought of as "Sir." His right hand curled instinctively around his knife as he reached with his left to unbar the door.

The mass of male humanity packed in the square seethed, primed by emotions Charles understood firsthand. Battle lust hovered beneath the surface, waiting to explode into action. He inched his way through the crowd, searching for Frances, as Humphrey swaggered over to Crillon and planted himself before the commander's horse. The square quieted, and the tension heightened. Men leaned forward, their attention riveted on the newcomer. No doubt they wondered if he would supply their excuse to fight.

"The Duke of Guise advises you to retreat." Humphrey spoke in ringing tones.

Watching the confrontation from the corner of his eye, Charles wove his way among the troops.

Crillon stared at Humphrey with undisguised dislike, clearly irritated with Humphrey's failure to use his title. "How is it you come as his spokesman, Englishman?" he snarled. "Do you speak for the duke?"—he paused deliberately and glanced around at his men—"or do you really speak for Spain?"

A low murmur of shocked approval at his bold accusation rippled through the French guardsmen.

"Bravo, Crillon," several shouted. "If he works for Spain, we'll see him cast out of France."

"*Non,* we'll see him dead!" yelled another.

"I work for England and no other," declared Sir Humphrey, drawing up his bulk with dignity at the insult. "I am here to lend diplomatic aid. The duke's commander stationed at the Sorbonne asked me to visit you with this advice. Your king is about to do the same thing."

Crillon scowled as Humphrey gestured toward the barricade over which he'd come.

A man in the king's colors waved at Crillon from the other side of the barrier, where he'd been forceably detained by the duke's supporters. The two monks, who were leaving the square, partially blocked his view as they climbed the barrier, their wooden yokes and empty buckets dangling. One of them hopped to the ground on the other side. The other crouched low, frozen in place as the trunk on which he stood wobbled and threatened to fall.

Crillon spurred his horse toward Humphrey. "Let His Majesty's messenger come forward and deliver his dispatch.

How dare you detain him," he berated the duke's men on the other side of the barrier. "He comes from your king."

Charles picked up speed as he slipped around a tight knot of men. He had checked for Frances in every doorway and cranny of the buildings edging the square. His lips twisted with a silent curse as he covered more ground but failed to find her. At least this business between Crillon and Perkins occupied everyone's attention. As he skirted another clump of soldiers, one of them elbowed him and laughed.

"Will you look at that! That clown of a monk is going to take a fall."

Charles glanced back at the barrier where the king's messenger had mounted the row of barrels, intending to go to Crillon. As he did so, he bumped the second monk, who was already unbalanced.

The monk sprawled flat on his face across the trunk. His robe flew up to reveal a woman's gown and a slim, female leg.

Men burst into guffaws. Charles froze in his tracks.

It was Frances.

With every eye in the square trained in that direction, Humphrey Perkins wouldn't miss seeing her. He would know at once why she was there, in disguise.

"Stop that woman," Perkins shouted. "Stop her accomplice, that other monk. They're spies."

The other monk grasped Frances by both arms and jerked her frantically. Frances tumbled headlong from the trunk to the far side of the barricade.

With a mad oath, Charles burst into a run, heading not for the barrier but the abbey. With the crowd and the barricade separating him from Frances, he would never get to her this way. He would go through the abbey, come out on the other side, and meet Frances. But only if someone would let him in again. With a gasp for breath, he hoped someone had decided to watch.

Just then a small door to the left of the main entry opened. *"Ici,"* hissed the kitchen lad. Relieved, Charles dived for the door.

Frances shook off the unwieldy wooden yoke and scrambled to her feet as Anne Roche, disguised as the other monk, hauled her up. At Sir Humphrey's shout, terror sliced through her midsection as neatly as a new-whetted knife through raw meat. In response, she grabbed up her habit's hem and stumbled after Anne.

All around them, the duke's supporters leered and chuckled. "Why don't you show us more of your leg, good brother?" one of them chaffed her good-naturedly. " 'Tis most shapely."

"Why stop with a leg?" another demanded. "Show us more. Is your friend female, too."

Several students groped for both Anne and Frances.

Anne smacked away their hands as she elbowed her way down the street. "You heard the elegant Sir Humphrey Perkins. He says we're spies," she shouted at the men. "He's one to talk, when he's not even loyal to Guise, as he's led you to believe. He's completely in the pay of Spain, and once Guise gets on the throne, he intends to assassinate our duke and put King Philip of Spain in his place. King Philip of France. How do you like the sound of that?"

The mood of the duke's men shifted abruptly. Their angry response broke out, rocking the crowd.

"Assassinate Guise?"

"We don't want Spain on the throne."

"Then you'd best take up the issue with him." Anne pointed at Sir Humphrey as he strode up to the barrier. "He's the traitor of France. Don't let him hurt our country any more than he has."

Sir Humphrey puffed up to the barrier and leaned against the other side. He gestured at the men who had moments ago welcomed him as a messenger from their duke. "Seize that woman, I say. She's a traitor and a spy."

"She says you want to assassinate Guise," bellowed one of the duke's supporters. "Is that true?"

"Nonsense," Sir Humphrey protested. "You must all understand—"

"Don't listen to his lies!" cried Anne. "Keep Spain off France's throne."

Not waiting to hear more, the supporter leveled his pistol at Sir Humphrey and fired. He missed and one of the king's soldiers in the square beyond fell like a stone.

Chaos erupted as men on both sides of the barrier lunged for each other's throats. Frances ducked her head and ran. Gunfire and battle cries peppered the air in her wake.

"Is he after us?" she panted to Anne as they ran.

"Not now." Anne paused to let Frances catch up. "So the

salaud betrayed you, did he?" She snorted in disgust. "I never trusted him. He would appear regularly when I met with your uncle, to pinch my ass and hint at bedding me, as if I should give my favors away free. This way."

They hurried past the alley leading to the nunnery kitchens. They cleared it and debated briefly which way to go when a figure leaped from the shadows by the wall.

Frances shrieked in terror as she recognized Sir Humphrey's servant, the same fellow who had fetched her things only days ago. She staggered and fell beneath his weight as his fingers closed around her neck. Fear and the insidious pressure of his hands on her throat paralyzed her. Her lungs screamed for air. She knew she was going to die.

Suddenly, a figure blotted her view of the sun. Her attacker was lifted from her bodily, as if he were a mere rag. He sailed through the air and crashed against a wall, where he sprawled at an unnatural angle, either unconscious or dead.

Frances stood up unsteadily and met her rescuer's gaze. "My God, Charles," was all she could say.

"Damn it, Frances, you should have told me what you were doing instead of going into that square alone."

Her knees wobbled and threatened to collapse as she stared at him in mute relief. He loosed a string of vivid curses as he caught her around the waist with both arms.

"Your language is getting as bad as Pierre's." She grinned up at him weakly. "Mind your manners, now, and meet my uncle's friend. Anne, this is Baron Milborne. Charles, meet Anne Roche."

"Delighted," he muttered. "Now if you'll dispense with the formalities, I'd prefer to get us out of sight." He hustled Frances down the deserted street. "We're for the barge again." He motioned for Anne to follow, then increased his pace. "We'll hide there until we can leave Paris. We must wait to see how bad the fighting gets."

"I have a better idea," Anne said. "We'll leave now. Under cover of a load of cloth bound for the country."

Frances grinned to herself as Charles sent her a sour look, but didn't disagree. Like most men, he probably abhorred anyone having ideas better than his. But she couldn't trouble herself with his feelings just now. She inhaled deeply, filling her lungs completely for the first time in hours as they hurried toward the river. It felt good to breathe normally again. Her masquerade as a monkish water bearer had been dangerous but successful. What a relief! The worst was over now.

Or was it?

Dismay filled her as she realized she must now cope with Charles's plans for their marriage. She hadn't worried about it before when she had honestly believed she would either be taken prisoner or killed.

Now she must decide. Should she take the security he offered and give up her freedom? Or would they make each other so miserable, she would be wiser to refuse?

"We must make for the coast west of Le Havre," she whispered to Charles as they approached the riverbank. They slowed their pace while Anne searched for her friends' barge. "They'll expect us to try for a port farther east. If we do otherwise, we'll throw them off our trail."

He nodded and handed her onto the barge Anne indicated. With a sob building in her throat, Frances bid her home of nine years a final and silent farewell.

Chapter 23

Violent illness seized Frances during the Channel crossing. But they were fortunate to be crossing at all, she advised herself as she gripped a basin. Vessels making a night run to London were not easily come by in small French villages, especially not to people lacking ready coin. Two young boys and a caged hawk raised the price higher still.

"Here's a fresh cloth." Charles entered the cabin and knelt beside her bunk. "We should see land within the hour."

Frances lifted her head in embarrassment, having just completed another bout with the basin. "My thanks, but I'll be happier when we actually touch land, not just see it." She covered the basin with the cloth and set it on the floor. Oriana screamed from her perch in the corner, letting them know she, too, disliked the tossing ship.

"I'll see you escorted to my sister's town house as soon as we arrive." Charles patted her shoulder with tender concern. "You can go straight to bed."

"You're jesting, of course." She lifted an eyebrow at him, hoping that was the case.

He didn't answer immediately. Instead, he took a turn around the cabin. His posture and movements suggested nothing untoward, but Frances watched him warily for the signs of temper. The way he casually uncorked the water jug and tilted the vessel to drink told her nothing. But he rammed the cork home with the heel of his hand when he was done—a gesture that illustrated his pent-up frustration more eloquently than words.

He was as tightly closed to her as that jug, Frances observed with a defiant shrug. She couldn't even fulfill the legacy her uncle had left her without quarreling with Charles. Given that, how would she dare broach the subject of his marriage offer? Yet it had to be discussed, for she couldn't accept. Yes, they quarreled about every and any subject that arose. They were about to quarrel right now, she thought dismally, as she braced herself for the storm.

"Frances, you're being impractical and unreasonable," he began decisively as he swung around to face her. "If you refuse to guard your health, I must do it for you. You're ill; you belong in bed."

Frances leaped to her feet in outrage. "And who's to deliver my messages to Her Majesty?" she cried. "You?"

"Why the devil not?" he stormed back at her. "You act as if I'll go to the Spanish the minute your back is turned."

She lifted her chin mutinously. "You'll not take my place. I swore to my uncle to keep everything I knew about his business private. And I can't possibly sleep until I've seen Her Majesty. You can go to your sister's and sleep if you like."

"If you're going to court, I'm going as well."

"Good. You can watch the boys while I talk to the queen."

Charles compressed his mouth into a hard, unyielding line at her directive. Disapproval leaped from him like sparks from a stirred-up fire.

"If you would prefer to accompany me, do so." She turned away and groped for her equipment bag lying on the bunk. Its smooth, worn leather beneath her fingers reassured her. She must not let him ruffle her feathers. "But my business with the queen is just what I said . . . private. I've already told you more about it than anyone else. I've violated my uncle's trust. Even Pierre and Louis know little except that the Spaniards are out for my blood."

"Which brings us back to that pair of ragamuffins," he shot back at her. "If you insist on bringing them with us, I'll not play nursemaid to them, Frances. They can't even obey simple commands. Pierre uses his sleeve for a handkerchief and swears like a porter. Louis will probably burn down your house one day."

Frances shrugged one shoulder and refused to answer, convinced he was just jealous because the boys had fussed over her since they set sail and she took ill. He had expelled them both from the cabin when her condition worsened, insisting on caring for her alone. His obvious envy of the boys had amused her then, but not now. He had profited from her boys' help, but still couldn't love them—which didn't surprise her. He'd proposed marriage to her, but never mentioned the word *love*.

"Frances, you refuse to recognize what you're doing. Those boys learned thievery at an early age. They may never change, no matter how hard you try to make them." He stalked over to stand in front of her. "But since you insist you can't live without them, I won't tolerate stealing. If they don't behave, they'll pay the price."

"I'll be sure to let them know."

He growled beneath his breath. She caught a smattering of words, something about his brother Jonathan, and in a fit of pique, she latched on to the name. "Jonathan will be most interested in the information I bring," she baited him. "And I, for one, will provide it to him gladly. Does he still work at his armory? I always liked the pearl-handled hammer he wears at his belt. Once he let me—"

"Stop right there." Charles looked every bit as angry as she'd expected him to be. "How do you know about my brother's pearl-handled hammer. Or anything else about him, as that goes?"

"Everyone's heard of *El Mágico Demoníaco*." She donned her most innocent air. "And he *is* the queen's most valued spymaster."

"What's that to do with you?"

"At his last meeting with my uncle, he—" The ship rolled. Her rebellious stomach twisted again, and she scrambled for the basin, her teasing abandoned.

"You might as well admit it," he ordered as she gagged over the container. He steadied her shoulders to keep her on target, holding her with possessive hands. "You're working with my brother. He knew you had access to these secrets all along."

She moaned as her throat convulsed, but nothing came up. And a sudden rush of guilt plagued her. She shouldn't tease him, but his expectation that she would gladly hand her work over to him angered her beyond belief.

"Duped again." He sounded not the least surprised and only slightly disgruntled. "I told you older brothers are a curse. Off I went on my errand, thinking you were just a poor, orphaned waif. I had no idea the pair of you were working hand in glove."

"We aren't, exactly," she admitted as the heaves subsided and the firm clasp of his hands stirred her in quite a different way from the tossing of the boat. "Jonathan doesn't know about the messenger. Word came from her after his last contact. When my uncle learned she was coming, he told no one but me."

"Which left you in charge. What an exquisite coincidence."

"If it is, don't blame your brother. He could never have known my uncle would be killed." Suddenly, the memory of last night's venture in the churchyard hit her, its impact worse than the seasickness. She bent her head and let the tears come. "Oh God, he's gone."

"My poor fledgling." His voice softened, and he cradled her in the shelter of his broad chest and arms. Ironically enough, within seconds of their disagreement, she welcomed his touch.

"I let myself hope, for a day, that he was still alive"—she sobbed—"that I had only to let the captain lead me to him. How stupid I was, believing whatever I was told without question. He's gone. I'll never see him again."

"Hush, hush," he soothed her, his hands working their magic. "I know it seems impossible at first, to lose someone who protected you and cared for you. Eventually, you'll accept it. The bad memory will fade, leaving only the good."

"I know. I've lost . . . others . . . before." Drained by her physical exhaustion and emotional pain, she leaned against him and swallowed her tears. "How long since your father died?"

"Ten years. He was everything I admired in a man, as well as being our economic mainstay. Fortunately, Rozalinde, my older sister, kept the family business thriving so my mother could raise us younger ones. A woman alone can be defenseless against loss brought by death. My sister is, of course, a solitary exception." He took her hand, as if to remind her she was one of the defenseless types. "Have no fear for your future. I'll care for you now."

"I'll care for myself, thank you." She forced out the words, determined to make them true, though Charles tempted her to depend on him. His sheltering arms conjured up long-lost childhood memories of being with her mother and father, of feeling secure and cared for at Morley Place. Yet she must not fool herself. She could go to Morley, the place of her birth, regain her security, and still be free. But with Charles, she would lose her freedom. He would rule her the way he ruled Oriana—with a magic so powerful, it overcame her resistance like a drug.

"You can't care for yourself." He snapped her attention

back to him, reinforcing her fears with his words. "You haven't any money. You want security. I'll supply it."

In frustrated sorrow, she realized he believed her a helpless waif who couldn't care for herself.

"Come now, I'll see that you want for nothing. You'll have your own home and a place for Oriana. You can have more birds as well, as many as you like." He glided an arm around her waist and squeezed. "You need only accept."

Like the falconer, he swung the lure, tempting her innermost need. "Everything comes with a price. What's yours?" she asked, after she'd just decided not to bargain, too.

He studied her pensively, apparently unaware that his hand had wandered to her back, that his fingertips circled over and over, imprinting his possession on her flesh. "I do need something from you," he mused.

"You want to bed me," she said concisely. "Let us not mince words."

"You're so sure you know me. But that isn't all I want." His fingers tightened on her arm. A light kindled in his eyes, as if he would devour her with his gaze. "I require one thing as the term of our marriage, and I'll not mince words. I want your loyalty, Frances. All of it. To the end."

"L-loyalty?" She sputtered in stark disbelief, taken aback by his unexpected demand. "You ask for it as if it were a . . . a hat to be passed from hand to hand. It can't be given like that."

"That's the offer. I'll provide you security in exchange."

Moisture pooled in her eyes as she met his demanding gaze. He'd both shocked and touched her by making a request she could respect. She wavered on the brink of agreement, but finally thought better of it and drew back. "I must think on your offer." She turned away and furtively wiped her eyes. "What of children? You don't mention them."

"I do want an heir," he said promptly. "In fact, I would like to begin working on one with all haste."

Frances frowned as he raised his eyebrows meaningfully. One instant he touched her with his wish for loyalty; the next, he exasperated her with his arrogant demands. *His* appetite dictated that they work on an heir immediately. *His* need for a child must be fulfilled. He mentioned nothing about her needs. "*You* are entirely too full of yourself, master baron," she snapped. "Which is something I abhor in a man."

"That's not a straight answer to my offer," he clipped back at her. "Try again."

"I mean no!" she flared up at him. "I refuse your offer. Is that straight enough? You say you want loyalty, but you really want more. You want to own me, but I won't let you. Go away and leave me be."

Her words seemed to have no effect on him at all. "I'll give you two days to consider and give me a true answer." With a final squeeze of her arm, he rose, scooped up the basin, and tossed her the cloth. "I'm going to empty this," he gestured with the basin, "and talk to the captain."

"And what if after two days I still say no?"

"You won't." He grinned wickedly at her from the doorway. "Be a good girl now and don't move while I'm gone."

Frances sank back in the bunk and wiped her mouth with the cloth. How gracious of him. He wouldn't listen when she refused him. He left her alone in this bad-smelling cabin with orders not to move. And he generously provided her with two whole days to decide something she had already decided. In truth, she couldn't wait for this voyage to end so they could part.

Charles welcomed the cold night breeze of the Channel that greeted him on deck. He'd had to escape from Frances before he did something desperate—such as force himself on her. She'd looked so beautifully vulnerable when the seasickness first claimed her, he'd wanted to have her on the spot.

Ridiculous reaction, he chided, sure he'd taken leave of his senses. The woman was ill. She couldn't engage in pleasures of the flesh. How callous of him to be aroused.

Of course he had curbed his uncivilized appetite, holding her while she tossed up the contents of her stomach. Naturally he'd played the gentleman throughout, even cleaning up after her and chasing the boys away when they refused to sleep and became too loud. Yet he'd felt anything but gentlemanly inside.

In his mind, he had stripped away her garments, one by one, and tossed them to the four winds. He had tasted her warm lips while he pressed his lusting, mortal body against her smooth, cool flesh. Now that he'd stated his terms and her loyalty lay within his reach, the beauty of her unswerving devotion once she made a commitment burned like a vision before his eyes. The wonder he'd felt at their mating in the barge flooded back, startling him into awe.

He took his time rinsing the basin in a bucket of cold salt water. All the while he scanned the black water and groped to quell his raging need for the woman he'd known for only five days.

Listen to reason, he argued with himself. Although Frances offered many things he desired, her loyalty being chief among them, she had her bad points as well. For one, she made him utterly, gut-wrenching choleric half the time with her obstinate ideas. She made him want to tear his hair in rage. And this urge to tear off her clothes, regardless of the place and time, was bound to cause problems. *Thunderation,* she reduced him to a primitive whenever he was with her. Could he bear spending the rest of his life suppressing such a violent urge?

She also became angry faster than any woman he knew. At times, her sudden mood shifts drove him close to fits.

Mayhap he should just emigrate to the New World. Anything to escape this agony. Except that he wanted Frances in his bed with an urge that refused to be denied. He wanted her loyalty; he wanted her precious, seldom-given-and-therefore-holy trust. And all for reasons he didn't care to think about, for reasons he crushed beneath an iron heel so they couldn't see the light of day. They smacked of emotions, which he refused to acknowledge in his life.

He sought the captain then, as a distraction to stanch the flow of torturous thoughts. It was time to rescue the poor man. Pierre and Louis had pestered him unmercifully ever since they boarded the ship. Now they hung on the rail and bombarded him with questions while he steered the course.

"Run away, rascals," Charles ordered them with a jerk of his thumb as he approached. "The captain and I have business to discuss. And don't you dare to bother Mistress Frances. She's resting quietly at last."

The captain then agreed to sail them all the way up the Thames to Whitehall Palace, in exchange for a considerable sum. Charles would demand it from Jonathan. His brother owed him that much and more.

As he headed back to the cabin, he considered the two rascals. The pair had immediately returned to harassing the captain, one on either side. Charles had tried to settle them with Anne Roche when they parted company outside Paris. As far as he was concerned, they were French and belonged in France. But he had failed to prevail. Frances had insisted she couldn't live without them, so he was stuck with them for the nonce.

So be it. Their presence bound her closer to him. Yes, he would take care of her and her charges, and yes, he required something in return. He would have her loyalty, because she would promise it. And then he would seek a taste of that magic she claimed he inspired.

His resolve to wait wavered as he entered the cabin minutes later. Despite being tired, ill, and disheveled, Frances captivated him as she sat at the table, her long hair trailing loose around her shoulders, her good cheek propped in her palm. His hands itched to explore the slope of her petal-fine flesh just where her smock met her shoulder, tempting him to . . .

He cut off the fantasy before it took over. He strode to the washstand and refilled the basin with fresh water. "Let me wash your face for you. Lie down."

"I can manage."

"No, I'll minister to you." He clasped her arm to help her rise.

The minute he touched her, she pulled away and moved quickly to the bunk.

He covered her with a woolen blanket, then sat by her side, the basin steadied between his feet on the floor. He wrung out the cold cloth and placed it gently across her bruised cheek.

"Did anyone ever tell you you have pleasant hands?" she murmured, closing her eyes.

"Yes"—he took up the cloth and cleansed the other side of her face—"Did anyone ever tell you you have beautiful hair?"

She grinned wanly. "Sorry, but you're not the first. Did anyone ever tell you you have a chest like an ox?"

"Oh ho, now we're getting personal," he teased. "You must be feeling better to make such an observation. Yes, I do recall someone mentioning the breadth of my chest, though they put it more prettily. I believe it was accompanied by an inspection. Would you care to indulge? No?" He chuckled as she shook her head. He lifted the cloth and wiped away a smudge of dirt at her temple.

Her forest green eyes reflected both caution and desire. He stopped sponging her face and captured a tendril of hair stuck to her wet cheek. "Did anyone ever tell you how bewitching you are when you fly your hawk? You look as if you're one with her, soaring among the clouds instead of being tied to earth."

The graceful arch of her brows shot up. "No," she breathed. "No one ever said that."

Well done, he congratulated himself. The other clods had missed the best thing about her. Unable to resist, he combed his fingers through her thick, dark hair.

A soft sigh escaped from her lips. She closed her eyes and snuggled deeper in the pillow. "I just realized"—she gave a small giggle reminiscent of her tipsy laugh at the monastery—"Pierre hasn't cursed once since we set sail."

Charles's mood soured. Pierre hadn't cursed in front of her, was all. "My high flown declaration of admiration inspired you to think of that?"

She opened her eyes and grinned at him. "I think about the boys all the time. They're like my own children."

"Why that particular pair, Frances? I'm sure you could have found any number of well-bred orphans elsewhere if you'd wanted to foster children. Why a ragged, lousy pair of thieves?"

She drew herself up and glared at him. "You've made your feelings about them perfectly clear, but I chose them because they needed me much more than those other orphans might have. I don't expect you to understand—you were always loved and cared for as a child."

"It has nothing to do with how I was cared for as a child. I just wanted to know why you chose them. I asked a civil question. Am I not entitled to a civil reply?" He didn't want a foul mood, but it rooted its way through his pleasure like a mole breaking through the earth.

"Do you call 'lousy' and 'ragged' civil?"

Damnation, they were bound to quarrel. Just then the door burst open, and Pierre and Louis tumbled in, saving him from further offensive words. "We've spied land, and it's white!" Pierre panted. *"Sacre bleu."*

"I've never been abroad," Louis chimed in, equally excited.

"You shall be now. What you're seeing are the white chalk cliffs of Dover." Frances laughed, sending them a warm smile Charles wished she would reserve for him. She held out both hands to them and gathered them into an embrace. "But we must go straight to Her Majesty after we land. No stopping for anything other than necessities. And I'll expect the very best behavior from the pair of you. No tricks and no purse cutting. Do you understand?"

"Hold a moment," Charles interrupted, not liking the drift of this discourse. "They're not going to the palace looking the way they do. In fact, they can't stay at my sister's until I give them baths and cut their hair. And I fully intend to burn those rags they're wearing. Rozalinde will have something they can wear until I buy them new clothes. They're not to go anywhere in public until then."

"Oh, thank you, thank you!" To his astonishment, Frances launched herself at him and smothered his cheeks with kisses. "You are so generous to take care of my boys. I couldn't think how I would manage new clothes for them."

"If it's going to be done, it must be done right," he muttered stiffly as he accepted her caresses. *By thunder,* the contradictions of this woman puzzled him. He proposed marriage to her and she never once thanked him. Yet he had only to propose new clothes for her urchin friends and her gratitude swelled to levels he'd never dare demand.

"I know you don't like them." She patted his arm almost shyly. "So I truly thank you for your generosity."

He grimaced at her blunt words in front of the boys. "Of course I like them," he admitted grudgingly. "They saved our lives. Do you think I'm an utter brute?"

She smiled at him, a brilliant eclipse that nearly blinded him with its beauty even as he realized she'd tricked him. The scheming wench, she made him admit to feelings, something he abhorred.

"Come now, I want you two to sleep. I'll lie down as well." She bustled around the boys, settling them with blankets and pillows.

He smoldered as Frances fussed over her charges. The constant presence of two children made being alone with her impossible. It wasn't that he disliked them, he insisted silently. *It's just that I want her all to myself.*

Then there was the problem of the boys' background. Mayhap it was cynical of him, but he firmly believed their early values couldn't be changed. Despite this, he would refuse to let them hurt Frances by letting her down.

The thought of their shaming her, of causing her pain or sorrow, infuriated him again. Then Louis wiped his damp nose on one sleeve, reminding Charles of what he personally disliked most about the pair. He would break him of that bad habit. And Pierre's language. In the first moment of excitement in polite company, the little savage would slip, Charles felt sure, even though he'd cleansed his vocabulary of the worst offenders in Frances's presence since they sailed. "Here is my handkerchief," he said sternly, pulling it out and thrusting it at Louis.

"What for?" Louis's thin, triangle-shaped face donned an expression of surprise.

Charles itched to cuff him. "Don't play the fool with me. You know what it's for. Whenever you feel a drip or a sneeze coming, you use the handkerchief. Now do as you're told, and if I see you use your sleeve for your nose again, I'll cut it off. Your nose, not your sleeve."

"Charles!" Frances protested. "Such a way to talk to children."

"They're to learn manners if they come with us," he thundered, unleashing his irritation. "When I give orders, they're to be obeyed. Otherwise, I toss them out. Understand?" He glowered at the pair, who had the grace to nod.

"Then call them by their rightful names if you expect them to be mannerly," Frances retorted, inserting herself into the argument.

"You keep out of this. What are your surnames?" he demanded of the boys.

The boys exchanged rapid words in French, then shrugged. "Got no other names. Pierre and Louis. *C'est toute.*"

"From now on, you are brothers, Pierre and Louis Sillington," he told them, frowning at Frances to let her know she was included in this directive. "It's pronounced Sill-ing-ton. Say it after me." He insisted they each repeat the name several times. "They are distant cousins on your mother's side of the family by marriage," he said to Frances. "We've done exactly what I told the abbot, taken in relatives who were orphaned."

Frances looked at him with wide, innocent eyes. "Does that mean you agree to foster them?"

"Damn it, it means they're to obey me implicitly!" Charles shuddered inwardly as he roared the words. *Ye gods*, he sounded just like his father. A father already, when he wasn't even wed yet. His life was being played out backward. It was almost too much to bear.

"You are wonderful to agree." She was so starry-eyed with appreciation, he yearned to collect on the favor. "I keep misjudging you. Is there any way I can make it up to you?"

"Yes, they're part of the bargain. If I foster them, you give me what we discussed earlier." He smiled wickedly, pleased that this time it was his turn to back her into a corner. He pulled a stool forward and sat down. "We'll disembark in about three hours, so here's what you must do. You're not attending," he chided Frances.

"Shh," she motioned to him. "Listen to the boys."

"*Diable,* you should have been there," Pierre said to Louis. "King Henri gave the Duke de Guise the slip and left Paris. No battle. *Tante pis.* I was hoping for some spoils."

"Enough of that sort of talk," Charles interrupted. "It's wrong to take spoils from people when they're busy fighting. Mend your mouth if you can't mend your mind."

"But King Philip does it," Louis argued. "If it's proper for the King of Spain, why can't we do it, too?"

"Can't you teach them to improve their discourse?" Charles demanded of Frances. "The French king losing control of his capital is no fit subject for children."

"It is unfortunate that they have such an acute knowledge of politics and their effect on people," she said, "but they're right. Spain has just improved her grip on France."

Privately, Charles wished he might improve his grip on the boys enough to hustle them out of the cabin. No chance of that just now, but he intended to take them firmly in hand once they arrived in England. They would cease monopolizing Frances's time, nor would they shame her or let her down. He intended to see to that.

"So if the Armada is victorious over England," Frances continued, 'twill advance Spain's position in France even more."

"The Armada will not be victorious. And you didn't tell me when it would sail. What did Anne Roche say?"

She had remained deliberately secretive on the subject. Nor did he fool himself into thinking she would confide in him now, especially not in front of the boys. So her next words took him totally off guard.

"The Armada's admiral received the blessed standard of the campaign and had orders to leave port on the ninth of May," she said grimly. "Today is the twelfth. That's why we must hurry to London. Her Majesty must call the country to arms."

Chapter 24

Frances swayed with fatigue as she curtsied before Queen Elizabeth Tudor in her private Whitehall apartments early the next morning. The sun had scarcely crept over the horizon and the queen, still garbed in night smock and waistcoat, hadn't officially arisen. "The Duke of Medina Sidonia received firm orders to set sail from Lisbon on the ninth of May to invade England," Frances said. "It is now the thirteenth of May, which means they have embarked. Majesty, I have also brought you, straight from Lisbon, the Duke of Medina Sidonia's full report of the Armada." Unslinging the leather bag from her shoulder, she opened the secret compartment and removed the papers she had protected with her life for five arduous days. Dizzy with exhaustion, she knelt and placed them in the surprised queen's lap.

"Christ's wounds!" Elizabeth shuffled through the papers, astonishment written plainly across her face. "Every detail about the fleet is recorded here. Names of ships and their commanders, their tonnage, number of gunners, cannon. You say it came straight from Lisbon?"

"It did, Your Majesty. My uncle had a network of reliable contacts. I took delivery of the papers after he died and brought them straight to you. Word of the Armada's sailing date came to me just yesterday."

"Your uncle has done us an invaluable service. I am doubly sorry to lose him."

Frances could scarcely acknowledge the queen's sympathetic hand on her shoulder, she was so drained of strength.

"If you were a man, I would see you knighted." Elizabeth paged through the papers, continuing to exclaim over their amazing information. "Since you are not, we will discuss a reward for your service later. Just now, I had best assemble my Privy Council. Russell! Carey! Come straight." The queen clapped her hands in a strident burst of sound.

Frances winced at the burst of sound as two ladies in waiting burst into the chamber, startled by the strident pitch of their mistress's summons.

"Russell, fetch Walsingham and Burghley as fast as ever you can!" commanded the queen. "Have them meet me in the Privy Council chambers in ten minutes. Carey, choose something simple for me to wear and send the ladies of the bedchamber to assist me. Hurry! We've no time to lose. Spain's fleet has set sail."

The two ladies didn't even bother to curtsey, so urgent was the queen's tone. The entire nation knew Spain's desires regarding England. With the eternal threat finally come to fruition, the women took to their heels.

"Damn Philip," Elizabeth muttered under her breath, gathering up the precious papers and bundling them together. "I should have listened to Sir John Hawkins. He told me to keep the navy armed last December, and I did not do it. Now here 'tis, a crisis." She started toward the door of her innermost private apartments, Frances forgotten.

"Doesn't that depend on how quickly they sail up the coast?" Frances asked, staying her.

"It does, my dear. Pray for bad weather and unfavorable winds. You have done well for us, especially given the circumstances. Your loyalty is appreciated. You say the messenger who brought you the news is safe?"

"I parted from her at Le Havre, Your Majesty, and she was safe then, but I believe there is a traitor in Sir Edward's delegation in Paris. One Sir Humphrey Perkins. He had a hand in my uncle's death, and he tried to prevent my bringing you this message. All along I had thought he was my uncle's friend."

" 'Sblood!" The queen swore, clutching the papers to the front of her sleeping robe. "I'll write the order to call him home or have him arrested if he resists as soon as I've talked to the council." She clapped a hand on Frances's shoulder so heartily, Frances staggered. "You're nigh done in, child. You say my Master Falconer brought you? Good. His sister will feed and house you at their town house. I would keep you here at Whitehall, but as usual we're packed to the rafters. Go to Lady Wynford and get yourself some rest."

"By your leave, Your Grace." Frances stayed her as once more the queen moved for the door. "May I accompany you to the council meeting? My uncle died for this cause," she protested as the queen prepared to deny her. "I pray you give me a task that will contribute to the demise of the Armada. I am an expert with birds and could work with your messenger flock."

" 'Tis highly irregular to involve a maid," the queen began, "but you may come along to the council meeting as soon as I am gowned," she amended, seeing Frances's agonized expression. "Are you really an expert with birds?"

"As expert as your Baron Milborne," Frances answered staunchly, forcing herself to stand straight and proud despite being near collapse. "Perhaps more so. I've had years of experience. My uncle would testify to my skill . . . if he were alive."

"Poor child." The queen clucked her tongue. "We shall tell Lord Admiral Howard to put you to work if that is your wish. Sit you down and await me."

The queen indicated a chair, then vanished into the adjoining chamber. Frances sank into the padded seat and stared numbly at the rich wood paneling and silk wall hangings of the queen's private apartments. The frightening succession of events in France, coupled with the miserable crossing, caused a wave of delayed terror mixed with nausea to swirl through her head and aching body. Pressing her fingers to her painfully pulsating temples, she wondered exactly how angry Charles was with her. Probably incensed, judging by his tight expression and cold silence once they arrived at the palace. He'd abandoned her instantly, heading straight for the royal mews and his birds with Pierre and Louis in tow. But what, in truth, had she expected? For him to mope outside the queen's door while she met with Her Majesty? Did she expect to hurt his pride again and again?

No man abided such behavior from a woman, not without ill feelings. She wasn't fit to be a wife. Which meant they must part as soon as she was rested and ready to travel. She would take the boys and go to Morley Place.

But first she must receive her assignment from the queen and the name of her contacts in Dorset with whom she would work. After that, would Charles deign to fetch her once she left the council meeting or must she find the town house herself? Add to that the hour—it was still so early, she hadn't even broken her fast.

Frances groaned aloud. After so many hours of retching onboard ship, she wasn't sure what she needed most—her hungry stomach warred with her throbbing head, the one demanding food, the other begging her to lie down and sleep. Staring out an east window, she noted the rising sun, reflecting on the many panes of glass until they shone like diamonds. The Queen of England, Wales, and Ireland was like that sun, she thought, the rays of her rule gracing the land. Unless a Spanish storm cloud blotted it out.

A short time later, Frances stood at the queen's elbow in the richly attired room known as the Privy Council chamber. The queen's eldest minister arrived a minute later.

"Your Majesty, what's amiss?" William Cecil, Baron Burghley, Lord Treasurer and Elizabeth's chief counselor, saluted the queen, puffing from his hurry. " 'Twas well I slept at the palace last night. I came in all haste."

"The Spanish have set sail for the invasion," Elizabeth said. "The Armada had orders to leave Lisbon on the ninth, and if all went well, they did so." She turned as Sir Francis Walsingham, her chief secretary, appeared at the chamber door. "Ah, Francis, enter. I've already sent off word to Lord Howard at Plymouth. The other ministers have been summoned. We must mobilize straightaway."

"What is the source of this news?" Walsingham questioned, as if reluctant to hear any disastrous details. "There was no word last night."

"Here is the messenger. And here is the invaluable document she brought, delivered to us straight from Lisbon."

Frances felt the queen's hand on her back and stepped forward. Once more she stated her source of information and how she came by the Spanish report. Burghley and Walsingham paged through the Spanish propaganda and exclaimed at the detail it gave.

"There are other copies, you may be sure, Your Majesty," Frances warned. "It will be common knowledge everywhere within a fortnight. But I knew you needed this information, so I brought it to you straight. I understand it was prepared personally by the Duke of Medina Sidonia."

"I'm glad you brought it," the queen declared fiercely, eyes blazing. " 'Twill allow us to muster our forces in like manner. Burghley, Walsingham, the duke received official orders to cast off on May ninth. We must get to work."

"We still have that time to prepare, Majesty," Frances assured them as panic lit up the two ministers' eyes. " 'Tis said the weather is foul for May. With some one hundred

ships in Spain's main force, they'll have trouble weathering
the journey up the coast."

"Merely a breath before the storm breaks," the queen muttered. She seated herself with a swish of her severe black
gown, pulled her ink pot toward her, and readied a quill.
"Lord Howard will lead the fleet on board the eight hundred-
ton *Ark Royal.* Raleigh says 'tis the swiftest ship he ever
designed. We have forty-two guns aboard the *Revenge.* But
we'll need every minute to assemble munitions and food.
Burghley, how long will that take?"

"A fortnight. Mayhap a bit longer," the minister ventured.
"That's what it took last fall. We have ample men from each
county in the local militias, every one of them prepared to
fight on behalf of the Crown."

"But, young mistress," Walsingham interrupted, speaking
to Frances, "are you sure 'tis not a false alert? They were to
set sail November last, but nothing came of that plan. We
spent a great deal of money in preparations, all for naught."

With effort, Frances defended her information. "A great
mass was said on the twenty-fifth of April in Lisbon, to bless
the standard of the expedition. 'Twas general knowledge in
Paris that the fleet's departure was imminent. That doesn't
mean they *will* sail on that specific date if weather or other
problems intervene, but be assured, they will sail eventually.
The orders are a royal command."

" 'Tis safest to assume they're on their way." Burghley
ended the argument by seating himself at the table and, like
his mistress, taking up a quill. "I'll begin the orders to the
commander at Deptford so they'll be prepared."

"Do so." The queen gave a visible shiver. The Deptford
force would protect Her Majesty's person should the Duke
of Parma's Spanish forces from the Low Countries land. By
no means was the Armada meant to undertake the invasion
alone. Forty thousand troops under Parma's command were
to cross over from the Spanish-occupied Netherlands, pro-
viding the man power to lead the attack. The Armada was
both a convoy and a means of sea attack.

More members of the Privy Council arrived. The council
chamber buzzed with hasty greetings and agitation.

"I knew the Spanish were coming," Her Majesty muttered
to Henry Stanley, the Earl of Derby, as he bowed and kissed
her hand. "I felt it in my bones, Derby. Philip wants to make

a blood bath of my kingdom, but I'll defy him. I swear I will."

"We won't permit it," Derby assured her staunchly.

"You won't permit what?" the Earl of Leicester demanded as he entered, followed by Sir Christopher Hatton.

"Robert!" The queen hurried to her favorite courtier. Despite his increasing age and growing paunch, not to mention his disgrace in wedding with Her Majesty's cousin five years back, Elizabeth let Robert Dudley enclose her protectively in his arms. "The Spanish have set sail with their Armada," she said in tortured tones. "We just received word from an infallible source."

"The devil they have!" the earl swore roundly, tightening his embrace. "I'm for the south and Lord Howard within the hour. Our fleet can match theirs with ease. We'll run circles around their stupid, lumbering galleons. Haven't I told you we have the superior force, your grace?"

"Aye, you have, Robert," sighed the queen, pulling away and hurrying back to her papers at the table. "So we'd best get it in place and be prepared to fight. Gentlemen, pray be seated. Cecil, what ready funds does the treasury have?"

Frances found herself forgotten as a barrage of business ensued. Withdrawing to a stool in a quiet corner, she listened to the work progress. After a few minutes, the queen cast her a glance and informed the council that Mistress Frances Morley would work with the royal Master Falconer and the Lord Admiral to organize communications on the southern coast, using messenger birds. That said, the queen signaled for Frances to leave.

Work with Charles? No, by God! Her head spinning with fatigue, Frances groped her way to the door and quit the chamber. The heavy oak panel swung shut behind her, and she leaned against it, staring at the floor, immobilized. The queen hadn't mentioned Charles earlier. Now she wouldn't be quit of him, as she'd intended. Bewildered by this abrupt change of events, she pressed a hand to the bruised side of her face and tried to think what to do next.

"So, you wheedled Her Majesty into giving you a part," an audacious voice accused.

Lifting her tired gaze, Frances beheld Charles, lounging on the stairs at the end of the corridor. Other than sporting soiled, unpressed clothing, he looked none the worse for the crossing that had changed her into a bedraggled waif. And he seemed to know exactly what had taken place in the council chamber.

Unfolding his long legs, he sauntered down to stand before her. His hands settled on her shoulders, weighing her down, too possessive by half. As he inspected her face and person closely, his gaze intimate, she felt her flesh grow hot.

"Frank, you look done in," he observed.

He drew her toward him to cradle her against his chest, but she pushed back and lost her temper entirely. "You didn't tell me you were in command of the messenger birds for Her Majesty," she cried. "And how did you know I would ask to work with them, too?"

"I *am* the queen's master of birds. Who did you imagine would command?" He frowned at her for the first time, suggesting she had indeed angered him by requesting a place in the venture. "As for your part, one of Her Majesty's ladies brought me word."

"I knew it. They were listening at the keyhole, for they came mighty fast when Her Majesty called. They had no right to repeat what we said." She smoldered with resentment, debating over which angered her more—Charles or the rattle-tongued women.

"All the queen's ladies do things for me." His brown eyes were like twin paths, beckoning her to enter a forest and lose herself entirely.

"I can just imagine what those things are," she said, her taunt acerbic. The image of Charles lovemaking with another women—or an entire bevy of women, one after another—caused her queasy stomach to churn with jealousy. What was wrong with her? She meant to refuse his offer of marriage, yet something within her rebelled at the thought of leaving him to other women. And how would she work with the messenger birds and still avoid Charles? He put her in an impossible position. Clasping both arms across her middle, she squeezed her eyes closed. "Oh no, I think I'm going to be—"

"Don't you dare be sick again." Without a by-your-leave, he swept her into his arms. "Enough, madam baroness. You've proved your stamina, dragging yourself here after that voyage, but you're going to bed now. You are indeed," he chastised over her protest. "My bed. Oh, never fear. I'll let you sleep for now. But you are going. Did the queen ask you to remain? Of course not. Then you're coming with me. No more arguments, wife." He favored her with a stern look.

"I'm not your wife yet," she rebelled.

"We'll talk about that later," he said firmly, heading for the door. "Just now, I'm getting you home."

"I suppose the queen's ladies also told you when I would be dismissed from the council chamber."

"I can't help it if they like me."

"You could," she muttered angrily into his shirt front as he bore her away. He was too possessive, he had to be first in everything, and a hundred women wanted him. It was entirely too much to be borne.

Chapter 25

Frances opened her eyes to golden sunlight streaming through a many-paned window near her bed, setting the sapphire bed curtains aglow. Still groggy with sleep, she parted the translucent silk fabric and was delighted to behold Oriana on a tall perch. Upon seeing her mistress stir, the bird bobbed her head and chuckled with pleasure. *'Tis about time you awoke and paid attention to me, slugabed,* she seemed to say.

Frances smiled and stroked the bird's back in greeting as she struggled to remember where she was and why. The escape from the Spaniards, the exhausting ride to Le Havre, the tumultuous Channel crossing—all reeled through her head in slow motion until she remembered.

She was in Charles's bed. And he would be angry once he found out about the papers she had smuggled to the queen.

Both ideas alarmed her. If she remained here, he might catch her in this state of partial undress. He would play on her needs with penetrating insistence until she gave him her body and her promise to wed. She had best rise and dress.

"I was beginning to wonder if you would sleep the day through."

She whipped around to find Charles seated at the far end of the chamber. His dark hair lay in sleek, wet wings against his head. His chin and cheeks had been pared smooth of whisker stubble, proof that he had just come from a bath and a shave. A sleek silk shirt the color of new whipped cream enclosed his torso in soft folds, molding to his muscles. With legs crossed, leaning back against his chair cushions, his head tilted as he examined her, he reeked of lazy, sexual allure.

And here she sat, in bed, wearing nothing at all but the thin night smock.

She yanked up the coverlet to her chin. "How long have

you been here?" she demanded, self-consciously pressing her bare thighs together beneath the linen sheets, denying the glow that started at her core.

"About an hour. You've slept well past the dinner hour. How do you feel?"

A note of warmth in his voice lulled her to relax her guard. If he was angry with her, he didn't show it. "Much better," she admitted, glad to avoid the subject of the messenger birds if he did. "How do I look?"

He surveyed her critically. "Your face is greatly improved. Your color is better. Your hair is as wild as ever." He grinned as she groped for her braid and found it half undone. "You could do with a good meal. Don't move. I'll serve you in bed." He rose with that languid grace of his that made her shiver beneath the coverlet. Several of his lanky strides took him to the door, where he summoned a servant.

A short while later, he nestled a tray on her lap and plumped cushions at her back.

Then he sat on the bed beside her, which further troubled her sense of propriety, what was left of it. They weren't wed, this was his sister's town house, and here she was in his personal bedchamber. In his own bed, no less!

As for the state of his temper, no matter how hard she studied him, she couldn't judge where she stood. Did he know about the papers or didn't he? With a sigh, she decided to deal with that problem later. Her stomach came first.

She attacked a bowl of steaming porridge that dripped with cream and honey. It slid down her throat like a dream, light and hot and filling. Halfway through, another bowl containing a cache of garnetlike cherries begged for her attention. Popping a fruit in her mouth, she closed her eyes as its sweet-tart flavor exploded in her mouth.

Charles watched as Frances ate. The entire time she had slept, his displeasure with her behavior had built to the bursting point. But before he told her about it, before he put an end once and for all to her wild antics, he had wanted her rested. He wanted to see her consume food and keep it down. "No one is going to steal it from you," he warned as her spoon moved more rapidly than he thought wise. "If you bolt your food, it may come back up."

She made one of those tiny moues that so infuriated him. "Did you feed Oriana?" she asked.

"I did. Fresh pigeon on my fist. Not so much that she

won't want to hunt on the morrow. She was quite greedy about eating it, too. Just like you." He watched intently as she indulged her appetite. While she feasted on the porridge, he couldn't avoid feasting his eyes on her. Midnight hair against almond-pale skin, her hands soft and fluttering as she lifted the spoon to her rosy lips. Arrayed in a spare night smock of his sister's, Frances looked decidedly virginal, white lace against delicious white flesh. A violent urge filled him, to strip back the coverlet and join her in bed. And not because he wished to help her devour breakfast. "After you've had your fill, I'll see you bathed and your hair washed," he said brusquely. "I've requested heated towels along with the hot water and lavender soap."

"You speak as if I'm your new toy." She daintily removed a cherry stone from her mouth and placed it in the bowl before fixing him with a stare. "I'm not."

Charles clenched his jaws to bite back a snarl. She was right, but the darkness of his need flared within him, over-coming reason. The thing he feared most in his life had come to fruition—he'd let a woman back into his life. Now he must fight with all his strength to control the blinding obsession she aroused.

"What news of the Spanish?" she asked as silence grew between them.

His temper smoked as she reminded him of that unwelcome subject. Any pleasure from examining her half-naked in bed vanished. Rising, he plucked a sheet of paper from the nearby table and tossed it in her lap. "You owe me an explanation for this little item, and it had better be a good one, because I'm not at all pleased."

Frances glanced at the paper. "It's a broadside. What's that to do with me?" But after examining first one side, then the other, a guilty expression crept across her face, and she grimaced. "Oh dear. Are you going to scold?"

"I'll do worse if you can't give a favorable account of yourself," he all but shouted, pushed well beyond his limit. "I travel half the length of France and all the way across the Channel, offering my very life for your safety, and what do you do? You paper the streets of London with the highly secret, official Spanish report of 'La Felicissima Armada.' It's being discussed in every shop and tavern from here to Shoreditch, and I wasn't favored with a single mention of this important secret you carried the entire way."

"I didn't print it and pass it out in the streets," Frances protested, wide-eyed. "Her Majesty must have shared it with someone who did. I had no idea that would happen. I swear."

"She had no idea," Charles said with sarcasm to Oriana. The hawk tilted her head and observed him, as if listening intently. "She carried important papers for five days without mentioning them, delivered them to the queen, and I was told nothing. I suppose you knew about them, too."

"I'm sorry." Frances cast down her gaze and folded her hands in her blanketed lap. Charles waited with anticipation for the rest of her apology. "But I did what I thought was right," she finished serenely. "I didn't think you should know."

"What?" he exploded, unable to believe his ears. "Haven't I earned your confidence yet? Do I have to be sliced into little pieces for your sake before you'll tell me a blessed thing you're doing? What would have been the harm, had I known?"

"The harm," she replied, with an infuriating primness that drove him halfway to murder, "would have come when you confiscated my equipment bag and guarded it with such care, the Spaniards would have known straightaway it contained something of value. But since *I* carried it about with me, they assumed it was full of fripperies. I did have a few, just in case they checked. My comb and handkerchief, as I told you. I'm only a woman, after all."

That is eminently apparent, he thought, as his entire body tensed with awareness of her, compounded by his fury. The shape of her thighs beneath the light coverlet roused his response the way sight of prey drew a hawk. *Blast,* but Frances always did this to him. First she lit a flame in him until he burned with need for her body, then she provoked him until his temper flared.

"There will be no more of your antics," he ordered coldly, determined to control her before she controlled him. "You're to behave properly from now on, especially once we wed. I insist you curb your behavior or I shall have to step in."

"Proper?" Frances sat up straighter, clearly outraged by his order. "There's nothing improper about the way I behave. You're the one who's put me up in your own bedchamber, in your own bed. That's improper, if anything is."

"You're not understanding me on purpose." He glowered at her, wondering how long he could avoid going mad. At this rate, he might as well go on down to Bedlam and ask for a room. "I mean you're to stop taking dangerous risks. You've fulfilled your uncle's wishes. You have no further excuse."

"Ah, Charles, there you are." His tirade was interrupted as the door swung open and his sister Rozalinde rustled in. She glanced at him coolly, clearly chiding him for being alone with an unwed female guest in his own bedchamber. She'd probably heard them quarreling as well.

With her heavy crown of chestnut brown braids and her pure, noble face, his sister might look fresh and lovely, Charles thought in irritation, but appearances were deceiving. Despite being five and thirty years old, with three children borne, she still took on tasks that belonged to men. With acute displeasure, he realized she and Frances were much alike. He hadn't considered that until now.

"Welcome, Mistress Frances. We are delighted to have you as our guest." Rozalinde moved around the chamber in a whirlwind of energy, straightening draperies and picking up dropped linens. "I looked in on you earlier, but thought it best to let you sleep, since—Troth!" She broke off in mid-sentence as she got a good look at Frances, her welcoming expression changing to one of horror. "My dear Frances, whatever happened to your face?"

"Courtesy of our Spanish friends, I fear," Charles told her with a snort of derision for his enemies. "We both had some unpleasant interviews with them. But that particular party won't trouble us again. We're quit of them for good and all."

"Charles! How terrible." Rozalinde embraced him. "I had no idea this journey would be dangerous to you. Frances will want some of the same comfrey salve I gave you. 'Twill help the bruises. I'll send it up before I go to the quay. I would stay longer to see to your needs, my dear, but we have three cloth shipments due in from foreign ports."

"My sister loves her duty, running the family business," Charles quipped to Frances on a sardonic note. "Don't let her suggest she does not."

"You are well enamored of yours, so don't accuse me," Rozalinde tossed back at him. "Mistress Frances, bathwater is being heated for you even as we speak. Ask Mistress Fetiplace, my chief woman, for anything you desire. My husband, Lord Christopher, may return from court ere I do. We will all sup at seven of the clock. Now, little brother, take yourself off and let this poor girl have her bath. Don't let him torment you," she added to Frances. "He's quite good at it, I assure you. As little brothers go, he's always been the worst."

Charles rose and snagged one of Rozalinde's thick braids that drooped from the neat cornet wrapped around her head. She had dominated him when he was young, but he had since learned how to manage her. "My sweet *elder* sister," he said, emphasizing the word *elder* in a tone so sincere it was cloying, "my first greeting from you in a sennight and you are graciousness itself. My elder sister generates such a windstorm with her activity," he explained to Frances, "that she blows her own hair down."

"You wicked man," Rozalinde scolded, fumbling at the loose braid. "I'm not so elder as all that. You make me sound a hundred years old. Troth. I can't find the pin."

"You sometimes *act* a hundred years old." He turned her about, found the pin, and anchored the loose braid. "*Now* I shall leave you two to your gossip. But I must needs talk to you later, Rozalinde," he added. "And to you, too, Frances. You will kindly remember what I said."

Frances had remained as quiet as a mouse during his entire exchange with his sister, he noticed, staring at them with her thickly lashed eyes wide. Being a lone child, she probably wasn't accustomed to grown siblings and their spates. Which reminded him of the not-yet-grown boys in his charge. "You will be pleased to know that Pierre and Louis had a splendid rest," he informed her, remembering with distaste the struggle he'd had. The pair had been so excited by the elegant town house, he'd had to hold them down until exhaustion finally overcame them and they slept. "Then I had them fed, bathed, and trimmed. They're a sight cleaner than they were before."

"Troth, yes," added Rozalinde. "Charles pinned them down while Mistress Fetiplace scrubbed them. But I told them there was not to be a louse in my house, and if I found one, they were out on the street. They actually had the audacity to say they *preferred* the street, impertinent rascals. Where did you find them, Frances? I'm amazed their bellowing for mercy didn't disturb your sleep. One would think we were killing them rather than bathing them."

Charles rolled his eyes toward the ceiling as his sister launched into a detailed description of the boys' cleansing

ritual, along with his prominent role in it. Once she was well
into a story, there was no stopping her, so he quit the
chamber. But as he descended the marble staircase, his
thoughts moved to Master Dickon and Arcturus. Dearly
would he like the company of his favorite hawk and the old
man who had taught him everything about hawking, but he
dared not leave for Dorset without the queen's permission.

Just the same, he longed for Master Dickon and the chance
to discuss this overwhelming mystery—this desire for
Frances that was so intense, he broke his sacred vow to
remain unwed.

Until then, he shrouded the thought, quieting it the way
the hood did a hawk. That done, he sought out Jonathan. He
had a score to settle with him.

Chapter 26

"So, Charles, you're back."

Charles narrowed his gaze at his older brother as he paused in the midst of a fencing exercise. After a search, Charles had tracked him to London's most fashionable school of defense. The huge, covered arena echoed with the activity of men practicing in pairs with rapier and épée. "You're damn right, I'm back. No thanks to you."

Jonathan whipped the air with his rapier in a last defensive stroke, then stepped back. "Master Gilbert"—he bowed slightly to the master coaching him—"we must continue this exercise later. My brother wishes discourse."

"Say rather I wish a few rounds with you myself," Charles snapped. "I'm angry with you, Jonathan. I'm furious enough to cut out your entrails and display them in the town square."

"Dear brother, didn't you enjoy your journey? You're behaving like a spoiled brat complaining about his chores."

"It's not the chore," Charles snarled back at him. "You didn't tell me the truth about it. So humor me just this once."

"Oh, very well. A rapier for my brother, Gilbert," Jonathan called. He stopped and scrutinized Charles more closely. "One with the safety tip on it. I think he's out for my blood."

"Some of your blood would be just the thing right now," Charles muttered as he stripped off his jerkin, tossed it to an assistant, and rolled up his sleeves.

Within minutes he circled his brother, moving over the bark-covered floor, rapier at the ready, looking for the best angle of attack. He was of a height with his maddening older brother, which made them evenly matched, except that Jonathan had eight years on him. That meant Jonathan had more experience but less flexibility. Charles knew his brother's clever style with a rapier, but he, too, kept a few tricks in reserve for moments such as this. His blood heated in anticipation of the satisfaction he desired.

"What happened to your face, brother mine?" Jonathan queried as they circled.

Charles lunged suddenly, forcing Jonathan to leap back to escape his blade. "I ran into a Spaniard's fist," he drawled, putting plenty of sarcasm into the words as he recovered his stance. "*Four* Spaniards' fists, to be exact. None of them with the least compunction about beating me bloody. Why didn't you tell me, you rotting worm?" He slashed at Jonathan's lower right. Their rapiers clashed as he executed the mandritta and Jonathan parried. Both recovered and circled again.

"I suppose I should have," Jonathan conceded. "But I had hoped you would meet Mistress Frances, leave with her quickly, and all would be well. I regret things didn't turn out as I had wished, but I expect you were late."

"Understatement always was your strong suit, Jonathan." Charles jumped in again with a furious stoccata attack, enraged by his brother's accurate assessment.

Their rapiers crashed as Jonathan defended himself against the rapid, upward cuts, but his answering shrug was still nonchalant as he recovered from their clash. "Things still turned out for the best. Your sojourn with the Spanish put Mistress Morley in the perfect position to receive that recent message. The pair of you did well."

"You've spoken with Her Majesty already?"

"But of course. While you slept, young one."

"Next time, be solicitous before you send me into danger, not after." Charles attacked with a vengeance.

"If you don't like it, take me to the law," Jonathan teased, dancing out of reach.

"The law takes years. I prefer something more immediate," Charles parried, wishing to spend his anger and be done with it. "I think I'll shred that fancy shirt of yours."

Jonathan glanced down at his shirt, which was beautifully trimmed in discreet lace accents, white on white. "Margaret made this shirt for me with her own two hands. I'm rather fond of it."

"Good. Consider it forfeit." Scowling, Charles launched an all-out attack. Whipping his rapier in rapid feints and parries, he drove his brother across the arena, fighting wide and wild, unleashing his full anger. All activity ceased as men cleared the way. Some huddled to make wagers, particularly the more fashionably dressed since the school of defense was *the* place to be seen in London. When the Cavandish brothers fought, particularly Charles, the betting was high. So was the noise level in the arena as shouts rose, urging one or the other of the pair on.

By then, sweat prickled Charles's forehead, and he stretched himself farther to extend his reach. His feet danced in rapid tempo as he rose to the challenge. With a twist, he attacked Jonathan's back and caught his shirt with his rapier. Despite the protective tip, as he thrust upward, the fabric tore. With a wrench, he slashed the shirt from bow to stern. His supporters burst into a raucous cheer.

Charles drew back and waited for the flood of satisfaction. But despite his victory, nothing happened. As he stood panting, pleasure evaded him, just as it had before the match.

"Are you satisfied now?" Jonathan paused also, his chest heaving. "You've destroyed my best shirt."

"You're fortunate to be my brother," Charles said between gasps for air. "I would have destroyed more than your wardrobe." He glowered at the bark-strewn floor.

"But even that wouldn't be enough, would it?"

At his brother's well-aimed question, Charles suddenly struggled in a pit of anger, overwhelmed by its bottomless depths. If only he could blame Jonathan, no matter how unjustified that would be. But the more he tried, the harder his anger squeezed, until it reached a pressure not to be borne. "The shirt will have to do," he gritted out. For the benefit of their audience, he stalked over to Jonathan and, with studied nonchalance, lifted one of the shirt shreds for display to the crowd. "I didn't touch you or the lace. Considerate of me, wouldn't you say?"

"More than considerate," Jonathan agreed, his glance suggesting he didn't believe Charles's feigned composure for an instant. "Have I your promise not to murder me when my back is turned?"

"At least until next time you do something despicable." Unable to get enough air, Charles yanked open the throat of his shirt.

"If you didn't have such a temper—" began Jonathan.

"If you didn't treat me as if I were still eight and couldn't understand anything," Charles snapped, "I wouldn't be angry with you all the time."

"Yes, yes, point made." Jonathan signaled for Gilbert to take the rapiers.

He waved away the men crowding around to congratulate Charles and ushered him to the tiring room. There, Jonathan signaled an attendant to remove his ruined shirt. Declining aid, Charles shrugged out of his own sweat-drenched shirt. Water was poured for them each, and they lathered the musk-scented soap into rich suds to wash away their sweat.

"So do you plan to wed Frances?" Jonathan asked unexpectedly as Charles bent over his basin, eyes closed, about to rinse his face.

Charles reared up and glared at his brother. "Is that why you sent me for her?"

"No, but I would be pleased to see her settled. You're dripping. Wipe your chin." Jonathan threw him a towel.

Charles caught it and gripped it fiercely. "Damn you, Jonathan, how could you plot against me like that."

Jonathan finished his own washing and dried off, maneuvering the towel across his broad shoulders with obvious relish. He motioned the attendant to hand him a clean shirt, then sent him away for clean stockings. "I wasn't plotting. It's just that I knew it wouldn't be easy for her here. The women at court imagine she was whoring for state secrets. It disgusts me, but gossip spreads like a pestilence at court. She needs someone to protect her from their barbs."

"She needs someone to tie her down and keep her out of mischief." Charles toweled his face vigorously, seething with resentment.

"You'll be good at that."

"You forget," Charles reminded him ascerbically, "I'm not free to wed."

Jonathan pulled the shirt over his head. "If you imagine yourself still pledged to that bitch in the Caribbean, forget her. Rest assured she's wed to someone else by now."

"You don't know Inez del Calvaladosa," Charles muttered, beseiged by the remembrance of Inez's dark passions. He flicked the towel to dry his damp shoulders, wanting to flick away the unwanted memory as well. "She never forgets something she's owed."

He reached for his shirt, but as he did so, a hand fell on his shoulder. The pressure of his brother's fingers conveyed sympathy, compassion, and more. "Take one of my clean shirts," Jonathan said quietly. "Yours is soaked."

Charles fastened his gaze on the folded, pristine white garment, unwilling to meet his brother's eyes. He imagined the forgiving expression waiting for him, and a stab of self-loathing for his churlish behavior pierced his gut. It was no use laying blame on his older brother.

Yet his spirit rebelled. How could he willingly bend to the insane chain of events that threatened his peace of mind . . . even his very life?

"You can't hide from them any longer," Jonathan said, as if reading his thoughts. "Spain is coming to us this time. We have no choice but to fight." He pressed Charles's shoulder once more, offering painful sympathy.

Charles accepted the shirt with little grace and slowly drew it on, barely able to think clearly through his haze of resentment. From the morass of confused plans clouding his mind, one thought emerged, as clear as the city's church bells. "What in heaven will I do with Frances while I'm gone? Will Rozalinde keep her at Wynford House, or should I ask Margaret, instead?"

"So you are going to wed her." Jonathan plunged straight to the heart of the matter, as usual.

Charles jerked around to confront his brother. "Yes, blast it. What did you think?"

"I thought you would take her with you to Dorset, to work the messenger birds."

"She isn't going." Silently, Charles dared Jonathan to contradict his statement. "She stays here, out of trouble where she belongs."

Charles thought a smile hovered around Jonathan's mouth, but it never materialized, and his brother's next question sounded perfectly serious. "Has she agreed to stay behind while you go to fight the Armada?"

"She'll do as I bid her once she's my wife." He hated Jonathan's blatantly skeptical expression as his brother pulled on his doublet and waved the assistant forward. The man bent to fasten the long row of gilt buttons up the gold-embroidered front.

Charles shrugged into his own plain cloth jerkin and shooed away the man offering to assist. Rapidly fastening the horn buttons, he headed for the door.

"Where are you going? Shall I come?" Jonathan called after him.

"I'm going for a walk," Charles gritted. "Alone."

Charles stalked from the school of defense and into the brightly lit London street. The sun's glare stabbed at his eyes, forcing him to squint. With a grimace, he shifted his hat low over his brow and turned south toward the river, setting a fast, furious pace.

He didn't want to start again; he wanted to be left alone. But circumstances, or fate, or whatever one cared to call it, left him no choice. Once more he must face the hated Spanish to defend his country and all he held dear, despite his personal desires.

Can you really live without Frances while you're gone? his inner voice harassed him. Without mercy, he examined the question with a cold eye. He was well and truly obsessed with her after their few short days together. Too late to turn back. He couldn't give her up.

What was it that forced him to crave her, wrenching him out of numbness and back into life?

Even as he denied it, he knew. It was her maddening ability to see and feel things he'd decided to shut out of his life. And his inability gnawed at him as he advanced down the street, weaving among men and women without noticing who or what they were, hawkers, merchants, churchmen, or women marketing. He strode on blindly, knowing only that he didn't want to feel again.

Pure magic. The words Frances had breathed hovered again in his ear, as if blown by the wind to within his reach. How they tempted him, how he yearned to leap high in the air and capture the essence of those words. All because he needed her magic in his life. But to have it, he had to feel.

Otherwise, the magic she had touched him with so briefly would continue to elude him with all the cunning of the devil's own kin.

Chapter 27

She wasn't glad to be back in England, Frances reflected as she soaked in the bath after Rozalinde had left her. The kind countess had directed an obliging maid named Annie to prepare a bath for her. Now Frances sat alone in the steaming tub, clean hair bundled on her head, and soaked away her aches. How she had hoped the safety of her homeland would banish her problems, but instead, she had more.

The threat of the Armada hung over the country, inspiring some to panic, others to fierce preparation for battle, still others to gloom. Despite the danger, she burned to take on the hated enemy and drive them to their knees.

Spain had seduced her uncle's friend to turn traitor, then murdered her uncle. Spain had sent Captain Landa to abduct her, then turn her over to the Inquisition. These firsthand, ugly reasons pushed her to wish the Armada scattered and wrecked beyond repair.

But how would she work with the messenger birds *and* with Charles? They did nothing but quarrel. If she refused to wed him, would the queen deny her the work?

She prayed for an answer to her dilemma. Mayhap she should avoid the entire issue by leaving London and going to Morley. She could take Louis and Pierre with her, and together they would bring the old estate to life once more.

But then she couldn't defeat the Armada. As a solitary woman on her own, she knew Lord Admiral Howard couldn't permit her a part in battle plans.

Crushed between her choices, Frances swung from one to the other. Should she risk her future happiness and wed Charles, which would allow her to claim her rightful place with the messenger birds? Or should she flee him and return to her beloved Morley, thus losing her only chance to strike back against Spain?

She felt sure she could make a difference in stemming the

invasion. How many times had her uncle told her the lord admiral of the Spanish forces had never been to sea. Nor was he a military man. More rumors came from the Netherlands, where the Duke of Parma commanded King Philip's troops. "Parma's the man to watch," her uncle used to say, wagging his finger at her solemnly. "Mark my word."

"But he's negotiating peace with the queen's emissaries," Frances had protested. "Do you suggest that he lies?"

"I suggest that there's no love lost between Philip and Parma, his nephew," her uncle had answered. "But time will tell."

Frances's thoughts darted swiftly between these ideas. Short of ships and supplies . . . no love lost . . . Surely there were ways to play on these weaknesses so that England might win the day.

She counted the number of days a normal voyage from Spain to England took, then prayed for more foul weather. Even under the best circumstances, so large a convoy required a week to make the journey. England still had time to prepare, but not much. She must go straight to work and not let Charles distract her from her goals.

"Mistress, do you require more hot water?" Bearing a kettle, Annie peeked around the wooden screen that shielded Frances from the rest of the room.

"That would be welcome." Frances beckoned the girl forward, grateful for the attentive care of the house staff. As a heavenly cloud of steam rose, she sighed, glad to be clean again. If only her cares would float away as easily as the dirt from her skin.

"Would you care to have your back washed with her ladyship's lavender soap?" offered the girl.

"That would be marvelous." Frances leaned forward, rested her arms on the far side of the pretty brass tub, and let Annie work. She had a comfortable way about her as she rubbed a fair quantity of lavender soap on a cloth and ran it over Frances's back.

Closing her eyes, Frances drifted on the scent of lavender. The sweetness enfolded her, reminding her of verdant fields lush with growing things. How she longed to run free with Oriana in the countryside, the way they had outside Paris.

Her father and Uncle Ned had teased her about behaving like a young heathen each time she returned dirty and tousled, her hair trailing down her back in a half-loose braid, Oriana on her fist.

But they both had seemed to understand, for neither stopped her from wrapping a bit of bread and cheese in a kerchief and going out for the day. And when the hawk spread her wings and shot after her prey, Frances would fly, light-footed, across the land after her, full of love for her soaring bird and the joy of running free.

Only after several days of such release did she settle back to copying documents for her father, while he lived, and then her uncle. He, in turn, grew to depend on her loyalty. State secrets never strayed from her safekeeping, and he relied on that fact.

Frances expelled a long breath as the pleasant memories mingled with Annie's ministrations and the soapy cloth circled between her shoulder blades. Ah, that did feel good. Annie seemed to know just the right way to rub sore muscles. As the cloth slid along her arm, Frances glimpsed the hand that washed her. Strong, blunt fingers gripped the cloth, the back of them flecked with dark hairs.

"Charles!" Water splashed as she whirled around. "What are you doing?"

"Washing your back for you."

"But what happened to Annie?"

"Her arm got tired. I sent her downstairs to rest."

He was masterful, as usual, even on one knee by the tub. A ray of sun from the window gilded his face and hair, turning him angelic, though his purpose here couldn't possibly be innocent. She knew he intended to influence her decision. Beneath his calm exterior, she sensed the fierce hatred smoldering, for himself and for the Spanish, and she suspected he'd also come to drown that hatred in the frenzy of sensations they created together.

Her suspicions were confirmed by the way he inspected her, with a lazy look that set her on fire as his hand, along with the cloth, caressed her breast.

"That's not my back," she said caustically. Already he attempted to enthrall her by weaving stimulating patterns across her flesh.

"For certes, it isn't." By his grim expression, she knew he was still angry with her. And his eyes glowed, as if lit from within by a dark craving that threatened to devour her whole.

"By thunder, but I saw far too little of you in the barge."

His voice husky, he cupped her breast and studied it with avid interest. "Mmm, I want to put my mouth just here." He swept his thumb back and forth across her nipple.

Frances inhaled sharply as her flesh contracted. Excitement exploded in her middle, sending shards of pleasure spinning to her extremities. Tiny gooseflesh sprang to life across her shoulders and arms.

"I think you should leave," she managed, in agonies over her reaction to him. Heavens, how she wanted the opposite of what she asked.

"I like washing you."

"I . . . don't think you're washing anymore," she gasped as his thumb began its intricate dance again.

"I don't suppose I am."

Desire became excruciating, but fortified by her earlier thoughts, Frances refused to give in. "Charles, stop!" She flung up her arm to knock away his hand. Water flew and spotted his silk jerkin. She splashed him again, hitting him deliberately in the face. "Away, you horrid plague."

"Sweet Frank. Attack me like that again." He laughed as he dodged out of range.

At the innuendo in his tone and his hungry stare, she glanced down at herself. Without realizing it, she had risen from the water and was exposed clear to the waist. "The devil with you!" She sank back as guilty pleasure tingled through her center in the most appalling manner.

Far from obeying, he drew closer, as if encouraged by that one glimpse of so much flesh.

"I'll splash you again," she warned, inching to the far side of the tub. Any contact with him would sway her choice.

"I don't care." He leered diabolically.

"I'll soak you through. 'Twill ruin your jerkin."

He sank to one knee beside the tub and begged dramatically. "One more look. 'Tis worth any price."

" 'Tis highly improper," she argued, resisting the mad urge to rise to her feet and show him everything. Never had she felt this way before.

"So is living intimately with me for five days, which you've already done." He hooked his fingers over the edge of the tub and brought his face near hers. "So is refusing to marry me afterward."

"And that entitles you to persuade me by fell means?" She sank lower in the tub, but it wasn't big enough to shield her.

Unquestionably, he could still see a great deal. "I didn't live with you on purpose."

He sighed deeply at that and leaned over the tub. Grasping her firmly by both shoulders, he covered her lips with his.

He explored her mouth gently, brushing his lips against hers, as if testing her texture. Warm and demanding, he sent her the message: he wanted her. At his silent bidding, she straightened until she also knelt, with nothing between them except water and the brass tub.

He tasted delicious, of fresh tamarisk bark that he must have used to clean his teeth. His touch spoke of forest magic, echoed by lavender scents from the soap. Startled by the sudden introduction of his tongue to their lip play, she flinched and broke the kiss—not because she disliked it, but because she liked it all too well.

And he evidently intended to stoke the fires further, for with both hands he claimed her waist. As the master of hawks drew her to her feet, she wanted to stretch and flex her body beneath his gaze. She felt sleek and dripping, like a bird from its bath. His look told her she was eminently ready to be devoured.

His expression beckoned, inviting her to devour in turn. His eyes were the color of forest paths, shadowed brown and deepening into mysterious, intriguing thoughts. Yet the painful darkness in the heart of that forest discouraged her. If only she could drive it away.

"You know what must happen next, don't you, my fledgling." He ran his hands over her naked hips and breasts and belly, as if he couldn't get enough of her.

"What?" she asked, breathless.

"We will wed two days hence. On the morrow, you must choose your wedding gown."

She frowned. "If I agree to wed you, will you let me lie alone in my bed?"

He looked appalled, as if she'd proposed he commit highway robbery. "You've no wish to lie alone. Nor have I. You want me to pleasure you, as I'm going to do right now." He bent forward to lend his words emphasis. "And then again tonight, and again on the morrow, and again after that." He claimed her lips once more.

Frances leaned into the kiss and imagined how it would be to live in harmony with this man. Was such a thing possible?

Her body wanted it. She felt ripe and ready, like the full bud of grain about to burst under the golden eye of the sun.

But her mind didn't believe it. In harmony with Charles? That was a grand jest. As it was, he rushed her, demanding they wed in only two days.

Wed in two days! Old memories leaped inside her, sparking old fears. Once Antoine had promised marriage, then taken her to bed. Two months later, in an incense-scented church she had stood, a bride lacking a bridegroom, waiting for someone who never came.

Never again will I give myself to a man.

For three years, she had said this nightly, a litany like a prayer.

It brought reaction faster than reason. She pushed Charles away in sudden panic. Unbalanced by her own thrust, she stumbled backward and fell.

Everything blurred. A burst of pain erupted in her right shoulder as she crashed into the screen. It toppled with an ungodly clatter, and she fell clean out of the tub. She stared, stunned, at a skinned, stinging elbow and wondered why Charles wasn't laughing. She must look foolish, lying naked on the screen.

She searched for him and, with horror, discovered him sitting on the floor, his legs splayed as he clutched his head. He looked more stunned than she felt.

"Oh, no!" She crawled over to him on hands and knees, afraid to trust her legs yet. The screen's end panel, set at an angle, must have clouted him when it fell.

He muttered angrily, feeling his crown for damage. "Is something like this going to happen to me whenever I want you in bed? First the Spanish beat me bloody. Then I'm attacked by a screen. Or did you make it do that?" He looked at her with suspicion.

"Charles, I'm sorry." She stretched out a quaking hand. "Let me look. Did it hit your old wound?"

"I can't tell where the old one ends and the new one starts."

He appeared confused, which worried Frances. Rising carefully, she grabbed a clean smock from the foot of the bed, pulled it on and started for the washbasin. "Let me get you a drink of water. 'Twill revive you, I'm sure."

"I believe I've had enough water for one day. And don't you dare say you warned me." He lurched to his feet, staggered, then righted himself and stood, supporting his head in one palm. "I am going to lie down now. In another chamber. You're to decide what you want for the wedding while I rest. And no arguments."

"Wedding? What wedding?" she asked innocently, hoping the knock on the head might have driven the idea from his mind.

"Your wedding to me, my shrewsome."

"Charles, earlier you said you would do anything for a look at me." His reproachful stare didn't daunt her. "You said it was worth any price."

"I got the look, and I believe I just paid the price for it. Now I want more than a look."

Frances's mouth dried like the sands of the desert as he studied her smock-clad body. "Are you sure you're capable just now?" she asked quickly, hoping he was not.

"I might not even be alive if you keep getting me knocked in the head. But when I get over this one, just you wait. Only two more days."

His veiled threat brimmed with suppressed passion, like an overful cup, awash with rich, intoxicating wine, but she quelled her response. "I'll wait," she promised, glad of the reprieve.

Still holding his head, he gave her a tight, pained smile. "And before I forget, tomorrow night the queen commands us to her revel. We're required to appear."

The last thing she wanted was to appear at court where nobles and courtiers would gape at her, where all Charles's women would stare. "But I have nothing to wear to a court event," she protested, horrified by the prospect.

"Rozalinde will see you properly gowned. When Her Majesty decrees, you obey. She intends to announce our betrothal then."

"But why?" This news astounded her. How had the queen suddenly become involved in their marriage? And to tell an entire room of strangers. Frances cringed at the thought.

"In case you didn't realize, Her Majesty wishes to honor you by giving you a baron in return for your loyal work."

Hadn't their marriage been Charles's idea alone? The thought leaped, unbidden, into Frances's mind, along with a great gush of disappointment. "She chose you for my bride-groom? But why—"

"I can't take any more just now, Frances." He waved his free hand to silence her arguments. "My head hurts like the very devil."

An excited squeal burst from the doorway. There stood two lads Frances hardly recognized, they were so clean and well garbed.

"Frank," cried one, "you're better, God rot my soul!"

"Don't we look the coxcombs!" the other shouted at the same time.

The pair pelted into the chamber and fell into her arms, laughing and hugging her. Frances hugged Pierre and Louis in return. How could she fail to recognize her boys for an instant?

"Yes, I see that your hair has been cut." She smiled and smoothed Pierre's dark locks. "It well becomes you. And Louis, you look manly in that jerkin, so don't complain 'tis stiff. And look at your netherstocks. No holes or sags." She admired and cajoled, flattered and ordered them, enjoying the sight of her boys tricked out in clean, honest garb. She almost didn't notice when the door bumped shut.

Then she remembered Charles and looked up. He had slipped out.

A stab of fear pierced her heart, but reason reminded her to be stalwart. He had asked her to wed before the queen decreed it. Partially because they'd been too intimate, but another reason must exist as well.

Pure magic . . . the swift beat of wings whispered in her mind, like the glimmer of jewels in the night sky. Their only salvation might lie in that magic. He evoked it in her. Could she possibly learn to conjure it in him?

It seemed entirely too much to hope for. Mayhap she grasped at straws as they scattered on the wind. Mayhap continued knocks on his head would have better effect.

As she dressed in a clean kirtle skirt and bodice supplied by the countess, then sat down to cakes and ale with the boys, she took comfort in them.

Pierre's little face looked younger and more innocent with his dark hair cut straight across his forehead to reveal his gypsy dark eyes. Eagerly, he downed the cakes as fast as he could chew, yet he clearly curbed his sloppier impulses for her sake. The napkin she had spread on his lap stayed in place. Once he would have shucked the linen aside without a thought.

As for Louis, he looked older rather than younger, now that his thick, nut brown hair was shorn to reveal his brow. His lanky legs had lengthened in the last year, defying her efforts to keep him in netherstocks. Now, in properly fitting, fully matching clothing, he seemed to her all that might be expected of a young gentleman, hale and healthy, saving his best smiles for her.

If she could change the lives of two lads from the gutter, might she not be as successful with Charles?

She would take the risk, for she loved him. As surely as she loved her lads, she admitted at last, she loved Charles Cavandish.

With a hard swallow, she fought past the lump in her throat and faced the inevitable. She had fallen in love with him that day on the marsh, and had loved him ever since.

Chapter 28

"I don't want to go to the queen's revel, and I refuse to wear that monstrous thing."

Charles winced as Frances rejected the Spanish farthingale before her and turned a defiant gaze his way. After being hit by the screen yesterday, after lusting after another taste of Frances's magic but not getting it, he burned with the extremes of his desire.

But instead of having the chance to assuage his dark hunger on her forgiving body, he had to engage in mental wrestling instead. He had brought Frances to his sister's silk-hung tiring chamber, thinking she would enjoy selecting some finery for the revel. As usual, his wild bird refused to behave like her domesticated counterparts, claiming instead to scorn the things other women loved.

Damn it, she'd been permitted to run wild far too long. Although he'd traded everything for the right to tame her in bed, he had hoped to avoid forcing her to conform to social requirements. The last thing he wanted was another quarrel.

He shifted his gaze away from Frances and her pouts to the whalebone and tape structure before them. It did look ridiculous, unwieldy, and heavy, but she had to dress properly for the queen's court revel. Every important noble and official in London would attend, their nerves tuned to fever pitch as the English fleet and the entire nation armed for battle. Despite news earlier today that the Spanish Armada hadn't even left Lisbon, it would eventually. It was only a matter of time.

Charles considered the reprieve no more than temporary. The feather-brained might feast and frolic, but he saw work to be done. And one task was to get Frances through this revel. He didn't want her torn to pieces by the court gossip-mongers. They could be heartlessly cruel to anyone they considered odd.

"All the court ladies wear Spanish farthingales," he explained in the most reasonable tone he could muster. "They consider the new shape a beautiful style."

" 'Tis just like the Spanish to invent such a thing. It's a torture to women, not a delight."

"You must wear one to be accepted and fit in."

She mantled fiercely at his words, like a bird crouching over its kill, threatening all who approached. "Then I'll never fit in," she snapped, showing him her talons as well. "If they're all stupid sheep, following a leader and failing to use their own wits, I don't want to be accepted by them. If you want a woman who is, wed one of your bevy of devoted female followers. You've tried out all their beds. You've only to choose the one you liked best."

Charles rolled his eyes heavenward and all but cursed aloud. So she had heard about his former bedding practices. He'd wondered how much she knew. But he hadn't touched another woman since their return. He'd scarcely had a chance to touch Frances the way he'd wanted to, except for that moment in the tub earlier with its disastrous results.

His head still throbbed. His temper throbbed also, combined with his desire, building to a painful pressure.

He didn't want a wife who continually questioned and refused to obey. He refused to cajole and cozen her every time he required something and she disagreed.

Damn it, they probably weren't suited, but he refused to break off with her. For one thing, it would cause complications with the queen, who expected him to take Frances off her hands. But most of all, he would lose his only chance to rc-create that astonishing moment with Frances in the barge. He craved her pure magic at any cost, as he'd already proved, asking her to wed after the briefest taste of her charms.

What folly had he committed?

With sinking spirits, Charles saw she appeared not the least inclined to respond to his need. Yet catastrophe would follow if she waited too long. He had unending patience with war strategy, but his endurance with Frances ran short all too fast.

Adjusting his trunk hose, he gripped his temper firmly and counseled himself to remain calm. That's what Master Dickon would advise him. "You're prone to exaggeration," the old master often said. "Rule your passions. Don't let them rule you."

The words of St. Augustine's abbot sprang into his mind as well. Frances differed from other women. She would resist eating from his hand, choosing instead to fly free, seeking acceptance her own way.

"You choose what you'll wear tonight," he said gruffly, gesturing to the bright silks and velvets strewn around the chamber and peeping from trunks and clothes presses. "I won't say a word. Take what pleases you and leave what does not. Attire yourself in any way you wish."

Her expression was skeptical as she lifted a velvet bodice. So she didn't trust him. Wild birds continually bated off the fist when first caught, stubbornly refusing to believe their new masters meant them well.

"You're sure?" she quizzed him, as stubborn as he'd predicted. "You won't insist on that monstrosity? Nor one of those iron bodices that can crush your ribs?"

"I doubt my sister even owns one of those, and I insist on nothing." He held up both hands in surrender. "You can go to the revel stark naked if it pleases you, though I wouldn't advise it. The men would plague you all night."

"Very well." She stood up and dismissed him with a flick of her hand. "Leave me and I will decide."

It infuriated him to be sent off like a child whose opinion counted for nothing. To show his mastery, he caught her around her soft waist and sought her lips. She remained stiff-armed and unresponsive as he kissed her, which infuriated him even more.

Hot with vexation, he headed outside, grabbed a spade, and shoveled bird-soiled sand from his brother-in-law's mews until sweat ran down his face and soaked his shirt. Finished, he sank onto a stool and complained aloud. Ordinarily, he would talk his problems over with Master Dickon and Arcturus. Lacking them, he addressed the earl's oldest peregrine, a majestic bird that sat its perch, both eyes closed. But Charles knew from the way it shifted its feet and scratched an occasional louse that it wasn't asleep.

"Irritating female," he said to the falcon. "She's had little money for finery over the years. So thinking women craved such things, I arranged to deck her out in silks. And what happens? I offer enjoyment, but she refuses to enjoy. She tells me women who like such things are sheep."

The bird opened one eye and gazed solemnly at him without blinking, as if questioning his story. "Oh, very well,

she didn't say they were sheep for liking the finery," he
admitted. "She said the farthingale was stupid, and any
woman who thought so but wore it anyway was a sheep." He
stroked the bird's sleek back and decided the clothing was
the least of his worries. He was fortunate Frances had agreed
to attend the revel at all. If she chose to wear her smock and
nothing more, at least she would be there.

What troubled him was how she would fare in polite company. What outlandish thing might she say or do, especially
if the gossips proved unkind?

"My lord, I am sorry to disturb you, but we require your
assistance at the Whitehall mews," a voice interrupted.

Charles turned and recognized his royal assistant falconer.
"Robert, I didn't hear you come in. What's wrong?"

"The queen's favorite falcon has had an accident. He
requires your care."

Charles leaped up, ordered a horse saddled, and left for
Whitehall before remembering to leave a message with
Frances. No matter, he thought as he rode. He would be back
in time to escort her to the revel. She need not even know
he'd been gone.

But as he traveled west toward the palace, a refrain repeated
over and over in his head. Irritating though Frances was, he
didn't deserve her. He was the one who carried a black rock of
despair inside him. He was the one who had once behaved like
a fool at a crucial moment and could well do so again, would
definitely do so if he allowed the intelligence-robbing idiocy
called *love* to claim him and rule his mind.

He refused to give in to it. Never again would he permit
weak, womanish feelings to transform him into a powerless
bumbler. He would have Frances, but he refused to succumb
to love.

"Baron Milborne, you're late," Frances greeted him caustically some hours later when he finally returned to the town
house. "Now that you're with your birds again, will it be like
this all the time?" Arms crossed, slippered foot tapping, she
regarded him from the superior position of several steps up
the foyer stairs.

He absorbed her words with barely contained anger as he
brushed past her on the way to his room. Her displeasure
might be justified, but hardly welcome. He'd forgotten the
revel entirely once he'd become engrossed in his work.

Robert had returned from supper, but even then he hadn't remembered until his assistant began chattering about the fine folk gathering in Her Majesty's banqueting chamber. Horrors and hellions, he'd hurried back to Wynford House, expecting to find a disgruntled Frances.

She was all that and more. Despite her silence as she followed him into his chamber, he could tell.

" 'Tis bad enough I have to go to this foolish thing," she railed once the door closed, "but now we'll walk in late and everyone will stare at us. And I hate being stared at. I hate it worse than having to put on these fripperies. I hate it worse than . . . than wearing shoes in summer instead of running barefoot in the fields."

Her comparison tempted him to smile, though he didn't. No use getting her more upset than she was. "But you did enjoy playing with your fripperies, didn't you?" he placated, eyeing her low-cut neckline. He could enjoy playing with them, too, given a chance.

"Not as much as you enjoyed playing with your birds."

The dark shadow of his need for her gripped him with sudden, unexpected strength. She had no idea what she was talking about if she thought he preferred his birds to her, no inkling that he burned for another taste of her warmth. "I had to go," he growled. "A broken feather can't wait."

At the smallest mention of a bird's distress, her face transformed from wrath to concern. "Oh, a broken feather is very bad. Which one was it?"

"A right primary on the queen's favorite falcon. I mended it, but it took some doing."

"Thank the bright heavens for your skill with thread and needle. There's nothing worse than a broken primary. Well, the earl and your sister went ahead to the revel. They sent the coach back for us, but I wouldn't mind staying here."

She looked so hopeful, he would have liked to oblige her. But he didn't dare ignore the queen's command and fail to appear. Being late was bad enough. Besides, Frances was garbed appropriately at last, so he wasn't about to excuse her. He looked closer, taking in her new attire. Like a slow sunrise, her beauty dawned on him. She looked as radiant as the spring. Clasping both hands behind his back, he strolled a full turn around her.

She endured the inspection with little grace. "Well, say something." She glared at him over her shoulder as he paused behind her. "Do I look a fright? Fit for mucking out the mews or carting ash?"

"Hmm." He forced her to endure the suspense of his silent judgment, enjoying every minute. Even more, he enjoyed feasting his eyes on her. She had chosen a rare mix of the conventional and the exotic, subtly blended to produce a highly provocative vision to drive men mad.

He paced around her and paused, this time with arms crossed at his chest and head cocked, as if he couldn't make up his mind whether she would do or no. As she turned and swayed, following his perusal, she looked first anxious, then irritated, then anxious again. He would make her wait for his opinion.

He also had a fleeting glimpse of the delectable forest nymph he'd first met in Dorset. She had chosen a forest green kirtle skirt, not a hard emerald color, but a soft, rustling silk, muted and inviting like the woods. The full skirt frothed and whispered as she moved. Charles suspected she wore a bum-roll instead of the scorned farthingale under her many petticoats. The padded bolster tied around the hips supported the layers, forming a pleasing, bell-like shape. Glimpses of silk underskirts peeked out like undergrowth from beneath woodland trees, offering artful glimpses of silk-embroidered blue gillyflowers and gentian gold. How he burned to rent the green protective covering and possess the sweet reward of her fairy-soft thighs.

Steady now, he cautioned himself, feeling his loins tighten. He didn't have time for seduction just now. He crossed his arms over his chest as he returned to his original position and met her face-to-face.

For a kirtle bodice, she wore soft shorn velvet of a green so deep it reminded him of ancient oak leaves gilded with gold embroidery. The shining thread glittered in the light, emphasizing the magical beauty of her form. The bodice molded to her as tightly as a knit silk stocking to the hills and valleys of her breasts and waist. How he would like to travel that land with his hands. Her neckline further invited such a journey, revealing her creamy half-moons of breasts.

After that, he tried to admire the sleeves she had chosen, all green and gold with red ribbons and white spangled gauze foaming from the cuts. But his gaze wended back to the twin moons of her breasts. How he wished they would rise for him tonight.

"Pray look at my hair," she demanded. "You insisted I have it braided. Does it meet your strict standards, lord baron, sir?"

The richness of her ebony hair drew his attention like a lodestone drew a compass point. Someone, probably Annie, had twined her braids with gold satin ribbons embellished with sparkles, then wound them around and around her head. The rich mass gleamed in the candlelight as she moved. Against her forehead lay a circlet of gold adorned with a single emerald that matched her eyes. And tucked in the circlet was a crowning touch fit for a fairy queen—two snow-white heron plumes.

"A woman's clothing looks best when it heightens the man's desire to remove it," he pronounced, and was satisfied to see her mouth curve into a smile. Only then did he realize she had painted her lips with a shining gloss. No wonder their rosy plumpness enticed him beyond endurance.

His trunk hose suddenly felt too tight, pinching him in a critical spot. "I have to wash and change. Why don't you have the coach brought around," he said hoarsely, knowing he must be rid of her before he ravished her on the spot. "I'll be down anon."

"Does that imply I'm acceptable?"

"You're unusual." He poured water into the washbasin and motioned for her to go. "The gallants will wheedle you into alcoves and behind staircases to beg for kisses. Some won't bother to beg first, so have a care."

"Only the gallants?"

She pursed her sleek lips, and his trunk hose pinched him worse than ever. He cursed the tight, diminutive style of the damn things.

"Get along with you," he growled. "We're late enough as it is."

With a last moue, she flounced from the room.

Alone in his chamber, his arousal subdued as he lathered soap and rinsed, then dried and shrugged into clean clothes. But desire seized him again as he handed Frances into the coach. Her sly, sidelong glances were knowing, as if she understood all about his suffering. She teased him on purpose and enjoyed the game, though how could he begrudge her the pleasure. Her days of gay, girlish flirtation had clearly been too few.

At the same time, he had to tighten every muscle to hold

his control. He had best ensure she didn't take this too far. "Frances, we are under threat of an invasion from beyond our borders," he warned as the coach rolled down the drive of Wynford House and turned into the Strand. "Men are ready to fight on the least provocation. Women are testy. Tongues will wag."

Her eyes turned as cold as the gem on her brow. "You don't believe I'll behave."

Charles wanted to kick himself for a dullard. Of course she immediately perceived what he had only half admitted— that he didn't trust her in company, though mayhap for good reason. If she refused to dress like the others, she probably wouldn't behave like them either. "I just don't want you hurt," he explained. "Pay no heed to anything you hear. Some people use gaiety to dispel fear. Others use gossip. Our kingdom will be under a full-scale attack by the Spanish in a matter of days. No one knows how 'twill end, and one wrong word or action can make tempers flare."

"The gossips will find me fair game. Is that what you mean?"

"The men will admire you," he hedged.

"The queen approved of me when we met."

"Of course she did. You've performed a valuable service to her and the country. But the reigning beauties won't feel the same."

"I won't challenge them," she pouted. "You said I was too 'unusual.' Wasn't that your word?"

She was unusual, and more. And she would challenge them with her mere presence, because he'd chosen her to wed over the rest. "Just stop your ears and refuse to listen," he counseled, pushing back into a corner where he could brood. Despite her difference—no, because of it—she exuded an aura that would draw men like hawks to fair game. The women would hate her for it, and she didn't need to be wounded further. She wasn't a virgin, yet she retained a purity of spirit that he didn't want tainted. Evidence of that purity shone in her eyes as the light from their coach's torches played across her face and her dark, beribboned hair, heightening the beauty and mystery of her appeal.

No, he thought, he had done his best to protect her from the Spanish, and would be forced to do so again, but he couldn't protect her from everything. Sharp barbs surely awaited her at court.

Chapter 29

Frances repeated to herself Charles's advice as she stood in an alcove of the queen's grand banqueting chamber, waiting for him to return later that evening. It hadn't seemed important at the time he gave it, but now she understood exactly what he'd meant. If only he would bring the cooling cup of malmsey he'd gone to fetch, but she could no longer see him in the press of people thronging the room. She was alone at the queen's revel, at the mercy of the gossiping wolves.

A pair of ladies squeezed by her on their way to the refreshment table. Although their huge silk skirts rudely brushed against Frances, they offered no apologies. Their veiled glances at her dripped with venom as they passed.

A strong desire to bare her talons and attack seized Frances, but she stifled her anger and confined herself to a deadly glare aimed at their retreating backs. Haughty bitches, she'd been introduced to them earlier in the queen's presence, and they had greeted her cordially. Now, given the choice in private, they deliberately cut her.

She squeezed her handkerchief spasmodically into a ball and wished to be well away from this foolish revel. Her dislike for closed spaces stuffed with too many people preyed on her nerves. That was bad enough. It was worse to discover that the few dances she knew were performed differently here in England. Worse still, her head ached from the dazzle of lights, rich food, and her initial, majestic greeting from the queen.

But the epitome of torture had come when the queen called for attention. The music had halted, the chamber had stilled, and every eye had fixed on her as Her Majesty announced Frances's pending marriage to Charles. A pillar of ice—that was how she had felt, struck through to the heart by her reception from these cold English. With fervor, she had prayed to melt so she could drip between the cracks in the floor and disappear.

Frances edged deeper into the alcove and wished the window draperies would swallow her entirely, even as she appreciated the chamber's gilded ceiling and white-painted plaster ornamenting. Given other circumstances, the atmosphere could have been pleasant. Festoons of branches ladened with thick green foliage ornamented the room in celebration of May. Huge urns of flowers released their fresh scents. Joyous music and the excited ripple of voices covered what really lurked beneath the surface—envy, suspicion, and jealousy.

In contrast to the women's disdain, the men bombarded her with attention. As Charles predicted, they flocked to her like wasps to jam.

"Mademoiselle Morley, may I partner you in the couranto?" inquired a youth in a pea green doublet with monstrous gold buttons.

"I thank you, but I do not dance the couranto." Frances adopted a tone of finality. "Nor the galliard, nor the pavane," she added as he opened his fleshy lips to ask another question. "In short, I do not dance."

"Ah, then we shall discourse." He proceeded to talk until her head ached more than ever, the wisp of his first beard waggling so, she yearned to yank it and run.

Then she realized that as he talked, he peeped down her bodice front as if he were on grand tour and she was the scenery. *Pharaoh's foot,* she cursed. In France, the men never did such things, though in France, she admitted, they didn't have to. At court, men didn't confine themselves to mere glimpses of half-naked flesh. They plucked the women they liked from public places, took them somewhere private—even semiprivate would do—and had them. There was no comparison, she supposed.

With a sigh, she wished again for Charles. Where had he gone?

She rose on tiptoe and strained to see over the crowd, hoping to catch a glimpse of him. Why did he not come back?

Without warning, the youth grabbed her by the waist. As she stumbled off balance, he yanked her behind the draperies, pulled her close, and gazed at her with amorous calf eyes. His mouth descended toward hers.

Frances snapped her head to one side and gave him a mouthful of hair. Then she wiggled away and kicked him squarely in the shin.

His shout of pain throbbed in her head as she bolted from behind the draperies and barrelled into a distinguished-looking, older gentleman smoking a tobacco pipe.

"Mistress Morley, is aught amiss?" He steadied her by the arm, removed the pipe from his mouth, and studied her in some surprise.

Frances realized one of her braids hung askew from her tangle with the youngster. "Nay, but my thanks for asking." Self-consciously she repinned the braid. "I'm simply not accustomed to such large events and so many people." Her outrage at the youth's pawing calmed as the gentleman released her and tucked the pipe back in his mouth.

"Isn't this at all like the French court?" he inquired politely. "You must have gone there, your father and uncle being in the ambassador's train."

Frances shivered as she remembered the sinister aura of King Henri's court the few times she attended with her uncle. "It's not the least similar, at least I hope not. People died so unexpectedly while visiting at the French court."

"People were poisoned?" He removed his pipe and blew a stream of fragrant gray smoke that circled above his head like a question mark.

"No one could swear to the cause, but they did die."

"Well, well, then England is different. Forward young men and gossip have their bite, but they won't kill you, I suppose."

Although he spoke without a smile, she caught a sympathetic twinkle in his eye and realized he knew exactly what was amiss. She might be able to like this gentleman above the others. It was on the tip of her tongue to ask his name when a snippet of the gossip Charles had cautioned her to ignore drifted to her ears. And despite his warning, she listened. Some sick fascination made her do it. The pair of women who had brushed by her so disdainfully stood beyond the drapery, chattering like magpies. Did they know she could hear?

Within minutes, she realized they did. What she heard made her blood boil and her heart pound so hard, a red haze swam before her eyes.

Swept by the heat of foul humors, she excused herself to

her new friend, gathered her skirts, and stalked toward the women. Blast and beshrew them both.

"Lord Milburne, sir, Her Majesty is asking for you. I . . . You'd best . . . that is, she requires you, straight." A page bobbed hastily before Charles where he conversed with Jane Manners about her merlin. The tiny bird on his fist seemed in health to him. Not the least ailing, though Jane had lured him to her distant chamber, claiming it refused to eat. The lad, on the other hand, looked stricken and required attention right away.

"Here you are, Jane. There's naught wrong with young Pippa," he said as he urged the bird from his fist to hers.

"Can you not stay?" begged Jane, holding her arm at an awkward angle, as if the bird smelled bad. She hadn't wanted one to begin with, Charles speculated. She'd merely wanted an excuse to summon him for assistance. Repeatedly.

"I regret I cannot when the queen bids me to her presence," he explained. With a bow, he quit the chamber behind the lad.

"What's amiss?" he asked the lad as they crossed the courtyard. Then he remembered. *By thunder,* he'd left Frances standing alone in the banqueting chamber, waiting for him to bring her some wine. One mention of a sick bird and all other thoughts deserted him. Under no other circumstances could Jane have lured him away.

"I'm not sure what's amiss, my lord." The lad held a door for Charles. "I saw Mistress Morley discoursing with Lord Admiral Howard. He was actually smiling at her, and you know he doesn't often like the ladies at court, but he seemed to like her. A short time later there was a great deal of shouting, and Her Grace said you were to come straight."

That did it. Charles burst into a run. He should never have left Frances alone with the gossip-hungry wolves.

As he approached the main entry to the banqueting chamber, out stalked the queen, Frances gripped tightly by the arm. Her Majesty's glittering costume of vivid black and gold tissue lent grandeur to her fury as she thrust Frances into his arms.

"Here, Master Hawk, take your betrothed and leash her. She's utterly unruly. Whatever they taught you in France, child, I can't have cat fights in my banqueting hall."

"I begged your leave to retire, Majesty." Frances wore her

stiffest expression and refused to yield. "I told you trouble would result."

"You are required to stay until *We* bid the company god'den," snapped the queen imperiously, shaking her wigged head. She grabbed the feathered fan chained to her waist and waved it furiously in a vain attempt to cool her dangerously red face.

"I was tired, Your Majesty."

"You were not too tired to quarrel with Mistress Digby. What was it about?"

Frances stared at the floor. "She said something unspeakable about my uncle. I told her what I thought of her." Charles saw her mouth tremble. "After that, she pulled my hair, claiming it was false. It isn't, so her pulling hurt. I shouted at her to leave off, but I did nothing to her in return, I swear."

The queen crossed her arms, the click of her tapping foot audible from beneath her huge farthingale. "What exactly did Mistress Digby say about your uncle?"

Frances looked up from the floor, her eyes full of pain. "I dare not repeat it aloud, Your Majesty, but I will whisper it if you insist."

Elizabeth nodded permission. Frances stood on tiptoe and leaned across Her Majesty's wide skirts and starched ruff to speak in her ear.

As she drew back, the queen frowned so that her white face powder creased. "We heartily regret you should be subject to such wickedness, but your reply must have been equally bad if Mistress Digby then pulled your hair."

Frances studied first the queen, then Charles, uncertain how much to say. Elizabeth had calmed considerably, but Charles hadn't. His tight expression and the way he gripped his rapier, knuckles white, showed he was still furious with her, and for the first time, she was afraid. Quickly, she whispered to the queen once more.

The queen pursed her lips in displeasure. Her gaze dropped to the farthingale she wore, then fastened on Frances's skirts. Suddenly, she threw back her head and let out a startling guffaw, deep and hearty like that of her sire. "You said that to Mistress Digby?" she roared, clutching her side with one hand and leaning on Charles with the other for support. "No wonder she tried to pluck out your hair by the roots."

"I beg your pardon for causing a stir, Your Majesty." Despite the queen's amusement, Frances desperately wished to escape. "As I said, I am truly not fit for court life. I would rather get on with the work to which we agreed."

"Your Majesty, a messenger has arrived." The Earl of Leicester joined them in the corridor, a tall, solid figure, his glittering court costume a strong contrast to the grave expression on his face. Heedless of what business the queen might be transacting, he thrust forward a cloaked, booted man who fell to one knee before the queen.

"Your Majesty, I come from Plymouth and Sir Francis Drake." The fellow had obviously ridden hard to do so. Dust mottled his dark clothing, and fatigue showed in his eyes. "He bid me deliver this letter into your own hands."

Elizabeth took the letter and tore past the seal. Her brow knit with concern as she scanned the message. "Rise, friend. No need to kneel. You have Our thanks for your loyal service." She caught the attention of a guard at the door. "You there. Take this man to Walsingham. He is to be well rewarded for his pains." She waited until the pair were out of earshot. "The news is both good and bad," she said to Leicester, who had assumed a protective stance at her side. He shot a glance at Frances and Charles, as if asking whether they should hear.

Elizabeth turned to Charles. "You must leave for the coast soon. Drake brings further word of the Spanish fleet. It is indeed detained in Lisbon, but word comes out of the Netherlands that the Duke of Parma prepares forty thousand men. Only days ago he swore to my peace emissaries that he wanted accord between our countries. He lied."

Charles let out a low whistle. Leicester looked grim.

Her uncle's words flashed in Frances's memory. *Watch Parma. Watch Parma.* "Will you tell the company now, Your Majesty?" Frances asked, indicating the reveling subjects beyond the door in the banqueting chamber.

The queen considered for a minute. "Nay," she said at last, "let them feast and be merry. On the morrow, we will withdraw our commissioners from the Netherlands and prepare in earnest. Leicester, let us return and make the most of our final hours at peace. I wish to pretend nothing has happened, at least for tonight. But within a fortnight, I expect to declare war."

Elizabeth took Leicester's arm, but before she left, she

caught Frances by the hand. "Behave yourself, Mistress Frances," she warned. "Or the next woman you anger may do worse than snatch you bald." Though she sounded stern, Frances thought she glimpsed a twinkle in the queen's eye.

"I shall strive to improve," Frances promised meekly, not meaning a word of it. Anyone who dared malign her uncle deserved what Mistress Digby had gotten.

"Charles," she said softly as the queen left them, "will you show me the royal mews?"

"If you think to distract me, I refuse to allow it." His anger leaped forth all too readily. "What were you thinking, to cause such a stir? You insulted the Earl of Landsdowne's daughter, the queen's chief maid of honor."

Frances stared at him, full of regret that she couldn't be sorry. She, the untamed, unruly daughter of a nobody had hurt his reputation at court, had made a spectacle of herself so everyone would mock him for taking a foolish woman to wife. But she couldn't help it. The tears that she had refused to shed earlier when Elinor Digby first let loose her shocking insult now prickled behind her eyelids. Before she let them fall, she must find solitude. Whirling in a mass of moss green skirts and sorrow, she ran for the mews.

Chapter 30

"What did she say about your uncle? I insist you tell me!" Charles's demand resonated through the semidark of the royal mews, rousing the birds leashed to their perches. Dozens of wings rustled as the birds shifted and fluttered, disturbed by the anger and concern in their master's voice.

Too distraught to answer, Frances sank to her knees before a stool and buried her face in her hands. She hated Charles's question, but she hated herself more for her outspoken reply to Elinor Digby. Even the queen's opinion mattered less to her than his, but the queen had forgiven her. Charles, it seemed, would not. "Please," she pleaded, feeling the scalding prick of embarrassing tears. "Leave me be."

He knelt beside her on the sanded floor. His hands closed on her arms, their heat startling to her chilled skin. "The entire palace knows," he rasped. "Why do you insist on keeping secrets from me?"

For once, she hadn't meant to be secretive. And she did want him to know how horrid his English friends could be. Uncomfortably aware that tears had ruined her pearl face powder, she lifted her face to met his gaze. "She said my uncle was . . . was swiving me, that he had been for years, and my father permitted it. There. Are you satisfied? You can retract your fine offer of marriage," she added bitterly, wiping the tear tracks on her cheeks and further smearing the powder. "I refuse it anyway. I'm not fit to be wife of the queen's Master Falconer, sister-in-law to an earl, sister-in-law to the queen's chief spymaster. I can't control my wild tongue, and my family is full of scandal of the worst kind."

The pity on his face hurt worse than she'd expected. She didn't want him to think her a charity case, but it seemed mortifyingly clear that he did. "I'll take myself off to Dorset on the morrow and trouble you no further. You must forget about me and go on as you were before."

"You can't go to Dorset alone. I won't permit it." His hands tightened on her arms. "You have nowhere to stay."

"I will live at Morley Place. 'Twill not be in good order, but I'll enjoy setting it right and seeing the land planted again." She felt braver as she remembered the beloved old house and the endless beauty of green fields stretched out on all sides. "My father left me a bit of money that I can retrieve through his London lawyer. I'll survive."

"Frank, I'm telling you, you can't go there."

Something ominous in his tone sent fear spiraling through Frances's belly. The cake and spiced wine she'd taken at the revel shifted uneasily. "Why not?"

"Don't you remember what Humphrey Perkins said?"

"I don't want to talk about him," she cried, unable to bear more torment. "I'll leave for Morley on the morrow and there's an end."

"Frances, you must listen. Someone sold Morley Place. A Master Ralph Stokes lives there now."

"What?" She leaped to her feet, propelled by fury at the prospect of a stranger living in her family home. "That can't be."

Charles rose slowly to stand opposite her. "I'm sorry, Frances. I'd hoped to spare you the pain, so I didn't mention it. But now you have to know. Stokes moved in last March, saying he bought the estate from Master Sillington."

"He's a liar!" Grief almost too vast to bear filled her. "My father left the estate to me."

"Do you have the deed to the land, properly signed and witnessed? Do you have your father's will?"

"Of course I have them. In my trunk . . ." Realization halted her, and she gasped in dismay. "Sir Humphrey has my trunk. I'll wager he never shipped it back to Dorset. He said he wanted to help me, but all the while he swindled me and wished me dead." She collapsed in a heap of hysterical sobs. With Morley stripped from her, she belonged nowhere. Her last hope of refuge exploded, the pieces raining around her in useless shards. "I hope he roasts in sulphur," she wept, pounding the sand with her fist until the needling grains punished her flesh. "How could he do such a thing?"

"My poor Frank." Charles gathered Frances into his arms, cursing her ill luck. Once back in England and out of immediate harm's way, he'd counted on the rocky way turning smooth for her. Instead, fortune dealt her yet another harsh blow.

As he offered comfort, he again pondered the capriciousness of fate. After two days back in England, he positively ached for Arcturus and Master Dickon. He'd never been separated from them both this long, and in the past, nothing would have stopped him from rejoining them, neither bedmate nor duty. Yet he didn't go to them now.

He'd sent word to ask how Arcturus did, learned he was well enough, and stayed on in London to be with Frances, putting her needs and her business first. *Damn it,* he couldn't understand his compelling need to help her ... which went hand in hand with his mad urge to marry her. In fact, the temptation to take advantage of her troubles and press her to wed right now sorely tempted him. Robbed of her home, she might give in.

The fatal words refused to pass his lips. For some reason, it was suddenly important that she *want* to marry him. Otherwise, he would have to live out his life, knowing he'd coerced her. "I'll confront this person who claims to be the owner," he declared, focusing on the problem at hand. "I'll demand to see his documents. They must be forged if what you say is true."

"Of c-c-course they're forged." Her bent shoulders shook with anguish. "You saw Sir Humphrey try to destroy me. If he had his way, I would be rotting in prison even now. If he has his way, I will be yet."

"He won't touch you," Charles insisted as he recognized his other problem. He must keep her in London, out of harm's way, though he hadn't undertaken that battle with her yet. Nor would he just now. Sitting on a stool, he settled Frances on his lap. Her vulnerability communicated a need that clawed at his innermost grief. While he rocked and consoled, he pulled out his handkerchief to wipe her eyes, steadying her chin with one hand. All the while, he scrupulously avoided her gaze because the taste of her sorrow stirred old pain within him. Yet hers was far worse, being fresh and ever present in her life, while his was many years in the past.

He paused with the handkerchief in the air. Suddenly, he realized he still tortured himself for an error that was three years in the past and continuing to age. He changed nothing by doing it. While here was Frances with a wrong to be righted, awaiting his aid.

"Frank, you must stop this crying." He crushed her against his chest. "You'll make yourself ill."

"W-who cares?" She shuddered.

"I care," he whispered, so low he scarcely heard the unfamiliar words himself.

"No, you don't." She caught a ragged breath and stumbled on. "You pity me. Don't mistake that for something as intimate as caring, or for anything else. And don't ruin your life by chaining yourself to me. I'll destroy your reputation at court. You might lose your post. And the Spanish want to kill me. After they conquer England, I know what they have in mind for me. The stake."

Charles's patience slipped. "Enough of your ugly predictions."

"But I can't just forget about them."

"Nor I, but I don't intend to hang myself on tenterhooks and agonize about them every minute. Furthermore, stop telling me what to do. As if I would leave you to the Spaniards. I've asked you to wed, and if you won't agree, I'll drag you to church and force you to say yes." He winced as his noble intentions flew out the window. But the order just slipped out, confirming what he already knew—he would take Frances on any terms.

"How noble. Does that mean you're in love?" she asked sourly. Her tone implied a complete lack of confidence in the likelihood.

"Does that mean you agree?" he countered, equally determined to avoid her question, yet force her to answer his.

"It doesn't mean anything. I told you to be patient and we would see."

Charles glared at Frances. She hadn't said no, exactly, but she hadn't agreed either. Even after the queen announced their impending marriage before an assembled company, she refused to relent except on her own terms. "I hate arguing with you," he ripped out.

"Then don't do it." She returned his glare, as if unafraid of the consequences of his displeasure. "I'll answer you on the morrow and there's an end."

"Tomorrow is the wedding."

"If I come, that will be your answer. But you'll be sorry if you wed me," she predicted darkly. "Don't say I didn't warn you."

"The devil with your warnings." He captured her chin and forced it up. Her crying had subsided into a series of painful gulps. By the light of the moon, her eyes appeared swollen, and her sweet, upturned nose was reddened. Yet she looked beautiful to him. *Damn it,* apparently he must wait for her answer, but he would do everything possible to convince her to agree in the next four and twenty hours.

Firmly, he brushed away her tears and launched into his new campaign. "Put away your tears and tell me"—he cast about for one of her favorite topics—"if Pierre and Louis saw you in your finery before we left."

The burst of pride shining in her eyes at the mere mention of her boys told him he'd chosen his subject well, though it rankled at the same time. "That's better," he said grudgingly. "Did they like your gown?"

"Aye."

"I'll wager they never saw you so beautifully garbed. What did they say?"

She tried out a tremulous grin. "Roughly translated, Pierre said I looked better than the best bloody bawdy basket he'd ever laid eyes on."

Privately Charles wished to clout the boy for his language, but he forced himself to return her smile instead. "We're going to have to whitewash that child's speech."

"I rather like it."

"He should learn appropriate language for a small lad."

"And Louis must learn to use a handkerchief before you strangle him," she put in with a choked laugh.

"Indeed." He'd made her laugh, Charles thought with relief. Her moment of extreme despair seemed to have passed. Now if she would just agree to wed . . .

"Thank you for taking them under your wing." She twisted his handkerchief and dropped her gaze, as if ashamed to accept help for both the boys and herself. "I owe you a great debt, especially since I know you don't like them."

"Blast it, will you stop saying I don't like them. I would like them if they tried to be likeable, instead of rubbing my nerves raw all the time."

The smile on Frances's face slipped. "I'm not particularly

suited to improve them in that area. I've made a poor start at court."

Exasperation threatened Charles. He had limitless patience in planning battle strategy. He could spend hours with a recalcitrant bird, coaxing it out of its doldrums and into its best flight. Yet the boys and Frances tested his patience beyond bearing at times. He wasn't sure he was going to survive being a husband and a father at the same time. "You are entirely likeable when you want to be," he pointed out. "I'm told, for instance, that you were having a perfectly reasonable conversation with Lord Admiral Howard, and that he liked you well."

Frances frowned, as if puzzled. "I was talking to the lord admiral?"

"Of course you were. A gray-haired gentleman, very distinguished. Often smokes a pipe." He gave her a moment to let her success sink in. "For another example," he continued once he thought she had absorbed the importance of having pleased the leader of England's defense fleet, "you made the queen laugh. And believe me, if she doesn't like a person, she won't laugh, no matter how amusing they are." As he touched on the subject, curiosity gnawed at him once more. "Come, share the secret," he wheedled. "What did you say to Elinor Digby that made the queen laugh so?"

The two snippets he'd shared must have improved her mood, for she now seemed inclined to tease him. "I had best not tell you." Maddeningly prim, she folded both her mouth and hands and sent him a coy glance.

"Why the devil not?"

"You'd give me a hiding."

"I never have."

"You wanted to."

Damn it, he had. He wanted to right now. His fingers itched to shake her for keeping secrets. There were other things he wanted to do as well, but he restrained himself from those, too, until the time was ripe, though as far as he was concerned it was ripe all the time. "On my honor, I won't raise a hand against you," he swore, "even if you deserve it, which you certainly do."

"Well . . ." She drew out the suspense until he realized she was teasing him again. There it was, the sparkle of mischief that bubbled from her, a contagious humor he longed to share. "Well," she drawled again, sending him an impish, sidelong glance, "you wouldn't have liked to see her face when I told her 'twas no wonder she loved the new fashion in skirts, since it disguised that her rump was as big as her farthingale was wide."

"My stars!" Torn between horror and admiration, Charles stared at Frances. "You said that to Elinor Elizabeth Mary Digby, the second daughter of the Earl of Landsdowne and one of the wealthiest heiresses in all of England?"

"One of the nastiest shrews in all of England." Frances pouted her delectable lips.

His horror shifted to hilarity as he imagined Elinor, always so self-indulgent and demanding, her plump, haughty face squeezed into an expression of incredulous outrage. The image was so ludicrous, he threw back his head and roared. He laughed until he almost jiggled Frances off his lap and tears rolled down his face. She was a rare wonder, his Frank. "By thunder, I can't tell you how many other women wished they wore your shoes at that particular moment, Frank. She's a hard dose to swallow, is Mistress Digby. No wonder the queen was amused."

"I didn't say it to amuse anyone."

"No, you didn't. Give me that kerchief."

She insisted on wiping away the tears of merriment for him, and he used that moment to advance his campaign to win her consent. "I wish to start anew," he proposed. "You can help. If you'll be so good as to stop asking me what happened in my past . . ." He wavered, but pushed aside the old guilt and continued, "I will move forward. I can't mend a torn cloth, but I can try to create new."

"Odd, your using tailor's terms," she said, straightening and looking around the mews. He thought her expression skeptical, as if she didn't believe he could do it and wanted to talk about something else. "Can we have our bit of fun now?"

"With pleasure." Relieved, he fastened greedy hands around her waist and leaned forward to taste her full lips.

"That's not what I mean." She turned her head abruptly and gave him another taste of her hair.

"By thunder, will you stop that? I hate kissing your hair. It's dark and thick and . . . hmmm, on second thought . . ." He ran his lips along her hair, raining kisses, slipping down to kiss her ear. "Mayhap I like kissing your hair. Mayhap I—"

"Enough!" She bounded to her feet, laughing and shaking

out her moss green kirtle skirt. "I mean let us have our fun by going hunting. I would like to, just now. Wouldn't you?"

He would like to hunt, but not for game. Blood pounded in his ears, and his senses were tuned to Frances's every move. With reluctance, he followed her eager gaze to discover the snowy owl, leashed to the corner perch, well away from the other birds. Alert and ready, the night hunter awaited the chance to fly by light of the moon.

Frances dangled the idea before Charles like a tempting toy. A lightning image flashed through his mind—of roaming the night-dark woods with her, the thrill of the hunt racing through his blood. "I'll get Caesar's equipment and change into boots. But what of you? You can't go in those clothes." He would be delighted to help her remove the tightly molded bodice if she would only let him. "There are spare clothes over there. Some of them belong to the younger lads and might fit." He indicated a trunk in the corner, then pulled on a heavy glove and urged Caesar onto his fist. The owl came to him eagerly, anticipating fresh prey.

She rummaged through the trunk with a smile on her face, faintly illuminated by the sickle moon. "These will do," she announced, holding up trunk hose, netherstocks, a shirt, and a jerkin. "Turn around so I can change," she ordered. "And don't you dare peek."

Chapter 31

She'd warned him not to look, but he hadn't agreed. Instead, Charles strolled into the equipment room, Caesar on his fist, and pretended to search for an extra leash while stealing illicit glimpses without her knowing.

The sweetness of those glimpses taxed his control beyond bearing. Smooth white thighs emerged from rustling silk. Her full breasts strained against linen, pressed high by a lightly laced busk. Off came her chemise. Away flew the busk. The garments released her porcelain flesh, and for an instant she stood, a vision of nude perfection, before she dived into a shirt.

With a low groan, Charles leaned against the wall of the equipment room and closed his eyes. His arousal filled his trunk hose to the point of discomfort. How he longed to fling Caesar to the wind and have Frances with the ferocity of a mating bird.

Fortunately for Frances, she changed quickly. But the sight of her clothed in the new garments was almost worse. The tight netherstocks molded to her legs, showing every curve of her calves and thighs. A white shirt tucked into loose trunk hose displayed more of her hips and derriere than when she wore skirts. And as if she couldn't bear to part with them, she had retucked the white plumes into the gold band encircling her hair, an exotic contrast to her boy's clothing. In fact, if they didn't get moving right away, he couldn't vouch for what he might do.

He barked orders for Frances to bring the game bag and strode out of the mews.

Minutes later they raced across the open meadow north of the palace, following Caesar as he hovered above them on silent, slotted wings. As he flew, the owl would search the ground with his sharp eyes and listen with his keen hearing, alert for the slightest move of his prey in the dark.

Charles felt sure his senses, tuned to Frances's every move, were as keen as any owl's. Feverishly, he hoped the heat of the chase would heighten her desire until it matched his.

Stretching his legs, he worked his lungs and body in a temporary effort to outrun his passion. Frances flew beside him, a flurry of muscled legs and engaging eyes that gleamed in the dark. The sounds and scents of her magic crept through his senses, casting him back to the first meeting in their youth. The sorrowing young woman she had been earlier vanished. Once more she was the way he loved to see her, a child of the earth and sky, running wild and free.

Catching her hand, he sprinted forward, following the blur of wings that coasted above them, gleaming white against a midnight blue-black sky. The hunt was on, and his prize was the heart of the untamed nymph who raced at his side.

Suddenly, the great owl dipped. Wings folded, he hurtled for the ground. A field mouse shrieked, followed by silence as nature took her course. Charles halted and drew Frances close beside him, signaling for silence. A hush hung over the meadow, except for her labored breath as she shifted her hand and gripped his arm.

Their gazes locked, and an almost palpable desire sizzled between them—the moment had come. The hunt's enthralling message pulsed in frantic measures through her veins.

While Caesar slaked his appetite on the field mouse, then relaunched once more into the jewel-spangled night sky, Charles drew Frances into the welcoming forest shadows, eager to feed as well. The trees bordering the meadow whispered of deep enchantment, teasing him to partake. He was starving for her lips, her arms, and although he didn't deserve it, the gift of her wild heart.

The swollen moon was a pulsing crescent of light, reminding him of Frances's creamy breasts mounded above her gown. As clouds raced across the celestial sphere, temporarily dropping them into blackness, he drew her close and fit his body to hers.

Plucking the pins from her braids, he loosened her wealth of midnight hair until it hung around her shoulders, a sharp contrast to the white plumes and gold circlet around her head, lending her a wild, untamed air. The emerald on her forehead winked as he gazed into its hard depths. Quickly, he sought the softer depths of her eyes, and discovered a more gentle green, laced with need for him, as she raised her face to welcome his kiss.

Sweet and shocking, her caresses tortured him. He couldn't get enough. She tasted of wild berries she'd eaten at the revel, and she smelled of fresh air. As he deepened the kiss, she parted her lips for him, until he felt like a man drowning, and Frances, the air he needed to live. With his fingers he traced the softness of her throat where her flesh ended and the shirt began. As always, she turned him fourteen again, reckless and driven. Like a savage, he tugged her to the woodland floor and settled her in his lap.

What a feast she offered, of silky lips and lush breasts. Above their heads, leaves shifted, admitting moments of moonlight that silvered her creamy flesh—flesh so tempting, it drove him to kiss and stroke while she moaned and enjoyed. The sense that his arousal made her frantic heightened his response further. He would be just like the owl, strong and fierce, taking from the wild what he needed to live.

"Let me shield you from the cold ground, Frank." He leaned back and coaxed her to lie full length upon him. She wriggled to arrange herself, teasing him with her body revealed so well in the boy's clothes. The rounded swell of her bottom beneath the paned trunk hose demanded his touch. Her waist was spare above the loose waistband, and he counted each of her ribs deliberately. Then without ceremony he yanked out the lace restraining the neckline, threw it away, and kissed her everywhere—her mouth, her cheeks, her jaw, her throat. His hands stole beneath her shirt and sampled her precious womanly flesh.

Her reckless response to him, her own exploring hands and rubbing hips, brought him all too quickly to the edge.

"Mercy!" He dropped his head back on the ground and writhed in torment. "Leave off or take the consequences."

"Trouble, baron?" She braced an elbow on the ground, clearly inclined to tease him. "Crying foul so soon?"

"Not foul. Mercy. You're doing me in." He closed his eyes and drew great breaths of air.

"You admit I'm the most provoking? I can hardly believe my ears." She clucked her tongue, obviously pleased by his admission.

"Believe it," he insisted. "And because of it, you must agree to become a Cavandish on the morrow." Time was passing, and danger gathered on the horizon. He couldn't risk losing her. "Say yes, Frank. Say it now."

She dismissed the idea with a shrug.

"Don't be saucy." By now, he recognized when she wasn't serious. "Say yes or I'll . . . pluck out your feathers."

"Then I can't fly." Her hand flew to her hair, but it was too late.

He attacked. Tickling her ribs, which convulsed her with laughter, he grabbed the feathers with the other. "You can't escape." To make good his threat, he twined both legs around hers. "Ha. Got one." Victorious, he brandished the feather above their heads. "Careful!" he warned as she stretched for it, breathless with giggles. "You'll not have it until you agree."

"I don't have to agree. You swore to wed me whether I agreed or not. Give me my feather, Baron Millstone . . . Oh!" He glared as she said the name, and she giggled nervously behind one hand.

"You taught the boys to call me Millstone!" he accused.

"But you *are* like a millstone." She lunged for the feather and missed as he shifted it to his left hand. "As hardheaded and as burdensome as a stone. Sometimes I think you're worse."

"I am hard, but not in the head."

Chuckling, she gathered herself for another snatch at the feather.

"Come now, Frank," he badgered, waving the feather tantalizingly out of reach. "Call me any name you like, but give up this nonsense and marry me."

"I'm not ready," she grumbled, shifting her weight in the new direction. "First you have to give . . . me . . . my . . . feather!" With hands, legs, and feet, she shinnied up him like a tree. Her flat belly, then her lower body, rubbed against his hardness in her haste.

"Would you be still?" he complained, though he thoroughly enjoyed the sensation.

" 'Tis your own fault." She swiped at the feather. He jerked it away just in time. She collapsed full length on him. "My property, if you please, Baron Millstone."

"Why do you want it?"

"I told you, so I can fly."

"So you can fly *away* from me, you mean. Because I frighten you, pressing you to wed and share my bed."

Maneuvering her body, he renewed the tickling to distract her. While she thrashed with laughter, he tucked the feather in his trunk hose, knowing she wouldn't reach for it there. Then he wrapped both arms around her, hugged her to him, and rocked back and forth.

"Worm pate," she cursed, eyeing with annoyance the place where her feather had gone. "You'll crush it there."

But she halted her struggle and let her body soften, her curves collapsing delightfully against him—soft breasts against his chest, hip bones bumping his, tangles of clean hair, and rich, female-honeyed scent.

"Be rid of your fears, my dear," he urged her, still rocking. "When we bed again, remember our agreement? You'll manage how 'twill be."

He knew quite well by her face that she did remember. She would particularly remember their intimacy in the barge, which must have embarrassed her, because she dipped her head and hid against his chest.

He gazed at the shifting leaves overhead and rubbed her back, a rhythmic motion to lull her to relax. Night wind ruffled the forest and set the branches tossing, revealing glints of stars through the ink-dark web. The brisk chill of shadowy woods invaded his senses—the scent of damp moss and wet ferns mingled with the flower freshness of her cool flesh. "What else troubles you about wedding me, Frank?" he murmured, wanting to overcome her reservations. "Tell old Millstone and rid yourself of its plague."

Wings of breeze stirred her hair so that it played around them, tickling his cheek. A rock gouged him in the back, but it was nowhere near as hard as the rock of his passion. Surprisingly, she didn't flinch, though she must have felt his craving. Summoning patience, he waited.

"How many other women have you asked to wed? Beyond the one, that is?"

Her stark question released flocks of memories, another raven-haired woman prominent among them. Brusquely, he ordered them back to their mews, herded them in, and locked the door. Enough of melancholy dumps, he tired of thinking about Inez. He could do with some humor instead. "So you think I offered to wed every woman I bedded?"

"Antoine did."

"No, he didn't," he explained patiently. "He asked only the virgins, I assure you. And I've bedded no virgins, so you're safe. In fact, most of the women I bedded were wed already. Does that answer your question, my nosy sweet?"

"You're a disgusting tease, Baron Millstone."

"I am." He laughed outright, surprised that his new name on her tongue now amused him. "But my point is, I've never asked a woman to wed besides the one, and naught came of that. Antoine, on the other hand, must have thought of virgins the way many Frenchmen do. They're a banquet; he wanted the first taste. He knew others would eat after him, but he didn't mind after he'd had his fill." He captured her face between his palms and met her gaze. "He and I differ in a thousand ways, but especially in that one. Because I'll never have my fill of you, Frances Morley. Never if I have you a thousand times. Once we're wed, you can count on finding me in your bed for the rest of your days."

Charles's sudden fervor nearly jolted Frances from her perch. He hadn't declared love, but she desired what he offered almost as much. Deep inside, she hungered to be wanted. And for whatever the reason, Charles wanted her. His demanding lips against her throat proved it beyond doubt. The renewal of his ardent onslaught threatened to sweep her out of control. Arching her exposed neck, she encouraged him to enjoy.

In keeping with his usual insistence, he merely took it as an invitation to bolder measures. He loosened the band of her trunk hose and sent his wandering fingers to visit places she normally wouldn't have allowed. Down between her legs he delved, until he found her center. With eyes closed, she savored the feeling. She'd never craved anyone like this before.

"Mercy!" she cried at last, the word half smothered as his mouth blessed hers again.

Obligingly, he completed the kiss and pulled back. "Am I provoking enough?"

"Provoking is an understatement. I would term you madly seductive."

Mirth danced on his face. "I shall continue to be just that until you agree. Marry me, Frank."

She stuck out her lip and baited him. "No."

"You shall say yes." In a flash he wrapped his legs around hers in a wrestler's grip and attacked her again with his maddening fingers.

Heavens, she'd never known she was so ticklish. For a

minute, she tussled with him in a frenzy of frantic arms as he clamped her legs tightly. She squirmed and twisted and laughed like a lunatic. "Yes, I like mutton stew," she gasped, desperate for air.

"That's not the 'yes' I wanted." He tickled her ribs on both sides.

She convulsed with laughter. "Yes, I'll play quoits with you."

"Still wrong."

Frances bent double, helpless with hilarity. "I have never laughed so hard before."

"Not even with Louis and Pierre?"

"Not even with them. Charles, stop!" She shrieked as his fingers found the most ticklish spot of all between her thighs. "Pharaoh's—"

"Pharaoh can't save you. Don't call on him and his useless foot."

The tickling stopped suddenly, giving her a chance to right herself on his chest, though he didn't release her legs. Catching her attention, he riveted her with his next words. "I'm the one who wants you, Frank. If I can admit it, at least you can say yes."

His entreaty touched her. In the madness of the moment, he put words to his wanting, showing her a tiny glimpse of his heart. Dozens of women at Queen Elizabeth's court, many wealthy and titled, all of them beautiful, begged to wed him, the queen's Master of Hawks. But he declared he wanted her! Frank, the odd one. Frank, the savage, with her outspoken manners and unruly ways, was desired by Charles Cavandish. She wanted to say yes with all her being. But she couldn't yet. "I have to ask you something, first."

"Ask away."

"Tell me about Inez," she said, realizing this was the moment. Now, when he had bared his need to her, when he was vulnerable and his defenses were down. Now, because the shadow of Inez that stood between them had to be destroyed.

Charles reared up his head as his ardor wilted. "You promised not to speak of her," he flared, stunned that she brought up the forbidden subject at such a time.

"I promised nothing." All teasing abandoned, she faced

him, serious. "Charles, there's something odd about the story you tell me. It can't be right."

"I told you what happened," he gritted, furious to lose the moment of passion to nonsense. "I pledged myself to Inez del Cavaladosa forever. Then I jilted her, as you were jilted by Antoine. Isn't that cause enough for blame?"

"But how did she behave when she learned about Richard? If she'd been torn between the two of you, she should have been devastated. Was she?"

"Of course she was."

"Are you sure?"

Charles searched the foggy corner of his memory where Inez reposed, veiled in mists of youthful idealism, and realized he couldn't remember a thing about how she'd reacted. He'd been too swept away by his own torment, by his own futile efforts to defy his company commander's orders and attempt the impossible, to save Richard from an impregnable prison and certain death.

"Did she weep?" Frances persisted, renting the layers of protective covering swathing the memory. "Did she visit the garrison and try to stop his torture? Did she beg the commander to set him free?"

"I was too overwrought to notice," he snarled, stung by the pain of remembrance. "I don't recall what she did." But he felt the seeds of doubt, then, trickling from Frances's hand into the soil of his mind. "I believe she asked her father, to see if he could help."

Frances pulled a face, utterly disbelieving. "What good would that do if her father had no jurisdiction over the garrison?"

Charles moved his lips, trying to form an answer. He couldn't accept the idea that Inez hadn't cared. Yet in all truth, he couldn't remember any reaction from her. Was it his bad memory, or had she not shed a single tear?

"Answer." Frances probed the wound further. "Could her father have helped?"

"No!" he cried in anguish, the full significance of his response tearing into him. "Her father was a planter with no military position. He couldn't have done a thing."

"And so *she* didn't do a thing, did she, Charles?" Frances's face hung above him, sad but earnest. "In her place, I would have visited the commander and bartered for the Englishman's freedom. Or I would have smuggled him out. Or I would have—"

"Stop!" He rolled her off and pulled into a sitting position, overcome by the grief that tore through his mind. For the first time, he questioned someone's responsibility to Richard besides his own. He questioned Inez and found her lacking. "Inez didn't have your kind of loyalty," he grated, but even that statement slammed him to a halt. Few people had Frances's kind of loyalty, but what kind did Inez have? "She remained steadfast to her father and her heritage," he said, convinced of that much. "She refused to run away to England with me. She wanted me to stay there with her."

"But you implied she refused you," Frances argued.

"Not exactly. She . . . wanted me to work for her father, to become essentially a Spaniard. I couldn't do it. I'm English through and through. Oh, God." He embraced her suddenly, anguish driving him to seek comfort. "Don't ask any more, Frances. I pray you, leave off."

"I can't yet, Charles. I need to know what words of consolation she offered after you lost your best friend. Think, Charles, what did she say?"

"All she said," he remembered painfully, "is that it wasn't my fault Richard was a fool."

"That's no consolation. And to call the man she almost wed a fool."

"She didn't almost wed him; she chose me."

"Did she?" Frances persisted, walking with him along the dark paths of his soul as he relived the night of Richard's death. "Consider this, Charles. Consider the possibility that she pledged herself to Richard first."

"That's impossible." He rejected the idea. "I just told you she chose me."

"Did Richard congratulate you on your good fortune?"

"No, but we both knew . . ." He froze as he realized for the first time that no such conversation with Richard had ever taken place between them. He'd assumed Inez had rejected Richard when she pledged herself to him. He'd assumed Richard's kindly acts of friendship throughout the subsequent days had been a silent admission of honorable defeat.

Frances drew closer, as if to deliver a final, devastating blow. "Don't you see. She chose Richard, thinking he would agree to her terms, but when he refused to become Spanish, she had to dispose of him. She couldn't wed two men. So she asked him to meet her at the bay, then told the garrison where he was."

Charles opened his mouth to protest, but Frances flew on with her startling train of thought. "I know you'll say she could have denied she pledged herself to him. Her father would have supported her. But I'll wager she had given up her virginity, mayhap even before Richard. No decent Spanish lord would want her once she was deflowered. And she wanted to be married. So after Richard disappointed her, she decided to try for you."

It could be true. With new clarity, Charles recalled how Inez had cursed him when he denied her wish to work for her father and join with Spain. Her phrases had been far more colorful than he'd expected from a virgin's lips. But then she hadn't been a virgin. He'd learned that fast enough the night they sealed their pledge with lovemaking. She'd told him she'd been raped as a young girl, but now he considered she might have given herself to Richard earlier. Or, as Frances pointed out, to another man long before.

Another unpleasant vision unfolded from his memory—of Inez, the night of their final argument. He'd come to her, his nose still bleeding from his commander's disciplinary blow. Over and over he had begged his superior to let them attempt Richard's rescue. His behavior had been so unmilitarylike, the man had finally struck him. Inez had scoffed at him for enduring the punishment. Then she had demanded they visit a priest that very night. On the morrow, she wished to present him to her father as a man who had changed his allegiance from England to Spain.

Aghast, he'd refused. At that, she'd flown into one of her famous rages, throwing porcelain pitchers and glass ornaments, making such a noise, he'd had to flee. After that, she'd barred her window against him. They had never met again face-to-face.

The seeds of doubt, planted earlier in his mind, began to sprout.

"Charles, admit the things you've been avoiding." Frances's voice steadied him, holding him in the present. "She pinned her final hopes on you, believing you would be so overjoyed to have her, you would forget all else. But she didn't count on your loyalty. Nor had it occurred to her you would blame yourself for what she'd done to Richard."

He shook his head, confounded by so many new ideas. For so long, he'd believed he'd been disloyal—though he'd been faced with an impossible dilemma, damned no matter which choice he made. He'd loved a woman who begged him to desert his country. His friend had died at the hands of her people. If he joined them, he was a traitor. If he didn't he jilted his love. Dazed, he reviewed Frances's arguments and admitted she might be right.

But they had no proof. None at all.

Still, his burden lightened. As a young man with few resources, he had been unable to rescue a wounded man and spirit him from a strong blockade, especially against his commander's opposition. But even had he managed, now he considered that Inez might have stopped him. She'd known exactly where he was, trying to help his friend.

It didn't solve all his sorrows. He had misjudged Inez badly, thinking her someone she was not, which was his fault, not hers. Now he saw he had probably misjudged Richard's thoughts and feelings as well. Poor judgment had led him down the path of pain, and could well do so again.

Yet if Inez had sent Richard to his death, her actions absolved him of many things.

Frances had remained at arm's length throughout their discourse. Now she placed both hands on his shoulders. "Charles," she whispered, "put away your past. Let it go and let us truly begin anew."

He looked into her woods-darkened eyes and more guilt tumbled away. Regret would stay with him forever. Pain for his lost friend. But now he believed the death was not entirely his fault.

Frances hastily rubbed away tears of her own as she finished telling Charles her suspicions about his past. Unwrapping his memories had ripped the covering from her own. They tore at her now, excruciatingly painful. All too well she understood the despair when a beloved fell from the pedestal of glory and became unworthy. The night Antoine had held her hand and declared his love had been a treasured moment in her life, until she waited alone in the church for hours and he had never come. Yet she had blamed herself for her poor judgment as much as she blamed him for his deceit. Perhaps more.

"You've been hurt worse than I." Charles's voice reclaimed her as he took her hands reverently in his own.

And at that moment she knew Charles possessed a loyalty that ran as deep and true as her own, if only he could come to recognize and trust it again.

"Yes," she whispered, lifting one of his palms and carrying it to her cheek. "Charles, my answer is yes."

"Yes, what?"

"Yes, I'll wed you on the morrow, Charles Cavandish," she said clearly, carrying his palm to her lips.

"You're sure? This isn't a trick?"

"No trick. I'm very sure."

"Thank God." With an urgent motion he pulled her to him, found her mouth, and kissed her hard, as if he were dying and she, his last hope. And she kissed him back with all the passion that rose up inside her, demanding release. And while they kissed, she felt him tuck the feather back in her hair.

"Let us fly together, Frances," he whispered, devoid of jesting now. "I promised we would soar, and we shall."

"Yes, let it be now."

Together, their hands fulfilled the promise. Memories from the night on the barge repeated in Frances's mind, but with a marvelous difference. Tonight the magic of the forest surrounded them. Groves of thick ferns lurked at her elbow. Arches of green leaves formed their roof, and the rich brown of moldering leaves formed their floor. And Charles, with his clever fingers, spoke to her needs.

She would take the dangerous plunge, she would become his bride. Because now, hope bloomed within her. She had pecked away the first fragment of the barrier between them. It had fallen, and through the tiny hole, she saw the shining light of the sun beyond, someday to be hers.

Let me fly wild and free.

Charles stripped away her shirt and loosened her trunk hose as she urged him on, enraptured by their mutual sharing. His hands were everywhere, preparing her to fly. Her breasts tingled with excitement. Moist heat rose between her thighs.

She gave in to impulse and tore at his clothing. His shirt disappeared into the ferns. Her fingers delighted in exploring his body—the lean planes of his muscles, the power of his torso, chest, and hips. In response to her demands, his trunk hose yielded his arousal. She closed her fingers around him and laughed when he groaned.

She leaped to straddle him and then eased her hips down. A shout of delight burst from his lips, and she reveled in her power, in his obvious thrill. He wanted her. He craved her. And she needed him. Who cared if he couldn't love her? Tomorrow the Spaniards might invade and they both could die. Until then, the passion that bound them together refused to be denied. The excitement in Frances rose as Charles stroked her breasts, yet he yielded the control to her with a knowing gleam in his eye. He knew exactly what he did to her, playing on her wild instincts. And as she directed their pleasure, she also bent to his will.

But it was her will, too, and she took mad pleasure in it. Stroking his chest and clinging to his thighs, she rode him in jerky movements. What other man could provoke her to such lunacy? Certainly not Antoine. Not any other man she knew.

Then all thoughts faded and sensation ruled. The glory of their friction rose inside her, bold and brilliant, like a hawk on the wing.

She savored the way he filled her with feral intensity. His hands gripped her waist, his face transformed by euphoria as his thrusts met hers. For this moment they became two equals, flying under the wing of magic.

He shouted his pleasure when he found his climax. Elation crossed his face, and with a gasp, she hurried to find her own release.

The leap from her own heights stole her breath away. Her muscles convulsed as Charles's pure magic seized her in its grasp.

Reach for the heavens. Covet the stars. Anything was possible. Life was blessed.

Like a child in the arms of its mother, she trusted. Tonight, she yielded to the dream and gave her heart away.

In the aftermath of their passion, Charles lay spent and exhausted on the woodland floor. A rock gouged his back, but he didn't care. The shadow that usually stood between him and Frances had melted. It might be only temporary, but he welcomed any breach in its dividing power. Tonight he had felt the magic she had spoken of on the barge. Only the tiniest taste, yet enough to whet his appetite for more.

Indeed, the miracle was, he had *felt* something for the first time in years. For an instant during their mating, it was as if a guiding star hung overhead, blessing their union. For years he had carried twin burdens of guilt without even realizing it, his and Inez's. Now, partially released, he had reached for the magic with Frances and almost claimed it for his own.

It was little enough, yet he breathed a sigh of thanksgiving. She had agreed to marry him. At last she was his, and she would keep the hope for magic alive in his life.

Chapter 32

The shadow was back the next day. Frances retreated behind it, frightened by what she had done.

She was caught, snared at last.

Based on a flimsy hope, she had sold herself into slavery. People couldn't change each other; they had to change themselves. How had she ever been so foolish as to think otherwise?

Fear tightened within her as she realized, too, that Charles had taken her heart and flown away with it, when what she wanted was his, given in return.

Even more immediately, she was now caught in Rozalinde Howard's silken bonds, as the countess put it, being attired in garments fit for a bride.

Frances stood in the elegant tiring chamber, feeling as hollow as a stuffed form for the clothing rather than full of joy. She had made a terrible mistake, tying herself to a man, much less one with a vast family of important social standing. She hardly dared move for fear of committing a faux pas.

"Of course we wish to assist you in selecting your wedding garb," Rozalinde had said, laughing in answer to Frances's not so polite protests. "We're to be your kinswomen."

"And you're to be ours," added Margaret Cavandish, Jonathan's wife, who struck awe in Frances with her bright beauty of golden hair and amber eyes.

In Paris, Frances had heard much about these two legendary beauties, but never had she dreamed of becoming kin to them. She stared at the pair, tongue-tied, clad in naught but an embroidered chemise and a mountain of petticoats, letting them select for her as they would.

They were aided, or mayhap impeded, by a curious, giggling girl of perhaps five or six years whom Margaret lovingly called Mercy. "Gracious, Mercy, put that back," she said every time the child did something unwarranted. First the child adorned herself with too many of her aunt's jewels. Then she overbalanced and tipped headfirst into a trunk. "Gracious, Mercy," Margaret had cried as she rescued her daughter. "Gracious, Mercy" continually punctuated their attiring session. Frances felt sure the child must think Gracious her first name.

But in no time at all, Frances found her own cautions to Pierre and Louis rivaled Madam Margaret's gentle scoldings of Mercy. The boys, present at Frances's insistence, rummaged through the intriguing chests and painted boxes of rainbow silks and sarsanets, enjoying themselves as much as Mercy.

"Look at this!" Pierre held up a golden chain. "I'll wager this is real gold. I could sell it for—"

"Put that down"—Rozalinde snapped it out of his hand—"If you can't behave, Master Pierre, you're out on your ear. You're only here by the grace of your friend. Why she wants you, I'll never understand. You lack manners, that's for certain."

Margaret laughed, a silvery, trilling sound. "Let him root about, Rozalinde. He means no harm. Though you can't sell the countess's things," she added sternly to Pierre. "There are rules for the streets and rules for here. No selling anything you find in this house, do you understand?"

"Indeed, or we'll give you over to the Spanish," Rozalinde admonished. "Which reminds me, Margaret, Christopher sent word from Plymouth that the wind blows like the Furies over the Channel. I hope Lisbon is being blown off the map."

"Be assured, the wind blows in Lisbon, too," Frances put in, now that they mentioned the topic most on her mind. "The wind had just started when we left France, so Spain is getting her share."

" 'Twill keep the Armada anchored at Lisbon for days." Rozalinde plucked a ruff from a pile of laces and held it against Frances. She frowned, not liking the effect, and put it aside.

"Let us hope they stay anchored for weeks," Margaret agreed. "But do not be troubled," she added, as Frances's face filled with concern. "Our ships are swifter than theirs. Our guns have a longer range."

True enough, but Frances wasn't sure that meant England

would triumph against almost two hundred enemy vessels that intended to deposit forty thousand and more soldiers on their shores. She tried to show interest in the colorful bodices Rozalinde offered. But silently she wished to get on with war preparations. She had met the Spanish firsthand, and she knew their ruthless tactics.

"Spain's fleet is greater in numbers than ours," she ventured. "Aren't you worried? Don't you wish to be in Plymouth, helping to prepare?"

Rozalinde shivered and focused on several bodices that seemed to be her final choices. "I would like to be in Plymouth, but I cannot. I have three young children to protect, and I won't leave them."

"And I am expecting again, so I'll not stir a step," Margaret put in. "I refuse to lose this child, as I did our last one." She laughed blithely at Frances's exclamation of worry. "Have no fear. This child is four months along and feels well rooted in place. You may soon find yourself with child as well, so you're best off here. Which of us would you like to stay with, me or Rozalinde? Or would you like some time with each of us?"

Frances tore her gaze away from Margaret's slim waistline that showed no hint of her being with child and answered the last question. "I thank you both kindly for your generous offers, but I'm for Dorset immediately after the wedding. Her Majesty has agreed I should work with her messenger birds."

She frowned as Rozalinde and Margaret exchanged significant glances that boded ill. "I *am* going to Dorset," she said a bit too loudly. "Why do you look so grim?"

Rozalinde rustled to her side and put on her most soothing manner. "Didn't my brother discuss with you the possibility of your staying here?"

"No, and I'm not staying," Frances said resolutely. But inside a burn of fury swept through her. Charles had apparently planned to leave her behind without even consulting her. And to that, she would never agree.

"Oh dear, how like my brother," Rozalinde sighed. "He has much to learn." She sighed again and fussed among the bright fabrics, clearly embarrassed.

Frances pressed her lips together and refused to comment. She was going to Dorset, and if Charles failed to make travel arrangements for her, she would make her own.

"Is Jonathan coming from Dover for the wedding?" Rozalinde asked Margaret, unexpectedly voicing the very question Frances had been pondering.

"He's on his way, even as we speak," Margaret said. "He always swore if Charles decided to wed, he wouldn't miss it for the world."

"Papa is coming! Papa is coming!" Mercy chanted, clapping her hands and grinning from ear to ear. "He wouldn't miss Uncle Hawk's wedding."

Frances grasped at the information, knowing Jonathan might serve as her hoped-for travel escort. "Is he returning to Dover after the wedding?" she asked as innocently as possible.

Apparently she didn't fool Rozalinde. "He's off to Plymouth to join my husband at the lookout point," the countess said. "And whatever you do choose to do, Frances, have a care. Charles has a worse temper than these unseasonable storms."

Not the least contrite but determined to hide it, Frances submitted while Rozalinde dressed her long hair. But the sight of Louis with a candle in the next room caught her attention.

"Louis, stop!" Frances bolted through the open door and caught the lighted candlestick just as Louis dropped it. Snatching the taper from the bed, she pinched out the flame.

"The coverlet might have caught fire," she admonished. "Don't you dare fiddle with a candle near a bed and its hangings." She stuck both singed fingers in her mouth. The lad looked repentant, but from experience she knew it wouldn't last long. "You got wax on her ladyship's bedding. You'll be required to pay for the damage." Seizing his hand, she marched him into the dressing room. "Stay here where I can watch you or you'll have to go below stairs."

"Troth," exclaimed Rozalinde, "these lads. Must they be here?"

"They're all the family I have." Embarrassed but defiant, Frances pointed to a stool and Louis sat.

"Yes, sit there and tell us which bodice looks better on Frances," Rozalinde said. Frances recognized the countess's obvious attempt to keep the boy occupied. "This"—she held a brilliant blue bodice in front of Frances—"or this?" She exchanged it for the emerald green satin Frances had considered and rejected for last night's revel. "Margaret, what do you think?"

"They both look like horse turds," Pierre piped up from where he rooted through a chest with Mercy.

"Pierre!" Frances cried, mortified to the tips of her toes. "You're not to say that word. Never again, do you hear?"

Pierre grinned, showing a charming set of dimples that had previously been so hidden by dirt, Frances had forgotten he had them. "Pardon, countess," he said, standing up and giving a little bow, first to Rozalinde, then to Margaret, proving he could behave if he wished. "What I meant to say," he went on, mimicking the proper speech of the house servants, "is that they are both as ugly as the droppings of a horse."

Frances closed her eyes and groaned. "Pierre, you're impossible. What am I going to do?"

"Wear this," cried Mercy, dancing over to Frances. She laid across her lap a bodice of soft creamy velvet decorated with wonderful, curving patterns in moss green ribbons and matching curlicues of braid. "In this, you'll be a beautiful bride."

She would be one frightened bride, Frances thought with trepidation some hours later as she stood in the Chapel Royal, wearing the beautiful bodice and waiting for Charles, who was naturally late.

For his own wedding, she thought dismally. Or mayhap, like Antoine, he wouldn't come at all.

No, that couldn't be. Her worst fears would not come true. She concentrated instead on Charles's vast family that had assembled for the event. Hordes of people crowded the room, among them five of Charles's six siblings, nieces and nephews galore. Even Charles's old mother who, despite her rheumatism, insisted on being present for her third son's nuptials. The only people related to Frances were Pierre and Louis, who had been scrubbed within an inch of their lives and suited up in clean doublets and hose.

Charles finally arrived, late on account of an ailing hawk, and Frances grew even more terrified—down to the tips of her toes, which were now adorned by beautiful slippers that matched the green and cream bodice. The three Cavandish men—Jonathan, Charles, and Roger—loomed at the altar, forbidding figures with their imposing height. Even Roger,

only fifteen and short for a Cavandish, frightened the wits
out of her with his fierce, good looks.

As she walked down the chapel aisle, the Cavandish
women clustered before her, Rozalinde and Margaret leading
the way, Frances pushed down her fear and followed, feeling
tongue-tied and terrified. What should she say to all these
people? How did they expect her to behave? Desperately she
wished she could run to the mews and hide with the hawks
and falcons, whose ways and wants she understood.

As she curtseyed to the queen and her ladies, she praised
heaven that one thing didn't frighten her. She need not fear a
prolonged encounter with Charles in bed, which would
remind her further that she had given away her heart. Her
earlier precautions would solve that problem, at least temporarily. She just hoped Charles wouldn't be furious at what
she had done.

Chapter 33

"What do you mean, we ride for Dorset within the hour?"
Charles roared at Frances mere minutes after the wedding
ceremony concluded. He confronted his new bride outside
the Chapel Royal, not caring who heard. The rest of the
family and guests had tactfully moved on to the queen's banqueting chamber for refreshments, leaving the couple to their
quarrel. A rounding good one, too, if he had his say. Though
Frances dazzled him, looking like a goddess of the woodland
in her leaf-colored greens and cream, Charles was in no
mood for nonsense. Their mating in the woods last night had
raised his need for her to fever pitch, and he had looked forward with barely suppressed eagerness to their first time
together in a real bed.

"We'll have a wedding night first," he told her succinctly.
That was the way to handle her, clear but firm. "After, we'll
discuss what you're to do while I go off to fight."

"My regrets," she said glibly, turning to follow the others.
"I ride with your brother. If you wish to accompany me, pray
do, but I can't ignore the queen's command. I intend to train
those birds."

"You requested that assignment. The queen gave it only to
humor you." He stalked after her, itching to grab her, but
seeing no place to do so—she was all over puffs of expensive fabric, slashed and pearled and covered with braid or
lace. With no free space left, he clasped her by the waist
from behind and whirled her around.

"That's not true," Frances stormed at him. "She agreed
because she recognized my skill. And you're afraid to com-
pete with me because I might be better at it than you."

Charles narrowed his gaze at her, enraged by her insult.
"Skill is not the issue. I won't have you endangered again.
And I won't have you sneaking behind my back."

"You did it first," she accused. "You made an important decision without including me."

"It's the man's place to decide. I did what was required." He stood firm in the knowledge that he was now her husband. The quarrel would end here.

She apparently recognized his new determination, because she changed her demeanor suddenly, turning soft in his arms and sincere. "Charles, we're acting like children, but this is serious business, so please listen. I'm sorry I criticized your skill. I shouldn't have done that." Her voice caught on the last word, and he was suddenly aware that she trembled beneath his hands.

"Go on." Though she had infuriated him with her slight, she had apologized. And he recognized the tremendous effort it had taken to admit herself in the wrong.

"I'm terrified of what's about to happen. Isn't anyone else? Our country stands on the brink of war. Our lives may be forfeit and our children become slaves to Spanish lords, but I'm the only one who seems to notice. You act as if the Spaniards were coming for cakes and ale and then intended to go merrily home."

"Panic serves us naught," he reminded her. "Of course we're all concerned."

"Then let us act," she pleaded. "Let us leave for Dorset now so we can prepare for the Spaniards. I want my house back, as well, but I know there will be trouble over it, so I want to begin sorting it out. I can't sleep another night in London, knowing there is so much to do. I *need* to go." The fever of her need filled her voice as she closed her eyes and gripped his arms. "Don't you *need* things in your life, Charles? Don't you have a burning need for Arcturus? Isn't his absence an emptiness clawing at you inside? These things claw at me. They hurt."

Something did claw at him. Charles's insides writhed with it, but it wasn't wanting Arcturus or his old master. He *did* want them, but since returning to England, he'd discovered his need for Frances overwhelmed all else. Last night in the woods, she'd soothed his conscience like nothing before, as if drawing a hood over his ugly past. When he held her in his arms, he lit up inside with a need every bit as intense as hers. The thought of being without her for a protracted period did hurt—more than he had imagined it would. "If I let you have your way in this, Frank, I demand something in return," he growled in her ear, feeling her shiver, all pliant and soft in his arms. "I would have you obey me for a change. And I'd have something else as soon as we arrive in Dorset. You know what it is." He kissed her forehead, her cheek, then moved to claim her lips.

"Despotic toad." She evaded his mouth by turning her head aside.

"Despotic, am I? If you think I'm despotic now, just wait until I get you in a real bed. I won't let you out for a month." He followed her movement, avoiding hair in the face by nuzzling her neck instead. His nose bumped the little pearls swinging from her ear as he inhaled her honeysuckle and rose scent. "Tell me you agree."

"I agree . . . if your decisions meet with my approval."

A delicious expanse of bosom bared by her bodice tempted him unbearably. "Not good enough. In matters pertaining to the Spanish and your safety, you must obey me implicitly. Agree to that."

"Oh, very well, I agree to that, but nothing more. Your orders must pertain directly to my safety and the Spanish. Can we be off now?"

"Don't forget the other part of the bargain. When we arrive, you're to—"

"Yes, yes," she cried with impatience. "I hear you. Now please, may we go?"

"After one last kiss." He nestled her closer against him, despite her stiff gown, and kissed her closed eyelids, then her cheeks and her mouth. He was torn between anger at her sneaking behind his back and sympathy for her desire. He was wrenched between his own burning need and the importance of her safety. "We will ride, just as you wish."

But he wouldn't like it, he resigned himself to that. Especially when he found her heart set on taking the boys. Dorset would take several days to reach, even if they rode like the very devil, changed horses often, and stopped only long enough to catch a few hours of sleep. It meant dirt, exhaustion, and the continual presence of the boys, since Frances refused to leave them alone at night. And it meant no privacy in bed.

As their small party rode south, the horns of his dilemma jabbed Charles, worse than the rocks that had poked his ribs last night. But he would suffer them for a small taste of

Frances's magic. In fact, he wanted a great deal more than a taste.

Setting his jaw grimly, he prepared for the worst.

That "worst" took the form of Louis's constant questions, as Charles soon found out. The more the lad asked, the older Charles decided he was.

Eleven or twelve, Frances had originally told him. But Charles had scrubbed the boy clean in a tub personally and judged him to be older. Though small for his age, Louis had to be thirteen at the least, based on the signs of maturity his body bore.

Charles adjusted his reins and led their party across a small stream. The late day sun shone pleasantly warm on their shoulders. Frances rode behind him with Jonathan beside her and Oriana perched on her fist.

The boys rode on either side of Charles by his express order. They were unaccustomed to riding, so he wished to keep an eye on them.

Actually, he was rather proud of what he'd done with the pair, he decided, surveying them critically as they traveled through the broad valleys south of London. Washed, trimmed, and properly dressed, no one could tell they were street urchins until they opened their mouths. Pierre was doing decidedly better on that score and remaining silent, mayhap because he was younger and more malleable. But Louis still let his tongue flap all too frequently for Charles's taste.

"So, Baron Milborne, you're well and truly caught." Louis smirked at him from his shorter gelding at Charles's right side. "You're a husband at last."

Charles bit back a sharp reply. "You seem pleased about that fact."

"I am pleased for Frank. I told you you wanted to kiss her. You see, I was right."

Fourteen, not thirteen, Charles swore inwardly. The boy had to be at least fourteen. He should have realized it from the first. He reached for his water flask, popped out the cork, and put the vessel to his lips.

"So, you've made her your wife," Louis continued. "When are you going to make me a knight?"

Charles choked, spewing water everywhere.

Pierre, who was caught in the spray, loosed a string of French oaths.

"Enough," Charles roared at the child, wiping water from his arm. "And don't pretend there was nothing wrong with what you just said. I know foul language when I hear it, even if I can't translate the exact words."

Pierre pouted. Frances clucked her tongue from behind them, verifying his guess that the curses were strong ones. "There'll be a punishment for you when we arrive in Dorset," he said.

"Do you intend to whip me, baron?" Pierre asked sullenly.

"No, every time you curse unsuitably, you'll have an unpleasant chore to perform." Charles smiled in private satisfaction, thinking of just the task for the boy. He had hated mucking out the stables as a lad, but he'd gotten that assignment every time he showed disrespect for his father, which had been all too frequently when he was Pierre's age.

The memory became uncomfortable as he realized how he inched closer to his father's behavior daily. Was he changing into an old man already? My God, what a miserable thought.

And there was still Louis's extraordinary question to be dealt with. He turned to the waiting lad. "Exactly what makes you think you've the makings of a knight in you?" He met Louis's dark gaze straight on, expecting him to recognize himself as unworthy and look away.

The lad didn't flinch in the slightest. "Frank says I can do it. She says I can be anything I want."

"She forgot to mention a certain essential part of the process," Charles said caustically. "Firstly, you are too young to be a knight, so you'll have to wait. Secondly, although you've shown bravery and ingenuity in the face of danger, there's more to being a knight than that. A knight performs his duty loyally and without complaint, as ordered by his superiors. A knight learns to judge situations and understand unfailingly exactly what to do when required, even if he lacks his superior's direction. If you'll work on those things, you might someday be worthy of a knighthood. I would then be more than happy to help you secure a chance to earn one."

Charles didn't know why he held out hope to the lad, but as the boy's face lit up with excitement, he realized he'd spoken the truth, and the truth by itself held out the hope. Louis had indeed shown bravery and ingenuity in the face of danger, giving his all to rescue Frances from certain death. If only he could learn the judgment required, if only he could avoid reverting to the bad habit of stealing taught by years of survival on the streets, he might indeed be a knight some day.

"I will learn the judgment, I swear it," Louis cried, his dark brown eyes shining.

A sudden shot of pain forced Charles to look away as he recognized that he, too, had once been young and bursting with the hope of achieving great things. That was before misfortune and poor judgment had beaten him down. If he had failed so miserably, if the possibility of his doing so again still lay strong within him, how could a poor gutter waif ever hope to succeed?

The memories troubled him all the way to Dorset. Though he now saw Inez more clearly, thanks to Frances, he still blamed himself for his bad judgment. And his own punishments were more severe than any he would ever impose on Louis or Pierre.

Several whirlwind days later, Frances and her traveling party approached West Lulworth. The Dorset road was far from quiet. As they neared the coast, they met companies of men mustered by the local commissioners and drilling in preparation for invasion. Charles explained that Sir John Norris, the queen's general, had issued orders for three thousand Dorset men to be organized under the authority of five captains located throughout the county. They passed carts ladened with victuals, weapons, and ammunition for the companies. Messengers moved purposefully past on important errands. Charles was greeted by scores of people he knew.

One man going in the opposite direction stopped them and doffed his hat. "My lord baron, we're right glad to see you back among us. Will you lend a hand in drilling my company? They could use your expert advice."

They talked so long, Frances barely managed to hide her chaffing. An invisible Morley called to her from across the fields and beyond the woods and marsh.

Home. The single word sang in Frances's mind, and she wanted nothing more than to set off for Morley this minute, if only to view it from afar.

After what seemed a millennium, they reached the Cavandish family home, and she dismounted stiffly from her mare in the stable yard. Pierre and Louis hopped down from their horses and fell to exploring their new terrain. But Frances stood and rubbed her back while clucking to Oriana, wondering how she could persuade Charles to let her visit Morley soon.

"Ho, there, lads. A Cavandish comes," Charles called to the stablemen, who appeared with cheerful salutes. "I want a bath," he told Frances, guiding her with a firm hand toward the house. "But first I have to see Arcturus and Dickon. You and the boys have the first round of hot water. I will join you anon."

So he *did* need Arcturus, Frances noted. He also needed his old master, who would be with the bird. The sudden light in Charles's eyes told her this and more—light kindled by the warmth of the home fire burning strong in his soul. Though he refused to admit it, he needed his bird as badly as she needed hers.

More than that, his roots flourished, in the form of a living man and bird eagerly awaiting his return. How she envied his good fortune. Her home, though it awaited her, was only an aging hulk, now empty of human warmth.

Desire to share his warmth burned so hot in Frances, she suddenly couldn't wait to know this marvelous master firsthand. So after Charles had escorted her into the great half-timbered house and turned her over to the housekeeper, Frances instructed the boys to take their baths first, then excused herself to the good woman.

As she slipped out the back door, she felt distinctly lax, turning their bathing over to a stranger, especially when it might be a tussle, but she couldn't help it. With Oriana still perched on her fist, she entered the garden in back of the house.

Even from this new vantage point, the house exuded an aura of comfort and calm. Some parts were additions; all of it rambled. Roses climbed on its southern wall, not yet in bloom, and a huge kitchen garden flourished before her, pungent with herbs. A pigeon loft nearby rustled with wings and the cooing of its inhabitants. Frances imagined seven laughing, jesting Cavandish children bursting from the kitchens to romp in the garden, playing games and pranks on one another. She mourned for her own childhood spent only a few miles north—isolated. Alone.

Ahead, she glimpsed Charles's back as he walked a stone

path curving toward an outbuilding set some distance away. Frances followed stealthily, hiding behind broad tree trunks until she realized he was so intent on his destination, he was unlikely to look back.

He disappeared into the building, constructed of mellowed wood with perfect corner joins. Long rows of windows made it a perfect mews for birds. Smoke rising from the chimney at the building's far end told her it also housed a keeper's lodging. Master Dickon must live here.

Creeping up to the door through which Charles had disappeared, she grasped the latch.

With hinges oiled and silent, the door swung open, just wide enough for her and Oriana to pass. Like a thief, she tiptoed through the dim interior, across the pristine layer of sand and many perches. Hawks and falcons greeted her, ruffling their feathers, chuckling in their throats. "Shhhh," she warned them uselessly, one finger pressed to her lips. Another door loomed at the far end of the mews.

Ear to wood, Frances strained to hear through it. Male voices rumbled. With any luck, they would be so engrossed in their reunion, they wouldn't know she was there.

With great care, she pried the door open and peered into the room.

Chapter 34

The scene that met Frances's eyes touched her greatly. On one knee, Charles paid homage to an older man. The gentleman wore a heavy leather jerkin, the shoulder of which was marked by birds' claws. His face was wreathed by a thick, bushy beard the color of forest bark flecked with snow.

A male goshawk, large for its sex, perched on Charles's fist, preening in a sunbeam that burnished its feathers to cream and gold. The three of them drew together, deep in discourse, some of their words human, some of them clicks of the tongue and chuckles exchanged with the hawk, who shifted and bobbed, glad to see his master again.

As Frances watched in fascination, the old man ruffled Charles's hair with a fatherly hand. That touch, the way Charles leaned into it, affected Frances as much as the hawk's rich golds glinting in the sun. Here was a bond of love, abundant and tender. Master Dickon's face reflected it, along with a bluff good humor and tolerance for youthful ways. In a flash she saw who had honed Charles's magic. Here, wisdom transferred from teacher to pupil. She had sensed the spellbinding strength in Master Dickon the second she opened the door.

"So, Shikrah," the old fellow murmured, "you've gone and got yourself wed." Frances shook her head in bafflement at the unusual name he called Charles. "About time," he went on. "And I see, from your look, 'tis for love."

"I would not gainsay you at our first meeting, master," Charles answered, "but you know there's little love left to my heart."

"You've said that before, but hearts change. Otherwise, why did you wed her?" The master's magical hand smoothed Arcturus's feathered breast. The bird bent toward him, seeking a repeat of the caress. Frances stared at the master's work-worn, roughened hands and yearned to feel their approving power bless her as well.

"Because she requires care," Charles insisted. "I seemed the best one to give it."

"Is that all?" probed the master.

Charles bowed his head, as if admitting it was.

Frances's heart contracted. She'd known this truth about Charles, that he couldn't give what she most craved. But his silent admission to another whittled at her heart. Holding Oriana closer, she sought the bird's fragile warmth.

"Noble sentiments to offer your protection," Master Dickon continued, "but have a care, my lad. A woman requires as much tending as your hawk. Don't ruin her with neglect."

"I won't neglect her. I swear to that."

The heat of passion burned in his voice. Frances heard it and sighed. At least he needed something from her, and offered the white-hot burn of his desire for her in return.

Master Dickon must have recognized it, too, for as Charles shook his head wearily, the master rested one gnarled hand on his rich brown hair, now glinting with bright gold from the sun. "Let them go, Shikrah. Let the old thoughts go. Make room for the new."

"That's just it. I can't."

"Shall I give you another penance to cleanse the soul? I have a new one that will do you a world of good, Shikrah."

"What now?" Charles sounded resigned, as if he frequently took unpleasant orders from his master, striving to escape his grief.

"Let your lady order the training of the messenger birds."

Charles's head snapped up. "Why should I do that?"

"Why do you let your bird decide when it will fly and when it will not?"

"Because I respect his instinct. If Arcturus refuses to fly, 'tis for good reason. I can't force him, nor would I wish to."

"Exactly. What would happen if you tried?"

"He would hate me. You can't force a wild thing to work against its will. What does that have to do with which of us trains these birds?"

"You can't force a wild thing to work against its will," the master repeated. "But when you ask of it something it loves . . ."

His unspoken meaning weighed on Frances. She could see it did on Charles, as well. The master of birds was never really a master—the two were equals, each offering something to the chase.

"But Frances knows little of this venture," Charles protested. "I know the ships that we'll work with. I know the coast."

Master Dickon scoffed in a friendly manner. "You will be called upon to serve in many ways, Shikrah. Leave the training of the birds to someone else. Teach your lady what she needs to know and trust her skill. It must be great within her, else you would never have taken her as your wife."

"And how will it help?"

"I think you know the answer to that."

Frances caressed Oriana and thought of her bond with the bird. Bird and handler must trust and respect each other before they could work as a pair. Never could she hope for such a relationship with Charles.

Apparently Charles thought the same way, because he said something too low to hear, and the master murmured words of solace. "Let your lady help you. Women can bring great comfort with their care."

"I don't deserve comfort. I deserve the same torture my friend had. And she"—he paused as if despairing, then plowed on—"every time I think I'm getting close to her, a shadow falls between us. Always a shadow."

Frances rested her head against the door frame, full of sorrow. It was true, ghosts haunted them both.

His ugly legacy was the blood of his friend, staining his hands. And hers brought the shadow to stand between them. She couldn't help but it was the shadow of her own painful past, following. Always following. She turned away quietly, intending to go, when Master Dickon spoke her name.

"Mistress Frances, join us if you please."

Frances jumped. Oriana sidled on her glove uneasily, and Frances blushed at her rudeness. Listening at door cracks! She'd stooped to new depths. And he'd known she was here the entire time.

Seeing it was useless to deny her guilt, she pushed open the door and stood in the entry. Charles had leaped to his feet, holding Arcturus. From the angry expression on his face, *he* hadn't known she was there.

"A shy flower, just as you said." The master cocked his head to one side as he examined her.

"I said she was a *wild* flower."

Master Dickon ignored his pupil's surly tone. "Come here, my dear."

The second Frances entered the chamber, Oriana lowered her head until it was level with her tail, bobbed up and down, and cackled repeatedly. With a start, Frances realized Arcturus was doing the same.

"They greet each other." Master Dickon's broad face lit up with humor. His thick beard split with his smile. "With great ceremony, too, which is better than we are doing. I am Richard Pennington, at your service, madam baroness." He heaved himself to his feet in a ponderous movement suggesting joint pain and bowed his stocky frame from the waist. Frances curtseyed in return to this magical teacher. Her gaze moved from the strength of his stocky legs clad in brown stockings, to his broad, leather-covered chest, capable hands, and weather-pale eyes. Clearly he had spent years following birds, and by all appearances, still did. Pain or no, nothing would keep him from the hunt.

"Frances Morley, at yours," she said. "I mean Frances Cavandish." She blushed furiously at her blunder. "Why do you call Charles 'Shikrah'?" she blurted out.

The master ran a hand through his snow-tipped hair, his face thoughtful. "The word means sparrowhawk and comes from a country far to the southeast, where the land is desert and scorched by the sun. I was teaching him to fly his first hawk when he was a lad, a game little sparrowhawk twice as fierce as its size. We named it Shikrah, but eventually the name transferred to Charles and stuck. Apt, is it not?"

"Shikrah." She tried out the name, liking the way it rolled off her tongue. Suddenly, she saw Charles as his master did, as he had once been, as he was meant to be—loving and loyal. How she wished she held the key to unlock his pain and scatter it on the wind just as the ashes of their enemies had dispersed when Charles exploded the French inn.

It was on the tip of her tongue to ask if she might call him Shikrah as well, when Master Dickon spoke again.

"I understand you have a home to recover." He plucked a jar of oil from a shelf, dipped two fingers in its contents, and lubricated Arcturus's jesses to keep them soft. "Never have I liked that man living at Morley. Nor do the others in Lulworth. We all wish him gone. I pray you call on him and challenge him to prove his claim."

"I shall," Frances declared, heartened by this support from an unexpected source, "first thing on the morrow."

"And I shall accompany you," Charles reminded her. "I'm convinced that Stokes's claim to Morley is false."

Chapter 35

"That signature is a forgery!" Frances whirled away from the hearth and paced the well-appointed chamber belonging to the Cavandish lawyer, the learned Master Carew. At Charles's request, he had agreed to assist in her case, but the immediate prospects of recovering her land looked dim. Charles stood by in silence by the big oriel window while she spoke. "No, 'tis worse than a forgery," she cried, knowing she was raving but unable to help it. "Whoever wrote it didn't even attempt to duplicate my father's writing. And Stokes seemed to take an inordinate satisfaction in showing it to me, as if he'd been anticipating the moment when he could see me helpless to prove him a liar."

"I am prepared to believe all that you've said." Master Carew smoothed his long gown and riffled the pages of a law book. He was flanked by his two clerks, whose quills scratched as they recorded the discussion. "We have little liking for Master Stokes in these parts. He has made enemies at every turn. First he enclosed part of Morley land with fences so it couldn't be used for common grazing. Then he wanted to take anyone caught hunting on his property before the courts. I refused to assist him though, so he put out traps like the one that caught the baron's hawk. I assure you, baroness, none of us likes him. But the difficulty is, without your father's will, the false nature of his document cannot be proved."

Frances ground her teeth in frustration, having already explained that the will lay in other hands. "The queen sent dispatches before I left London, recalling Sir Humphrey. I enclosed my directive that he bring my trunk, which contains the will. But we have yet to hear from him, and I suspect he's gone to Spain by now. I know not what to do."

"Haven't you some other document with your father's signature?" Charles asked. It was the first thing of substance he'd said since they'd returned from Morley. Frances had wept in rage and despair during their return ride, while he had remained silent and grim.

"That would answer the problem," Master Carew agreed. "If you had an official document or personal correspondence with an earlier signature, and it bore no resemblance to that held by Stokes, I would have grounds for ordering him to vacate the property. Of course he could contest it, and you would both end by going to the law. It could take years to sort out."

Frances squeezed her eyes shut and thought as hard as she could. "There must be a signature somewhere."

"Mayhap other deeds of sale or purchase of land," the lawyer put in helpfully, "or dispatches he wrote to the queen or her servants while in her service."

"There are most likely papers with his handwriting in London," Frances began, "but I didn't think to ask while we were there. To fetch them and return would require a week's journey. Add to that the time it would take to search the royal records. . . . I think instead I could find some letters at Morley," she said thoughtfully, a plan forming in her mind. "We had some things packed away in the garret. Stokes wouldn't know about them."

"We'll look there," Charles said decisively.

"Yes," Frances interjected, delighted to find him in agreement. The idea of searching the house beneath Stokes's ugly nose both terrified and delighted her.

"Don't be caught if you venture this," Master Carew warned them. "Just now he has the law on his side."

"No fear of that." Charles looked as grim as Frances had ever seen him, except for the time Diego came at him with the bar shackle. The fire of blood lust had burned in his eyes then. Now another glimpse of the killing instinct heartened her as she realized that impulse leaped in her as well. She would fight to recover her land. But more than that, the will to fight would be unleashed in all Englishmen and women when the Spanish finally arrived.

Charles could have murdered Stokes with pleasure. Naturally, he wouldn't, but he would willingly do the next best thing if Stokes caught them and threatened Frances. He recognized the malice in the man and was immediately suspicious. Why should Stokes feel anything but concern that he might lose his land? Why should triumph gleam from the whoreson's eyes?

Then, too, he'd had no chance to bed Frances. No wonder his foul mood colored their every discussion. No wonder his temper flared. A full night in his own bedchamber with her, where the bed was soft and the linens clean, and still he hadn't had her. He'd teased and provoked as far as possible, but she hadn't responded. It put him half out of his wits.

If he hadn't realized she was terrified of the experience, he might have thought he had lost his touch.

Yet what could he do to assuage her fears? She had responded passionately to him in the barge and the woods. He hadn't stood her up at the altar, like the miserable Antoine. She'd promised him solemnly to let him bed her once they reached Dorset. Yet the minute they had entered the bedchamber where they might take their pleasure, she stiffened and became as responsive as his hawk's wooden perch. Much as he loved his hawk, the demeanor of the perch failed to inspire him. Not to coupling, at least.

He also wanted to ravish her whenever she called him Shikrah. Tonight, as they walked beneath the Dorset stars, making their way across the downs by a roundabout path toward Morley, he felt surprisingly like that young Shikrah again—clean and new like the wind whispering through the trees. He reached out to recapture who and what he'd been as a boy, wishing he could start over again.

As they approached the marsh where they'd first met, his need for Frances intensified. In this well-loved country of his youth, in the boggy, blessed land where he had first craved her, he imagined being unsullied, as he'd once been, waiting for her to enter his life.

"Hold a minute." He arrested her as she balanced on a log, about to cross to drier footing. "Isn't this the spot where—"

"Where I first bested you, Shikrah? 'Tis the very spot." She grinned at him, an outrageous elf, seeming not the least touched by his sentimental memories.

"A goshawk and a marsh hawk should never be pitted against one another. 'Twas never a fair contest. If it had been, I would have been first."

"If we had both flown the same birds and started together, I still would have bested you." With a pert wiggle she slipped across the log and raced ahead.

"Minx!" He pelted after her, water flying beneath his

boots, just as it had that day long ago. "You teased me then and you tease me now. You were every bit as interested in me as I was in you."

"I didn't like you in the least." Her voice streamed over her shoulder, reminding him of the way her hair had streamed around her at age thirteen.

"You didn't *like* me," he insisted. "You *loved* me on sight."

"You were careless with your bird." She laughed at him, twitching her skirts flirtatiously as she ran. "You didn't even call her back yourself."

"That's why you fell in love with me."

"Because you were careless?" she taunted.

"Because I was more interested in you than anything else, even my bird." He stepped in a wet spot and sank to his ankles. As water seeped into his boot, he cursed and sprinted forward. With immense satisfaction, he caught her by the arm.

Frances shuddered as Charles captured her and whirled her into his arms. As their bodies flew together, she yielded, letting him claim her lips in a joining that rocked her to the core. Suddenly, the fear and restraint she had felt in the house, in the rigid bed like the one where Antoine had taken her, dissolved. Urgent need rose inside her, fueled by this place's memories. She wanted to best him. She wanted his body. She wanted to rule him and be ruled in return.

The touch of his hands drove those thoughts and all others from her mind. With the grace of wings, wind-light and airy, his lips explored hers. Offering, teasing, nibbling, and pleasing—just as they had wanted to do long ago. She felt as if she had come home at last.

Yet how could that be?

Home, a voice whispered inside her. Here the spirits of her mother and father seemed strongest, united at last in death. She had sensed them when she visited the house with Charles earlier, though Master Stokes ruined her chance to commune with her parents. Never had she met a man with uglier teeth. His mouth had split to reveal them, dark and crooked, probably just like his soul. Despite him, the quietude of the old house had spoken to her, chanting the sheltered peace and love of her youth.

"Help me, Charles," she pleaded, turning away from his kisses. Her need for home merged with her need for him, confusing her utterly. He didn't hold the key to happiness. He couldn't give her what she'd once had, could he? For an instant, she wished he could. His kisses promised so much, and yet . . .

Wrapping both arms around her middle, she hugged herself, unwilling to trust her instinct. "Charles, I must have my home back." The cry welled up and burst from her lips. She tugged at him with sudden urgency. "I must! We must go now."

With a groan that rang with despair and frustration, he obliged her. She couldn't help it—she had to be within her own walls once more before she could think clearly. Morley called to her across the marsh and woods. As the passion between them subsided, she sighed deeply. Taking his hand, she led him onward, up the hill and through the wood, toward the old half-timbered house that was the place of her birth.

"How do you intend to get in?" Charles asked as they crouched in the unkept gardens a short time later.

"Stokes will be in the front parlor, I would guess. Or in the front bedchamber if he has retired." Frances pressed against Charles's side, unable to still her trembling from fear and excitement. The thought of Stokes sleeping in her parents' bed, sitting at their table, violated the sacred memories of her childhood. Her primitive urge to fight surged within her, as in a female hawk protecting her brood. "We will go to the opposite end of the house and climb the tree there. I used to do it regularly as a child and go in the house through a garret window."

As Charles followed Frances around the house, her excitement infected him. He felt like a mischievous child up to a trick. Yet this trick carried a life-and-death meaning to it. If Stokes caught them, he might do something drastic. Somehow it heightened the thrill, to defy the whoreson. At the same time, it worried him. The man would probably delight in killing them, given the chance.

The old oak proved an easy climb. No wonder Frances had done it at age seven and eight. Bringing her back skirts between her legs, she tucked them firmly in her waistband, forming breeches. Then he helped her reach the first limb, his lust running rampant as his hand cupped her bottom before he boosted her up.

With a leap, he followed. The shudder of fragile branches beneath his weight brought him up short, reminding him to have a care. They were here to find papers, not for a bedding. Yet he was all in a lather for her, as excited as a stallion.

He let her climb ahead while he waited, seeking to quell his arousal. The smooth oak bark gave off its woody fragrance, and he breathed it in, grateful for the night air cooling his heat. So to his business. Yet as he heaved himself up to the next level, he knew the stern reminders were for naught.

She climbed above him with airy grace, her body too tantalizing. Nearing the top, she poised on a branch, inspecting a window. A pity that window was so high. She couldn't possibly get to it. Nor could he, since the higher branches were too slim. Yet he felt as if he could touch the stars, his exhilaration had so heightened. The brilliant points of light peering at him between the shifting canopy of leaves seemed to agree, for they winked at him. Just out of reach, his beautiful fairy hovered above his head.

"Shikrah," the fairy hissed at him in most unfairylike syllables, "can you knock a hole in the window pane? The one nearest the latch so I can reach in?"

"No doubt I can," he answered in an equally loud whisper—though he might break his neck doing it, he added silently, eyeing the distance to the window. Happily, fortune was with him. Having anticipated the eventuality, he had brought a long dowel with him. Drawing it from his belt, he edged along the branch, holding fast to the limb above his head. Just below the window, he paused and stretched upward. He could just reach the pane with the dowel.

The glass proved thick. He drove the dowel several times before it shattered. He winced at the racket it made, and waited, breathless, hoping no one had heard.

"How will you get across?" he queried with concern. "Your branch doesn't reach far enough."

"I'll lean across and grab that bit of trim above the window." She retucked her skirts with matter-of-fact motions.

He assessed the ornamenting strip skeptically. "You can't hang from that."

"I often did as a child."

"You've gained weight since then. And stature," he

informed her dryly. "Beyond that, you're like to be out of practice. It's been more than ten years, you know."

"Shikrah, you should have studied the law." She linked one arm around the branch beside her and grinned down at him. "With your arguments, you would win every suit." So steadied, she spit on her hands and rubbed them together.

As usual, she had the last word. Before he realized what was happening, before he could argue out the details with her and come to a decision, she leaned from the branch and plummeted into empty space.

Chapter 36

Charles's heart slammed into his throat and stuck there, nearly cutting off his wind. Horrified, he leaned out as far as he dared and groped for her, knowing he couldn't possibly catch her.

Frances's fingers closed on the trim above the window, and she dangled like a spitted rabbit above the fire. Her feet clambered for purchase on the ledge below.

"I'm coming," he called, at a loss as to how he could fulfill that promise. He inched out on his own branch, feeling it give dangerously beneath his weight. It would either break or throw him off if he ventured farther. Which would leave him swinging from the slender limb above.

"Stay away," she snapped, finding her footing suddenly. Her left hand snaked through the hole he'd made in the glass and flipped up the latch. Before he could blink, she shoved in the window and disappeared into the dark garret beyond.

"Thank God." Relief flooded his mind. Inching his way back toward the tree trunk, Charles settled on his branch. It irritated him that Frances went off, leaving him to wait in suspense. Then he noticed for the first time that his dark shirt clung to his back and chest, soaked with sweat, a vivid reminder of his fear for her. Which irritated him more.

"Damn," he muttered. He felt like an acorn, swinging from a precarious twig in this blasted tree. Here he sat, helpless as a babe, forced to wait until she returned.

Frances picked herself up from the attic floor and surveyed her past with wholehearted joy. She forgot Charles. She forgot danger, haste, or stealth. The climb up the tree, the leap that carried her into a private, secluded part of her own home plunged her back in years. Suddenly, she was seven again, sitting on the floor of the old garret, the place she had transformed into her private realm.

In the musty, warm darkness, she felt her way to a little table. It nestled in its familiar place beneath the eaves, waiting for her. The narrow drawer grated as it slid open, the way it always did. Her fingers discovered candles, just where she'd left them. Their scent had faded, but their wicks stood ready. She groped for the tinder box, then produced flint and steel.

The spark jumped. The lint ball flared. Warm and comforting shadows of the old clothespress and her mother's trunk leaped around her as she lit the candle—familiar forms, beloved forms. Her own little chair, made by her father—she touched it in awe as the veil of her beloved past descended and wrapped her in its memories. Her child's heart remembered, despite the layers of dust and passage of time.

Here she had reigned supreme, queen of her own domain. So strong were her memories, she scarcely noticed she had cut her wrist on the window. Blotting away the blood with a careless finger, she remembered how she had sat here and crafted a nest for her own special dreams. No one would gainsay her, no trace of sorrow. Secure in her parents' love, she ruled here.

With breath held, Frances reached for her special trunk. Her fingertips touched the heavy leather, its once pliant surface now dry and cracked. The cool feel of the brass bindings chilled her momentarily. But then the lid creaked open, and a rush of her mother's scent surrounded—the faint trace of orange water wafted from her mother's old dress, a well-worn, favorite plum silk. The fabric crackled as she lifted it, dry and brittle. With reverence, Frances brought it to her cheek while hot tears welled.

Imagination. That's what Charles gave her! Suddenly, her imagination sprang to life again, and she dared hope for the future, the impossible. She saw Morley like the Cavandish house, filled to the brim with hordes of laughing, rollicking children. Children playing pranks and getting into mischief. Children eating and drinking and growing strong and healthy. Children cherished and hugged by their mother. And she . . . she was their mother. She, the one who nurtured and loved.

The image wrapped her in a grip so strong, she trembled with excitement. This was what she wanted! This was what she had dreamed of at age eight as she played in the garret!

And Charles gave her the chance to live the dream. For that reason alone, she would cleave to her husband. And she must reclaim Morley. Spurred by the new thought, trembling with happiness, she put the silk aside and searched the trunk again.

An old-fashioned fan, its feathers shedding. A book of sonnets by someone long dead. And finally, what she sought. Letters. Her father's love letters to her mother in their youth.

Each one had a date and the place from which it was written. Each one had directions for delivery to her mother. And at the end of each letter, her father's signature, first and last name, not to be denied.

The details were too complete to be forgeries. The contents of the letters too intimate, too personal, to be false. Quickly, she counted, touching each fragile parchment. This was her proof. Her irrefutable proof. In the circle of her candle's gold light, she bent her head and read.

Tenderness, she found there—love in profusion—between a young, budding woman and her gentle knight. Once again the image of her mother rose before her, smiling and lovely, with her delicate touch and her kisses so sweet. She, too, had lost her father, just like Frances. Then the aunt who had raised her had died, leaving her alone, but for her brother Edward. At the death of her caretaker, her mother had married her knight, despite her youth and her lack of funds.

A last line caught her eye. "What were we put in this world to do, if not to love. We must seize the chance and never let it go."

With trembling fingers, she folded the letter. Searching the trunk for an old handkerchief, she wrapped it securely with the others and placed them in the pouch at her waist. Suddenly, she needed Charles, with a burning need that could not be denied.

The longer Charles waited, his gaze riveted to the window, the shorter his patience grew. He rose eagerly in his place as Frances appeared at the window.

"I found it."

"Found what?" He strained to see if she held anything in her hands.

"My father's signature, many times over. Irrefutable."

"Excellent." As she flung one leg over the sill, he waved

at her madly. "Stop. Don't move. You can't come back the
way you went in."

She surveyed the distant branch ruefully. "Oh dear."

Worse than oh dear, he thought to himself. *Thunderation.*
"You'll have to go out through the house. Do you think you
can manage?"

She nodded. "That should be easy enough, unless he's still
awake."

"I'll look first. Don't you dare move until I return," he
ordered, sliding to the branch below. "Watch for my signal.
And have a care, will you?"

"I'll meet you at the scullery door."

"Don't meet me anywhere until I tell you. Stay put." He
said it again, slowly and deliberately, pausing in his climb,
one leg thrown over a branch, hands curled around different
limbs. "Do you hear me, Frances? Answer me straight."

"Despot."

Her pert insult wafted down from on high. At least she
hadn't called him a toad this time, he muttered, incensed at
the danger. "Don't you dare disobey me. Promise."

"I promise."

Given no choice but to trust her, he had to be contented
with her vow. By the time he'd swung from branch to branch
and leaped to the ground, he was thoroughly aggrieved with
himself. How had he let her go in the house alone?

He scouted the first level of Morley, pressing his nose to
the glass of each window, taking the time to check carefully.
Front entry hall, parlors, private chambers, kitchens. All
appeared dark below and above stairs as well.

Completing his lengthy circuit of the house, he returned to
Frances. There she sat at the window, chin in hand, gazing at
the mist now covering the moon. Her tipped-up face suggested she wandered in a dream. Eager to reclaim her attention, he scaled the tree again. "He must be abed," he
informed her, once again at her level. "No lights anywhere.
But be careful. Take the safest route. And don't linger!"

Without a word, she nodded and swung the window
closed. After that, he could only climb back down and walk
around to the scullery door. Crouching at the ready in the
shadows, he steeled himself to wait.

A millennium passed. *Thunder and damnation,* what was
taking her so long? Stray rain drops pelted his face, and the
night turned darker. When the door jiggled, as if stuck, he

tensed every muscle. It popped open suddenly like a cork
released from a jug.

"Charles?"

"Here." Relieved, he reached for her and drew her into an
embrace. For the second time that night, he was fervently
glad to see her safe.

A light suddenly struck him full in the face. His joy evaporated like water on a hot pan, dispelled by the rays from a
swinging lantern. The cold metal of a militiaman's musket
pointed their way.

"Hold," came a voice, as rough and grating as the stuck
door. Charles knew it immediately. He'd heard it earlier that
very day. "Hold, trespassers, or I'll fire."

Chapter 37

"So it's the great baron, is it?" Stokes's snarl had a nasty edge to it. "This came for you. Here." He flung something at them.

Charles ducked, yanking Frances with him. A white paper fluttered down on their heads, and he captured it. "What is it?" he demanded while Stokes laughed.

The man's eerie mocking filled the still Dorset night. "Take it with you and you'll see. Now get off my land and don't come back."

The weapon exploded, its shot whizzing over their heads. Before Stokes could recover from the gun's recoil, Charles dragged Frances away, stuffing the paper in his shirt. They plunged over the low wall and into the bedraggled garden, slipping and sliding. Making all kinds of racket, he pushed her ahead of him, over the opposite wall at the other end. Running feet pursued them, and they raced, hell-bent, for the wood.

"This way." She tugged him furiously toward the left. "He won't follow us into the marsh."

He charged after her down the hill, winding around trees, crashing through bracken. Their only hope was to put distance between themselves and Stokes's gun.

The shouts behind them receded, still coming from above, at the top of the hill.

When they reached the marsh, he halted. "We can't cross here. The water's too deep."

"I know a pathway," Frances whispered. "The water is shallow. Follow me."

Slime closed around his ankles as they squelched through the muck, but it grew no deeper. Once he blundered off the path. His leg sank to the knee before he pulled back and recovered the path. Frances caught his hand and led him after that. He placed his feet directly behind hers.

They reached the far stand of woods in safety. Frances stopped and tilted her head. They both listened. Nothing but the rasp of their own breathing sounded. The call of a nightingale echoed through the trees. The scamper of small animal paws sounded on the forest floor.

"We did it! They've given us up." An exuberant whirlwind, Frances kissed him, missing his mouth in the dark. Her lips pressed wetly to his chin.

He corrected her error gladly and claimed the warmth of her lips with all the vigor brought by danger, tension, and mutual need. And by heaven, that same vigor must have taken hold of Frances, because she was a glutton for his kisses. She flung herself into his embrace with a vehemence he couldn't refuse.

"What is it, sweetling?" he groaned, wanting her on the spot, whether that spot was mucky or no.

"I want to make love to you," she cried. "I want you to make love to me."

"Here? Now?" Her unexpected demand amazed him. "I mean yes!" He couldn't correct himself fast enough. Wasn't this what he'd wanted? Frances, hot and panting for him? Begging to be his? But what a place she'd chosen. He hadn't been serious when he thought of having her in the muck. He wanted her in a soft, clean bed.

"Don't move." Her excited breath flared against his cheek. "I want to be rid of this bodice."

Anything, he thought fatalistically. He would do anything to have her. He would couple with her in a mud hole. Bruise himself on roots and stones while doing it. Be stuck by pine needles. He watched in fascination as she stripped off her bodice and dropped it on a bush.

Without question, the nymph had returned to this marsh. Slender and lovely, she stepped across the forest floor to meet him. All the desire he'd held inside these past days, all the despair he'd spent on Inez, boiled within him, threatening to explode. He needed this woman, this queen of the woodland. He needed her forgiving love.

"Away with your doublet." With unsteady hands, she released the buttons. When he shrugged out of the garment, she laughed and tossed it away.

"Frances, I'll never find it again in the dark."

"Good." Her laugh trilled through the wood, pure and liquid like the song of the nightingale. She reached to loosen the throat lace of his shirt and peeled the cloth away. As it skimmed over his head, the letter from Stokes fluttered out. He ignored it as she bent to kiss his arm. Fingers gliding, her lips traveled upward. Then she passed behind him, her mouth gliding across his shoulder until his blood ran hot. When her teeth nipped his neck, when her hands found the fastening to his trunk hose, an overwhelming shock of pleasure fanned through him. Summoning his will power, he controlled his urge to grab her. He had sworn to let her decide how far and fast to go.

But if she didn't speed up the pace, she would be sorry. The silk of her soft lips addled his wits so, he couldn't think straight. When she moved to unfasten her skirts and petticoats, he ripped off his remaining clothes with the speed of a hawk's dive. Fueled by his need, he reached out to clasp her, only to have her dance beyond reach.

"Not yet," she teased, rolling down a stocking. With a laugh she flung it away, then chased it with the other.

He stalked her through the bracken. When something sharp gouged his foot, he barely winced. Naked and aroused and marvelously glad of both, he tracked her laughing retreat. Pausing in a moonbeam that filtered through the trees, she pulled off her white smock and tossed it away. It settled on a bush like a snowy owl. Which left her beautiful body bared to his eyes.

The white heat of desire blinded him to anything else around them. "I can't wait another second to have you," he growled as he pursued her. "You'd best stand still, nymph."

Frances felt the eagerness exuding from Charles and delighted in it. Thrilled to provoke him, excitement coursing through her, she led him deeper into the wood.

"Damn it, Frances, I've kept my promise. I've let you decide. Now stop," he panted, crashing after her.

"Who's begging?"

"I am," he admitted with clarity. "Are you happy? You're far more provoking than I, Mistress Nymph. Come here at once, and I'll make you mend your ways."

"Shan't," she tossed at him, along with a saucy flirt of her bare shoulder. Plucking hairpins from her hair and losing them into the darkness, she sent her locks streaming down her back. Laughing, she led him a merry chase. "You must come to me, Shikrah," she teased. "Come to me, my millstone."

He was just as hard as the namesake she'd given him.

Despite the darkness, she could see that quite well. Imperiously, she held up her fist, as if he were a bird to be summoned home.

Even as she did it, she knew the truth of the matter. The falconer served the bird, and the bird served its master. A working pair must bond. And just now, she craved such a bonding and all it meant. A fierce fire lit within her, setting her imagination ablaze. Tonight, she would break through the last barrier. She would tell him of her love, here and now.

With a muted moan, she welcomed him as he reached her and whirled her into his arms. Their bodies twined, and they tumbled to the forest floor, Frances on top, her hair raining around his face. With possessive arms, he melded her to him. His eyes ignited with craving. For her. Only for her.

With a laugh of ecstasy, she gave them both their desire.

His frenzied groan rewarded her efforts. Head flung back, hands gripping her thighs, he looked the picture of pleasure. Shivers of heat careened through her body with each move and thrust they made.

Joy of the heavens. Power of the winds. Suddenly, she felt freer than she had in years. Despite his reticence about his emotions, Charles took her soaring; he had promised her this.

"Charles, I love you. I swear, I do."

He rose up in answer and, with a powerful joy on his face, without breaking their union, tumbled her on her back. She laughed, arched her hips, and urged him deeper. Teasing, she struggled, and they rolled again, ever thrusting, ever joined. Now on top. Now on the bottom. She nipped his neck as they tumbled, until at last, with a breathtaking swoop, she ended on top. He responded by rhythmically squeezing her thighs with both hands. The slippery, thrilling friction built between them, taking them higher into the glorious wind.

They both reached the heights at the same moment. Clasped in each other's arms, they flew high, as if straight into the dazzling force of the sun. Frances squeezed her eyes shut and cried out her pleasure. Charles took her to the bright heavens with the urgency of his touch. Her imagination kindled, and she saw the tapestry of her future laid out before her, a picture of beauty and peace.

Let us make a child, she prayed in silence. She yearned to be a mother. This was the future she desired with the man she loved.

* * *

Charles lay on the bare ground of the marsh, the heat of his passion for Frances and hers for him temporarily spent, and marveled over what had just happened. She loved him! She had said the words with conviction, and he believed her. It explained why, for the second time in a matter of days, she had mated with him so fiercely, so ardently, she astonished him. Here in the marsh, she had all but torn away his clothes in her urgency, flung them away, and had him with a zeal so marvelous, he hardened again at the mere thought. It was almost an identical repeat of their London coupling, complete with the chilled bare ground and the tree root that jabbed him in the back. Only this time the blasted thing threatened to puncture his lung.

Not that he was complaining! Charles congratulated himself for remaining silent on the subject. To do otherwise might subdue Frances's ardor, and he didn't want that. He'd had a taste of her at her coldest, most distracted, earlier in his bedchamber, where they might have taken their ease on a luxurious feather bed. She had turned to an ice maiden with him, giving him a hint he was forced to heed. God knew, he wasn't a dolt. The woman had told him in all but words that she chose the time and place.

Lord, it had been worth the wait. She'd more than conceded to couple with him. The wench had initiated it without a hint from him, throwing away his clothes with such enthusiasm, he wasn't sure they would turn up again. Was he doomed for the rest of his life to risk walking home fully naked because his wife had scattered his clothes hither and yon?

Marvels, but the wench was wilder than he'd thought, refusing to mate like a reasonable woman, in a bedchamber, on a soft feather bed. Nowhere but the woods or marsh would do for her.

Once his stiff sense of propriety would have been appalled, but in truth, his need for her drove him so, he no longer cared where he had her, as long as he did. Because in that moment of glory when they had culminated together, she had finally said the words he longed to hear. As she'd admitted she loved him, he'd felt the magic. He had reached for the heavens with Frances and glimpsed their beauty. He would do anything for the chance to capture some of his own.

"Anything?" Frances queried, her face hovering over his, her dangling hair tickling his cheeks. "You'll do anything at all?"

Unaware that he'd spoken aloud, Charles blinked up at her night-softened face. "Love me like this always, Frances, and I'll give you anything you want, your whole life through."

"Anything?" Her playful tone suggested she meant to tease him.

"Anything," he vowed, determined to gratify her as much as she had gratified him.

"Children, Shikrah," she pronounced, gripping his hands with sudden eagerness. "I want a dozen children, and I want to raise them at Morley. I want a house full of them. If I can't bear all dozen myself, I want to take in abandoned strays and waifs to add to ours so that the old house rings with the laughter and joy as it never did when I was a child. Do you agree?"

"If that's your wish, then you shall have it," he swore. "I'll give you the 'children' part with pleasure, though we must have a care for your health. As for the other . . ." They both knew she couldn't have her home until they pried Ralph Stokes out of it, and he stuck to the house as tightly as a physician's leech. "As for ousting the old coney, what papers did you find to strengthen your case?"

With a flick of her dark hair, Frances crawled away on her hands and knees to grope among the ferns for her discarded pouch.

Teasing words about the foolishness of her earlier abandon sprang to his lips, but Charles repressed them. He liked that abandon far too well to discourage her from indulging it.

"Let me show you. I found the perfect thing." Frances returned, fumbling with the purse catch, and pulled out a fat bundle of letters. "My father's letters to my mother," she enthused, settling cross-legged on the ground, completely at ease. "At least a dozen, all with signatures. We have an irrefutable case."

"We'll see the lawyer on the morrow." Charles pulled her into his arms. And if their case wasn't irrefutable, he refused to voice lack of confidence. Because for the first time, she had given herself to him without the slightest reserve. For that, he would do anything, as he'd truthfully told her. Fight a dozen Ralph Stokeses; beat off the entire Spanish attack. She was his. His spirit soared.

Frances nestled against Charles, full of their shared pleasure, hope springing in her heart. Finding the letters, visiting her beloved home, however briefly, and declaring her love had revived her faith in her future. Even their narrow escape from Stokes didn't discourage her. Most of all, although Charles hadn't said he loved her, she knew he cared deeply for her. He showed it over and over—especially tonight. Careful, orderly Baron Milborne had made love to her in a muddy, coastal marsh and not complained once.

At just that moment, Charles shifted, letting her know he desired her again. A note of joy sang in her veins.

This time they used less haste and more gentle attention to one another. And when they reached the heights together, Frances knew that Charles soared with her. He, too, must feel the majesty of the moment when their bodies bonded. Now that bond remained, as strong and sure as the invisible loyalty that linked her with Oriana, drawing the hawk back to her side after every flight. She realized now she had offered Charles her loyalty from that first moment in Paris, when he was forced to defend her. She would give it again and again, returning to his side each time until she had no more breath left.

But now, with matters of the spirit temporarily settled, practical matters insisted on attention. Her feet had grown cold, and her bottom was undoubtedly muddy. It was time to find their clothes.

She bid Charles stay where he was and strolled through the woodland, plucking garments from thickets and ferns. With most of the pieces collected, she returned to sort them out.

"Here's one of your stocks, your trunk hose, canions, and doublet." She tossed them into his lap, then struggled into her own smock and kirtle skirt. "I've missed your shirt somewhere. Don't move. I'll wager I know where it is."

A moment later she returned with his shirt and her bodice. "What is this letter from Stokes?" She held it up, trying to focus light on it but with little success.

"It's probably a warning to stay off his property." Halfway into his clothes, Charles held out a hand for the letter and bent to read the name scrawled on the front. His shoulders tensed. "God's blood!"

"What's wrong?" Frances's heart leaped into her throat at his unexpected vehemence.

Without answering, he tore past the seal and read part of the letter. "Damn." He threw it aside, his voice thick with a venom she had never heard before.

Hesitantly, she retrieved the letter and stepped into a shaft of moonlight to read it. The dark ink script stood out, written in a feminine hand.

"My beloved Charles," the letter began.

Fear clutched her belly. Frances scanned the letter, searching for some clue as to its author. Another sentence leaped out at her. "Now that Spain is about to conquer England, we can be reunited, my husband. I have secured the promise of high places for us. You will live at my side, as was meant." Sickened, Frances turned to the next page and scrambled to find the signature at the end—Inez del Cavaladosa de Cavandish.

With a cry of despair, Frances flung the letter away from her. Her worst fears had come true. For the second time in her life, she had fallen in love with a man who already had a wife.

"It means nothing, you know," Charles said, bitterness against Inez showing, despite his denial. "You can't believe I'd desert you for her."

"Of course I trust you, Charles," she cried in torment. "But don't you see? She's working with Stokes. How else would he be the one to deliver your letter. And if Spain conquers England, Inez's claim becomes the superior one, a claim she fully intends to exert."

"But Spain won't conquer England. We're going to fight them and win."

"We will if I have any say in it," she muttered darkly, tugging on her bodice. "I intend to get to work straightaway."

Chapter 38

On the thirtieth of May, word came that the skies had cleared at Lisbon and the Armada had set sail amid great pomp and ceremony. Any Englishmen or women previous claiming the Armada would never reach England closed their mouths and joined in the preparations. To Frances's grim satisfaction, the entire country fell to its defense arrangements with a haste unknown until now.

From the Lizard in Cornwall all the way up to County Devon on the eastern coast and inland, captains trained and drilled men fitted with pikes, bills, muskets, and arquebuses. Gentlemen provided horsemen according to their means, mounted and equipped. Beacon signals were stoked with tinder on every promontory along the southern coast as well as inland to London. No one was immune to the threat of Spain's king. He intended to rule their land.

By then Master Carew had met with Ralph Stokes, and Frances paused long enough in her efforts with the birds to hear his report.

"I'm so afraid of what Master Carew will say." Frances shifted restlessly on her chair in the lawyer's chambers, too distracted to concentrate on anything properly. "What if Stokes refuses to—"

"Stop inventing trouble," Charles admonished. "See what he says, first."

Frances lifted her chin, determined to be brave.

Master Carew arrived and sat with them for a full hour, recounting his formal meeting with Stokes. "He laughed at me." The lawyer frowned at the stack of letters written by Sir Richard Morley. "I showed him the signature on one of the letters and challenged him to prove that the document he held was legal. And can you believe it? He laughed." The lawyer's face reddened as he spoke. "He said it made not a speck of difference what proof I had. 'Take it to the courts,' he said, nasty as you please."

"We will take the matter to the courts, then. Spare no expense," she heard Charles say through the haze of her anger. "Proceed with the paperwork to—"

Frances leaped to her feet, interrupting him. It was the height of rudeness, but she couldn't help it. She would explode into a thousand splinters of rage if she didn't do something—preferably smash Stokes's head.

Outside, she broke into a run the second she reached the street. Townspeople stared, and behind her she heard Charles pursue her. In a small corner of her mind, she regretted his need to apologize for her unruly behavior, but she couldn't just sit there and plan a paper attack. That villain possessed her mother and father's home, the home where the three of them had lived and loved.

The Cavandish house loomed before her, extending its welcoming aura. It must remain her home for now, because Morley might never be hers again.

She headed for the pigeon loft, seized a cage, and captured a fat pigeon. The birds cooed as she worked feverishly. At her back, she knew Charles watched, sorrowing for her, saying not a word of reproach.

Thank you, she wanted to whisper, but her mouth wouldn't obey. The new indignity from Stokes was too great to bear.

She snapped the full cage shut and hurried to the stables. Charles ordered the horses and fastened the cage to her saddle bow.

Frances set the pace, urging her mare into a hard gallop, heading westward up the coast. Her mind whirled in torment. Her beloved home—held under a false pretense by a villain and blackguard. It was her home! *Hers!*

The beat of the gray mare's shod hooves thudded on the road for two leagues. Spotting a suitable promontory, she guided the horse off the road and leaped from the saddle. With hair whipping her face, she scanned the broad, wind-blown Channel. Mountains of fog built in the distance, signaling the approach of late afternoon. Soon the sun would wane and mist would obscure all vision. And beyond, Spain restocked its ships and prepared to invade.

Grim with concentration, she loosened the lashings of the pigeon cage. Charles anticipated her, dismounting and moving forward to lift the heavy cage from her saddle.

Brushing off his attempt to help, she grasped the cage and lugged it to a grassy spot, leaving Charles to tether the horses. Without prelude, she opened the door and handled the plump birds, one by one. Their warmth crossed her palms for a bare instant as she launched them into the air.

"Home!" she cried, tossing a bird into the sky. It spread its wings and caught the wind. "Fly away home. I'll be waiting for you at journey's end." *Fly swift, fly sure,* her sorrowing heart echoed. *Fly away home, because I cannot.*

Each bird answered her challenge with a will. One by one they claimed the sky in a raucous dazzle of wings. They flapped and soared above her, now coasting on wind currents, now working to gain height. Without exception, they turned eastward and set their courses for the Cavandish home.

Frances stared after them until they dwindled into specks, only then noticing the scalding tears that poured down her face. She had wept throughout the ritual release of the homing birds, sorrow thrashing within like a storm.

When Charles put his arms around her, she pressed her face against his brown-quilted doublet and cried out her grief. "There's our proof that he's working with Sir Humphrey," she choked at last, her statement stark.

"We've been over this before."

"Yes," she said, angrily, "we've been over it, but I can't get over it. He knew all along I lacked the proper document to put him out of the house. And Inez . . . you can see that everything I suspected about her is true."

"She is unfailingly persistent," Charles agreed, as if she really needed an explanation.

"She's worse than persistent," Frances cried, distraught. "I resent her coming back into your life. Why isn't she married to someone else?"

"I don't know, and I don't care. I don't intend to yield to her."

"Nor I." She was so full of torment she boiled with it. "I'm going to fight back. I want some of our birds placed on Drake's and Howard's ships, and I want Plymouth and Dover birds brought here," she said. "I want some of our birds taken to Paris to speed news from the Continent. As for communications with London, I brought birds from the queen's royal lofts, but Her Majesty must have some of ours so we can relay news to her from Lord Howard and Drake."

For once he didn't contradict her. "Anything else?" was all he asked.

She faced the Channel and pointed in the direction of the Netherlands. "I want some of our birds placed with the English in Ostend. They must send me full reports of Parma's preparations."

Frances closed her eyes and heard her uncle's warning resound in her memory, as clearly as if he spoke at her side. *Parma is the man to watch.* "The question is, does he really have forty thousand men, or is the number a ruse?"

"You doubt they can inflict damage on us without Parma's men? They have nearly two hundred warships."

Her short-lived composure crumpled. "I'm terrified of what they'll do." With a cry, she yielded to another storm of tears.

Charles held Frances's shuddering body close and let her cry her fill. What he really wanted to do was to get Ralph Stokes alone on a dark night, cut up his heartless body, and scatter the pieces in the Dorset sea. As he considered how that might be managed, Frances suddenly lifted her head.

"Promise me something," she pleaded, full of urgency.

"Anything, sweet."

"If the Spanish come, promise you'll do whatever you must to preserve your life. Even if it means forsaking me."

The shadow fell between them, and he studied her with concern. "We just agreed we were going to fight them. What the devil do you mean?"

She stepped out of his arms and stared out to sea.

"Answer me. What kind of thing is that to say?" He whirled her around and gripped her shoulders. "Damn it, I won't forsake you. You're my wife."

She swallowed hard, as if struggling against another eruption of emotion. "Charles, I ask this of you because death follows me everywhere. Everyone I've loved has died."

"No one lives forever. I loved my father, and he died."

"But I lost my mother, my father, *and* my guardian. *Everyone* I loved. And now *she's* coming. She's been watching you and laying plans." Her urgency increased. "She sent Stokes here to prepare a place for the pair of you. Who knows what house or land he has his eye on—probably your brother-in-law's Lulworth Castle. This is no small plot of one, unimportant woman with little power, Charles. Her plans fit perfectly with those of Philip of Spain. I believe they'll use lies, trickery, anything to overcome us. Look at Stokes, flaunting his false document and taunting us to do our worst. He expects the Armada's landing to change everything. If Spain is in power . . . no, when she's in power, they'll desecrate my parents' home. They'll make us their slaves."

"You're hysterical." Charles captured her and held her tightly. "You go too far when you invent these fantastic futures. They're pure imagination. The Spanish will never come to power here."

Imagination. He saw it was her enemy and her savior. It plunged her into the depths of despair and it pulled her up again, renewing her hope. It had allowed her to see who had really caused Richard's death. And now it made her miserable as she foretold her impending doom.

And she was too restless to be comforted, so he let her pull away and race to the cliff edge. He watched, the torment churning inside him nearly equal to hers, as she hurled stones and mud clods into the sea. Let her work out the anger, he counseled himself. Let her calm herself down.

But his inner advice failed him when she whirled to face him. The western sun lit up her face, highlighting her fine lips and slanting brows. The breeze whipped color into her cheeks and tugged at her hair. A thick lock escaped from its knot and the wind raked the ebony strands. The green of her eyes glinted with untameable passions of anger, need, and love. If only he could remove the anger, leaving her the treasured emotions. If only he were more than human and could mend the troubles in her life.

"Make love to me, husband!" She flung the demand at him like a challenge. "Here! Now! I want to forget those monsters. Drive them from my mind!"

She shocked him, as usual. But *blast it,* he was up to any challenge she could issue when it came to mating with her. Anytime. Anywhere. She had but to say the word, and he would perform the deed with more passion and abandon than she could ask for.

He covered the distance between them in two of his strides. Face-to-face they stood, she with her chin tilted high and her fists knotted, he about to ignite from the incredible heat she stirred in his loins.

Then he could stand it no more. Like the waves crashing below, he curled his arms around her and claimed her the way the sea claimed the land. Here, on the coastal road he would have her, and she would have him, uncaring of who saw them. Before all the world, he swore aloud he was not wed to Inez del Cavaladosa. Frances Cavandish was his only bride.

Chapter 39

Tense days passed, and Frances dreamed at night of Philip of Spain. He sat like a spider in his web, spinning an ugly fate for her land. Like a miserable fly, she hung with the others, bound by strangling threads. The spider meant to possess her, her home, and everything dear to her heart.

On the twentieth of June, more news arrived from Portugal. Storms had driven the Armada to seek shelter in the port of Corunna. England drew a collective breath of relief.

In the wake of their temporary reprieve, the lord admiral sent his kinsman, Christopher Howard, to meet with officials in each coastal county and refine their battle strategy. Frances was permitted to attend the Dorset meeting, but Charles knew the outcome displeased her. Afterward, in the mews, he awaited her outburst. Sure enough, she let it loose, full force.

"I'm in charge of the birds. So why did you act as if you were?"

"I never agreed that you were in charge."

"You knew I believed I would have their ordering."

"I'll not argue with you."

"We're already arguing so we might as well finish. Do I have to write the queen and ask her to settle our dispute?"

He sucked in a breath, frustrated with her stubbornness, hamstrung by his rising desire for her. "We'll look like fools if we run to her every time we disagree."

"We could ask Master Dickon to settle it," she said a bit slyly. "You know what he said."

"You weren't supposed to be listening."

"But I did. And I won't give this up."

Charles narrowed his gaze and glared his fiercest, but Frances seemed unlikely to repent. She drove an impossible bargain, hinting she would dig in her heels until she got her way. But for once, he recognized her need. She clung to the work to fight her fears. And although in his opinion, women should obey, not give orders, he would let her have this. But he didn't have to like it.

"You win." He flung down a leash and stormed out of the mews.

She raced to catch up with him. "This isn't a battle."

"You're right," he growled, "it's a competition."

"It shouldn't be."

"Then we'll change it." He rounded on her. "You order the birds, and I'll order the boys."

Frances skidded to a stop, looking astounded at his statement. "But you don't like them. Why would you want charge of them?"

"Blast it, I do like them," he shouted, fists clenched, then realized what he'd said. Frances's face curved into a blinding smile at his confession. Maddening wench, she'd tricked him again. *Thunderation*, so what if he liked the urchins. "What I don't like is Louis visiting the alehouse both day and night," he said forcefully. "What they both need is lessons to keep them occupied, so they don't get into mischief. If you take over the birds, I'll want complete control of the boys' daily lessons and tasks."

The width of her smile increased. "Lessons? You'll see them educated like gentlemen?"

"The local vicar can teach them reading and writing, numbers, geography, everything they need, as well as riding." He was still irritated with her, but he had strong opinions about what he felt the boys needed. "I also want them to learn handling of the hawks and falcons. I'll teach Louis, you teach Pierre. They're also to help you daily with the messenger birds. And I don't want any arguments from you when I punish them for good reason," he warned. "They'll have disagreeable chores assigned if they don't behave."

"Whatever you say, oh lord and master," Frances said much too pertly.

With a grunt, he strode away, wondering what he'd been thinking, to imagine women would obey. The country was ruled by a woman. All the rest followed her lead.

Regardless of that, he now had to talk to Louis, so he gave the boy a lesson in falconry that afternoon, along with a stern lecture.

"Will nothing else please you?" Louis asked in response to Charles's demand that he not visit the alehouse again.

His thin face had filled out in the last weeks, changing his appearance vastly. But his love of the alehouse reminded Charles too much of his hardened demeanor in Paris, which he'd sworn to banish forever. "Nothing will do but your oath as a gentleman to stay out of all alehouses and taverns at all times."

Louis looked downcast. "But . . . I . . ." He swung one foot in the tall grass, lobbing off seeds. "I promise, I guess."

Charles smiled his approval and promised a reward if he kept his word.

Louis didn't brighten at the prospect. "I suppose I'll be punished if I don't."

Charles nodded, discouraged to think the boy might be so entranced with alehouse company, it put him in the dumps to give it up. He still didn't trust the lads, and if they shamed Frances, he would skin them alive.

"Might I still work as a night lookout at the beacon signal?" Louis asked. With most of the men in the militia, reliable lookouts had run short. Louis had begged permission of the mayor and been granted the task.

Charles had agreed with grave reservations. Assigning the flame-enamored lad to a task involving fire seemed foolhardy at best. He could just imagine the beacon flaring in a false alarm that would throw the militia along the entire coast into chaos. "You may," he said, "only if you behave, and if you stay away from the alehouse."

"I must go to Plymouth on the morrow to meet with Lord Howard and the other captains," Charles said to Frances the next day. "We have plans to discuss."

Frances scowled the entire way back to the house. No doubt he'd held back the news, knowing she wouldn't like it. *She* wanted to go to Plymouth, *she* wanted to discuss communications and strategy with Lord Howard, but in her zeal to take command of the birds, she had limited her freedom. She had to stay in Lulworth at her assigned post.

With Charles gone, Frances applied herself to her birds with a vengeance and soon saw the reward for her fervor. Birds flew from Lord Howard's ship to Lulworth, then relays went on to London and Dover. Her links were firmly in place with the queen's naval force.

A good thing, too, because English spies ferreted out the

news that the Duke of Medina Sidonia worked with single-
minded zeal to replace broken masts and spars, replenish bad
food and round up ships that had strayed in the storms. Spain
fully intended to relaunch when the weather brightened and
beat England to her knees.

In the meantime, false alarms, rumors, and hysteria waxed
and waned. Frances heard that Philip of Spain had drawn up
a black list of those he would put to death when the Spanish
conquered. It grew longer the more it was discussed, until
Frances's head spun with confusion and fear.

The only way to survive was to ignore the stories, so she
took refuge in her work. Each day she visited the airy pigeon
loft to talk to the birds, feed and water them, and dose them
with ground tobacco leaves for lice and mites.

The loft had been Master Dickon's domain for years, so
naturally he assisted her. Soon she noticed signs in the man
that disturbed her greatly. Dickon reeked of strong spirits in
the morning, and although he still performed his required
tasks, he joined her later each day and left her earlier each
night. She wondered if he'd always been this way. Surely
not. Charles would never have loved and respected a man
who drank too much.

Concerned, but unwilling to cause trouble, Frances
remained silent on the subject and watched.

She had fewer opportunities as the days passed. Master
Dickon assisted her less and less often, and Louis took over
more of his tasks.

"Look, there's Ivory," she exclaimed one day as a bird
pushed in the swinging panel of the bird door and reentered
the loft. "I told you she would be back first."

"Where is that Rex?" Louis groaned, having lost their
wager. "I guess I owe you tuppence."

"I refused to wager money, if you recall." Frances took up
Ivory and offered her a handful of cracked corn. The bird
eagerly gobbled her reward. "Listen, that may well be Rex
now."

The bird door swung open and a feathered head popped
through. Louis scooped cracked corn from the tin measure
and fed it to the bird. "What do I owe you if not money?"

Frances surveyed his accomplished handling of the bird
and congratulated herself on his rapid learning. "A kiss on
the cheek and a strong embrace," she answered. "I want
nothing more."

Louis poured the remaining corn into the bird's food pan, released Rex, and bestowed the requested prize. "I'm glad you ask for something reasonable. The baron expects me to turn into a model gentleman overnight," he said as he hugged her. "And I still think he doesn't trust me."

"Surely, you're wrong." With both hands occupied, cradling Ivory, Frances pressed her cheek against Louis's for a moment and sighed. "He's just preoccupied, working with our defense. He gets little sleep at night."

"I hope that's all it is." Louis straightened to his full height.

Frances released him with reluctance. Yet she knew she must trade her "mothering" ways for a more adult respect, just as she had replaced his brown fustian jerkin when it grew too small.

Tears threatened as she imagined him setting off on his own, and she quickly brought Ivory to her cheek, taking comfort in the fragile pulse of living warmth. "Charles trusts you as much as he trusts anyone," she said, wishing she could offer better, but at a loss herself. On the eve of an enemy invasion, she yearned to draw closer to Charles and cherish what might be their last days together, yet it seemed a hopeless dream. Especially when the person Charles seemed to trust least was himself.

"I hope *you* trust me," Louis said, his gaze solemn.

"I do, but I worry about your interest in the alehouse, Louis. Charles is incensed about it. Why do you wish to go there?"

"I just like it," he said with apparent candor. "The smell of the tobacco smoke. The lute player when they have him. The friendly talk."

"But you promised not to go again, didn't you? You'll keep your word?"

Several more birds popped in the trapdoor just then, and Louis moved quickly to reward them. Too quickly, it seemed to her. He hadn't responded to her concern.

She watched him with increasing worry after that, as they rewarded the other birds returning home. Then the hour of Louis's afternoon lessons with the vicar arrived, but he lingered, helping her change the water in the birds' pans. Suddenly, he turned, enveloped her in a fierce bear hug, then without a word of explanation, abruptly withdrew.

Distressed, Frances watched him as he hurried toward the

church, his lengthened stride more manly and determined than she had ever seen before.

Charles returned from Plymouth with new concerns on his mind. Who was bringing Spanish letters and messages into Dorset and sending them to other counties along the coast? Drake had captured a Spaniard recently who appeared to be one of the network. He admitted giving information to the Armada's admiral. With the multitude of ships plying Lulworth Cove and the coast, who could tell which were on legitimate business and which were not? In recent letters exchanged with Jonathan, they had decided Charles must help the local officials since they'd had no success stopping the information leaks.

On the night of July sixth, Charles saw Frances to bed and waited, stiff and tense at her side, until she slept. Then he dressed and left the house. He'd taken to making nightly rounds of Lulworth and the environs, going stealthily on foot. Tonight, he headed for the alehouse, hoping to learn something from the news exchanged.

Tobacco smoke cloyed the dim interior of the Nag's Head as he entered the large common room and surveyed the customers clustered at tables and around the fire. The host bustled over, wiping his hands on an ale-spattered apron, and welcomed him heartily.

Charles accepted a mug of small beer and settled on a bench where he struck up a conversation with several militiamen. A singer finished tuning his lute, then launched into a patriotic ballad about defeating the Armada, and Charles pretended interest in the performance as he scanned the guests.

"Baron, I'm right pleased ye've come tonight, because I've been meanin' to speak to ye." The host hauled up his loose-waisted trunk hose and peered into Charles's mug to see if he required a refill. "Best drink up and take yer friend home. He's dropped off one night too many here, if ye take my meanin'. The devil's own would have trouble rousin' him. I know I do."

Charles arched an eyebrow at him, puzzled as to whom he meant.

The host pointed. In a shadowed corner, Master Dickon sagged in a chair, his head tilted back. From the crack in his bushy beard emitted a loud, irritating snore. Charles stared, appalled. The man he'd never known to drink to excess, drunk? "On ale?" he asked, scarcely able to believe his eyes.

"He prefers the stronger spirits, if you take my meanin'." The host lumbered off to answer another call for ale, scratching his chest as he went.

Charles wove his way through the throng of guests. Was everything to go wrong of late? Tonight Frances had frozen up on him, clearly troubled about Morley, Inez, and the impending invasion. And now his best friend, cupshotten in the local alehouse?

He leaned over and shook his master by the shoulder, feeling dismal as the shake failed to rouse him. Charles shook him again, harder.

Dickon lifted his head, looked around groggily, then smiled up at Charles with half-lidded eyes. "Ah, lad, thee's come to see me home?"

Charles reared back, struck by the blast of wine fumes. Thoroughly disheartened, he hoisted Dickon to his feet and guided him through the room. Amid good-natured jesting, Dickon tripped and staggered, leaning heavily on Charles's arm. From the other guests' behavior, no one found Dickon's condition unusual. No one save him.

As they emerged into the clear night air, someone within called a greeting to another. As the door swung shut, Charles glimpsed a slim lad emerging from the kitchens to join the men clustered around the fire. It was Louis.

A haze of outrage fogged Charles's brain. What painful handout did fortune hold for him next? Embarrassed and pained, Charles guided Dickon back to the mews. Without a trace of guilt, his friend sank into his feather bed, asleep even as his head hit the pillow.

Charles pulled up a stool and sat, head buried in his hands, sick at heart. His friend's weathered countenance, creased by the valleys of time, had once radiated experience and wisdom. Charles had relied on that wisdom most of his life. "This can't be true. I don't believe it," he whispered aloud, the deep affection he bore the man welling up inside him like a fountain of pain. *Don't fail me. Not when I need you the most.*

There was no answer but the shifting of birds on their perches in the next room.

Charles rose and squared his shoulders. He would talk to the old man in the morning. But just now, he must face the next unpleasantness. He must confront Louis with his transgression and mete out punishment. Frances would be upset. Her tears always wrenched him in two, but he must not let her stop him from doing what was right.

Chapter 40

"Louis, did you go to the alehouse this eve?" Charles stepped out of the parlor and surprised the lad just as he started up the stairs several hours later.

His voice roused Frances instantly. She floated down the stairs and herded them into the parlor, where Charles repeated his question. If Louis lied, Charles would be doubly disappointed in him.

Louis looked him square in the eye. "I went, Baron Milborne, but I had a good reason. I swear I did."

"What possible reason could there be to go back on your word?" Shame for the boy gnawed at Charles, cutting a deeper swath than he'd expected. A sidelong glance showed him that Frances's mouth trembled, though she didn't weep. She would, though, as soon as he pronounced his judgment and the punishment. He hoped she wouldn't oppose him, but for the first time, he felt strong disciplinary measures were required. Breaking one's word of honor had been a serious crime in the Cavandish household. It was the sole transgression for which he and his brothers had been whipped as they grew up. They had learned quickly that one's promise must be kept.

"Louis, I hope you understand that you have earned a severe punishment," he said, wishing the boy would explain why he had gone. If only he would give a reason, even a poor one, so he might lessen the penalty.

"Don't you want to know what his good reason is?" Frances interrupted.

The catch in her voice all but broke Charles's resolve. He wanted to know more than anything, but Louis seemed determined to thwart him. Despite this, he tried again to give the boy another chance to confess. "What is your good reason?"

Louis hung his head. "My lord, I regret that I am not free to say."

Charles pressed his lips into a tight line. "You realize you leave me no choice. I can't choose a lesser penalty if you refuse to tell me why you went."

"I'll take the punishment, my lord."

"You shan't whip him," Frances cried, gripping Charles's arm.

He knew they were about to embark on their worst argument yet. Sending Louis to wait in the kitchens, he closed the parlor door and prepared for the clash.

"Frances, he broke his word," he began reasonably.

She flicked her long braid over one shoulder. "Choose another punishment. Anything. Make him scrub the scullery floor."

"My father whipped us for breaking our oaths, and we learned the lesson thoroughly. What was good enough for my brothers and me is good enough for him."

"But Charles, can't you just trust that his reason is good?"

Charles looked away from her imploring face, beautifully flushed with her passionate belief that she was right. "If you know what this reason is, tell me."

"I've tried to find out, but he's been too secretive."

"Do you approve of his having secrets from you?"

She didn't answer. So strong was her faith in someone she loved, she didn't question. But that was exactly why she'd been duped as a young woman. Charles shook his head, firmly believing he was in the right. "Go upstairs to our chamber. You may see him when it's done."

Her head drooped in defeat, the dark mantle she'd thrown on over her night smock hung from her slim shoulder and trailed on the floor. They were only an arm's length apart, yet their differences had widened into a gap that seemed impossible to breach. Slowly, she walked to the door, then turned, her eyes blazing. "I'm so angry at you for doing this, Charles Cavandish, no matter how correct you may be. I wish I didn't love you." She whirled and ran from the room.

Frances's words hurt Charles the way he knew the branch he trimmed from the willow behind their house would hurt Louis's backside. As he chose the switch, not too heavy, and trimmed the leaves with his knife, he grimaced. She hadn't said she didn't love him, but it was almost as bad.

It couldn't be helped. Just when he'd decided Louis might indeed have a future as an educated man, just when he'd caught Frances's enthusiasm for helping the boy, to imagine using his own advantages of position and education to help him, this had to happen. Remorse cut him to the quick.

In the parlor, Louis leaned against the table as bidden. Charles raised the switch for the first blow. He didn't strike his hardest, he hadn't even required him to lower his trunk hose, but the switch cracked as it met Louis's backside. The boy flinched and an involuntary cry broke from his lips. Pain snaked through Charles, as if the blow bit into him. His hand faltered after he delivered the second stroke. As he drew back his arm for the third, his gaze was riveted by the boy's expression.

Louis awaited the next blow bravely, feet planted, knuckles whitened as he gripped the table edge. Face in profile, his lips trembled. Tears welled in his eyes.

Seven more blows were required, but something in Charles snapped. Who and what was he? He felt as if Lucifer had stepped into his skin and subtly altered his will. To Louis he must seem so, regardless of whether he was right or wrong.

With a curse that shook the walls, he smashed the switch across his knee, breaking it in two, and hurled the pieces into a corner with all his strength.

Louis half turned to stare at him in frightened surprise.

"You're confined to the house for a week," Charles shouted at him. "And no more night watch at the beacon. Go to your chamber and stay there."

The lad didn't move.

Palpable pain sank its fangs into Charles. "It's finished," he roared. "That's all. Go!"

The boy didn't wait for a second order, but bolted for the door. As his feet pounded on the stairs, Charles sank into a chair and buried his face in his hands for a second time that night. How he'd wanted the boy to succeed. He hadn't realized how much until now. For Frances's sake. And, he admitted, for his own.

It hurt to think he had failed, the pain as startling and fresh as the bloody pulp of his broken nose had been when his commander had refused to endanger the entire division by attempting to rescue Richard. Over and over he had begged and demanded, his behavior so unmilitary that his superior had finally struck him. He ran his fingers over the permanent bump marring his nose and remembered the horror of those days.

Surely, this couldn't begin to compare. At least Louis was alive and could try again. Yet now the boy must do more than prove his worth. He must redeem himself first.

Oddly enough, Charles had a niggling feeling that he, too, must start again. Because for some insane reason, he had the impression that Louis was as disappointed in him as he was in the boy.

"I couldn't go through with it." Charles slammed the door to the bedchamber so hard, the walls rattled. Frances jerked around and stood, bathed in a pool of candlelight, an ethereal beauty cloaked by her onyx-dark hair against lily-white skin. Unfortunately, the midnight of her hair reminded him of the blackness of his soul. He sat down, jerked off his boots, and flung them on the floor. "I hope you're satisfied."

At his admission, she smothered him with a hug. "You do love him after all."

Stiffly, he disentangled her arms from around his neck. "Go to bed. I'm going to read for a while. We can draw the bed curtains so the light won't disturb your sleep."

"I'm going to see him." She padded for the door as he moved the candle to the small table by the window seat, took up a book, and sat down.

"You don't have to acknowledge feelings," she said softly, peeping around the edge of the door. "I know they're there."

"Go away, Frances," he said gruffly. "I don't want to talk about it."

But as he sat by the window pretending to read, he brooded. If it was love he felt for Louis, he didn't recognize it, and it gave him no pleasure. Pain and disappointment seemed the primary things in his life.

If the first letter from Inez had complicated things between him and Frances, Charles reflected the next morning as he sat at his father's desk, this second one might just tear them apart.

He stared at the unopened, water-spotted vellum and considered flinging it in the fire. Of course he opened it eventually, but after scanning it, he committed the sheet to fire. As flames licked the paper's edge and turned it to ash, his hatred smoldered. The bitch intended to land at Weymouth-Melcombe Regis. He was to meet her ship. Whether Spain triumphed or no, she wanted him. They could leave England, if necessary, and live somewhere else.

In a black mood, Charles removed the ashes from the grate and buried them in the garden. With them, he wished he could bury Inez. Bad enough that she had ruined his life. He wouldn't let her destroy Frances's love for him as well.

After that, he tried to get on with his daily tasks, but melancholy claimed him. For the first time in his life, he couldn't discuss his problems with Dickon, because his friend was now a problem as well.

With agonizing clarity, he relived the affectionate reunion they'd had when he first returned to Dorset. Nothing had seemed changed. But since then, he saw his friend had changed considerably. His work habits, his stamina, his attention to detail—all had deteriorated since Charles had seen him last.

A sense of grief dogged him all the next week, as if the old man had left Lulworth permanently and would never come back. In a sense he had. They had grown apart.

Louis, at least, behaved himself, following his orders scrupulously during the period of confinement. He was an apt pupil in hawking, learning everything Charles taught him. Reports from Frances about his work with the messenger birds glowed. For this reason, Charles renewed his permission for the boy to stand night watch on beacon hill. They would both begin again.

Something in his life had to begin again, for his relations with Frances seemed to crumble around him. The more he wanted her, the less he got—except for those rare moments when the mask hiding her love was swept away by the storms of her passionate love.

Frances believed Charles when he told her Master Dickon visited the alehouse every night. It explained the reek of spirits she smelled on him. It explained why he rose late each day. One day he didn't join her at all to care for the pigeons. After several inquiries of the servants, she found him in bed.

"Why do you go to the alehouse?" she demanded, after he insisted he wasn't ill. "You must stop."

"I have to go." He struck his chest with conviction. "It's a need within me."

"I don't believe you."

He lifted his head to study her. As Frances met his gaze,

she swore he examined her with all his former knowledge and wisdom flickering in his eyes.

He masked it instantly. Or had she imagined it was there?

"You don't know me well." He rolled his head to one side, voice feeble. "I'm old."

She snorted with impatience and pushed back her stool to stand. "Charles needs your strength."

"What Charles needs is to believe in himself as much as he believes in Arcturus," Dickon said with sudden clarity.

Frances spun around at this speech, but the flicker of the strong master disappeared. The weakling returned.

Try as she would, Frances could coax no repeat of the lucid moment from Dickon. "At least let me wash your clothes for you," she said, taking up his shirt and trunk hose. "They reek of ale."

He protested, but she took the clothes anyway and left his chamber. She lingered in the mews and let the tears fall. Why, she wondered as she stroked Oriana, did she long for people around her to change at this time of her life? Her mother, her father, and her uncle had been perfect just as they were. But first she had worked to change Pierre and Louis. Now she wanted Master Dickon to be different. As for Charles . . . she had married him hoping he would change. Yet she had no way of knowing if he could ever love her the way she desired.

Foolish dream, hoping to change another.

Time might change them both, but not necessarily for the better. Look at Master Dickon. She wept after mere minutes of talking to him, torn in two by the change in him. And if losing Dickon to drink and old age hurt her, she imagined how Charles must feel.

Chapter 41

The night of Friday, July twenty-eighth, Charles sat at supper in the wood-paneled dining chamber, at the head of the table, where his father had once sat. Frances took the foot, in his mother's former place. He even blessed Louis and Pierre as they knelt before him, just as his father had done him and his siblings so many years ago.

Lord, he thought heavily as he pulled the great chair up to the table, had his father felt this same plague of responsibility weighing on his head? Had he moved through the mundane ritual of checking the children's hands and nails for cleanliness while he blessed them, even as he feared disaster from other quarters? The part was more than he wanted, turning him old before his time.

Of course the heaviest care centered around the Armada. Earlier in the day, a bird had come from Ostend. Frances had told him with great satisfaction that the Duke of Parma might not have forty thousand men. "Many are sick with dysentery," she'd said. "And he hasn't enough ships."

"He doesn't need ships," he'd reminded her. "The Armada has enough for both."

"But the Armada may never get close enough for a rendezvous if we manage things right. Neither Flushing nor Ostend will let them land. And the Armada can't enter the ports of Dunkirk or Nieuport—they're blocked by shifting sand and the Armada's hulls sit too deep. So even if they reach the Netherlands, they may not be able to ferry all those soldiers out to their ships. And all Parma has is flat gunboats. They can't cross the Channel in those."

He hadn't wanted to dampen her enthusiasm. So he'd not mentioned that the twenty thousand soldiers on board the Armada were enough to take London, kill the queen, and hold the government while the others found their way across.

Bad enough he'd had to report to her the result of an investigation by the mayor and town aldermen of Ralph Stokes.

Suspicious of the growing number of servants he kept and his rich style of dress, a visit had been paid. Nothing could be proved against him. He had readily agreed to provide two mounted horsemen for the war effort when asked. He had consented solemnly to support a merchant ship converted for the war. The mayor had left Morley, still suspicious of the man's unexplained prosperity, but unable to find fault.

Frances had not complained when he told her, but he felt her unvoiced pain, more tangible than words.

World-weary, he finished the supper ritual, saw Louis off to his turn at signal watch with another man, and Frances to the pigeon loft, then left the house. With no particular purpose in mind, he struck out for the woods beyond the mews.

Once he had thought to crush all feelings from his consciousness. To feel nothing meant peace. Now he recognized that his years after the Caribbean hadn't been peaceful. As he had alternated between animal-like bedding habits and rigorous attention to his role as master of hawks, he had succeeded in crushing the good feelings. But the bad ones had still remained.

Back at the house, he met Frances returning from the pigeon loft. Just then Pierre ran out of the house and into her arms. "He didn't go to the lookout," the lad said, clinging to Frances and looking frightened. "He went to the alehouse. I'm afeared for him, Frank. That man will kill him next time Louis follows him. I know he will."

"What man?" Frances drew Pierre close to sort out his confused story, but Charles's mind numbed to all else. Louis had gone to the alehouse? After he'd trusted the boy and let him go to the beacon watch?

By the gods, his rage knew no bounds.

Frances must have guessed as much, because she moved quickly for the house. "I'll get my cloak and go find him."

"You'll do nothing of the kind. You'll remain here with Pierre." The bite of his command stopped her in her tracks. "If there's danger, I'll see to it."

With that curt order, he strode around the house and headed into town.

As Charles walked the mud lane into town, the church bells tolled the hour of eleven. Most houses and places of business were dark, except for the alehouse that stood apart, overlooking the cliffs. As he approached the establishment, with its lights and raucous laughter drifting from the windows, a man came out.

Unable to bear meeting with anyone, Charles slipped into a recessed doorway, meaning to wait until he passed. But he recognized the rickety gait at once, as unsteady as a derelict wagon. It was Master Dickon, suffering the ill effect of his cups.

Charles bowed his head, intending to wait until his friend was well out of sight. But suddenly, as Dickon approached the place where the lane met with Lulworth's main street, he straightened. His pace changed. Head up, shoulders thrown back, he moved forward like the old Dickon, his pace firm, sure of himself.

Astonished, Charles stepped out of his hiding place and stared after him, torn between pursuing this mystery and rescuing Louis.

Rescuing Louis won out, for Pierre had said the lad was in trouble. Still pondering the oddity of Dickon's change, Charles approached the alehouse.

"Louis, I'm a fair man, but I'm losing patience." Charles had entered the alehouse and collared Louis without a word. The walk home had been accomplished in devastating silence. Now he confronted the boy, once again in the best parlor, Frances beside him, her expression pained.

"Charles," she pleaded, "must you do this again?"

"Silence," he roared. His head ached nigh to splitting, his anger was so great. "I'll give you one last chance, Louis," he said with a ponderous show of patience. "Tell me why you were there."

To his astonishment, instead of cowering, Louis faced him with confidence. A slow smile spread across the lad's face. "Now I can tell you why I went, my lord." With a twitch, he flicked a thick letter from beneath his loosely belted jerkin. "Here," he said, his matter-of-fact tone failing to hide his self-satisfaction. "Read this."

Puzzled, Charles took the letter and tilted it toward the candelabra to read the name on it. Frances pushed up against him, her hair rubbing against his cheek as she leaned over to see.

"My God!" Before he could even focus, she pounced on

the letter and ripped it open. "It's to Ralph Stokes!" Finding the closing signature, she flourished the letter at Charles in triumph. "And it's written by Sir Humphrey Perkins from the Armada. Louis, whoever's purse you picked tonight, well done!" And she pulled the boy into a breath-stopping embrace.

"It's nothing to celebrate," Charles said as soon as he'd recovered from the shock of the revelation. "It means the Armada has to be within a day's sail or less."

"Not necessarily," Frances contradicted him, as usual. "Is there a date?"

"Just read the letter, would you?" Charles fumed. "What does it say?"

Frances read aloud through the opening and other formal greetings. "Where's the meat of the letter," she muttered, scanning down the page. She stopped abruptly and pressed one hand to her cheek. "Merciful heavens, the Armada intends to stop at Weymouth for ammunition. They're going to rob us to fuel their side of the war."

Charles narrowed his eyes as his thoughts shot off in an entirely different direction. He doubted the Spanish intended to take English stores. More likely they had a private cache of ammunition in Weymouth that English authorities knew nothing about.

Charles intended to find that cache of ammunition, and he would begin by leaving for Weymouth that very night. But first, several things remained to be done. For one, he and Louis had to talk.

Reading his intention, Frances inched toward the door, intending to withdraw, but he stayed her. This was for her ears as well.

"Louis, I owe you an apology. I'm sorry I judged you wrong." He spoke with dignity, willing to admit when he had erred.

"Forgiven, baron." Louis met his gaze with equal composure. "But I do hope you'll trust me next time."

"You accomplished the task you chose, but there won't be a next time." Charles eyed him sharply. "You're dealing with dangerous people. You could have been killed."

"But I wasn't."

"You could have been, and you could be yet," Charles pointed out. "From whom did you take the letter? Do you know his name or can you show me where he lives?"

"I believe the man conveys things from one source to another for the money," Louis said evasively. "I can't think he's aware of the contents."

"All I require is his name," Charles said impatiently.

"Don't you think it would be better if he continued to relay his letters and I relieve him of them?"

"Absolutely not. You'll cease going to the alehouse. Your promise still stands."

"But why?" Louis cried.

A glance at Frances told Charles she once again sided with Louis, but he stood firm. "There's the rather important matter of your life. Do you think we want you dead?" He tried to put some warmth into his words, but they sounded stiff, even to him. "You may stand watch at the beacon signal. In fact, I believe that's where you're supposed to be right now," he continued more gently, "but stay away from the alehouse. Do you hear?"

Apparently Louis understood, despite the stiffness, because the lad finally nodded grudgingly. "I promise not to go to the alehouse, and this time I'll keep my word."

"I trust you will. And when you're ready to give me the man's name, let me know." But Charles was beginning to understand Louis, and it seemed evident the boy did not intend to talk. And to Charles, Louis's protecting his source of information seemed as odd as Dickon's suddenly resuming his former, jaunty walk.

Charles dreaded parting from Frances, for the encounter promised to be as stormy as the Dorset sea at its worst. But it had to be done, for he needed to be on his way.

"You think to find that ammunition cache," she said after Louis went to his beacon watch and Charles informed her of his intent. She paced with restless steps to the window and peered out. "But you can't do so without taking more risks." She whirled to face him, her emerald eyes glittering with fear. "Charles, please don't go." The passionate plea in her face, the sweet siren's song of her flesh, urged him to stay. "I was so proud when you apologized to Louis, I thought at last everything was going to be better. I thought we were going to work the birds together. I thought you actually might . . ."

She trailed off at his look of warning, and Charles knew exactly what she'd meant to say. She still wished for something he couldn't give, probably never could, and he refused to offer her false hopes.

Her lower lip quivered, reminding him of her tantalizing softness and how he longed to feel her body against his. How he would relish one last, passionate mating with her before he stepped into danger's path. "Promise to watch after Louis while I'm gone."

"Of course. And Pierre, too." She held her tears in check, but her tragic expression gnawed at his core.

"I don't mean it that way," he said. "Pierre is still a child and content with a child's pastimes. But Louis is almost a man. If you see any sign that his life is threatened, let Captain Henry Ashley know."

"But Charles—"

"No 'buts'!" He swept across the room, suddenly needing to press her hands and convince her. Just as he'd misjudged Inez, he'd been wrong about Louis. Self-doubt ate at him, feasting on his errors. But this, he knew, was right. "You love him, don't you? Then don't let him be involved. Let him grow up first."

A sharp response sprang up in Frances. *You didn't wait,* she wanted to cry. *You were too young when you went to the Caribbean.* That very choice had changed who he was for all time, and she didn't want that for Louis. "Very well," she said, convinced at last. "But I . . . I am disappointed you're leaving. I had thought we were going to work the birds together. Can you tell me why you changed your mind?"

He waved one hand vaguely, as if embarrassed. "It would never have worked. Our ways of doing things are too different. We can work together in other ways."

"Such as?"

A flame ignited in his eyes. Without words, he drew her near, and she knew his answer. He wished to visit the woods where they had pleasured each other before.

They stood for a full moment, gazes locked, then suddenly bolted for the door, both of like mind. They might never work pigeons together, but Charles was right. This was better. This, they could share.

Outside, she raced him, through the garden, past the mews and toward the woods. Like eager children, they removed each other's clothing, and Frances felt her passion for Charles flame as brightly as the beacon fires would soon burn.

They loved each other in a mad haste that bordered on frenzy, as if they could never get enough. And after it was over, Frances caught a glimpse of fire winking through the trees. She moaned deep in her throat.

Charles twisted to look. "So Louis has at last found the right time and place to light a fire," he jested, as if unwilling to face the gravity of what the beacon meant.

But they both knew. While they had loved in the woods, the invading force had been spotted off the English shore. All along the coast, from distant Cornwall to Dorset, and from there inland clear to London, the warning beacons would flare, the chain of fire lighting up their land like a string of fiery gems.

With their destiny hanging in the balance, Charles reached for her again, and she went into his arms. And as they once more made love, slowly, sweetly, she knew that her love for him and for each person in her life was like that chain of fire, linking the people she cherished with the blaze of her love that could not be quelled, no matter what. England would fight for her freedom. And she would fight for her loves.

Chapter 42

"What do you mean, you lost my letter?" At Morley Place, Ralph Stokes dropped so hard into his desk chair, it quivered beneath his weight.

The man sitting across from him fumbled at the hat in his lap. "I don't know what happened, Master Stokes. One minute I had it. The next, 'twas gone. I can search for it."

"Never mind," Stokes interjected angrily. "You'll not be paid this time, is all. I'll write back to say the message was waylaid and you can deliver the letter as usual. You can do that, can't you?"

His sarcasm was not lost on the humble fellow opposite. Head bent, he nodded.

"Good. Go wait in the kitchens while I write it. I'll be leaving for Weymouth on the morrow and won't require your services again." Stokes picked up a quill, effectively dismissing the man.

"But sir," the man ventured hesitantly, "you'll be needing messages carried from Weymouth back here. I can do that for you, sure. I can also help load the ship."

"True, we'll need as many hands as we can find. You might help." Stokes scrutinized the old fellow for several minutes. "What's in it for you?" he asked at last, pushing back his chair to rise.

The old man rose also and stood, his hat cradled in the crook of his arm. "I've worked hard all m'life and have little to show for it under current rule," he said with some dignity. "I'll serve you well when Spain rules. I've not erred once except for tonight, and it won't happen again."

Stokes sat down again and took up his quill. He needed men desperately, and this one had performed well until now. "Deliver this message tonight. Then get yourself to Weymouth and meet me at the Blue Falcon at noon on the morrow. I'll have a letter for you to carry back. Or you can help with the other work." He stopped writing suddenly and looked up. "Does anyone in your household suspect you?"

A ghost of a smile split the old man's beard. "Not in the least." Then, with a show of subservience, he bowed and withdrew.

Charles tore himself away from West Lulworth with reluctance, but he had to go. He thought it best to leave Arcturus, but first he went to say good-bye. In the mews, he took the bird on his fist and talked to him for some time. Oriana and Arcturus both stayed in the mews these days, now that they had each other. Frances said she hoped they would eventually mate.

Bidding Arcturus a last farewell, he headed for the door, but memory of Dickon's surprising gait stopped him. Retracing his steps, he tapped at Dickon's door.

No one answered, so he lifted the latch and looked in. The bed, where he expected to find Dickon, stood empty, as if it hadn't been touched all night.

Puzzled, Charles swung the door wide and entered. The bed drew his gaze again. Its empty state, along with the unexpectedly sure-footed walk, merged to form a vast question in Charles's mind. Something odd was up with his friend.

Frances ached at losing Charles at a time like this. But he was gone, and early the next morning, with fear hounding her, she set to work. First she sat down and wrote a brief message to Lord Admiral Howard at Plymouth.

"Intercept all messages from the Armada to Parma using hawks to attack their messenger pigeons," she directed with urgency. "The Dover fleet may stop messengers that slip away from the Armada, but we must also stop messages sent by air."

To her way of thinking, the admiral would order the master of some nonfighting ship to carry out this task. The small ship would edge its way ahead of the Armada and watch for the morning release of any messenger birds. As she folded the message into a thin strip, she prayed the admiral would receive her instructions before his ship left to engage the enemy. She must launch a bird with all haste.

At the loft, she selected one of the Plymouth-bred pigeons and bound the paper to the bird's leg. Then, with the cage tied to the saddle, Frances rode for the headlands. The sun cut through the morning mist like a blade renting a veil of platinum lace. A clear day lay ahead—perfect weather for flying if one was a bird.

Frances opened the cage without even dismounting. The bird hopped into her hands, and she held it close, its tiny heart fluttering as she whispered a prayer to speed it on its way. At her swift toss, it flew from her hands and mounted the air, sending a pang through her heart. How she longed to rise on strong wings, to join her love in Weymouth, but instead she was chained here. Without Charles, magic fled from her life.

The bird circled higher and higher, then struck out toward Plymouth where it had been born. Frances tilted her head and watched until the mist swallowed it. The mare shifted her feet and whickered impatiently.

"I know, girl. You want your oats. Let's go home." Frances patted the mare's warm, dappled neck, attempting to shrug off her melancholy. But it was no use. Somewhere, Charles risked his life, and she was not permitted to help.

She encountered not a soul during the ride home. By order of the queen, once the beacon fires blazed, all those not fighting were to stay inside.

By the time she returned to the house, it was eight of the clock, yet no one stirred. The cook, the two kitchen maids, the housekeeper, Louis, and Pierre, all must still be sleeping, worn out by the excitement and fear of last night's warning beacon.

That left her free to compose her own message to Parma. Using Sir Humphrey's letter as a guide to his style of phrasing, she informed Parma of the Armada's position and its plans to arrive at Calais.

"Heed not what His Excellency, the Duke of Medina Sidonia, says of ammunition," she counseled. "I have ammunition aplenty hidden at Weymouth. I will inform him that he can restock the Armada from there. You may ignore his requests."

She congratulated herself as she visited Captain Ashley and requested an expert in forgery. After all, she told no lies. Sir Humphrey did intend the Armada to replenish at Weymouth. She just ensured that Parma answered none of his fellow duke's requests.

The town bustled with men assembling on the town green

as Frances reached its center. She caught Henry Ashley, booted and spurred, just about to leave his quarters. In response to her request, he stared at her, as if trying to decide whether to comply or not. "Should you send this letter of your own volition, baroness?" he asked, a slight edge to his question. "Shouldn't it be reviewed by the lord lieutenant first?"

"Guide me to him, and I'll show it to him." Frances donned her most obliging expression.

"He's at Plymouth with the lord admiral and the fleet."

Frances rolled her eyes toward the ceiling. "Then he can't read it, can he? Besides, Her Majesty told me to write this letter," she lied without shame. "Shall I show you her order? I have it at the house."

"Madam, I have not time to look at it. I must move my force to Weymouth. The armies are commanded to rally there."

"Then pray be so good as to lend me your man," she said as prettily as possible, "so I can fulfill the queen's command."

Ashley sighed, found the man, and sent him to her house. He copied Sir Humphrey's style of writing to perfection, complete to the signature flourishes.

That task accomplished, Frances gave the man a shilling and sent him back to his company. She carried the forged document back to the mews and selected a pigeon from Ostend. The English garrison commander regularly intercepted messages coming from Parma's headquarters nearby. This time, she would ask him to slip in a message. Spies abounded in both camps. An Englishman need only boast to the wrong companions that he had intercepted a Spanish message meant for Parma, and it would be stolen from him with all speed.

She took Louis and Pierre into town at midmorning to see the militia off to Weymouth. Clutches of women and children with frightened eyes watched from the doorways of shops and houses. No one gossiped anymore about how the Spanish king planned to set his daughter on the throne and rule through her, as they had a week ago. The chatter subsided about how the Inquisition would be instituted and all non-Catholics would have to convert, flee the country, or beware. With the country's future hanging in the balance, it was time to stop gossiping and fight.

As the last man tramped away to the shrill sound of the fife, Frances herded the boys home. She couldn't wait to return to the pigeon loft. Pierre and Louis trailed her, aware of the danger, though neither of them mentioned it. Somewhere, two of the mightiest navies ever gathered in Christendom prepared for battle, with England to be the prize.

The minutes lengthened into hours and the hours passed from early afternoon to late. The lack of news wore at Frances like a chafing sore, and she had to clamp her mouth shut to keep from frightening the boys.

Every moment, she prayed feverishly, hoping to hear from Charles.

Just before dusk, a bird popped into the loft. Like twin cats leaping for their prey, Frances and Louis lunged. Louis got there first. He held the bird while Frances removed the message with trembling fingers and unrolled the paper strip. The date and hour recorded were early that morning.

"The Armada was spotted last night off Plymouth by Sir Thomas Fleming," Charles had written in a tiny, terse hand. "Our fleet left Plymouth harbor on the evening tide, most difficult in the face of the wind. The admiral intends to capture the weather gauge and gain the superior battle position. Pass the word on to Dover and London as quickly as you can."

With a sob of horror, Frances buried her face in her hands and wept. The first battle loomed before them, complete with its bloody deaths.

Up and down the coast that night, the chain of beacon fires lit up the darkness, signaling the enemy attack. Frances sat up suddenly in her rumpled bed, unable to sleep. A premonition of danger prickled within her. "Please, Charles," she whispered into the empty darkness, "have a care, my love. Trust yourself and stay safe."

Chapter 43

Charles crouched on the cold shore with the other men and awaited orders to load. Clouds scudded across the midnight sky, and the sea growled restlessly as it swept the smooth stones of Chesil Bank just north of Portland Bill. A perfect place for a galleon to shelter, he speculated with apprehension. Soon, he would know if he had guessed rightly about the contents of one hundred barrels sitting in the nearby cave. The question tore at his nerves, which were already ragged from lack of sleep, but he dared not show any interest in the barrels. Soon enough he would know what they contained.

"Care for a smoke?" The man next to him produced a tobacco pouch, apparently forgetting the prohibition against smoke or fire.

"Thanks, but no."

Charles's companion filled his pipe and reached for flint and steel before he remembered. "Blast, can't do that," he muttered. "Might be spotted. What's a body to do to pass the time?"

If the half dozen others commiserated, they did so in silence, shifting in their rocky hideout behind the wall of gray stones. Charles rubbed his chin where two-days growth thickened and hoped he wouldn't be recognized. His name was known in the adjoining port towns of Melcombe Regis and Weymouth, but not his face, and based on that, his plan had evolved. Before reaching Weymouth, he'd stabled his horse in the town of Sutton Poyntz, bought ragged clothes, roughed up his face and hair with a bit of dirt, and walked the rest of the way. In the port town, he'd sought an inn rumored to harbor pirates. It wasn't hard to find.

A one-eyed sailor with no patch over his mangled socket had struck up a conversation. Charles encouraged him by buying multiple pots of ale. One-Eye had asked a hundred questions, all of which Charles answered with oblique hints that he would do literally anything for money. Which brought him here to freeze his backside on a desolate, stone-studded shore between the decaying castles of Portland and Sandsfoot.

He'd stumbled into this blindly, skeptical because it had been so easy. He damned well hoped he wasn't wasting his time. But everything about the venture suggested he wasn't. And the ease came because the Spanish were desperate for hands to load this cargo. A hundred barrels couldn't be loaded with evil intentions alone.

Hours passed, but at last the rattle of oars in their locks shook him from a fond dream of his boyhood. The expected ship had crept up on them without a sound. The modest-sized pinnace stood offshore, awaiting its cargo. At the signal, the men rose and fell to work.

The instant Charles hefted a barrel, he knew by the smell, the shift of the contents, its weight, that it held gunpowder. Others probably contained shot. Going purely on instinct, he'd found the cache. The question was, could he accomplish his next dangerous gambit before the Armada arrived?

He grunted as he maneuvered the weight onto his shoulders, then set out for the water's edge. The shadows of the others moved around him as they lugged their loads from cave to shore. On his twentieth trip to the cave, Charles snatched a minute to rest. Blowing from his exertion, he labored to fill his lungs while he reviewed his plan.

A man entered the cave behind him, grasped a barrel, and headed out again. Charles watched until his scrawny form disappeared. Of the ragged, motley crew, none of them seemed to merit his attention while they worked . . . save one. Swathed in a ragged cloak that flapped at his heels, one man walked with a gait that struck Charles as familiar, although in the dark, who could tell?

Like the rest of them, the man trained his eyes on the ground most of the time as he navigated the rocky shore to the boat. His hood drooped to conceal his face. Even if it hadn't, none of them were eager to stare each other straight in the eye tonight. No one wanted to be remembered for what he was doing.

Partially revived, Charles grasped the iron hoop rimming

one barrel's top. Rocking it onto its side, he rolled the barrel toward the mouth of the cave. He would move it this way and perhaps save his back some strain.

"Taking the easy way? You'll find it doesn't work well," the man in the cloak said congenially. "Too many big rocks for the casks to roll."

The familiar voice froze Charles in his tracks. "What the devil are you—" He clamped his mouth shut abruptly as another man entered behind them.

As if their exchange hadn't happened, the cloaked man grasped a barrel, as did the other. Left with no choice, unable to ask the hundred questions that surged to his lips, Charles hefted the barrel onto his shoulder.

But as he stumped his way to the shore, his spirits soared. His old friend Dickon was back with them, exactly the way he'd always been, minus his thick beard. Suddenly he understood perfectly the incredible ruse he'd witnessed for the two months past. The entire time Dickon had pretended to suffer the ill effects of drink, he'd been working in secret for their country. Charles wanted to shout with pleasure at his friend's cleverness. Except for the two clues, he'd been almost completely duped.

And what did Dickon do but dupe him again tonight. Thinking back, Charles searched his memory for a time when he'd seen Dickon without a beard. Never. Not in the fifteen years he'd known him. He'd had no idea what his friend's chin and cheeks looked like under all the hair.

He looked ten years younger without it, Charles decided, working to hide his elation. *By heaven,* but it felt good to have his friend back. It felt even better to know that Dickon was here for the same reason he was, and that now they would work together to destroy the ammunition cache.

As dawn broke over the horizon, Charles heaved the last barrel on board the small pinnace and stepped back. His exhausted companions slumped or lay helter skelter around the poop deck, husbanding their strength. They would need it to transfer these hundred barrels to the designated Armada ship. The first battle would undoubtedly take place today, and after, the Spaniards would be low on munitions. But before the barrels were moved, he and Dickon would destroy them.

He hadn't decided how yet, but they would. Preferably without destroying themselves as well.

"All ashore who're going ashore. Last chance," called the captain of the pinnace, opening his purse to indicate he would pay any who wished to leave.

"Go." Dickon suddenly grasped his elbow and guided him toward the boat. "You're needed onshore."

Charles struggled out of his grasp, taken by surprise. The protest he meant to utter died in his throat as he saw Dickon's worried expression. "What do you mean?"

Dickon abandoned all attempt at secrecy and pulled him aside. "You're needed in Weymouth by noon on the morrow. Inez has sent word to Frances telling her you're there, wounded. I can't think Inez is up to any good."

Charles winced at this incredible story. "How do you know all this?"

"I just know."

How could he know? Charles stared at him, suddenly forced to question everything he'd concluded in the last hours. Before God, had he assumed wrongly about Dickon? Those three words shook his faith in his own judgment like no others. Common sense and logic fled as memory roared to take over his mind.

Black ink of tropical midnight. Heat bore down with the strength of an enslaving fist. Blood from his broken nose trickled down his lip and into his mouth, the acrid taste a bitter reminder—swollen with love for a woman, he had made a fatal mistake when his decision mattered most.

Once more, a decision hung over him, sharp and unforgiving as the executioner's blade. Was this the man he'd known for fifteen years and trusted implicitly? Or was he someone else? Did he want Charles off the ship for malevolent reasons, using a lie about Frances to make him go?

Incoherent emotions fought to control rational thought. His past errors loomed large and threatening. The pressure in his head built, urging him to decide. But he couldn't decide. He didn't know. He wanted the truth, but truth evaded him, as slippery as the strange native men who had lived in the poison green jungles of Hispaniola. Was truth outside of us, or within? Desperately he struggled to see the way ahead.

Suddenly he felt Dickon's hand on his shoulder. He lifted his face, and their gazes met.

Deep in his master's eyes, he found other memories. He remembered, at age eight, staring up with awe at the huge master of hawks his father had hired. They had tramped the

Dorset downs together, Dickon's fierce hawk on his fist. Most of all, he remembered Dickon's magical hands—those hands had taught him how to hold a hawk on his own fist, how to hood and unhood it deftly, how to coax a frightened, bating bird to trust him and obey. And when he was ready, those hands had taught him to launch his own winged partner at its prey, to bring down a quail or a heron, then reward the bird as his equal and his friend. Dickon had shared his knowledge, his wisdom, his heart. Later, Dickon had held him when he lost his father, while he wept bitterly night after night. Arms he trusted. Arms that drove away the cold knot of his fear of loss.

The truth—he loved this man. Just as he had always loved Frances. And he knew with surety that Dickon was no Spanish spy.

Doubt evaporated. With a rush of elation, he admitted the depth of his feelings, for Frances . . . and for the two boys. No longer would he play the coward and hide his love.

Dickon apparently saw his realization reflected in his expression. "I have told you for three years to trust your instincts, the way your hawk trusts his."

Charles nodded decisively. "I'm staying," he said firmly. "We have time to load the powder and to meet Frances on the morrow." Turning to the captain, he motioned him to raise the boat. He and Dickon would remain together. For the first time in years, he felt full of purpose, strong and renewed.

Chapter 44

Sunday morning dawned clear and brilliant in Lulworth, with sun sparkling on the sea. Numb from worry and lack of sleep, Frances launched messenger birds in every direction. The world to the citizens of Lulworth looked the exact opposite of the weather. Pierre brought word of the fear among the womenfolk, their concern for husbands, sons, uncles, and more. Frances felt the same things, but ignored them and worked her birds.

"Fly swift, fly sure," she whispered to the bird raised in London as she launched it into the bright morning sky with Charles's news. "God speed you on your way," she blessed the next one headed for Dover. The last one, meant for Ostend, carried another special message to Parma, assuring the duke the Channel would be cleared of the English fleet in time to sail across in his boats. That finished, she helped Pierre and Louis dress for church and insisted they pray for the success of their navy, because at that very moment, a battle probably raged between the two fleets.

On board the *Bark Diana*, Charles clenched the rail and watched the first encounter rage between the English and the Spanish. They had rounded the Bill of Portland earlier to discover the Armada, its ships arrayed in a huge, dark crescent that spread over seven miles wide. Far away, a haze of smoke clouded the scene as the English fleet stormed the Armada's rear wing. Unfortunately, he couldn't see well enough to tell who was winning. Helpless to assist, agonizing inwardly because he couldn't fight, Charles watched all afternoon while Dickon napped below deck, pretending he didn't care.

By afternoon, no one had won. Both sides had incurred losses, but no ships had been boarded by the enemy. With a stalemate established, the Armada sailed on eastward.

In the aftermath of the battle, Charles scrutinized the numerous small ships plying about the English and wondered frantically if his friends and relatives were well. But he had to hide his interest as his moment approached. The *Bark Diana* adjusted her rigging and sailed toward the Spanish fleet.

The nearest ship greeted their captain's hail with a hearty welcome. Munitions were needed, without a doubt. They were directed to the supply urca called the *San Salvador*. They loaded barrels steadily for the next hours.

It was approaching four in the afternoon when they finished. Charles leaned against the rail of the *San Salvador*, sharing a wine skin with the old man with the pipe. Others joined them.

"I'd like that smoke now, if you've a mind," he said jovially to the old fellow. "To celebrate, now that we're done."

The gap-toothed smile lit up the man's face as he fumbled for his pouch. They passed the fragrant pipe between them for several minutes.

"Time to go," the captain of the *Diana* announced. "All those returning, come on."

"I have to visit the scuppers first." Charles exchanged glances with Dickon. "Mind if I borrow the pipe?"

The owner of the pipe chuckled slyly at the implication. What could be better than relieving oneself while enjoying a smoke? Charles didn't give a damn what he thought.

He headed for the poop and entered the powder storage area. Without hesitation, he knocked a hole in a barrel he'd noticed was rotted, sprinkled a thick, long line of powder on the floor, then lit it from the pipe.

Back on deck, he thanked his comrades for waiting and returned the pipe. It was his turn to descend the rope ladder into the ship's boat when a shrill cry halted him.

"Charles!" a woman cried. "Oh, Charles, is that you at last?"

He whirled to encounter Inez in all her sultry glory. Age had not dimmed her lush beauty. Instead, she had ripened. She wore a tight bodice that pushed up her breasts and whittled her waist. She laughed in triumph as she hurried toward him, arms outstretched, her face transformed with joy.

Charles's entrails twisted. The powder line would be dwindling. With a firm hand, he grabbed Dickon, mounted

the rail, and the pair of them jumped straight into the sea.
Not a second too soon, either. As they hit the water, a
tremendous explosion of fire and smoke rocked the world.

At nine of the clock, just as dusk was falling and storms
brewed, a messenger bird popped into the trap at the Cavandish pigeon loft. Frances hastened to reward the bird and
retrieve the message.

"Come at once to Weymouth," the terse message read.
"Charles Cavandish has been wounded and wishes you at his
side."

Frances surged to her feet, a cry of agony on her lips.

Unable to leave Lulworth by dark, yet unable to sleep,
Frances paced the dining chamber. How badly was Charles
wounded? Would she arrive in time to nurse him back to
health? Or might he die before she even got there?

The torment of not knowing ate at her all night. To calm
her mind, she sat down and composed several more false
messages to Parma, this time signing them simply "MS" for
Medina Sidonia. In one, she instructed Parma to bring his
entire army to mid-Channel in barges, a clearly impossible
feat for Parma's boats that were meant for water no rougher
than a canal. In another, Medina Sidonia ordered Parma to
join him in engaging the enemy so they could capture the
Isle of Wight and bring the Armada to port. Again, it was
clearly impossible. Parma had no navigable ships able to sail
clear to the Isle of Wight, let alone join the fight.

The next message bemoaned Parma's poor communications and demanded to know why he had not written. "I send
by messenger bird because of your silence. You cannot have
received my other letters, else you would write back," she
wrote in Spanish script so tiny, no one could tell if it was the
duke's handwriting or not. She wrote a half dozen more
equally contradictory messages and folded the paper into the
required strips.

She must rely on the Ostend captain's ingenuity to drop
them in Parma's lap, each by a different route so he couldn't
verify their falsity. But if Parma received even half of them,
he would think Median Sidonia a madman and the campaign
an impossible dream.

Before the sun had fully risen, she sent the first three messages, kissed Louis and Pierre, and enjoined them to send the

others, two or three per day. The housekeeper must look after them, and they were to care for the birds, both messengers and hawks. "It's a grave responsibility," she said to them. "I expect you to work together. Each hawk and falcon must be fed daily. I trust you. Tell the servants what they can do to help."

"I'll see to them, Frank," Louis told her with a hug. "I know how. You can trust me."

She kissed them each again, then set off for Weymouth alone.

On the *Bark Diana,* Charles lifted his head with a moan of exhaustion. They had almost drowned after the explosion on the *San Salvador*. Pure grit alone had kept him clutching the edge of the ship's boat while he towed Dickon, who couldn't swim. The other men had hung on to them, then boosted them out of the choppy, freezing sea and back on board the *Diana.* Now, frantic with sudden fear, he checked Dickon, who lay too still beside him. "Dickon, are you well?"

No answer. His friend had swallowed too much water, and Charles feared for his life.

His friend . . . how could he ever have doubted? Charles fumbled for Dickon's wrist, seeking a pulse. God, where was it? For an earth-shattering moment, he found nothing. He checked his mouth, put his ear to his chest. My God, he couldn't lose him now. Not when he needed to tell him so much.

At last he detected a faint flutter of life. Temporarily satisfied, he sank back on the musty pallet, exhausted by the effort.

"Charles." The whisper pulled him back to Dickon.

"I'm here. Can you breathe?" he asked with urgency.

"Aye. You know . . ." Dickon's body tensed as he swallowed with seeming effort. "I worked for both sides."

"Yes, I know. Don't talk now. I understand now how the Spanish information came into Lulworth and some of ours leaked out. It was a reasonable trade you made."

"Had to win their trust," Dickon gasped, "to make it work."

"And I love you for it, sacrificing our relationship for our country." Charles smoothed the old man's hair. "It must have hurt, not being able to tell."

"Aye." Dickon coughed, swallowed, and seemed to

breathe easier. "I hated hurting you, but you had Frances by then. I knew she would help. She's a good woman, with her ideas for fouling the enemy's communications. And she guessed, you know, that I feigned being drunk."

"How?"

"I couldn't force enough wine down to smell of it, so I soaked my clothes." He grinned ruefully. "Madam insisted on washing them one day, and I had to resoak. She noticed while my shirt was still wet. I could tell by her face."

Charles smiled. "She notices many things. I loved her for it from the start."

"You always did have good judgment."

Their gazes locked, and understanding flowed between them. Charles had tested his wings and found them strong. He believed in his power of flight.

They had cheated devil death, too, Charles reflected as they both rested, but by the morrow he had to get to Frances, and there wasn't much time left to regain his strength.

Chapter 45

The man who opened the door looked more like a jailer than a physician, Frances thought as she stood on the threshold of a small Weymouth cottage, facing the dim interior, but unsure how to proceed. Yet this is where the note had said Charles was housed.

"I understand you have one of the wounded here, sir. May I see who it is?"

The man held the door wide and stood aside.

As she stepped inside, she consulted the paper again, but it clarified nothing. With fear for Charles tearing at her, she followed the man through the humble cottage. Surely Charles would recover with her to help him. Surely he would, she assured herself with her heart in her throat.

Her host indicated another door and opened it to reveal a darkened room. Apparently the windows were covered, for she could see nothing after the bright outdoors. But after a moment, she detected a glimmering rush light burning at a rude bedside. The figure on the bed moved. *Charles?*

She started forward, terrified to learn his condition. But when he sat up, her courage broke. Sobbing, she rushed to kneel at his side, then reared back in shock.

A woman stared back at her, her face hideously burned, the flesh blistered and putrefied down one entire side and half her hair singed away.

A shaft of pain exploded in Frances's side. With a cry, she leaped up, but iron arms locked around her body from behind. She bucked, but the pain mounted. A blinding cloud of nausea assailed her, and through its haze, she felt her side grow wet. It had to be blood.

"Hold still and you'll go easier," the man holding her advised, and in horror she recognized Sir Humphrey Perkins. She would know that voice anywhere.

From the bed, the angry eyes of the woman who could

only be Inez del Cavaladosa burned into her. Frances's most hideous nightmare danced before her eyes. Her husband's first wife had arrived to claim him and eliminate her.

A sound like the swarming of bees buzzed in her head, threatening to blot out all else. Even as Inez sank back, clearly in mortal pain from her burns, nausea and weakness consumed Frances, and she slumped in her enemy's arms.

Suddenly, the room erupted into light as the window burst. The brittle sparkle of shattering wood and glass filled her ears. "Charles," she whispered weakly. She reached out one hand to him, grateful for his love, before the swarming bees carried her off into a black, forgetful world.

Charles exploded into the cottage, hunting knife drawn, and crouched, ready to fight. Inez recognized him and shrieked his name, but he focused on Perkins, who held Frances's sagging body, a sneer on his face and a blade to her neck. "A few more minutes and she'll bleed to death," he said. "You can stay back and let her go peacefully, or I can make it fast by cutting her throat."

"You're going to let her go."

"Nay. You're going to live in Lulworth Castle with Baroness Inez, and I'm going to court as a principal counselor to the new queen, King Philip's daughter."

"The Armada is beaten." Charles inched closer, scrutinizing Perkins for a weak point in his guard. Only a second's error, that was all he would need.

"The Armada is moving toward London as planned." Perkins glowed with confidence.

"But we've fouled communications between your two dukes," Charles said. "Their forces will never rendezvous. Your side's messages have been intercepted and others sent in their place. Part of it was done by Richard Pennington. He never worked for you and Stokes. He passed on every Spanish message he delivered to the English command."

"He what?" Perkins's broad face was transformed by surprise. His knife hand wavered from its mark at Frances's throat.

Charles lunged, snagged Perkins's arm in a death grip, and wrenched the knife sideways, away from Frances. Frances crumpled to the floor and the blade bit into Perkins's neck instead. A spout of blood mixed with his scream as he fell. The three of them crashed to the floor with Charles fighting for control of the knife. He flung his weight against

Humphrey's taut arm, jerking it back farther than it could go. The shoulder cracked, an ugly popping noise of the joint leaving the socket. Humphrey shrieked and lay still, mortally wounded.

Charles knelt beside Frances and pressed both hands to her bleeding side.

"Give me a heavy piece of linen," he ordered Inez. When silence met his demand, he looked up. Burned flesh the color of raw meat adorned her once beautiful face and the entire side of one leg. By their fiery color and the putrid odor, he knew she wasn't long for this world. Startled, he realized he felt nothing but pity for her. Her life must have been miserable after they parted, to center her future hopes around a relationship that had failed.

He groped for a towel from the washstand and hurriedly pressed it to Frances's wound. "I love you, Frank," he whispered, bending close. "Don't die now, just when I've learned to tell you how I feel."

The warmth of familiar voices enfolded Frances as she drifted back to consciousness. With eyes closed, she savored the soft, safe feather bed cushioning her body. The sharp odor of medicinal herbs reassured her. The pain in her side ached dully. It would probably hurt worse later, but for now, it told her she still lived. And Charles . . . he trusted himself at last. The hazy memory hung in her mind, of Charles kneeling beside her, speaking his love.

"Frank? Open your eyes, you deceiver. I see your lashes fluttering. You're awake."

She had to struggle against the lethargy that weighted her eyelids, but the fight had its rewards. Before her eyes could focus completely on the face hovering over hers, she knew it belonged to Charles. The warmth of his smile enfolded her.

"That's better. We'll get some good meat broth in you, and some red wine." He pressed her hand. "You'll be as good as new in a day or so."

"I love you, Charles."

He laughed with pleasure. "Just the words I wanted to hear. I love you too, Baroness Frank."

"You don't have another baroness?"

He turned suddenly serious. "Not for long, God rest her soul. Frank, did you honestly believe I would go to her instead of you?"

"Never. I trust the good judgment you've always had." She gripped his hand harder. "How fares the English fleet?"

"Today is Tuesday, and unfortunately the Armada is not yet defeated, but it's almost out of ammunition. Give it time."

"Your forged messages are working perfectly, madam," put in Dickon, stepping into her view. "You should read the intercepted communications coming back from Parma, asking Medina Sidonia if he's crazed. I also hear Parma wrote to King Philip, informing his most august majesty that his lord admiral had no idea what it took to effect an invasion and that his men would never make it to England with Medina Sidonia in command."

Frances sighed weakly. "I'm glad to hear that, but Charles, you must see to Louis and Pierre. I was so afraid to leave them. I must know they are well."

"Oh, they're well, I'm quite sure." Charles said almost carelessly. "Though Louis has disappeared."

"Disappeared? No!" Frances sat up, then clutched her side as daggers shot through her wound. "Charles," she panted. "Stokes has killed him for stealing his letters. I know he has."

"Steady now." Charles urged her to lie back. "Some of the Lulworth pigeons and a cage were gone also, as well as Arcturus. Stokes didn't get him, have no fear."

"My baby," Frances moaned. "My child."

"Frank, listen to me. He's joined the fleet and it's headed for Dover. We'll have a message back on the morrow. You'll see."

Frances wasn't at all convinced. "How can you sit there and do nothing?" she spluttered in dismay. "You don't know anything for sure."

"Oh, I've done something. You did, too. We taught him to care for the messenger birds. He watched you write and send messages and release the birds to fly home. We taught him to fly the hawks, and knowing full well what you intended, he's gone to intercept Medina Sidonia's messages so they'll never reach Parma. Without communications, the Armada will fail in its quest. Don't worry, Frank," he said tenderly. "He has Arcturus to work with. I'd trust them both with my life."

"Louis has gone to fulfill the legacy you've left him,"

Dickon added. "Your son saw how you valued your work and carries it forward for you. Be proud of him and rejoice."

Her son. Frances clasped Charles's hand and, despite her pain, willed herself to envision Louis, Arcturus balanced on his gloved fist. Suddenly, she knew they were right. If Charles would entrust his most beloved bird to Louis, and she knew his judgment was impeccable, then she must also trust.

She closed her eyes and imagined her boy, stepping forward proudly, the hooded bird hungry and eager in his hand, waiting for her master's signal to attack their chosen prey.

Fly swift, fly sure, she urged them in her heart, seeing them in her imagination, her gift from Charles. And as she wept, they prayed together for the safety and success of Louis and Arcturus.

Sunday morning, August seventh, Louis stood onboard the *Ark Royal* with Lord Admiral Howard, feet planted wide to mediate the swell of the ship and stabilize Arcturus. The early morning sun had burned away the fog to reveal the menacing crescent of the Armada, anchored ahead in choppy waters just off the coast of Calais.

Louis peered into the crescent to locate the sole ship that interested him—Medina Sidonia's flagship, the *San Martín.* Silence reigned onboard as every hand and every soldier watched him work.

"You're sure they'll send a bird at dawn?" The admiral bent toward him.

"Quite certain," Louis said, fully confident. "Messages are sent early, so the bird has time to fly home during the day." He knew exactly what he was doing. Hadn't he watched Frank, Millstone, and Dickon do it a hundred times before? Hadn't they taught him and he'd learned his lessons well?

Suddenly, a pigeon broke from Medina Sidonia's galleon, no more than a pinpoint as it rose into the sky. But Louis's keen eyesight caught the movement at once.

"It's away," shouted the lookout, who would have seen it with his spyglass.

Louis held up his fist and whipped away Arcturus's hood, just the way Frank had taught him. The bird shot into the air and mounted on strong, pumping wings. Within seconds, the hawk closed on the distant pigeon. Spiraling rapidly above the doomed bird, Arcturus sighted his prey, then fell like a stone.

"Bravo!" A shout of triumph burst from Louis's lips as the distant specks clashed in midair. As he loosed the ear-splitting whistle Dickon had taught him to call the bird back, he imagined Arcturus's razor sharp talons piercing the bird's body. A vast satisfaction filled him as Arcturus winged his way back to the *ArkRoyal* and settled with the pigeon on the deck at his feet.

"Let's see the message." An enthusiastic seaman leaned toward the hawk.

Arcturus mantled fiercely over his prey, talons and beak ready to attack.

"Leave him be," Louis cried, jumping to the bird's defense. "He's hungry. You have to let him feed first."

"Won't he destroy the message?" wondered the startled seaman as he retreated, staring warily at Arcturus. The bird settled back to his breakfast, tore open the breast with its sharp beak, and calmly dined.

"He knows better than that," Louis informed his audience importantly. "In a minute, when his appetite wanes, he'll let me take the message for Lord Howard to read."

Minutes later, he tendered the folded paper to the Lord High Admiral, who read the Spanish writing, then turned to the waiting men. "Medina Sidonia writes for Parma to bring out his army in all haste. He is ready to proceed," he boomed, his strong orator's voice carrying into the topsails. "I shall substitute a message to Parma in its place. I shall write that the Armada has been destroyed by fire ships and cannot rendezvous. Then tonight, we'll make it true. We'll send them a present they won't forget."

"Fire ships?" Louis looked up from where he squatted by Arcturus, watching carefully as Frank had taught him how much the bird ate. "What are those, m'lord?"

"Fire ships, Master Louis, are sailing craft covered with tar and resin, then doused with gunpowder and set alight. We'll send them directly into the Armada's midst."

"May I help prepare these fire ships?" Louis rose to face the admiral as he made his eager request.

The admiral clapped him on the shoulder. "Indeed you may, lad. We must prepare them well to ensure the Spanish ships catch fire. 'Twill be hard work, though."

"I don't mind, m'lord." Excitement leaped within Louis. "Fire is one of the things I manage best."

Epilogue

February 1589, six months later

"And then, Louis made the best fire ship of all, and it scattered the Armada!" Breathless with the excitement of his story, Pierre waved his arms to hold the attention of his audience. "And he helped beat them in the terrific battle at Gravelines. No wonder the Spanish were done for, with him onboard."

"Haven't we heard this story before, love?" Charles arranged the mantle around Frances's shoulders as they sat before the fire in Morley's cozy parlor.

She snuggled nearer to him, glad for the warmth to shut out winter's chill. "It's new to me every time he tells it." She smiled on Pierre and he grinned back.

"What of you, Louis?" Charles persisted. "Do you tire of this tale?"

Louis stroked Arcturus on a perch at his side. "Not as long as I'm the principal actor. Proceed, Pierre. What happened next?"

"A terrible storm scattered what was left of 'em!" Pierre pronounced, satisfaction stretching his mouth in a huge grin. "They were all beaten, the Duke of Medina Sidonia, the Duke of Parma, and that ..." He glanced at Charles, who raised his eyebrows as if in warning.

"And that son of a rotten peascod, the King of Spain."

Charles threw back his head and laughed uproariously. "What an inventive curse, my son."

"Good story, Pierre," Louis chimed in. "Now let's play blindman's buff. Come on, Frank."

"She can't play." Charles stayed Frances as she tried to rise. "Remember your delicate condition, my dear."

Frances sat back, pretending to be peeved, but unable to hide a smile. "My lord protector says I mustn't, but

Master D. will play with you, won't you, Dickon." She twisted toward the warm chimney corner from which a rasping snore trailed.

"Wake up, Master D." With uninhibited affection, Pierre pounced on the man and tickled him.

Dickon bolted upright, gripping his chair. "What ... who ... ?"

"Did you think I was a Spaniard?" Pierre giggled. "I'm not. I want to play blindman's buff."

Dickon relaxed and fingered his beard, which once more approached its former bushy fullness after six months' growth. "Master Pierre, you mustn't scare an old man so. I lived two lives for so long, I still jump at my own shadow."

"And to think, Louis protected your identity from me," Charles threw in, nodding to Louis.

"If he hadn't, my duplicity would have been revealed to the Spanish, and I would have been a dead man. He did the right thing, believe me." Dickon stood and held out his hand expectantly to Pierre. "Where's the kerchief for the blind? I'll be 'it'."

As Dickon donned the blindfold and Pierre and Louis ran shouting about the room, Frances rested one hand contentedly on Charles's arm, the other on Oriana, perched at her side. "We have done well with the boys, haven't we?"

"They deserve the credit themselves. Louis has served his new country well."

Frances twisted to look at Charles in surprise. "His new country?"

Charles chuckled. "I petitioned the queen to make them both English citizens and our legal sons. They will grow up Englishmen, with all the rights and privileges thereof."

"Oh, thank you! You are goodness itself." Frances landed kisses on Charles's cheeks, something she knew he loved, though he rarely admitted it. "You did help them, though." She resettled beside him on the bench. "You taught them, you clothed and fed them, you trusted them to learn."

"Not at first," Charles growled.

"Let's not talk about then." Frances brushed over their past troubles. "Let's talk about the spring planting instead. I'm so glad Stokes left Morley to join the Armada. He was ruining the fields. I wonder what happened to him, if he made it to port somewhere or drowned."

"As you said, let's not talk about then," Charles chided as

she unwittingly lapsed into the past. "Stokes is gone from our lives, so I say we stay quietly at Morley Place and plant my seed in you and raise a crop of babes."

Frances put a hand over her expanding belly and chuckled. "Can we raise a crop of eyas, too?"

"Arcturus and Oriana will do that." Charles dropped an arm around her shoulders and squeezed affectionately.

Content, Frances leaned against his strength and surveyed the chamber, its rich woods polished to a glow once more, the homey, comfortable furniture arranged to best effect. Once she had sat here with her mother and father, she reflected, secure and happy in their love. When she had lost them, she had thought never to recapture that happiness, yet Dame Fortune had smiled on her, giving her four wonderful people to cherish. "Am I still your Lady Shadowhawk?" she ventured to Charles.

"I hope the shadow is gone forever." Charles solemnly took her hand. "I propose an entirely new name for you. I intend to crown you Ruler of the Wind—Queen of the Sky and Air."

"Queen of the . . . oh, Charles, you're such a romantic." She nudged him playfully. "I think I'm more like to be Queen of the Smelly Tailclouts in a few more months."

"We do have a nursemaid to change the baby, when it comes," Charles admonished. "You're not to tax your strength."

"And what of your strength?" She leered at him teasingly. "You've taxed it nightly without complaint."

"I have indeed," he said evenly, "since you learned to appreciate a feather bed. I wasn't sure what I would do if you insisted on making love in the woods in this weather." He glanced toward the lead-paned windows, beyond which February's snows blanketed the gardens and woods of Morley Place. "And since we're speaking of feather beds, what do you say we go appreciate ours right now?"

Their gazes locked for a full second. Their hands clasped. Suddenly, they both rose and bolted for the door, of like mind.

Frances raced Charles for their bedchamber, laughing like a young girl. The gift of imagination, that's what he'd given her. Charles Cavandish had restored her faith in her future. They would fill Morley Place with hordes of laughing, playing, healthy children. And they would breed hawks in their mews, swift, sure birds of noble lineage and valiant hearts.

Fly swift, fly sure. The words she had spoken so often six months ago to her birds as they carried false messages to confound Spain sprang up in her memory. And as Charles's loving lips closed over hers, she embraced him with joy.

The name he had christened her with seemed silly, but in a way it seemed apt. Because as she and Charles made love on their soft eiderdown bed, she mounted the heights in their mating flight and saw the marvelous tapestry of her life spread out before her, a dream fulfilled. She truly felt that she wore a crown, as his equal, as queen of the sky and air.

Lynnford's Historical Note

Many people ask me what inspires my stories. The answer is history. As I read the annals of the English past, I imagine the men and women who inhabited that world, how they lived and loved, and for a fleeting moment, I walk in their shoes. I feel the things they felt. I love the people and the causes they loved.

Unfortunately, all too few women leap out of the pages of the history books as I read. Historians have done their best to uncover details about the contributions women made to shaping events, yet the number of records describing women's roles, in contrast to those describing men's roles, is sparse. Historians are limited by the materials at hand.

The fiction writer, however, experiences no such limitation. For this reason, each of my books in the Cavandish adventure series augments history. Based on the idea that every historic event has some aspect that remains unexplained, I insert my heroine into the gaps, thus explaining why things turned out the way they did. The result? Breathtaking, nonstop adventure and romance. And who knows, maybe events of the past did turn out the way they did because of a woman's touch. I like to think so.

At the same time that I augment history, I strive to make the known historical facts of the events portrayed in my stories as accurate as research can make them. The war of 1588 between Spain's Armada and England's fleet was indeed fought in a series of four battles in the English Channel. The final outcome was decided when the English scattered the Armada with fire boats the night of Sunday, August 7. The winds of fate did the rest, blowing the fleet into the North Sea. By then the Armada was totally depleted of ammunition and food and couldn't even consider taking London by storm. The main force thus circled Scotland and returned home by way of the Atlantic. Of the 130 vessels that set sail for England, not more than 60 returned to Spain. The others were either captured or sunk along the shores of England, Scotland, and Ireland. Despite this, King Philip II never gave up the idea of conquering England, and by the time news trickled back to him of the Armada's fate, he was busy planning his next attack. He never achieved his objective, but he did provide fodder for marvelous stories for centuries thereafter.

One of these stories, cited in most sources I consulted, is that a woman really was present on the supply urca, the *San Salvador*. Each teller of the tale across the centuries embellished the story as to who she was and why she was there. Most of the stories are some variation on the theme claiming she was the wife of a Dutchman, who was taken by a Spanish captain claiming *droit de seigneur*. The outraged husband blew up the ship for revenge. For whatever the reason, the gunpowder onboard the *San Salvador* did explode. Since we don't know how or why it exploded, I saw no reason why it should not have been destroyed on purpose by Charles Cavandish. And since no records remain verifying who the woman was, I took the liberty of making her Inez del Cavaladosa, come to reclaim her bridegroom upon Spain's conquest.

Historians also puzzle over why the Duke of Parma was not ready to meet the Duke of Medina Sidonia's mighty Armada. Some suggest Parma had never been adequately rewarded by Philip II for his services in the Netherlands and held a grudge. Never did the king offer him anything other than the usual respect accorded an officer, though Parma was his nephew and therefore of royal blood (he was the son of Margaret of Parma, the illegitimate daughter of Charles V, Holy Roman Emperor and Philip's father). Parma was expected to take all the risks of invading England but was offered no share of the spoils once England was conquered. For whatever the reason, although he followed his assignment to the letter, it seemed he purposely failed to go the extra length required to make the campaign a success. More than that, communications between the two dukes were abysmal. Both were given orders by King Philip, but apparently neither one communicated with the other until the rendezvous was upon them. In a classical case of upper-level mismanagement, none of the details had been worked out beforehand. In fact, the history books say Parma never answered any of the letters from Medina Sidonia, but I wonder. Might he have answered them, but his replies didn't survive? It seemed perfectly logical for me to insert the workings of a woman into these already weak communications links. A classic example is Parma's claim that Medina Sidonia asked him to bring out his warships and join the battle so they could fight their way into an English port. Medina Sidonia says he never wrote any such thing. Medina Sidonia also wrote several times to advise Parma that he was entering the English Channel and for Parma to have his soldiers ready for transport in a few days. Parma is documented as never receiving notice that the Armada had even left Corunna until August 2nd, by which time the Armada was upon him. No wonder he wasn't ready. As I said, inserting a woman and her hawks and messenger pigeons into this situation seemed perfectly logical to me.

Please note that the dates used in this story are the revised version of the Julian (Old Style) calendar, which puts it ten days ahead of the English calendar of the period. This new calendar was adopted in England later. Most of the history books used this calendar because we still use it today.

The Cavandish adventure series began with my story of the eldest Cavandish daughter, Rozalinde, in *Pirate's Rose,* and continued with Jonathan's story in *Lord of Lightning.* After *Lady Shadowhawk,* Charles's story, I intend to write Lucina's story (she's called Luce or Luci for short), tentatively titled *Firebrand Bride.* Each of these stories is about the power of love to change the world. Each day, if we lovingly help others, little by little, in small ways that sometimes only a few people see, we make the world a better place.

A portion of the proceeds from my books goes to support charitable causes in Columbus, Ohio, including the YWCA's Generations day-care center for homeless children. You can write to me at PO Box 21904, Columbus, Ohio, 43221. I love to hear from readers, I'll send you my periodic newsletter, and I sometimes conduct reader surveys. If you're interested, let me know. An SASE is always appreciated.

◆▽ **TOPAZ**

PASSION RIDES THE PAST

☐ **FALCON'S FIRE by Patricia Ryan.** Beautiful and impulsive, French-born Lady Martine vows never to fall in love after her mother dies of a broken heart. A powerful and handsome English lord, Sir Thorne Falconer also vows never to love. By arranging Martine's betrothal to his son, he is assured that a grand manor will be his. But he doesn't count on his overwhelming attraction to Martine—and her fascination with him. "A richly textured pageant of passion. A grand adventure!"—Susan Wiggs   (406354—$5.50)

☐ **THE RAVEN'S WISH by Susan King.** Duncan Macrae expected violence and rage when he was sent to seattle the ancient feud between the Frasers and the MacDonalds, but nothing could prepare him for the strangely haunting warnings of a girl who foresaw his death. For in his heart he knew that Elspeth Fraser would be his love, his life, his soul.   (405455—$4.99)

☐ **BLACK THORNE'S ROSE by Susan King.** Emlyn de Ashbourne knew that to give herself to the man of mystery known as Black Thorne was to plunge into outlaw love—but Emlyn was swept up in a heedless desire that burned all bridges behind her as she changed from a helpless pawn to a passionate player in a game of daring deception and desperate danger.
                                                                                            (405447—$4.99)

☐ **TIMELESS by Jasmine Cresswell.** Robyn Delany is a thoroughly modern woman who doesn't believe in the supernatural and who is also beginning to believe that true love is just as much of a fantasy—until she is thrust into 18th-century England.   (404602—$4.99)

☐ **NO BRIGHTER DREAM by Katherine Kingsley.** When Andre de Saint-Simon discovers that Ali, the mysterious young woman whose life he has saved while on his travels, is the long-lost daughter of his mentor, he promptly returns her to England. But Ali knows that Andre is her destiny and arranges his marriage—to herself.   (405129—$4.99)

☐ **NO SWEETER HEAVEN by Katherine Kingsley.** Pascal LaMartine and Elizabeth Bowes had nothing in common until the day she accidentally landed at his feet, and looked up into the face of a fallen angel. Drawn in to a dangerous battle of intrigue and wits, each discovered how strong passion was ... and how perilous it can be.   (403665—$4.99)

*Prices slightly higher in Canada

Buy them at your local bookstore or use this convenient coupon for ordering.

PENGUIN USA
P.O. Box 999 — Dept. #17109
Bergenfield, New Jersey 07621

Please send me the books I have checked above.
I am enclosing $_____ (please add $2.00 to cover postage and handling). Send check or money order (no cash or C.O.D.'s) or charge by Mastercard or VISA (with a $15.00 minimum). Prices and numbers are subject to change without notice.

Card #_____ Exp. Date _____
Signature_____
Name_____
Address_____
City _____ State _____ Zip Code _____

For faster service when ordering by credit card call **1-800-253-6476**

Allow a minimum of 4-6 weeks for delivery. This offer is subject to change without notice.

◆ TOPAZ

TALES OF THE HEART

☐ **CAPTIVE by Heather Graham.** When sheltered Virginia belle Teela Warren gets a taste of the lush, exotic Florida Territory, her senses are dazzled. But when she glimpses halfbreed James McKenzie, the most attractive man she's ever seen, her heart is in danger.
(406877—$6.99)

☐ **A MAGICAL CHRISTMAS by Heather Graham.** Jon and Julie Radcliff are facing the last Christmas of a marriage in trouble. The love they once shared has been tattered by time and torn apart by divergent goals. Their children are beginning to show the hurt and confusion of their family's turmoil. Can a Christmas spent in an idyllic village help them to discover that love lost can be found again?
(407008—$14.95)

☐ **A TASTE OF HEAVEN by Alexis Harrington.** Libby Ross came to Heavenly, Montana, hoping for a new start, a family, children and a good place to raise them. What she found was terrible. The cowboy who duped her into being his mail-order bride had died, leaving her penniless with nowhere to go. That's when she heard about Lodestar Ranch and its owner, Tyler Hollins.
(406532—$5.50)

☐ **ANGEL OF SKYE by May McGoldrick.** Alec Machpherson, famed warrior chief of the Highlands, has served King James IV of Scotland with his sword. Now he would give his very soul to protect Fiona, the spirited, red-haired lass from the Isle of Skye. But it will take Alec's Highland strengths pitted against a foe's cruel ambitions to prove, through blood and battle, which will reign—an army's might or the powerful passions of two lovers.
(406745—$5.50)

☐ **PRINCE OF THE NIGHT by Jasmine Cresswell.** The Count of Albion, sequestered in an Italian villa, hid his secrets well—until the beautiful Englishwoman, Miss Cordelia Hope arrived. Irresistibly drawn to this cloaked, commanding count, Cordelia sensed his pain and, in all her innocence, craved his touch. He would become her destiny— the vampire whose love she was dying to possess.
(405668—$4.99)

*Prices slightly higher in Canada

Buy them at your local bookstore or use this convenient coupon for ordering.

PENGUIN USA
P.O. Box 999 — Dept. #17109
Bergenfield, New Jersey 07621

Please send me the books I have checked above.
I am enclosing $_____ (please add $2.00 to cover postage and handling). Send check or money order (no cash or C.O.D.'s) or charge by Mastercard or VISA (with a $15.00 minimum). Prices and numbers are subject to change without notice.

Card #_____ Exp. Date _____
Signature_____
Name_____
Address_____
City _____ State _____ Zip Code _____

For faster service when ordering by credit card call **1-800-253-6476**

Allow a minimum of 4-6 weeks for delivery. This offer is subject to change without notice.

▨ TOPAZ

PASSION'S PROMISES

☐ **THE TOPAZ MAN FAVORITES: SECRETS OF THE HEART Five Stories by Madeline Baker, Jennifer Blake, Georgina Gentry, Shirl Henke, and Patricia Rice.** In this collection of romances, the Topaz Man has gathered together stories from five of his favorite authors—tales which he truly believes capture all the passion and promise of love. (405528—$4.99)

☐ **BLOSSOMS Five Stories Mary Balogh, Patricia Rice, Margaret Evans Porter, Karen Harper, Patricia Oliver.** Celebrate the arrival of spring with a bouquet of exquisite stories by five acclaimed authors of romantic fiction. Full of passion and promise, scandal and heartache, and rekindled desire, these heartfelt tales prove that spring is a time for new beginnings as well as second chances. (182499—$4.99)

☐ **THE TOPAZ MAN PRESENTS: A DREAM COME TRUE** Here is a collection of love stories from such authors as Jennifer Blake, Georgina Gentry, Shirl Henke, Anita Mills, and Becky Lee Weyrich. Each story is unique, and each author has a special way of making dreams come true. (404513—$4.99)

*Prices slightly higher in Canada

Buy them at your local bookstore or use this convenient coupon for ordering.

PENGUIN USA
P.O. Box 999 — Dept. #17109
Bergenfield, New Jersey 07621

Please send me the books I have checked above.
I am enclosing $_____ (please add $2.00 to cover postage and handling). Send check or money order (no cash or C.O.D.'s) or charge by Mastercard or VISA (with a $15.00 minimum). Prices and numbers are subject to change without notice.

Card #_____ Exp. Date _____
Signature_____
Name_____
Address_____
City _____ State _____ Zip Code _____

For faster service when ordering by credit card call **1-800-253-6476**

Allow a minimum of 4-6 weeks for delivery. This offer is subject to change without notice.

◤T◢ TOPAZ

SIMMERING DESIRES

☐ **HARVEST OF DREAMS by Jaroldeen Edwards.** A magnificent saga of family threat-ened both from within and without—and of the love and pride, strength and honor, that would make the difference between tragedy and triumph.
(404742—$4.99)

☐ **THE WARFIELD BRIDE by Bronwyn Williams.** None of the Warfield brothers expected Hannah Ballinger to change their lives: none of them expected the joy she and her new baby would bring to their household. But most of all, Penn never expected to lose his heart to the woman he wanted his brother to marry—a mail order bride. "Delightful, heartwarming, a winner!—Amanda Quick   (404556—$4.99)

☐ **WIND SONG by Margaret Brownley.** When a feisty, red-haired schoolmarm arrives in Colton, Kansas and finds the town burned to the ground, she is forced to live with widower Luke Taylor and his young son, Matthew. Not only is she stealing Matthew's heart, but she is also igniting a desire as dangerous as love in his father's heart.
(405269—$4.99)

☐ **BECAUSE YOU'RE MINE by Nan Ryan.** Golden-haired Sabella Rios vowed she would seduce the handsome Burt Burnett into marrying her and become mistress of the Lindo Vista ranch, which was rightfully hers. Sabella succeeded beyond her dreams, but there was one thing she had not counted on. In Burt's caressing arms, in his bed, her cold calculations turned into flames of passion as she fell deeply in love with this man, this enemy of her family.   (405951—$5.50)

*Prices slightly higher in Canada

Buy them at your local bookstore or use this convenient coupon for ordering.

PENGUIN USA
P.O. Box 999 — Dept. #17109
Bergenfield, New Jersey 07621

Please send me the books I have checked above.
I am enclosing $_____ (please add $2.00 to cover postage and handling). Send check or money order (no cash or C.O.D.'s) or charge by Mastercard or VISA (with a $15.00 minimum). Prices and numbers are subject to change without notice.

Card #_____ Exp. Date _____
Signature_____
Name_____
Address_____
City _____ State _____ Zip Code _____

For faster service when ordering by credit card call **1-800-253-6476**

Allow a minimum of 4-6 weeks for delivery. This offer is subject to change without notice.

WONDERFUL LOVE STORIES

☐ **SECRET NIGHTS by Anita Mills.** Elise Rand had once been humiliated by her father's attempt to arrange a marriage for her with London's most brilliant and ambitious criminal lawyer, Patrick Hamilton. Hamilton wanted her, but as a mistress, not a wife. Now she was committed to a desperate act—giving her body to Hamilton if he would defend her father in a scandalous case of murder.
(404815—$4.99)

☐ **A LIGHT FOR MY LOVE by Alexis Harrington.** Determined to make the beautiful China Sullivan forget the lonely hellion he'd once been, Jake Chastaine must make her see the new man he'd become. But even as love begins to heal the wounds of the past, Jake must battle a new obstacle—a danger that threatens to destroy all they hold dear.
(405013—$4.99)

☐ **IN A PIRATE'S ARMS by Mary Kingsley.** They call him the Raven. His pirate ship swoops down on English frigates in tropical seas and he takes what he wishes. Taken captive while accompanying her beautiful sister on a voyage to London, spinster Rebecca Talbot is stunned when the handsome buccaneer winks at her and presses her wrist to his lips. She daringly offers to be the Raven's mistress if he will keep her sister safe.
(406443—$5.50)

*Prices slightly higher in Canada

Buy them at your local bookstore or use this convenient coupon for ordering.

PENGUIN USA
P.O. Box 999 — Dept. #17109
Bergenfield, New Jersey 07621

Please send me the books I have checked above.
I am enclosing $_____ (please add $2.00 to cover postage and handling). Send check or money order (no cash or C.O.D.'s) or charge by Mastercard or VISA (with a $15.00 minimum). Prices and numbers are subject to change without notice.

Card #_____ Exp. Date _____
Signature_____
Name_____
Address_____
City _____ State _____ Zip Code _____

For faster service when ordering by credit card call **1-800-253-6476**

Allow a minimum of 4-6 weeks for delivery. This offer is subject to change without notice.

Did You Know?

There are over 120 *NEW* romance novels published each month!

♥ *Romantic Times Magazine* is **THE ONLY SOURCE** that tells you what they are and where to find them!

♥ *Each issue* reviews *ALL* 120 titles, saving you time and money at the bookstores!

ALSO INCLUDES

♥ Fun Reader Section, Author Profiles, Industry News & Gossip

Plus

♥ Interviews with the <u>Hottest Hunk Cover Models</u> in romance like Fabio, Michael O'Hearn, & many more!

ROMANTIC TIMES MAGAZINE
~ *Established 1981* ~

Order a <u>SAMPLE COPY</u> Now!

$2.00 United States & Canada (U.S FUNDS ONLY)
CALL 1-800-989-8816*

* 800 NUMBER FOR US CREDIT CARD ORDERS ONLY
VISA • MC • AMEX • DISCOVER ACCEPTED!

♥ BY MAIL: Send <u>US funds Only</u>. Make check payable to:
Romantic Times Magazine, 55 Bergen Street, Brooklyn, NY 11201
♥ TEL.: 718-237-1097 ♥ FAX: 718-624-4231

♥ E-MAIL CREDIT CARD ORDERS: Romancemag@aol.com

♥ VISIT OUR WEB SITE: http://www.rt-online.com